ULTIMATE CARE

J M FARMER

Characters

The Cabinet

Prime Minister	Jack Hawthorn
Chancellor of the Exchequer	Bill Travers
Home Secretary	Alistair Radley
Health Secretary	Charlie Warwick
Replacement Health Secretary	David Michel
Education Secretary	Alice White
Media Secretary	Peter Oaks
Transport Secretary	Jane Dawes
Communities Secretary	Steven Tucker
Under-Secretary for Health	Nick Everest
Jack's wife	Laura Hawthorn

The Daily Post

Steven's journalist friend	Mike
Junior reporter	Olly
Chief Editor	Gideon

Social Care

Polish care worker	Kasia
Kasia's flat mate	Stefan
Kasia's clients	Eric, Mary
Kasia's clients	Doris, Pete
Care Agency Manager	Annie
Nursery Proprietor	Julie
Kasia's parents	Zofia and Jozéf
Kasia's brother	Piotr

Table of Contents

Chapter 1

All eyes turned to the door as Charlie Warwick, the Health Secretary, entered the Cabinet Room, a little late and out of breath.

"Sorry," he mumbled as his overweight form sank heavily down onto his chair and he slapped a thick dossier onto the table, papers falling out as he did so.

"As I was saying," Jack Hawthorn, the PM, continued "today we're having an important discussion about the funding of the Health Service. I'm glad our Health Secretary could make it."

Charlie glanced up from his papers, expecting the sarcastic gaze of the PM to be beamed at him, but he was smiling.

"Charlie has some new proposals for cutting expenditure in the NHS and Social Care and I'll now ask him to run through those proposals. Of course, I've had some prior insight into them but they will come as a surprise to you. All mobile phones off?"

Charlie unbuttoned his jacket, loosened his tie, mopped his brow and looked up from the dossier to address the Cabinet.

"I'll not beat about the bush," he started, his Irish burr gentle on the ear. "We all know that the NHS cannot continue in its present form, and whatever election promises we made, we are going to have to renege on them if it is to survive in any form at all. Budget overspends are now so huge that all health trusts are bankrupt and there is no hope of government continuing to bail them out in the long term - or even in the short term."

"The government seemed to find the money to move mountains during the Covid-19 pandemic," said Jane Dawes, the Transport Secretary.

"And that is one of the reasons we're in such dire straits now. We are still paying back huge loans and demand continues to rise and rise - much of it for conditions which are not, strictly speaking, illness. We have to return to first principles, as drawn up in 1948, and drastic economies must be made. Drastic economies call for drastic decisions."

He glanced around the table to see if this had sunk in. He did not yet seem to have their full attention.

"OK, Charlie, you're not in the House now," grumbled Jack. "Cut to the chase."

Charlie continued "We all know that decriminalizing assisted suicide has had some effect on the cost of treating the chronically ill, but it's not enough. Charging for GP appointments has not proved economic to administer and we need to review it. Stopping IVF, gender-reassignment treatment and frivolous cosmetic surgery is just tinkering at the edges. We need to do something much more radical."

Now heads bobbed up and focused on him. He paused for effect.

"What I'm proposing now is the compassionate euthanasia of those with severe dementia who require 24/7 publicly funded care....." He held up his hand as the noise rose. "Also for those with certain degenerative neurological diseases. And, the cessation of cancer treatment for terminally ill patients who do not have more than six months to live, whatever treatment they receive. Those are the most drastic proposals."

An incredulous hubbub broke out. The PM was struggling to make himself heard above the racket.

"Ladies and gentlemen, please! This is not PM's Question time! Let Charlie finish."

Charlie fished out his hankie and mopped his brow again. "As you know, during that pandemic choices had to be made as to who would benefit most from treatment. We simply couldn't keep everyone alive, and the many of the very elderly with dementia and underlying health problems were given palliative care. The precedent was set."

"It's not the same thing at all," shouted Jane over the rising volume of protests.

Charlie held up his hand for silence. "There are other, less drastic proposals - severe triage at A & E departments so that we truly *are* treating just accidents and emergencies, and compulsory life-style courses for smokers, the obese and for diabetics. They *have* to take more responsibility for their own health so the side-effects of their lifestyles don't make up such a huge part of NHS expenditure. I also propose much more involvement of pharmacists."

Several pairs of eyes lowered to focus on Charlie's not inconsiderable girth. Glancing down at his straining waistcoat he murmured in a self-deprecating way: "Yes, and I'll be one of the first." He continued "The introduction of compassionate euthanasia" ......

"What on earth is *compassionate* euthanasia?" muttered Alice White, Education Secretary.

".....will greatly reduce bed-blocking. We have a crisis in Social Care. Nobody foresaw that the introduction of the Living Wage would result in the closure of quite so many nursing homes...."

"Well, some of us did," said Steven Tucker, the Secretary for Housing, Communities and Local Government. "But you wouldn't listen."

Jack glared at him. He was not going to admit that the government had failed to foresee such an obvious outcome.

"And," battled on Charlie "bed blocking is so acute we must deal with resource-consuming elderly people in a humane but definitive way."

Alistair Radley, the Chancellor, stood up, his face red with anger. "Can somebody remind me what year this is? For a moment there I thought I was back in Nazi Germany."

Charlie waited for the noise to calm down.

"Well," he said very quietly, "Does anyone have a better idea?"

Jack strode to the door and put his head round it. They heard him yell "COFFEE! NOW!" before the hubbub in the room rose to a crescendo.

A trolley trundled in, and when everyone had a cup in front of them Charlie got to his feet, holding up his hand for silence.

He continued "I know it sounds drastic, but we've done research which shows that a huge percentage of the population are worried sick about what will happen to them when they get old. Talk to anyone in their 60s and 70s about it and something many of them say is 'I don't want to spend my last days a dribbling idiot with dementia in a nursing home. Just put a needle in me.' Nursing homes are closing down at a horrific rate and the government just can't afford to allocate the resources needed by local authorities to keep them all going. Obtaining and keeping staff is a nightmare. Being a carer is hard work and underpaid."

Everyone shifted uncomfortably in their seats.

"Home care is sketchy, to say the least, and there has been very little success in getting local health authorities to merge care budgets with local health service budgets to solve bed-blocking."

"Then let local authorities raise Council Taxes," piped up Alice. "We can't cap them forever."

Charlie sighed. "We have reached the stage where demand is limitless and we'll never catch up. Life expectancy has risen exponentially, despite the huge rise in diabetes and obesity. They don't all die young. It's bankrupting the country. People now live long enough for enormous numbers of them to get dementia which requires a high level of care. Many of them are just existing. And it's costing billions just to help them to exist. We simply don't have the resources. And that is why I'm

4

proposing the option of a simple injection to peacefully end their lives. It will be done very tastefully."

"There's nothing tasteful about death," someone observed.

"But there is such a thing as a Good Death," said someone else.

"And you just said 'option' - this isn't going to be compulsory, then?"

"Er, well, if their care is full-time and being publicly funded they will not be given an option, but they'll be time for them and their relatives to get used to the idea."

"What about those funding their own care?" This was Alice.

"They can continue to do so, if they wish, nothing will change there."

"But only the rich will be able to afford it!" said Alistair.

"Yes, and their families will jump at the chance to bump them off so they don't spend
all their inheritance on care home fees" said Steven.

"Can you blame them?" interrupted Bill. "I've recently had to find a home for my mother. Took me six months to find a vacancy anywhere, let alone somewhere I was happy with. The annual charges are more than for my son at boarding school. We tried having a live-in carer in her home but she's so difficult to handle none of them stayed long, and the lack of continuity confused her even more. I think it would be a kindness to her, and probably thousands of others."

The PM took a deep breath.

"Obviously, Charlie and I have discussed the bare bones of this. There are still many details to be sorted out. Of course, there'll be opposition but I don't really see any alternatives. In 1948 nobody foresaw how medical advancements would mean that the public would expect every little thing to be fixed at the cost of the State. It was great back then for everyone to be able to get relatively simple treatments they would otherwise never have been able to afford, but think how primitive treatments *were* back then."

"Yes, and we've already pared down free dental, optical and audiology services to the bare bones," added Charlie. "So, as pre-1948, we again have citizens walking around with only half a mouthful of teeth. It's not what any of us really want, is it? I could go on, but I won't."

"No, please don't," grumbled Bill. "If I'd realized that this meeting was going to be so contentious I'd have cancelled my diary for the rest of the morning."

"Well, we're not going to spend any more time on this right now, we have a couple of other matters to discuss," said Jack, "but Charlie is going to hand out notes for you to peruse in your own time, and we'll come back to it in a couple of weeks. Of course it won't be popular. But Charlie and I are very serious about this."

Alistair exchanged looks with Bill. What Jack really meant was that *he* was serious.

Chapter 2

Kasia fumbled with the keys and tried unsuccessfully to open the front door. It was a sticky lock, and she was despairing of ever getting it open when a turn of the key combined with an almighty shove finally budged it.

"Who's that?" shouted Eric. There was nothing wrong with his hearing. "Who's that?" he said again, a quavering note in his voice.

"It's only me, Kasia. Carol can't come today, she's off sick."

She came in, dumped her bag in the shabby, outdated hall and wrinkled her nose. The atmosphere was none too fresh. She went upstairs to his bedroom.

"Good morning, Eric. How are you today?"

Eric regarded her with great suspicion.

"Who's Carol? Who are you? What do you want?"

"I'm your morning carer, Eric. You usually have Carol, but she can't come today."

"Oh. Do I need a carer, then?."

Kasia sighed patiently. "Yes, Eric, you have carers come in four times a day."

"Where're you from, then? Don't sound English."

"Poland. I've been here before. Probably you don't remember."

"Never seen you before. Still, I'm not one to turn away a pretty girl."

"Well, it's time to get up and get dressed, Eric. I'll help you."

Eric continued to regard her suspiciously as she assembled the cleanest clothes she could find. He was a tall man, stick-thin, with a beaky nose and milky grey eyes. He still had most of his hair, though, and he needed a shave. Kasia pulled back the bedclothes, and helped him to swing his legs over the side of the bed and onto his feet. As she did so she noticed that the sheets were wet and she knew that giving Eric a quick shower and changing the bed would hold her up. She was allowed half an hour with him but she also had to get his breakfast. She certainly wouldn't have time to shave him.

"Oh dear, we need to get you in the shower."

"I don't like showers," grumbled Eric. "I just want to get dressed."

"Well, your pyjamas are very wet so you need quick wash." She gently guided him out onto the landing and along to the bathroom with him protesting all the way. She whipped off his pyjamas with practised ease.

"Hey, steady on," Eric shouted. "Nobody but my wife's seen my wedding tackle, girl."

"All your carers seen it plenty times before, Eric" laughed Kasia, "you just don't remember."

"Too right I don't. Disgusting. A young girl like you…….."

She ran the water until it was warm, and helped him to sit on the seat affixed to the shower wall.

"Ow, that water's hot."

"It's just right." She grabbed the shower gel and, ignoring his protestations, lathered him up, then rinsed him off and helped him to his feet before wrapping him in a grubby bathrobe before he could protest further.

"When is your son coming again, I wonder," she said, more to herself than to Eric. "This bathrobe and your towels could do with good wash, and your clothes."

"What son? I ain't got no son."

Kasia laughed. "Eric, you have two sons and a daughter! I think it is son David who lives not far away. He usually comes at the weekend. I will leave him a note asking him to wash some clothes and towels. I will put the bathrobe in with the sheets this morning."

She steered him back to the bedroom and started to dress him, praying that he wouldn't have one of his tantrums about which jumper to wear. Luckily he was still puzzling over the fact that he had two sons and a daughter and meekly allowed himself to be dressed and helped downstairs. It was slow going. A couple of times she had to take his weight when he missed a step.

"This is hard for you, isn't it?" said Kasia. "I think maybe a stair lift would be a good idea? I will discuss with our manager.

"Stair lift? What's that?"

She saved her breath, not wanting to get into a pointless discussion.

Finally they reached the kitchen and she helped him into a chair.

"You'd like porridge today as usual? And tea?" She was already ferreting in the cupboard for the oats. Please don't let him want a boiled egg today, she prayed under her breath.

Eric considered. "Yes, all right, porridge today." Within three minutes Kasia had boiled the kettle, made the tea and cooked the porridge and set it on the table in front of him.

"The other girl....." he began.

"Oh, so you do remember Carol, then?"

"Of course I do." Eric was indignant. "She puts honey on the porridge. And the top of the milk."

Kasia laughed. "Top of the milk is something from the past, Eric. It all comes the same now, just milk, skimmed or full fat. No cream on top nowadays."

"Rubbish," said Eric. "Always been cream on top of the milk."

She got the plastic milk container out of the fridge and showed it to him.

"This is what it looks like now, Eric. It is full fat milk but no cream."

She poured some on the porridge for him and picked up the honey jar and a spoon. He grabbed it from her.

"I want to do it myself."

"OK." Kasia knew the mess that would ensue, but it was easier not to argue.

"And toast - I want toast. With blackcurrant jam."

Kasia and popped a piece of rather stale-looking white sliced bread into the toaster and hunted for the jam.

"I can't find blackcurrant jam – you can have some nice strawberry?"

"I SAID I want blackcurrant," said Eric petulantly, waving his honey spoon in the air and flicking a blob of honey onto Kasia's hair.

"There is only strawberry. You ask David to get blackcurrant at the weekend, yes? Would you like me to leave toast, butter and jam here for you to do, while I pop upstairs and change the sheets?"

"All right, but there's nothing wrong with my sheets."

Kasia was already half way up the stairs. She hoped there was some clean bedlinen in the airing cupboard. She wondered if they should start putting him into incontinence pads at night.

She found the last set of sheets and pyjamas and changed the bed, came down and put them in the washing machine. It wasn't really her job, but otherwise they would run out of clean stuff. She noticed that the washing detergent was almost finished. Incontinence pads would save a lot of work. She pulled a piece of paper out of her bag and wrote:

| ERIC |
| STAIR LIFT? |
| INCOPADS ? |

and thrust it into her pocket. On another she wrote:

```
BLACKCURRANT JAM
WASHING POWDER
BREAD
MILK
MORE CLEAN SHEETS ETC AND PYJAMAS
FRONT DOOR VERY DIFFICULT TO OPEN
```

and left it on the worktop for David. Today was Thursday, the bread and milk might just last until the weekend.

Turning back to Eric she was dismayed to find that he'd spilled tea down his jumper. Her fault, in her haste she'd forgotten his bib. There were blobs of jam on the table too, but at least he had finished. He was a fast eater.

"OK?" She wiped away the jam with economical movements, dabbed at the tea on his jumper and whipped away his plates to the sink for a quick rinse. Then she consulted the agency schedule to see if she needed to give him any drugs. There were three due at breakfast time but she couldn't find them.

"Eric, do you know where your medicines are?"

"No, I don't need any medicines. Feel fine."

Kasia looked in all the cupboards. "Where have they gone?" She muttered to herself. She checked her watch. She'd already been here thirty-five minutes. She started looking in more unlikely places and finally found them in the rubbish bin.

"Eric! What these doing in here? You must not put medicines in the bin!"

She put them in an egg cup, five pills in all and poured Eric another cup of tea.

"Here, take these with your tea, Eric."

He swept the egg cup off the table and the pills scattered far and wide over the floor.

"Oh Eric, no. Why do you do that?"

"I TOLD you, I don't need any medicines. I'm fine."

"Yes you do, they keep your blood pressure down and your heart steady. You must take them, doctor's orders. Or I will be in trouble."

She gathered up the pills and put them back in the egg cup. Eric stared into space, oblivious.

She sat beside him and gave him the mug of tea. She handed him the pills one by one and said firmly "Swallow it down, Eric. You don't want me in trouble with my boss, do you?"

"Don't I? I don't know your boss."

"She's been to see you a couple of times, to do assessments, you just don't remember. Here, last pill."

Kasia rinsed his mug and took his arm.

"Come, we get you into the sitting room."

She helped him to his feet and led him into the sitting room. She made him comfortable in his favourite chair and fetched him a glass of water from the kitchen and put it on the table beside him.

"Don't forget to drink some water during the morning. You want the TV on?"

"All right. I like that programme with the pretty girl."

Kasia guessed which programme he meant and flicked on the TV. Sure enough, the curvy female presenter with the blonde hair was there. Eric smiled for the first time that day.

"Here is your walking stick for when you go to the toilet. Don't forget to go, will you?

Here is the alarm; when you hear it, you go to the toilet, yes? A good idea of Carol's."

Carol had suggested setting the alarm every two hours and so far it had worked quite well. He wasn't very steady on his feet but the downstairs toilet was next to the sitting room and he could just about get there with his stick.

"OK, I'm going now." She patted him on the shoulder.

"Where are you going?" he shouted, alarmed. "I don't like being alone,"

"I have to go and help other people, Eric. My next call is Mary, across the road. You remember Mary? You used to visit her when you could walk better."

"Never heard of her. When are you coming again?"

"Probably not today, my work list changed because Carol and another care worker are off sick, but someone will come at lunch time. OK?"

He nodded vaguely, his eyes already fixed on the blonde's cleavage. KASIA hurried across the road to Mary, checking her watch as she did so. She had overrun her allotted half an hour by ten minutes.

Chapter 3

Kasia had no problem getting into Mary's house as Mary was already up and waiting for her. She had made slow progress to the front door on her walking frame but was there, watching for her carer to arrive. She was a very large lady of eighty-four with a wrinkly face, twinkly blue eyes and a beautiful shock of pure white, wavy hair.

"Oh, hello Kasia dear," she said, " I haven't seen you for a while. You're a bit late?"

"Carol is off sick. Also Pat. It's a busy day for me and I was too long with Eric so now I am all behind."

"Nothing serious, I hope, with Carol?" said Mary as she shuffled back through the hallway. Her house had long since been divided into two flats and now she had mobility issues it was lucky hers was on the ground floor.

"Well, actually, she is expecting. It's not a secret at the agency, so I guess it's OK for you to know that."

"Oh, that's a shame, she'll have to stop work soon, I expect."

"She will work up until baby's due, she hopes, she needs the money."

"In my day the women stayed at home and the men earned the money," said Mary.

"Very nice if you can afford it, but it's different now, Mary, both parents need to work. Anyway, you are walking better since I last saw you. It's been a while."

"Well, I'm a bit more mobile now, dear, I had a hip replacement since you last came."

Kasia looked at the agency's patient record on Mary. She had undergone a hip replacement three weeks earlier.

"Very good," said Kasia, "you are doing well. So today I need to help you shower, yes?"

"Yes, please, dear, I can't manage on my own yet. I'll go along."

Kasia continued to read her notes while Mary shuffled to the bathroom. She saw that she was supposed to look at Mary's leg ulcer and assess the condition of it.

"Not really my job," she thought. "I'm not trained nurse, how do I know about ulcers?"

There were also several medications to give; besides her arthritis, Mary was a type 2 diabetic, had a heart condition, high blood pressure and was prone to chest infections.

Kasia followed Mary to the bathroom and sat her on a stool while she carefully unstuck the sticky tape and moved aside the ulcer dressing on her leg to look at it. She hadn't a clue if it had improved or not, as she hadn't seen it before. This was the problem when continuity with carers couldn't be maintained.

"What do *you* think?" she said to Mary, who replaced her glasses on her nose and peered down at it.

"Looks drier to me," she said. "The nurse is coming on Monday. You just pop a clean dressing on it, dear, and you need to put plastic wrap over it while I'm in the shower, to stop it getting wet."

Kasia was relieved, and deftly re-dressed it. She thought what a good job it was that Mary still had all her marbles, and wondered how on earth she would have managed if Eric had these problems.

The water wasn't very hot so the shower was fairly brief and Kasia had high hopes of getting through the visit in record time.

But when she was half dressed, Mary asked her to leave the bathroom while she used the toilet.

"OK." Kasia went to the kitchen where she found Mary's various medications lined up on the kitchen worktop. At the end of the row was a nearly empty bottle of laxatives. She consulted her worksheet and dealt out the drugs which were due in the morning, ready for Mary to take, although she thought Mary was probably quite capable of managing her own pills. She felt that her visits were probably due to be axed soon, there were so many other people who needed more help than her. Then she returned to the bathroom and helped Mary put on the rest of her clothes.

Back in the kitchen, she made a cup of tea and gave Mary her pills.

"You have a cup too, dear," said Mary, pushing the teapot towards her. "There's some biscuits over there. You girls have such a busy day, you need to keep your strength up."

"It's very kind of you, but I really don't have time. And I hope the biscuits are just for guests? They told us during our training that biscuits are not good for diabetics, you know."

"Well, I've got so many things wrong with me now! I just have the odd one. I'm glad you got some training for this job, I have heard that some carers are untrained."

"Depends on the agency. Some are so desperate for workers they take anyone if they say they have experience. My agency gives two days training - not nearly enough. But at home, my grandmother lived with us, I helped to look after her so I have good idea what needs to be done."

"And did you work as a carer in Poland?" Mary asked.

Kasia laughed. "Oh no, I was teacher. But I cannot teach here yet, my English needs to get a bit better, and my qualifications are not quite right for the UK. Maybe one day. OK, I'm going now. Your usual lunch-time carer will come, I think."

"Yes, thank you dear. Off you go."

Kasia glanced at her watch. She'd caught up by ten minutes.

Chapter 4

The Cabinet sat patiently, chatting amongst themselves while they waited for Charlie to arrive. As usual, he was late, tumbling through the door and murmuring apologies. He sat in his usual chair and took a thick file from his brief case. He appeared to have lost a little weight, which Jack commented on.

"Been taking a bit of your own medicine, eh Charlie?" he chortled.

Charlie glanced down at his waistcoat, on which there was less straining on the buttons.

"Hmm, yes, I'm under strict instructions from my doctor to lose weight and get my blood pressure down. Must avoid becoming a type 2 diabetic at all costs, mustn't I!"

He beamed his winning smile around the room and flipped open his folder.

"I've got some facts and figures here. I hope that when you hear them you'll realize how much care of the elderly is costing, and why something drastic has to be done. Jack and I strongly feel that those who have had their lives and are living in a twilight world should make way for younger people. People whose health problems can be treated so that *they* can continue to be active and contributing members of the community."

Jack nodded. There was some muttering from dissenters.

"So," continued Charlie, "the figures for the cost of adult social care for the last year we have accounts for was around 20 billion pounds of which 9 billion was for the over 65s. Some of that 9 billion is for a variety of chronic and acute conditions and some, as I mentioned before, progressive and distressing neurological illnesses."

There were several sharp intakes of breath.

"Care homes and care agencies alike are going out of business. We are already in a situation where people who self-fund residential care are subsidizing the care of the local-authority funded elderly. Is this fair?"

He glanced around the room, a glint in his green Irish eyes.

"Statistic number two, for those of you fortunate enough not to have a relative needing full-time care yet: the rough figure for a care home fee in London and the south-east is £71,000 a year, somewhat less nationwide. Whilst local authorities get preferential rates, it's still a lot of money."

Alistair interrupted "Yes, but people are entitled to the dignity of end-of -life care. Most of them think they've paid for it in their National Insurance contributions and taxes. This is not going to wash at all. Every government for decades has kicked this problem into the long grass, but I don't think your proposals are what the public is looking for."

"Perhaps you'd like to suggest some alternatives?"

The glint in Charlie's eye was becoming fiercer. "Surveys have been carried out and preliminary results show that more than half of those interviewed, and almost all those over 70, were in favour of an exit strategy for patients with severe dementia and other terminal diseases such as cancer and certain neurological diseases. Their biggest fear is mouldering away in a care home."

"Hear, hear," chimed in Peter Oaks, Media Secretary. "I think Charlie's proposals are interesting and innovative. Our real problem is to sell them to the vociferous minority who think people should be kept alive for ever."

Charlie's glint became harder.

"I don't think you quite understand. These proposals are going to be implemented, whatever. The PM and I have discussed it at length and we know that with our slim parliamentary majority we have no chance of passing a Bill. It will just be implemented as NHS and social policy."

A collective gasp went up.

"Have you had talks with the medical profession?" asked Alistair. "What about the Hippocratic Oath?"

Charlie shrugged. "Well, that was replaced by the Declaration of Geneva after World War two. I suggest you all read it. If you do, you won't find anything there about prolonging anyone's life for the sake of it. It doesn't actually say it's OK to kill them off, either, but a doctor can take any decision he feels is in the best interest of the patient. At the moment they're hampered by managers, and fear of being sued. If a 'best interest' decision favours a painless and swift death to alleviate the suffering of a patient they should be at liberty to implement it."

"Exactly," said Jack. "We don't let pets suffer at the end of their lives. We give them a simple injection. What's wrong with doing that for a suffering human?"

"But what if doctors refuse to comply?" asked Alice. "You can't force them."

Murmurs went around the table.

"I think you'll find we can," replied Jack. "They may have their contracts terminated if they refuse. And there's also going to be a series of public information videos on BBC television commissioned by the Government explaining the situation around elderly care and what are the most sensible ways of solving it. If the families of patients who are selected for Compassionate Euthanasia object strongly they have the choice of funding care themselves. Or appealing in the High Court. It just has to become acceptable to do this in a first-world country which is running out of resources. I put this to you: Is all life sacred, always, for ever, at whatever cost?"

There was a lot of muttering. They all knew that the majority of people couldn't begin to afford funding elderly care themselves. But neither could the country.

"Has the PM completely lost his marbles?" muttered Alistair to Bill. Bill shrugged.

Chapter 5

Kasia had now been assigned to Eric and Mary for regular early morning visits. She decided to swap them around and visit Mary first, then Eric, as Mary usually took a little less time. She'd not slept well, and watched, yawning, through the glass pane in the front door as Mary, still on her walking frame, inched herself forward. A key would be useful, she thought. Eric had a coded box on the inside of his garden wall in which the keys were kept and all the carers had the code.

"Hello dear," said Mary. "Sorry I'm so slow, I expect they told you I've sprained my ankle badly and it's really set me back. The fall didn't exactly help my new hip, either. I could really do with help getting out of bed, it's such a struggle."

"I was just thinking that a key box like Eric's would be useful," said Kasia. She explained how it worked and Mary agreed that it would be a good idea and that she would speak to her son-in-law about it.

"He's very handy with the DIY, he'll fix it for me."

She shuffled towards the bathroom and they went through the shower routine. "How's your ulcer, has the nurse been coming regularly to do the dressings?"

"Yes, she seemed pleased with it, but these ulcers are terrible, they take months to get better."

"What's this?" asked Kasia, pointing to a leaflet and a collection of unfamiliar objects on the windowsill.

"Oh that, that's a test I've got to do for the nurse. I told her about my constipation problem." Kasia remembered the near-empty bottle of laxatives.

"And she said I should do this test to make sure there's nothing nasty going on in my guts. It's really tricky, I have to do three samples and put them under these funny little flaps on this piece of card."

"Well, it's a good idea to get tested."

"I suppose you're right, dear, but at my age I can do without any more complications, I have enough of a struggle getting through the day. I don't know what I'd do without you lovely girls."

Kasia laughed: "You might find yourself with a nice young man one of these days, Mary, the agency has just taken on two male carers."

Mary tutted. "I do hope not, dear, I wouldn't be comfortable with it. I know there are a lot of male nurses nowadays but women of my age don't want to be helped by men."

"Well, there are a lot of male *doctors*!" Kasia mused. "Dr Brinklow is your doctor, isn't he? He's a man."

"Doctors are different," said Mary firmly. "I don't want some whippersnapper helping me with *my* shower!"

"What is whipper - how do you say it?"

Mary cackled uncontrollably. "Whippersnapper, dear, it means a young, jumped-up person."

Kasia decided not to pursue it, and to look it up in the dictionary later. She helped Mary dress, set out her pills and made her a pot of tea. Mary said she couldn't face food first thing in the morning. Kasia pointed out that she needed to eat regularly for her diabetic drugs to regulate her blood sugar and persuaded her to have a bowl of cereal.

"I need two of those red ones, dear, not one, they're for my blood pressure. It's gone even higher so the dose has been upped."

"Upped? Oh, I see," Kasia laughed. "This English!"

"You're doing very well," said Mary firmly. "Please have a cup of tea and a biscuit, you look very pale."

Kasia sighed. "Yes, I will have a very quick one, I didn't have time this morning, I feel tired. I slept badly, my flat mates were noisy."

She poured a cup and took a couple of biscuits, glancing at her watch.

"It's always is a rush, " she said, "Not enough carers, too many patients. Not enough time with each patient. Before I came here I heard the NHS is very good but now I'm not so sure."

Mary nodded. "It's old people like me, dear, putting a burden on the system. But we paid our taxes and expect to be looked after. I never thought I'd live like this, though, depending on carers to help me just get through the day. So your flat-mates, are they Polish too?"

"Yes, we have two girls and a boy, and only two bedrooms. We use the living room as a bedroom."

"You share with a boy?" Mary was horrified.

"Nobody worries about that now, Mary, it's normal. And the boy is very useful - he painted the walls to cheer it up."

"Sounds a bit crowded."

"We cannot afford bigger flat, flats are so expensive to rent in London. It's not a very nice flat, the landlord doesn't care about mending things but the Stefan and his friend have fixed problems in the bathroom and kitchen. These boys have jobs in building, it's very useful."

She drank her tea quickly, glancing at her watch again as she got up to go.

"You are looking thinner, Mary, you have lost weight?"

"I don't know, dear, I haven't got any scales, but now you mention it my clothes are feeling a bit looser lately."

"Perhaps ask the nurse to bring some, and weigh you?" Kasia knew enough to make the connection between weight loss and change in bowel habits. "It seems odd you should lose weight when you are not very active at the moment."

"You're a clever girl, Kasia, you notice things. You should have been a nurse!"

"I loved teaching, Mary, I hope I will get back to it sometime. You have shortage of teachers in the UK, I think?"

"So I hear. When I was a girl teaching was a respected job, a job with a good pension. From what I see on the TV, teachers can't cope with the behaviour problems of the children nowadays, and so they don't make a career of it."

"Yes, I am hearing this too. In Poland, discipline is strict. Here, the parents do not seem to have control of their own children, so it makes things difficult for the teachers."

"You're right," sighed Mary. "Different from when mine were young."

"I must get across the road to Eric, now."

"How is he? He's a nice man, we used to share a cup of tea and a piece of cake quite
often, before his memory started to go, and he changed."

"Yes, it's very sad, he has bad dementia. Often when I see him he doesn't
remember who I am. He needs a lot of help. OK, goodbye, see you tomorrow."

She let herself out and crossed the road, hoping Eric would be in a compliant mood. The keys worked first time, Eric's son must have sorted out the locks.

"Morning Eric," she called as she entered the hall. "It's me, Kasia."

"Not you again," grumbled Eric as she climbed the stairs. "Oh, it's *you!*" he said when he saw her. "I thought you said you were Kasia?"

"I *am* Kasia! You are thinking of Carol, perhaps? I will be getting you up every morning now, Carol's not working mornings for the time being."

"Hmm, I don't know who Carol is. All these different people coming in and out. What do *you* want? What did you say your name was?"

Kasia took a deep breath.

"I'm Kasia, one of the carers from the agency. I've come to get you up and dressed. So let's get you out of bed."

She gathered his clothes together. They looked cleaner, obviously David had seen her note and done some washing for his dad.

As Eric sat on the edge of the bed he suddenly went very pale and was having trouble getting his breath.

"You OK? Can you breathe, Eric?"

"Oh, oh....." He froze, trying to catch his breath for about twenty seconds, then relaxed.

"It's OK, I can breathe now. I felt ever so funny."

Kasia wondered whether she should call somebody, but the colour came back into his cheeks and his breathing seemed normal again so she continued helping him to his feet and took off his pyjamas, gratefully noticing that he was wearing incontinence pads and that the bed was dry.

"So on with your pants and vest," Kasia cajoled. It was not one of his co-operative days. He flailed his arms around and nearly fell over.

"Hey, Eric, take it easy. Quick, put your underwear on, it's cold this morning. OK, now the shirt..."

"I want the blue one," he said stubbornly.

Kasia rummaged around in the wardrobe trying to find a blue shirt. It looked like it had been worn before and not washed recently, but she didn't have time to worry about such niceties and swiftly put it on him, following on with an aged pair of baggy trousers which seemed to be his favourites. She pulled a blue jumper from the chair and started to put it over his head.

"NO, NO, I don't like that one!" He snatched it from her and threw it on the floor.

"But it is blue, dark blue, goes with the blue shirt?"

"I want the red one. Find it."

Kasia tutted, exasperated, and went through the pile of sweaters in the cupboard. There was no red one.

"Eric, look, you don't have a red one."

"I want *that* one," he shouted, pointing at a multi-coloured jacquard knit on the floor of the wardrobe.

"I put it there because it needs a wash. And it is not red, it's lots of colours."

"I WANT IT!" Eric shouted.

"OK, OK, you can have it."

Finally, she got him downstairs and into the kitchen with him leaning heavily on her. His gait was getting even more faltering and she wondered how much longer she would be able to help him downstairs. Maybe she should suggest a male carer for him. He wasn't exactly violent - yet - but was becoming difficult to handle.

"I want a boiled egg," he stated as he started playing with the salt and pepper pots, sprinkling condiments all over the kitchen table.

Kasia deftly removed them from reach and put on the kettle and egg-water to boil.

"Would you like some cornflakes, too?" She hoped he would say yes as it would give him something to do while the egg cooked.

"All right," he said condescendingly. She sorted out the cereal, made the tea and counted out his pills while waiting for the egg to cook.

"And I want - what's that bread called that's warm?"

"Toast?"

"Yes....toast....." He rolled the word around his tongue, as if it was unfamiliar.

Kasia served up the egg and toast and went to get the butter and jam. There was a new jar of blackcurrant jam which she put the table.

"I don't want that," Eric roared, "I want the red one."

Kasia prayed there was some strawberry left. He was obviously having a red day. She took care to keep Eric's medications at a distance from him until it was time for him to take them, and gave them to him one by one. She had learned her lesson. He grumbled over every pill, insisting that he was fine, didn't need any of them. It was a slow process. Kasia thought it was a pity that they didn't have an effective pill for dementia.

She finally got him into the living room and helped him lower himself into his chair. As he did so, he clutched his chest, went blue, and groaned. He gasped for breath and whispered "Oh, my chest....."

Kasia wasted no time in finding her mobile and dialling 999.

Chapter 6

The tension in the Cabinet room was palpable as they waited for Jack to arrive. Charlie was for once seated and ready, brow mopped, tie loosened, sweating anxiously.

"Unusual for the PM to be late?" murmured Alistair.

Charlie shifted uncomfortably in his seat; his large frame seemed to be trying to shrink into the chair. He knew why Jack was late, he'd seen the BBC newsflash on his phone and he knew there would be an eruption to end all eruptions when Jack finally arrived.

A long minute later, the door flung open and Jack strode in, flinging a newspaper down on the table with a resounding thwack. He didn't often lose his cool, but today he was positively bristling with rage and venom.

"Who - WHO - let this get out?"

He held up the newspaper for the benefit of those who hadn't yet seen it, which was the majority, as the meeting had been brought forward an hour at short notice and most of them hadn't even had time for breakfast, let alone a look at the daily papers. Twenty pairs of eyes focused on the headline, which was in a huge font:

"GOVERNMENT PLAN TO BUMP OFF ELDERLY"
by Simon Chapel

A combined shudder went around the table. Jack reversed the paper and began to read.

Sources close to the government have leaked a plan to kill off demented elderly people, cancer victims and sufferers of certain incurable neurological diseases. They are going to call this outrageous measure 'Compassionate Euthanasia.' Interested charities and action groups have vowed that they will fight this to the bitter end. A spokesperson for Age Concern was beside herself with anger when interviewed for this paper.

"The government seem to think they can play God," said their PR spokesperson. "We can barely believe it. Our organisation is dedicated to improving the lives of the elderly, letting them live with dignity until the end of their days, whenever that may be, not killing them off."

When asked about the huge funding gap in elderly and social care and recent headlines about care homes and agencies going bankrupt, she simply re-iterated "Our organisation is all about dignified life in old age, and dignified end of life. It's up to the government to find a way to fund it - the problem isn't going away any time soon."

Asked whether she couldn't consider that a timely helping hand from the medical profession when quality of life was totally absent from a patient might sometimes be appropriate, she shuddered and emphasized "No, never. We shall be fighting this with all our resources."

Nobody from the Department of Health was available to comment, however, one Geriatrician interviewed said that 'there is a growing number of doctors who are frustrated by having to keep certain patients alive, especially some of the elderly, when there is no hope of a cure and no discernible quality of life. Many of us involved in end-of-life care would welcome new initiatives.'

There do not seem to be any draft bills regarding this, and it looks very much like this is either just an ugly rumour, or a top-secret government initiative which they are trying to smuggle through the back door. If so, we can expect massive opposition.

Jack put down the newspaper and gazed around the table. Everyone shifted uncomfortably in their chairs, eyes anywhere but on Jack's face.

"This is reprehensible - you were all warned not to let a word of it pass your lips, not to anyone. One of you clearly has. We have a mole in the cabinet."

The silence was painful, and eyes darted around the room. Nobody said a word.

"I'm sure none of you has knowingly spoken to the Press, but as you know, the Press often pose as someone else. And it's all too easy to mention these matters to spouses and partners thinking that they will keep them to themselves. However, as we all know, it only takes one comment to reach the wrong ears and all hell is let loose."

Several heads nodded. But Bill said "But you and Charlie are intent on introducing this and the public will know soon enough, won't they?"

The Transport Secretary admitted that she had mentioned it in general terms to her husband to canvass his opinion but that she had not said the government was considering implementing any such plans. The Media Secretary said he had done much the same thing and had actually emphasized that there were no such plans, he was just interested in his partner's reaction. Nearly everyone else swore they had not mentioned the idea to anyone at all. The only face which remained red was Charlie's. All eyes turned to him.

"Well, I suppose it *could* have been me," he drawled reluctantly in his Irish brogue.

"What? YOU?" Jack's face was black with fury. "How?"

"I was in one of the members' bars the other night, I'd had a few whiskies, and a group of us were discussing end-of-life care. Two had parents with dementia, and they were lamenting the fact that these people had no quality of life. One of them said "Come on Charlie, isn't it time that we started to accord the same criteria to humans as we do to animals? Why is it OK to put down your beloved family dog at the end of its life, or when it develops an incurable disease, but not a human? Maybe the Health Department should be thinking laterally." And I said "You know John, that's not such a bad idea!" And we all roared with laughter."

"Yes," said Jack quietly, picking up the newspaper and waving it in the air, "that's all it takes, Charlie, for the Press to make a story out of it. Shit. What are we going to do now?"

But there was one person in the Cabinet room who was keeping very quiet. It wasn't anything Charlie had let slip in the bar. There was a mole in the Cabinet, someone who was so disgusted with the proposals that he had had a chat with a journalist friend of his.

Chapter 7

Kasia waited anxiously for the ambulance and did her best to reassure Eric, who was looking very blue, breathing in short gasps and murmuring "Oh my chest!" every couple of minutes. She didn't really know what to do; she assumed he was having a heart attack. She held his scrawny, blue-veined hand in hers and whispered "Try to keep calm, Eric, ambulance is coming. Won't be long now."

In fact it was fifteen minutes before it arrived, blue lights flashing and siren blaring. Curtains twitched up and down the road and necks craned to see where it would stop. As she opened the door, Kasia could see that Mary had shuffled to her front window across the road and was pressing her plump, white face against the glass.

"In here......" she beckoned the paramedics. She was so relieved to see them, she hadn't really known what to do to help except try to keep Eric calm. "I think he has had a heart attack – he has pain in his chest and it is hard for him to breathe. Where have you been?"

"Sorry love, the ambulance service is always stretched, we came as soon as we could. I'm Tony, by the way. And this is Mike. And you are?" he asked, as he swiftly took various pieces of equipment out of his bag. He was solid, reassuring presence.

"Oh, I'm Kasia, his morning carer. He had funny turn upstairs before breakfast but then he was OK again. Then just as I settled him here after breakfast and was going to leave, he said he had a bad chest pain and turned pale and then blue, and his breathing was difficult. So I called 999."

"You did the right thing," said the second paramedic as he deftly attached Eric to a small oxygen cylinder whilst the other fixed leads to Eric's chest and started to run a portable ECG machine. They were talking to Eric all the time, telling him what they were doing and reassuring him.

Kasia tapped Tony on the shoulder. "He has dementia, quite bad," she whispered. "He can be very difficult. But he still understands quite a bit."

"OK, thanks love. Do you know who his next of kin is?"

"I know he has a son, David – he comes every weekend, but I don't have details. The Agency will know, I must call them anyway."

"Do you know how old he is?"

"Yes, seventy-five."

Kasia took out her phone and called the agency. It rang and rang and eventually went to voicemail. She tutted in frustration. The manager, Annie, was always rushed off her feet trying to sort out rotas and fit in the ever-increasing workload of patients, or clients as they were now called. Kasia called again and Annie finally answered, sounding harassed.

"What? Heart attack you say? Oh God, that's all I need this morning. Yes, hang on, I'll dig his son's details out of the file." Kasia could hear the other phone ringing as she held on. She wondered how long Eric would be in hospital and if he would be able to go home again. Or, if not, it would free up a slot, she mused. Terrible to think of things this way, but this was how tight things were.

"OK, here you are." She read out two phone numbers. "I'll contact him now but the hospital will want to know NOK details."

"NOK?" Kasia was confused.

32

"Sorry dear, next of kin. I think you'd better go with him in the ambulance but as soon as his son turns up in A&E you can carry on with your round."

Kasia said "Must I? It will make me very late for the others, I have four more patients to get up. It will be lunch-time before I get to the last two."

Annie sighed. "I know, I know. I'll see if I can get anyone in to cover a couple of them, but we're running at full tilt as it is. I'll call you back. I may have to send one of the two new Portuguese boys but they haven't really had a full induction yet. Who do you think they could cope with most easily, not too complicated?"

Kasia wracked her brains. They were all high-maintenance – nobody got social help these days unless they were in a pretty sorry plight.

"Well, maybe best if you give them the two men on my list, Sid Howes and Ahmed Abdul. Mary says to me that she doesn't like the idea of a male carer, maybe the other ladies will feel same?"

"OK, I'll see what I can do."

"But...." Kasia was not happy. "I don't like to let them down, they expect me. You know what old people are like, they don't like new faces."

"I don't......." she began.

'Yes, yes, I know all that." Annie sounded impatient. Her other phone began to ring again. "Must go." The line went dead. Kasia turned back to the paramedics. "The agency will inform the next of kin, I also

have contact details. They tell me to go with him to hospital, then continue my rounds when his son arrives."

"Great, well we're nearly ready to go now, we've given him some medication and I think he's stable enough to move him to the ambulance."

They lifted him on to a stretcher and then onto the trolley and trundled him into the ambulance. Kasia held his hand.

"Where am I going?" he asked, panic stricken.

"You're going to hospital, they will take good care of you there. I will come with you, then I hope David will arrive to be with you."

"David? Who's David?"

"Your son, remember?"

Eric shook his head violently, dislodging the oxygen mask, which the paramedic struggled to replace.

"Take it easy, mate, just try to relax. Won't be long now."

"Where am I going?" he repeated. "I don't like cars, they make me sick."

"You're ill Eric, remember, you have problem with the heart. We are in the ambulance, going to hospital."

Eric muttered. Kasia couldn't make out what he was saying. He started to thrash around with his arms trying to shout "No, no!" through the mask. The paramedic, Tony, restrained him with difficulty. The other, Mike was driving.

"Going to have to give him a sedative, I think Mike," he shouted to the driver.

"Yeah, OK, go ahead, these patients with dementia can be tough to handle."

But as Tony was drawing up the injection Eric suddenly stopped struggling, gave a twitch and became very still and silent. His left arm dropped off the side of the trolley and lolled there, and the left side of his face collapsed down one side.

"Uh, oh, think we might have a CVA situation here now, Mike."

"OK, full steam ahead."

The ambulance, which had been speeding along at a fair pace as the roads had been pretty clear, now put on its lights and siren and Mick pressed his foot to the floor. Tony bent over Eric; Kasia couldn't really make out what had happened or what he was doing. She was sweating slightly with anxiety.

"What is a CVA?" she asked Tony.

"Hang on a moment, I'm just trying to get an airway into him."

"There, that's in," he said and turned to her.

"It's short for cerebro-vascular accident - in other words, a stroke. Do you know about strokes?"

"Yes, yes, I understand, I have another client who has had one. So Eric has had a heart attack *and* perhaps a stroke now?"

"Looks that way." Tony took Eric's wrist and tried to find a pulse. He noted that, and his blood pressure, on a chart.

"Looking in a poor state," he called to Mike. "Pulse irregular and thready, BP falling."

"Should be there in five," replied Mike. "I'll call ahead to Resus."

Mike spoke into the phone: "Seventy-five year old male, severe MI at home, has had a query CVA en route in ambulance. Airway in situ, ECG irregular, left-sided hemiplegia. ETA five minutes."

Kasia had never really thought much about what paramedics did before. She hadn't realised that they could do so much.

"You a nurse?" Tony asked her.

"Oh no, I just do a carer's job here in England. At home in Poland I was a teacher."

"Tough job, being a carer. Hard work, and some difficult patients, I should think."

"We must call them 'clients' now," she said.

Tony laughed. "To me they're still patients. Whoa, here we are." They screeched to a halt in the ambulance bay and Mick and Tony jumped out and hurried Eric into A&E Resus. Kasia was left standing there, not sure what to do.

"Go to Reception" Mike called over his shoulder, "and give them Eric's details."

She did her best but the receptionist was impatient when she didn't know his date of birth.

"What relation are you?" she asked, rudely.

"Am NOT his relation, am one of his carers. He has a son, David, I will give you his details. He's coming here, my care agency has already told him."

"Oh. Sorry. OK, give me the son's name and number for our records."

She went to sit down and wait for David to arrive, impatiently looking at the time on her phone every couple of minutes. She didn't really understand why she had to stay, she had so many visits to do. Annie from the Agency called and told her that the two men on her list would be visited by one of the new male carers.

"How's it going?" asked Annie.

"We are at the hospital, Eric is in somewhere called "Resus" and he very sick. On top of the heart attack they think he had a stroke in the ambulance. David is still not here, must I wait? And what about my pay if I don't visit the other clients?"

"I'd feel happier if you had a quick word with David to explain what happened, after all, you were there. Let me know if he's not arrived in another fifteen minutes. When I spoke to him he said he could get there in half an hour, so he shouldn't be long."

"My pay?" Kasia reminded her.

"Oh, we'll sort something out. I'll speak to Jennifer." Kasia had no time for Jennifer Whalley, the agency proprietor. She thought her a hard-nosed bitch who didn't care one way or the other about the clients. All very well running a care agency from a desk, she thought, whilst keeping an eye on the bottom line.

"OK," she said, and put her phone back in her bag. She picked up a newspaper someone had left. Before she had really started reading the woman sitting next to her, who was with a man with a head wound which was bleeding profusely, nudged her and pointed to the newspaper she was holding and said

"Seen this, have you? Look what the government is going to do now."

"What?" said Kasia.

"Says here they're going to stop funding full-time care for people with dementia, and stop treating terminal cancer patients. And people with some neurological conditions. 'Compassionate Euthanasia' they're calling it. Look."

Kasia focussed on the article. Her eyes nearly popped out of her head. She had had three clients who had recently been admitted to care homes for full time care and she knew that that they had no private resources and were publicly funded.

"I can't believe it," she said. "Surely, it's not possible to just kill people off like this? Oh poor John, and Emily and Pat…..and what about Eric?" she added to herself.

The woman sniffed. "Seems like the government can do what it likes nowadays. But I bet there'll be public uproar, you wait and see."

"I hear that some things you read in the newspapers are not really true? It's called sen….sensation…."

"Sensationalism," the woman helped her out. "Sometimes it's just rumour, we'll have to wait and see, I suppose, but it does say that it came from a government source."

Kasia was wondering how true it could be when at that moment a fifty-something man arrived, breathless, and announced at Reception that he was Eric's son. Kasia hurried up to him.

"Hello, I am Kasia, Eric's carer. The agency told me to stay until you arrived. But I must go soon, I have other clients to see to."

"No problem. The agency told me you were there when this happened, is that right?" he asked. David looked like a kind man, and Kasia relaxed as she related the story.

"Yes, I was just settling him in his chair after breakfast when suddenly he couldn't breathe and had pain in his chest. I was very worried so I called 999. I am not a trained nurse," she emphasised to David. "I didn't know what else to do."

"You did the right thing. Are you the one who leaves me the notes?" he joked.

"Yes. I don't do all his visits, usually the morning and sometimes evening. He gets very upset if he can't have the jam he wants, or wear the clothes he's chosen."

"You don't have to tell me," David smiled. "He's not easy to look after, I know. I think you all do a great job. I never see any of you to thank you."

"It worries me about the stairs," said Kasia. "He finds them very difficult now, and I'm afraid he'll fall one day. I'm not strong enough to support him. Maybe you could think about a stair lift?"

"Perhaps. We'll have to see if and how he gets over this this first."

"Oh. Yes. Of course. It's all right if I go now? Oh, wait, I've got the keys in my pocket." She handed them
to him.

David nodded. "Sure, thanks for waiting for me."

Kasia hurried outside and looked about, unsure where to go next. She pulled out her mobile and called the agency.

"Annie? It's Kasia. Eric's son has arrived at the hospital. Who is my next client? Have the boys gone to the two men I told you about?"

"Yes, all organized. You've just got Mrs Baines and Miss Gardener to do."

"Annie, I just heard something terrible. This lady at the hospital, she showed me something in the newspaper. It said that people with dementia and some other illnesses who need full time care are going to be killed off if they can't afford the care home fees. I can't believe it's true."

"What? Are you sure? You can't believe everything you read in the newspapers."

"Well, I hope not. If it is, it's terrible, isn't it?"

'I'll check it out," said Annie. "It can't be true."

Chapter 8

Charlie rushed back into his office and read, and re-read the 'Post' article very carefully. He was puzzled. There was detail in there he felt sure he had not given away. It was a general discussion about bringing an end to the lives of those with dementia who had no quality of life. He was sure that nothing had been said about neurological conditions. He wracked his brains to remember exactly who he'd spoken to that day in one of the Commons' bars. He'd had a whisky or two but not so many he couldn't recollect. He drew a sheet of paper towards him and began to make a list. There were four names, and he started calling them.

"Hello, Bob, Charlie here. Have you seen this morning's Daily Post, by any chance?"

"No, dear boy, don't read that rubbish! Why?"

"There's an article in there stating that the government is planning to introduce what the paper calls 'Compassionate Euthanasia.'"

Bob whistled through his teeth.

"You remember that conversation we had in the bar the other evening? About dementia? Jack thinks someone has leaked it to the Press, who've made a meal of it."

"Well, I can assure you it wasn't me. It Isn't actually *true* is it?"

"We are discussing ways of reducing the massive bill for elderly care, that's all I'll say at the moment. Now, specifically, was dementia the only condition mentioned in our chat? This is actually very important."

"As far as I remember." There was a silence while he thought. "Yes, I'm sure that was the only thing. We were comparing it with putting down dogs, weren't we? All very light-hearted."

"OK, thanks. Could I ask you to get hold of a copy and read it, and get back to me?"

"Not sure if I can sink that low, but all right, I'll send out my secretary for a copy."

"Thanks, you're a pal. Bye."

Charlie called the other three and got the same reaction from them.

He then called Jack, whose personal secretary answered and kept him holding for ten minutes.

"You're not his favourite person at the moment, what on earth have you done?" she joked.

"Nothing," said Charlie grimly. "But I now need to convince him of that."

"Yes, Charlie?" the PM finally drawled. 'I don't really want to talk to *you* at the moment."

"No, listen, Jack. I've read and re-read that dratted article and it didn't ring true. I've called the chaps who were in the bar that night and they all swear it wasn't them, but, more importantly, there's a reference in the article to people with neurological conditions. They are all certain that nobody mentioned that, least of all me. Which means that someone else talked to that journalist. Somebody in the Cabinet, because nobody else knew those details."

Jack was silent for a moment.

"Oh, damn. This is disastrous. Who the hell can it be?"

"Several of them aren't happy about the proposals, as you would expect, especially the religious ones. I've had chats with a few of them but I wouldn't like to hazard a guess - although Alistair is very grumpy about it. Can you get the Press

Secretary to talk to The Post? Although I doubt they'd want to reveal their sources."

Jack's face looked grim.

"No, of course they wouldn't, but we could put the screws on. Whoever it was will be hung, drawn and quartered, when I find out. Meanwhile, we need to get out a press release denying it all."

"But….." started Charlie, perplexed. "We can't do that, and then implement it, can we?"

"Well, we can certainly say it's gossip, or it's something that may have to be considered, but deny there are any firm plans. Since when has politics been an honest game?"

Charlie put down the phone. A prickly sweat was breaking out under his suit and not for the first time he wondered whether politics was the job for him. The idealism he first felt was draining away fast. Euthanasia wasn't really his idea, Jack had whispered it into his ear and told him to think up a strategy. Charlie had sensed that many in the Cabinet would think it a step too far, never mind the population at large. His phone rang. It was Alistair.

"Charlie, can I come and have a chat to you about this euthanasia thing? I'm really very concerned about it."

Charlie's ears pricked up. *Really?* he thought. *Surely the mole wasn't going to 'come out?'*

"Yes, pop in now, if you want. I can't say I'm all that happy either."

~

"Want a coffee?"

"I'd rather be drinking a wee dram right now, but it's a bit early."

"Never too early, old boy."

"Well, it is for me. I'm trying to live by my GP's rules, remember?"

Alistair asked his secretary to get two coffees. Then he sat down and leaned across the table, talking very quietly.

"Now, quick, while she's gone. I don't want anyone overhearing anything more than is necessary. You didn't, by any chance, air your concern to a journalist, did you?"

Alistair turned a little pale.

"Me? I thought it was *you* who was indiscreet."

"No, it now seems not, since some of the details leaked were not mentioned during my conversation in the bar."

He waited. Alistair looked uncomfortable. Finally he said:

"Look, I'm not at all keen on the idea, and there will be a lot of opposition, but no, I swear I've not talked to the press. Although, to be honest, I felt like it. I find it difficult to believe that this is a serious consideration, especially from an ex-doctor like you, Charlie."

"Perhaps it's my experience as a doctor which makes me think it may be necessary," Charlie replied, "but I can't see either the public or the diehards of the medical profession liking it. To be honest, Alistair, I'll tell you in confidence, this was not my idea. And I don't need to tell you *whose* it was, either!"

Alistair snorted. "No prizes for guessing it was Jack - he's the most ruthless politician I've ever met."

"I've got an idea. We need to find out who leaked this. Presumably you've made no secret of the fact that you are against these proposals, so how about you deliberately bring up the subject with other dissenters and see if you can get any vibes about who the mole is."

They were interrupted by Charlie's secretary bringing in the coffees. They waited until she had gone before continuing.

"What I always say to people like you is, what alternatives do we have? I'm not comfortable with either politicians or doctors playing God, but this is bankrupting the nation. You know, when I trained, doctors made life and death decisions every day. Who would be resuscitated, who would get the last place in the renal dialysis unit, at what stage cancers were a waste of time and money to treat, and so on. The culture of litigation has made them too risk-averse and we need to start getting tougher."

Alistair sipped his coffee and smiled slowly.

"You leave it to me, Charlie. I'll put out a few feelers. In my mind I've already narrowed it down to one or two. Mind you, there needs to be something in this for me."

"What, for heaven's sake?"

"Jack won't last for ever as PM. I'd like to think I could count on your support when the time comes."

Charlie sighed. "I'll bear it in mind."

God, what a dirty business politics is, Alistair thought. At that moment his phone rang. Bill.

Chapter 9

Kasia was half asleep on the bus on her way to her morning call on Eric, her first of the day. The bus screeched to a sudden halt and she opened her eyes to see a crowd of people blocking the junction, holding placards and chanting. She screwed up her eyes, trying to decipher the words. Some read "NO DEATH SQUADS" and others "HANDS OFF OUR ELDERLY." Some wore Halloween-type masks, and others carried plastic axes and scythes. Some were chanting "Let God decide" and the police were struggling to move them on. Someone shouted an instruction through a megaphone and as one person they all sat down, totally blocking the traffic. The police stood around, arms folded, not knowing quite what to do. Kasia was torn between wanting to join them and being resentful that it would make her late for work. As the stand-off continued she kept glancing anxiously at the time. Eventually, police reinforcements arrived, some mounted, and eventually the crowd got to its feet and shambled off, shouting loudly and waving their deathly props.

At last Kasia let herself into Eric's house, her stomach knotted. He had not long been out of hospital; Kasia thought that he'd been discharged much too soon and since his admission he had become far more difficult. His heart condition had stabilised and his stroke had responded to treatment, but he was less mobile, taking more drugs, and far less predictable. He now had carers calling six times a day, and even that was not adequate.

"Hi, Eric," she called.

"Who's that?" a tremulous voice replied.

"It's your morning carer." She had given up telling him her name, it didn't mean anything to him. She trudged through the hall towards the stairs. Eric was now confined to his bedroom. His son had put an armchair and a TV there and that was where he now spent his days.

She was startled when a voice called "Hi, Kasia, is that you? It's David."

He emerged from the kitchen.

"Could you come in here a minute, I'd like a word with you away from Dad."

"Oh, of course. Not your usual day to visit?"

"Well, I wanted to catch you, to talk to you."

"OK…." Kasia cleared her throat nervously. She hoped he wasn't going to complain about Eric's care. David looked pale and worried. He was a pleasant enough man, as Kasia remembered him from the hospital. He visited Eric regularly, unlike the relatives of many of her clients.

"I wanted to talk to you about Dad, and the amount of care he's getting."

"Yes? You're not happy about things?"

"No, no, it's not that at all," said David quickly. "I think you all do a great job; I know he's not easy to deal with, especially since he came out of hospital. No, it's just that….well….."

"Yes…?" said Kasia slowly. She took a deep breath. She thought she knew what was coming; the demonstration was fresh in her mind. "You mean the number of hours he needs now?"

"Yes; the agency says he now needs full time care. Do you agree?"

Kasia sighed. She didn't want to be having this conversation.

"Well, yes, I agree. And that means going into a residential home - the agency can't give him the care he needs. He was difficult before, but now…..."

"The problem is….."

"The Council won't fund full time care?"

"Oh, you already know?"

"The agency have not said anything to me about Eric, but I know the rules have changed. I was worried it would affect Eric. But maybe you could pay yourselves?"

"Not possible, I'm afraid. Dad's got no savings and this house is rented. There's no chance of *me* funding a home either, we barely manage now. My wife works full time too. So I suppose you know what that means."

He glanced at Kasia, who was pale.

"Yes, I know what it means," said Kasia. She looked down at her shoes, unable to meet David's eye. Finally she spoke.

"This rule is terrible. Perhaps the government will change it? People are organizing demonstrations, I saw one on my way here today. That's what made me late. Nobody is happy about it."

"No. And we all think these things won't affect us - until they do."

David ran his fingers through his hair.

"I just don't know what to do." His voice became louder, and quite angry. " Dad's trapped in the new system and it seems I can do *nothing* about it. I went to see his GP yesterday - they need his GP's agreement. I found he'd already given it - no consultation with his next of kin, or anything. It's outrageous."

He sat down at the kitchen table. "His GP thinks that ending his life would be in his best interests," he said tersely. "In a way, I can't deny that, he's got no quality of life, but emotionally I just can't get my head round it."

Kasia didn't really understand what 'get my head round it' meant, but she only had to look at his face. She glanced at the time.

"Well, I'm really sorry. But it's time for me to get started with him."

"Yes, of course. Sorry to hold you up, I'll come up with you and say goodbye."

As they got to the top of the stairs the smell hit them.

"Oh dear," said Kasia.

"Oh hell," said David. I'd offer to help but I really need to get to work."

"Don't worry, we are used to it. It is just part of the job. But it's not - what is the word - dignified, is it? I feel sorry for my clients."

"You're a very kind girl. I really don't think I could do your job."

"You would if there was no other job for you. My parents are shocked that I'm working as a carer, I have a degree."

"So why did you come to the UK? Sorry, I don't mean to be nosy, I'm just interested."

"Well, it seemed a good move. I didn't realise I'd have so much trouble getting a teaching job."

"Well, Poland's loss is our gain!"

"Thank you, David. Now I must get on. Goodbye!"

David could hear her as he went down the stairs:

"Good morning Eric, time to get you up and in the shower."

Eric was more exhausting and un-cooperative than normal. She was trying to get him to take his pills - never an easy task - when he suddenly started flailing his arms around shouting something unintelligible - the stroke had affected his speech. Then he lashed out with his fist, catching her on her shoulder. He hit it so hard that she lost her balance and fell against the wall. He was surprisingly strong for someone who looked so frail. She leaned against the wall for support, and got her breath back. Tears pricked her eyelids.

All very well for David to say how marvellous we are but Eric is getting dangerous. I must report him to the agency. I cannot visit him on my own any more.

When she had finally finished with Eric she crossed the road to Mary's house, feeling totally drained. She let herself in. The tests Mary had had done a few weeks earlier showed that she had an advanced cancer in her colon. She was still waiting for an MRI scan to see whether it had spread. If it had, it was unlikely she'd get any treatment. She looked a different woman from the plump, round faced lady she had been a few weeks earlier. Kasia could see her declining day by day. She had a soft spot for Mary. She had a lot of problems but she still had all her marbles.

"Morning, dear," she called as she heard Kasia open the door. "You're a bit late."

"Sorry, there was a demonstration which held up my bus. And then I was delayed at Eric's. First his son was there and wanted to talk about him, then he was...." Impossible, was what she wanted to say. She still felt shaken up. She blurted out: "Very difficult. He pushed me....hard."

She immediately wondered if she should have told Mary this - confidentiality rules were buzzing around her mind but refused to settle.

"That's terrible, dear, you look all-in. Why don't you go and put the kettle on and make us a nice cuppa before you help me get showered? If you could just help me to the toilet first."

Kasia felt she could certainly do with a cup of tea and maybe one of Mary's chocolate digestives. As usual, she hadn't stopped for breakfast. Mary put out her hand and patted Kasia's. "Go on, nobody will know, will they!"

As they sat drinking their tea Kasia said "I'm not sure I should have told you about Eric. We are not supposed to discuss clients with anyone except the agency."

"Don't you worry about that, dear, my lips are sealed. I'm only sorry that things have got so bad - for him, and for you. You know, you should speak to the agency about Eric. You shouldn't have to deal with violence."

"Oh yes, I am going to. But he may not be there much longer, anyway."

"Going into a home, is he?" asked Mary. "Seems like a good solution."

"No, he...." Tears welled in Kasia's eyes again.

"What dear? What's happened? You're obviously very upset. Tell me, it won't go any further."

Kasia knew she was breaching confidentiality in a major way, she really didn't care any more.

"It's terrible, Mary. He can't afford the fees for a nursing home, nor can his son. He now needs 24-hour care so the local council will not pay his fees because of the new rules. You know about these new rules?"

Mary looked past Kasia out of the window. Kasia looked at her expectantly; silence was unusual for Mary. Finally, she said

"Yes. And I may be the next. They probably won't treat my cancer, because of my age and my other health problems. I can't blame them, I'm eighty-five and I've had my life. But people of my age, who remember when the NHS started, just can't believe it's come to this."

"Me too. But you could fight it? What about human rights?"

"Well, I don't know much about them, dear."

"No, nor do I. You need a lawyer. Two of the Polish boys I know are decorating a big law firm's offices. I will ask them to try to speak to somebody there, to find out how we can fight this."

Chapter 10

The Cabinet dragged their unwilling bodies into the Cabinet Room for an urgent 8am meeting and slumped in their chairs.

"Bloody Jack," said Alistair. "Feels like he's just riding roughshod over us. We're going to do this. We're going to do that. No disagreements allowed."

"I'm not sure how much longer we can tolerate him," agreed Bill. "There's going to be a bid for the party leadership soon, if he doesn't calm down. He's turning into a megalomaniac."

Charlie and Bill came into the room looking grey with fatigue. They had been up most of the night, and not had time to shave, by the looks of it. Jack flumped a pile of newspapers down on the table.

"I doubt any of you have seen today's news yet," he started sarcastically.

A few muttered "Seen the TV news" and "Checked out Sky on the internet."

"Good. So I don't need to spell it out to you. We have a major civil unrest situation. Not entirely unexpected. But it must be dealt with. And I thought that our esteemed Health Minister had soothed the hackles of the BMA. Now, as well as the public demonstrating about the euthanasia laws, we've got half the doctors refusing to co-operate."

"Some of us did warn you," said Jane. "You seem to forget sometimes that this is meant to be a democracy. You and Charlie thought you could stitch up parliament by getting the BMA to agree, and side-step the Commons, but I fear you may have got it wrong."

Jack glared at her. Then he turned his attentions on Charlie.

"So what's the latest?"

"As you know, I've been having talks with the BMA overnight. It seems that most of their members agree to carrying out Compassionate Euthanasia, although the few who don't are making life very difficult. By and large, doctors don't think they are contravening the Hippocratic Oath or the Declaration of Geneva. Most doctors think we should not strive officiously to keep alive those who have no quality of life, but at present they do so for fear of litigation. The ones who object are largely the religiously fervent, and so I finally agreed with the BMA that doctors can exercise their consciences when it comes to the crunch."

"But some of your own government don't agree," interrupted Alistair. What about *their* consciences?"

Charlie ignored him.

"I think I've now got the BMA where we want them." He sounded a lot more confident than he felt.

"Right. Sounds more encouraging. Now, Alistair, over to you regarding the unrest."

The Home Secretary stood up and shifted uncomfortably from one foot to the other.

"There have been demonstrations in all major cities in the UK. The new movement 'Let God Decide' seems to have been able to mobilise huge numbers of supporters. The police are stretched to the limit trying to contain them and, as you know, they're blocking city centres, demonstrating outside hospitals and GP surgeries, and generally making it pretty difficult for doctors - and the public, for that matter - to go about their business."

"We need to get tough with them," interrupted Jack. "We can't allow them to obstruct not just doctors, but their fellow citizens. We don't have a universally armed police force - yet - but it may have to come. In the meantime, I'd like you to instruct the police to use tear gas and tasers when necessary. We *have* to get this under control, and fast. Otherwise it'll end up costing more than elderly care."

Eyebrows were raised all around the table. Bill gave Alistair a knowing look.

"On the plus side," continued Bill "The latest Mori Poll has revealed that two-thirds of the population agree with C.E. The announcement that funerals for euthanized patients would be paid for by the government has been a good move."

"C.E?" exploded Alistair. For heaven's sake, if we've got the courage of our convictions please don't let's abbreviate it. Or is it so offensive?"

Jack sighed. "Look, I've already had to get rid one disloyal cabinet minister. Half this furore wouldn't have happened if he hadn't gone squealing to the press. Three quarters of you agreed when we had the vote on CE. As Charlie often says to those who disagree "Do you have any better ideas?"

"No. But I don't like this one. And I think we should think up a different name for it."

"OK, we can work on that. And this is only stage one. Progressive neurological disorders is the next condition on the list. How's that going, Charlie?"

"Hmm, a bit more difficult. By the time dementia patients need 24/7 care they don't have the capacity to object. But advanced neurological conditions are another matter, many patients can voice an opinion. And the relatives often strongly object; then we have a problem. Most doctors seem happy enough to help them to a pain-free and dignified death. But the prospect of numerous court cases looms."

"And how much might *that* cost?" interjected Jane.

Jack ploughed on without giving her so much as a glance.

"Right, we were also going to review GP payments today, too. What's happening there, Charlie?"

"As I said a couple of months ago, it's proving much more expensive to actually collect the money than we anticipated, and nothing's improved. Extra staff, etc., problems with credit card machines, the risks of receptionists taking cash to the bank, and so on. The only solutions are either to scrap it, or put up the fee. Which, at £15, is cheap. In Ireland they pay €60 for every GP appointment, and €100 for every A&E attendance., unless referred by a GP. With that sort of fee, people have a huge incentive to manage minor ailments themselves, or consult a chemist first."

"Interesting point." Jack looked pensive. "I bet there are a lot of happy pharmacists in Ireland. How about putting it up to £50?"

There was a universal sharp intake of breath.

"I'd love to, but we've had enough trouble setting the amount at £15," said Charlie.

"Yes, but," Jack persisted "maybe that's the problem - £15 just isn't enough for people to value the doctor's time."

"Well, you may have a point," Charlie conceded.

"Is it decreasing demand for GP appointments, though?" asked Alistair.

"Yes, though not enough. Chemists report more people seeking health advice, which we are encouraging. We really need to incentivise pharmacies more to treat minor ailments and to authorise them to sell more medicines which are currently prescription-only," said Charlie. "I'm sure they'd relish the opportunity."

"Well, work on that in consultation with the BMA," Jack told him.

"Could someone tell me why we're still calling this a National Health Service?" asked Jane. "Seems to me it's quasi-private already."

"We just can't continue the NHS as it is. I've got people looking into insurance-based schemes, which are successful in other countries. It has to come."

Some uncomfortable looks were exchanged around the table.

Jane stood up. "I would like it put on record that I am against Compassionate Euthanasia. And Private Health Insurance. Full stop."

"Hands up those who approve of an increase in GP and A&E fees?"

Nobody put up a hand. There was a babble of voices.

"Whoa," said Jack, raising his hand. "You've all heard what Charlie has just said about fees in Ireland. £15 is not an economical amount to charge. If we raise it, we can sort out the problems with collecting the money, and so on."

Faces were mutinous.

"What about the unemployed and low-paid workers?" Jane was aghast again.

"They will have health cards entitling them to free care," said Charlie.

"So once again, it's the squeezed middle classes who will end up footing most of the bill?" said Peter, the Media Secretary.

"Afraid so." Jack's expression brooked no further interruptions. He nodded at Charlie. "Raise the fee."

He glanced at his memo.

"Changing tack, how're the Public Information videos going, Peter?"

"The ones about advice on managing minor ailments are in progress and going well. I'll have something to show you very soon."

"Good. And the others?"

"Um, well, we've been getting tenders from film companies. No decision yet."

"For heaven's sake, man, get on with it! This is urgent. Of course we don't want to pay over the odds, but don't shilly-shally around trying to save a few quid."

"It's not just that." Peter shuffled his papers, avoiding Jack's eye.

"Well?"

"The others - the ones explaining the measures we're taking with" - he cleared his throat –

"Compassionate Euthanasia, if we must give it its full name - well, to be honest, we haven't yet found a company that's willing to make them. On moral grounds. But of course, we're still looking," he finished hurriedly.

"Good grief, I thought these media people would do anything for money," said Jack. "Find some kind of incentive. I can't believe they've all got scruples."

"You mean a gong, or something?" said Alistair sarcastically. "For heaven's sake, Jack. You seem to think you can bribe everyone."

"Money talks. Simple."

At that moment, there was a knock on the door and an aide came in and handed Jack a piece of paper. He scanned it rapidly and blanched.

"What?" Bill peered over Jack's shoulder to read the note.

"Oh shit."

"What?" the rest of the cabinet asked with one voice.

"A mounted policemen has been seriously injured patrolling the riots in South London. A protester waved his banner right in the horse's eyes and he bolted. The officer fell off and the horse trampled him."

"Oh hell, that's all we need." The disgust sounded in Alistair's voice. "How bad is he?"

"Not sure. Have to go and find out more."

Jack gathered up his papers and jerked his head at Bill.

"Apparently the press are baying outside the door. Time to enter the lion's den."

Chapter 11

Kasia finally reached her flat after another tiring day, one during which she had not had time for even a short meal break. She'd bought some date-expired sandwiches from a garage, and gulped them down between visits. The agency had contacted her and asked her to fit in two extra visits before she went home, both elderly people who had just been discharged from hospital without a proper care package in place. The agency hated to say 'no', even though they didn't have the staff to cover all their clients properly. The second of these, a woman in her early nineties, had been brought home by her daughter, much to the annoyance of the daughter, who did not feel that her mother was well enough to go home.

"I work full time, and I live a hundred miles away," she railed at Kasia. "I can't stay here and I just don't know how they think she'll manage on her own. She can barely get around even with her walking frame, and she has several different medications to take at various times of day. She can't possibly remember when to take them all."

"How did she manage before she went into hospital?"

"She hadn't broken her hip, then. She was great, for her age. Still shopped and cooked for herself. She's lived on the ground floor for a while, the bathroom's out beyond the kitchen like a lot of houses of this age and we made the back room into a bedroom. She's aged overnight while she's been in that place. Much more dependent, immobile, losing her memory. And her confidence."

The old woman, whose name was Doris, clung to her daughter's arm.

"Don't leave me, Susan!" she pleaded. "I need looking after. How am I going to manage the flat, and the shopping, I can hardly walk?"

"I know, Mum, I know," she said, extricating her arm. "But I have to go. I've got to see to Derek. He's been on his own all day. The agency will send in people to help you."

She started to put on her gloves. "My husband's got Parkinson's and he can't work now," she said to Kasia. "I'm the only breadwinner and I can't stay here and look after Mum. Someone will look in on her regularly, won't they?"

"If they've said they will do her regular care, I'm sure they will. But it won't be me, I normally cover another area."

"Well, you're here now."

"Yes," said Kasia carefully, trying to keep a lid on her anger, "but the agency called me as I was on my way home and asked me if I could do two emergency visits. This is one of them. I've already worked 11 hours today."

"What did you say your name was?"

"Kasia. But I can't stay for long. As I said, I'd finished my shift when the agency called and asked me to come here."

Susan sniffed. "Foreign are you?"

Kasia's temper was a breaking point. She counted to five before replying, "Yes, I am from Poland."

"Well, I just hope Mum can understand you. She's a bit hard of hearing, and an accent could totally confuse her."

"I will do my best. I think you will find that most carers in this country are foreign. Also many nurses. Not many English people want to do these jobs."

Susan bristled. "You can't tell me anything about looking after other people. As I said, I've a husband at home with Parkinson's."

"Well, then, you know how hard it can be. Don't worry, I'll put your mother to bed and settle her for the night. Someone else will come in the morning."

I hope, she thought. Goodness knows who, we are all so busy.

Susan kissed her mother on the top of her head and said "Bye, Mum. It'll take me two or three hours to get back in the evening traffic."

"Don't forget her drugs," she flung over her shoulder as she went out of the door.

Kasia heard her boots clacking off into the distance and fought back some tears. She wondered how long she could continue to do this job; it was stressful enough dealing with the clients, but when their relatives were so unpleasant it just got too much.

She turned to Doris.

"Well, Doris, let's get started, shall we? I'll help you into bed, and I'll see which drugs you need to take in the evenings."

"I really can't go to bed before I've had something to eat. I'm starving."

Kasia took a deep breath. "When did you last eat?" she asked, aware that Doris might not remember accurately. The last thing she wanted to do was prepare food.

"I had a bowl of soup and toast for lunch. Seems ages ago. What's the time now?"

Kasia glanced at her watch. "It's seven o'clock. I suppose you do need a bit of supper."

She rummaged around the fridge, which was nearly empty. Doris had been in hospital well over a week and the few things left were curling up or going green. There were three eggs, which were just in date, and some butter.

"It's going to have to be eggs, Doris, there's nothing else. Shall I scramble them for you?"

"That'd be lovely, something freshly cooked. There should be a bit of bread in the freezer compartment. And I always keep long-life milk in that cupboard, for a cup of tea."

She watched Kasia with sharp, bird-like eyes as she found her way around the unfamiliar kitchen.

"There's nothing wrong with my memory, you know, whatever Susan says. It was being in hospital that confused me. They have the lights on day and night, and there's always someone crying out at night, you can't get a wink of sleep."

"I have heard that from other clients. Most people can't wait to get home. How did you break your hip?"

"I slipped on an icy patch on the pavement when I was out shopping. Ooh, it was painful. 'ad to wait forty minutes for an ambulance, I did. Then when I got to 'ospital, I had to stay in the ambulance for an hour, because they 'ad no room in A and E. Then I was on a trolley in the corridor for hours, until the next day, when they operated on me. "

Kasia put the plate down in front of her. "That's terrible treatment, Doris. Really awful, for someone your age."

Doris shook her head in resignation. She turned her attention to the scrambled eggs.

"That looks lovely, dear. And I'm not going deaf, either. At my age, people sometimes pretend they can't hear when they don't want to. But I didn't think they'd send me home until I could look after myself better. I don't feel up to it yet. I only started walking with the frame yesterday. Bed-blockers, they call us, you know. It's not our fault we don't have anyone to look after us when we get home. When my Dad was poorly towards the end of his life he used to have someone in four times a day, and they did his cleaning and laundry and shopping, too."

Kasia nodded. "He was lucky, things have changed. Carers will maybe help you get up, and to bed, and have a bath or shower some days, but fifteen minutes a visit is normal now. If you don't have relatives living nearby you may have to ask your neighbours to help. But you could ask your daughter to order groceries on the internet and have them delivered here. Then at least you won't run out of food."

"What a good idea. I don't know how I'll manage the cleaning but I've got a washing machine, I can do my own washing."

"It's things like changing your bed-sheets that's not easy to do alone," said Kasia. "But I'm sure your daughter will come and help you do that."

"Hmm," said Doris, "you've probably gathered she'll do as little as possible! Selfish, that one. But of course, she's got her own problems too."

"Now, your pills," said Kasia, rummaging through Doris's medications to see which had to be taken at night.

Doris leaned over the table.

"The pink one, and the green and yellow capsule."

She pointed. Sure enough, they were clearly marked "Take one at night." She checked the labels but they were the only ones she needed right now. She smiled at Doris.

"You're right, there's nothing wrong with your memory!"

After getting Doris ready for bed and turning up the heating, she left and plodded home, almost falling asleep on the bus. She stopped at the Polish supermarket near the flat and bought some familiar, comforting food. She felt she needed something to cheer her up.

Her flat mate Stefan said "Kasia, you look terrible! What have you been doing?"

"I've just had a really long, tiring day. I can't bear to think I've got to get up at six-o'clock and start all over again."

"Well, I've got some good news that might cheer you up."

"Oh?"

"I spoke to one of the lawyers at the company we're working for. He says there are lawyers who are specialising in appeals against this, er..... euthanasia, and he's given me the names of two of them. Your lady, what's her name, Mary? should contact one of them, or ask her daughter to, and see if they think she has a case."

"That's the best news I've had all day!" Kasia gave him a hug. She had secretly been pretty keen on Stefan for some time and she felt happy for the first time that day.

Chapter 12

Unusually, Charlie arrived first for the Cabinet meeting. He was feeling very hot, not to mention bothered, and wanted to make sure he could sit as far away from a radiator as possible.

The others filtered in, clutching fat bundles of files. This morning's agenda was mainly on the Health Service, which was becoming usual for Tuesdays, and it was the one day of the week they all dreaded.

"You all right, Charlie? You look a bit off colour," said Bill.

"No, not grand, terribly hot," he muttered, his Irish accent always more pronounced when he was stressed. "Is it hot in here, or is it me?"

"Pretty chilly, actually," said Bill. "Perhaps you've got a bug."

"Wouldn't be at all surprised. Spent a fair amount of time in hospitals and GP surgeries recently. God knows what infections I might have picked up."

Jack entered, a flurry of flunkies in his wake, all talking at once. They skidded to a halt at the door and Jack waved them off peremptorily. He sat down and beamed around the table.

"Good morning! You all look very glum."

"It's Tuesday," said Jane.

"The business of government docs not inspire Jubilation," said Alistair. "It seems to get more and more difficult."

"Perhaps you just don't have the right attitude!" Jack replied. "Work hard, play hard, sleep well."

"I don't know how he can sleep at all," muttered Alistair to Bill.

"What was that?"

"Nothing, nothing. Shall we get started?"

"Right, but before we start on the NHS, I'd just like to ask our Home Secretary a few questions. First, can you run through the current measures the police are taking regarding the demonstrations. It seems things have been quieter lately?"

Alistair stood up.

"Yes, much improved. The new water cannons have arrived and been distributed, and every police officer now has a taser. Tear gas has been deployed in every major city in the country at least once, which seems to have had the effect of fewer demos being organized. The final reading for the Curfew Bill will take place next week, and although of course we very much hope we won't need to use it, it also will undoubtedly have an inhibiting effect."

"I would like it put on record," said Jane, "That I find all these measures repugnant. We're turning into a police state."

"Sometimes democracy gets tough," Jack said. "We have to keep control, somehow. If we didn't have demonstrations about Compassionate Euthanasia we'd be having them about the complete breakdown of the NHS."

Deep down, they all knew this, but few of them had Jack's ability to be so blinkered.

"You seem to have forgotten that the new nomenclature for CE is Ultimate Care," Jane reminded him.

"Yes, indeed, thank you. A good name, I think?"

Most of the Cabinet were appalled at the choice, but none had dared object.

"So, all in all," continued Alistair, "things are going as well as we can expect, contingency plans are in place, and the overall effects of the new measures seem promising."

"What about injuries to the police?" shot Jane at him.

"There have only been minor injuries since the unfortunate incident of the mounted policeman who was badly injured a few weeks ago."

"And how is he doing?"

"Sadly, he still hasn't regained consciousness despite surgery to relieve the compression on his brain. He's been moved to a private facility to avoid demonstrations outside the NHS hospital where he was originally. He's getting very good care."

"I've no doubt about that," snapped Jane, "but the tabloids are baying about it. They're asking what compensation his family will get if he doesn't recover."

Alistair said "He'll get what all officers get who are invalided out of the force by injury in the course of duty. I'll check it out personally."

Which they all doubted.

"We may have to start censuring the press before long," said Jack under his breath.

"I hope I didn't hear that, Jack," said Bill.

Jack cleared his throat. "Right, now onto Health. Progress on Ultimate Care, Charlie."

"It's being implemented slowly, to assess teething problems. So far, there have been few. The first few patients who fulfilled the criteria have been um....processed."

There was an uncomfortable silence. They'd all had complaints from their constituents.

"OK. Next thing is GP and A&E charges. Charlie?"

"Despite the rejection of raised charges for GP appointments by you all, I'm afraid that they will have to go up. £15 is not economic and Jack and I have agreed that the fee will have to be raised to £50." There was a lot of sighing and tutting.

"Of course, those on benefits won't have to pay. Wealthier pensioners will pay, but those receiving benefits will not. Children between 5 and 18 will have to pay £25. And we just *have* to introduce fees for A&E attendance, to discourage those attending who do not need to do so. I propose to follow Ireland's example so I'm suggesting £100."

"But...." Alistair protested "how can you charge people when it's an emergency?"

"This is how it will work. On arrival at A&E reception, patients will be triaged by a nurse. If it is thought they need A&E treatment they will have to give a credit card number. But as many as possible will be referred to their GPs or a Walk-In Centre. Or, indeed, a pharmacist."

"What if they can't get an appointment with their GP?"

Charlie ignored him.

"What about people who don't have credit cards?"

"I don't know what century you're living in, perhaps you haven't noticed that even teenagers have a credit card on their mobiles. And *everybody* has a mobile."

"And people who can't afford it?"

"Those on benefits will be exempt, as I've already said; they'll give their NI number until we can fully implement the introduction of Identity cards. Which should be early next year."

There was more grumbling. It was a measure few of them approved of.

"What about people who are unconscious, or so badly injured that they won't be in a fit state to do either?"

"We're still working on that one. I expect we'll have to wait until a friend or relative arrives to deal with it. We need to thrash out the details."

"And will they withhold treatment until that happens?"

"No, of course not," said Charlie.

He didn't sound very convincing.

"And what about drunks?" asked Bill."

"Ah, this brings me on to the next proposal."

A universal groan went around the room.

"Drunk tanks?" offered Alistair, sarcastically.

"Yes, actually! We'll basically be keeping drunks out of A&E completely, unless they are injured. People really need to start taking more care of themselves. Every emergency department will have a Portacabin drunk tank parked nearby where a small team, headed by a senior nurse, will rehydrate them and stop them choking, etc, and then send them home. The cost will be £80. Plus the taxi fare home. In a couple of towns where this has been trialled, it's been a great success, and frees up a lot of space in A&Es especially at the weekends."

There was a general buzz of approval. "Seems like a sensible idea," conceded Peter. "Should have done it years ago, really."

Charlie suddenly sat down.

"Sorry, feel a bit off colour today." He had gone very pale, and sat, breathing heavily for a minute. Then he stood up again.

"Pharmacies will have more power to sell certain drugs which are currently prescription only. We're discussing this with the GMC."

"What about antibiotics?" asked Peter. "We are constantly being told by scientists that we've come to the end of the line with antibiotic development. Since they're blaming the resistance on over-use for minor ailments, do we really want pharmacists taking responsibility for selling them?"

Charlie, who was looking hotter than ever, sighed.

"Yes, I admit this is a tricky area. It's being discussed. We can't have pharmacists selling antibiotics willy-nilly, but trying to assess whether an illness is bacterial or viral is not easy for a doctor, let alone a pharmacist. The guidelines will probably be not to sell any prescription drugs for the under-5s. Courses of antibiotics will be limited to one, after which the patient will need to see their GP. We are also working on a TV ad campaign to emphasise that colds and flu are caused by viruses, and that antibiotics are unnecessary unless there is secondary infection."

"And how can we stop them going to more than one pharmacy to get further antibiotics?" asked Alistair.

Charlie gave him a deadly look. "We're working out an alert system." He'd been working 18- hour days for weeks to try and sort out all the minutiae. There were problems at every turn.

"OK, thanks Charlie," said Jack, "but do try and hurry up these discussions, will you, there is some urgency."

Charlie glared at Jack. He opened his mouth to speak, and then shut it again. He hadn't the energy.

"So, Alistair, let's talk about the implementation of Ultimate Care in your department," said Jane. "I've had complaints from several constituents about the shortage of graves, and the lengthy waits for crematoria."

"Er, yes, funeral directors, cemeteries and churches with graveyards are all worried by the increase in funeral requests. The shortage of burial plots is already acute. The proposed Funeral Benefit will be solely for cremations. However....." He cleared his throat to cover his embarrassment and Peter jumped in.

"I've heard of funeral parlours overflowing and waits of eight weeks for cremation," he said. "Not to mention lack of mortuary facilities. This is unacceptable."

Well, you'll be pleased to hear that we now have contracts with industrial freezer warehouses to house the overflow of....deceased persons."

"Good grief, what do the relatives think about THAT?" spluttered Peter. "You mean they're lining them up along with the frozen peas?"

"Um, well, so far, we've kept it quiet. Funeral directors are allowing viewings of the deceased for two days only, then they are sent to one of several storage facilities until they can be cremated. The relatives don't know exactly where they are."

"What sort of delay are we talking about?" demanded Jack.

"Around eight weeks at present. But bearing in mind that at busy times in winter the wait in some areas was often around five weeks, it isn't as bad as it sounds."

"What about religious beliefs which dictate their deceased are buried within 24 hours?" asked Alistair.

"They are already subject to special status, and this has not changed. In fact, knowing on which day their loved one will have Ultimate Care means administered means they can plan rather better than before."

66

"I foresee problems with the *rest* of the population then," said Jane tartly. "And rightly. And what safeguards are in place to stop people being cremated who might later need to be exhumed? All these cremations seem to me to be a perfect way of avoiding any questioning about the cause of death. Have you seen the Twitter feeds about it?"

"If they're in cold storage for four to six weeks," pointed out Jack. "that's long enough to do a post-mortem."

"However much this offends your sensitivities, Jane," said Alistair, "these problems have to be dealt with. We are urging crematoria to open longer hours, and Sundays, but of course the unions are up in arms and saying crematoria will have to recruit more staff rather than expect the current staff to work overtime. You've no idea the unforeseen problems this has created."

"And I'm sure we've all had representations from our constituents about the length of time the paperwork is taking," said Bill. "We need more administrative staff to process it and I've authorized funds to recruit more people to do just that. We've created a whole new department. But we can't afford not to cross the t's and dot the i's properly, or we're laying ourselves open to all sorts of litigation further down the line."

Alistair laughed and turned to Charlie.

"And this is really going to save money on elderly care, is it? A whole new department, more crematoria staff, renting cold storage...need I go on?"

Charlie opened his mouth to respond but nothing came out. His eyes swivelled, then closed, his jaw dropped open and with a wheezy gasp of breath he fell sideways onto Peter who had trouble supporting his bulky form.

Bill and Alistair rushed over and helped lower him onto the floor. "Charlie, what's the matter?"

Charlie was way beyond speech. He was grey and his breathing laboured. The Health Secretary was about to become a patient.

67

Chapter 13

The next day Kasia couldn't wait to tell Mary about the lawyers. "Mary, I've got some good news!" she called as she let herself in.

"Oh, yes, dear?" Mary didn't sound as enthusiastic as she had hoped.

"Yes, I've got the names of two lawyers who are taking on people like you, if you are told that they're not going to treat your cancer."

Mary looked pale and defeated.

"The District Nurse came yesterday afternoon. She said there's still no date for my MRI, and that she's also been told there are no plans to operate on my bowel. Apparently, at my age, and with my other problems, I'm not a priority."

Kasia took Mary's hand. She was growing frailer by the day, and they both knew that if she didn't get treatment soon there would be no hope at all.

"I'm so sorry. But this is all the more reason to speak to a lawyer - they can maybe appeal the decision and get you some treatment before.....before...."

"It's too late," concluded Mary for her. "It may be too late already. My children are talking about getting together to pay for an operation privately. I don't want them doing that, they really can't afford it. But they've already made an appointment for me to have an MRI done privately, and an appointment to see the consultant afterwards. I'm grateful for you trying to help, but going to a lawyer will take time, and time is the thing I don't have much of. Not to mention energy."

"It's just not fair, Mary, there is nothing wrong with your mind, and you have things wrong with your body which can be treated."

Mary patted her arm. "Thank you, dear. I'm glad I haven't got dementia, like poor Eric. It sounds like he is difficult for you to deal with."

"Yes," said Kasia, "but he can't help it. It's not always the patients who are difficult either. Last night the agency sent me to two people who had just been discharged from hospital without a proper care package arranged. The daughter of the second person I saw was so rude to me, she treated me like a servant. She couldn't wait to get away. They sent this lady home to a cold empty house a few days after a major operation when she could hardly walk even with a frame. She's ninety-three!"

Mary tut-tutted. "That's terrible. Mind you, they don't keep anyone in for long now. But she's ninety-three, and she had an operation? And I can't?"

Kasia sighed. "It's different - how do you say - protocols? A broken hip isn't terminal, she will recover and not need full time care. Even now, she will only have a carer pop in two or three times a day until she can manage alone again."

She helped Mary get out of bed; she was very wobbly. Kasia helped her shower and dress. Her tiredness had returned.

"I'm not sure how much longer I can do this job," she admitted to Mary. "I'm sorry, I shouldn't have said that to you. But I feel under so much pressure all the time. We are not giving the clients the care they deserve."

"Well, perhaps you should try and meet a nice young man with a good job, and get married," Mary laughed. Do you have a boyfriend?"

Kasia thought of Stefan.

"Not really. There is my flat mate who I like a lot, but I don't know if he feels the same. I would like to have children one day, but not just yet. My parents want me to go home, they don't think I've improved myself by coming here."

"Maybe you could set up your own care agency?"

Kasia laughed. "Yes, I would earn more, but it might be almost as stressful! But it's an idea. I know a Polish girl here who had a manager's job back home, she would probably understand how to run it."

"And you have the practical experience from the carers' point of view. There you are, sorted!"

Mary's laugh turned into a cough, and for some moments she couldn't get her breath properly.

"Your chest sounds terrible," said Kasia. 'How long have you been coughing like that?"

"Only a day or two. But I've had chest problems on and off for a while."

"Sounds like you might have a chest infection. When's the district nurse coming again?"

"She's not due again until Friday, that's another three days."

"I will leave a message with her office," said Kasia. You can't wait that long."

She carried on with Mary's morning routine without saying much more. Fond though she had become of Mary, she was getting slower and slower to help each day and twenty minutes was a ridiculous amount of time. Suddenly the door-bell rang.

"That might be my daughter," said Mary. "She's been dropping in a lot more just recently. Must be worried about me." She gave a hollow laugh.

Kasia opened the door.

"Hello," she said. "It's Kasia, isn't it? So pleased to meet you at last. I'm Pat."

She held out her hand. *What a difference from last night,* thought Kasia.

Mary's daughter turned to Mary.

"Hi, Mum. You ready to go?"

"What do you mean, ready? Where am I going?"

"Your MRI, Mum. Today at 10 o'clock."

"But I thought it was tomorrow?"

"No, it's today, Tuesday."

"Oh dear." Mary was in a fluster. "I'm just finishing my breakfast. Lucky I'm dressed. When do we need to leave?"

"We've got about ten minutes. If you hurry." Hurrying was not something Mary was really capable of doing these days.

"I've just about finished," said Kasia to Pat. "Just the breakfast plates to clear up. Is it all right if I go? I'm running a bit late."

"Of course, off you go. You do a great job with Mum, she's always talking about you."

"Yes, we get on very well," said Kasia. "Goodbye, Mary, see you tomorrow."

She went across the road to Eric's, where Janet, another carer, was meeting her. She couldn't manage Eric on her own any more, although it was only a matter of time before his documentation was finalized. The key wasn't in its normal place, which meant that Janet had already arrived. She rang the bell.

When Janet finally opened the door to her she was out of breath and panic was written on her face. She was a very large lady with wild red hair, and a proud Cockney. She was regarded at the agency as 'a bit of a character.'

"Thank gawd you're 'ere, I've just arrived to find Eric on the floor in 'is bedroom. He seems to be unconscious, I've called 999."

Here we go again, thought Kasia. What could they do for Eric now that he'd been 'sentenced?'

Janet struggled up the stairs with Kasia close behind and they got Eric into the recovery position. Kasia frantically tried to find a pulse.

"So?" Janet was still panting.

"Think I can feel a faint one."

Janet put her ear to Eric's chest.

71

"He's breathing, but only just. We'll just have to wait for the paramedics."

"The thing is," began Kasia.

"What?" Janet's tone was sharp. "You mean he might die while we wait? What's wrong with that, then? "Hasn't he been assessed for euthanasia anyway?"

Kasia was upset and angry at the same time.

"We're supposed to call it 'Ultimate Care' now. Stupid name! I've looked after Eric for a long time. He's only seventy-five - that's not old, these days. I've watched him go from a man with memory problems to someone who doesn't know who he is any more, or who anyone else is. And who can be violent. It's so sad. His son can't afford the nursing home fees."

Janet sniffed.

"Well, I think he's just a burden on society. I don't see why the state should pay for 24-hour care to keep people like this alive."

Kasia was shocked. "Yes, but....." Her words were drowned out by the wail of an ambulance siren. She went downstairs to open the door.

Two paramedics came noisily up the stairs, carrying their equipment.

"Hi, I'm Liam and this is Dave."

"I'm Kasia, this is Janet; we're his carers."

Dave bent to see to Eric, and Liam started tapping into a tablet.

"New rule," he explained. "Every time we get called out to an elderly person we have to check with a central data base what their status is."

"Status? What kind of status?"

"Whether they've been assessed for euthanasia. Sorry, 'Ultimate Care.' Terrible, it is. I joined this service to save people's lives; now I have to ask if I can."

Even Janet was slightly shocked. Neither of them had seen this before.

"And what happens if he's on the list?"

"We take him to a palliative care unit, where his 'life will be shortly assisted to end.' That's what we've been told to say. Sometimes I feel I'm in 1984, you know, the novel."

Kasia didn't know. Janet nodded.

"So you mean, if he is, you can't do anything for him?"

"Mm hm."

He jabbed at the screen, frustrated. It seemed to be frozen. Dave stood up and said, "Looks like a heart attack. Has he had one before?"

"Yes, a couple of months ago," said Kasia. "He was in hospital for a while."

"Not sure he's going to recover from this one. What's the deal?" he asked Liam.

"Can't seem to access the website. "Probably crashed again. You don't happen to know, do you?" he asked Kasia.

Janet opened her mouth to speak but Kasia trod on her foot.

"No, sorry, we don't know," she said, quickly. Janet raised her eyebrows.

"Looks like A&E, then," said Liam.

The paras carried Eric down and into the ambulance.

Chapter 14

Charlie's stand-in, the Under-Secretary Nick Everest, was nervously preparing for the Tuesday Cabinet meeting. His first hadn't gone too well and Jack didn't seem to appreciate just what a huge task he'd had to take on since Charlie's stroke. Jack was taking his time about appointing a new Health Secretary; he was hoping against hope Charlie would be back at work before too long. He had chosen Charlie because of his medical experience - it was invaluable in understanding the medical world and negotiating with doctors and the BMA. There were no other medically qualified MPs of a high enough profile to replace him.

Nick was engrossed in his papers as the other ministers drifted into the Cabinet Room.

"You OK, Nick?" asked Bill. "You really have been thrown in the deep end, haven't you?"

Nick, who was a very bright young chap who had shot through the Civil Service ranks at lightning-speed, looked up.

"It's a huge headache, to be honest, but don't tell Jack. If only I could discuss things with Charlie, it would help, but I can't so I'm having to just charge ahead without consulting him."

"Charlie still not able to talk, then?"

Jack had been trying to keep the finer details of Charlie's condition from not just the Cabinet, but the media, and those who knew Charlie well enough had had to resort to asking his wife - not something they felt comfortable doing.

"No, the stroke's affected his speech badly. I went to see him yesterday. Between you and me, I don't see him returning to work any time soon, if ever. It's tragic. He's been essential in bringing in all the new protocols, and he and Jack have worked so closely together. He'll have to replace him soon. I'm doing my best but it's such a huge responsibility, and an unpopular one. I can't wait for someone else to take over."

"I'll try and deflect him, if I can," said Bill, "But you need to stand up to him."

"Can I ask you something, in confidence?" asked Nick. Other ministers were filing in and he leaned closer to Bill.

"How much longer do you think Jack can be PM? He's riding roughshod over the Cabinet, and he's making fundamental changes to with no authority from either the electorate or the Commons. He's successfully sidestepped all opposition to get these euthanasia protocols instituted even though half the Cabinet doesn't agree with him. I'm not surprised Charlie's collapsed from the strain - he doesn't agree with half of it either, and he's had to persuade the medical profession to co-operate! Jack's turning into a dictator. There's a lot of dissent around, you know - Jack's so full of hubris he just doesn't see it."

Bill nodded. "Many would agree with you. But don't worry, we're keeping an eye on him. It's only a matter of time before a motion of no confidence is passed and we'll be looking for a successor."

All conversation stopped as Jack appeared and took his place.

"OK, we'll start with the Health Service, as is usual for a Tuesday."

'Health disservice, more like it," someone muttered.

Jack ignored it.

"Nick, in Charlie's absence I'm relying on you to keep us up to date "

"Yes, of course." He was trying to sound more confident than he felt; appearing flaky in front of Jack was instant death. He drew some papers towards him. "Being unable to speak to Charlie is, naturally, making things pretty difficult for me."

Jack tutted impatiently. "But you're his deputy - you must be abreast of events."

"I'm afraid he was having talks with the medical profession to which I wasn't privy. Particularly about the cessation of treatment for terminal cancer patients. He was using his close contacts to discuss the details, and I didn't accompany him to those meetings."

"Well, really, I can't believe there are no records," said Jack.

"It's a very sensitive subject," interrupted Alistair. 'I can understand that he wanted to initially deal with it on his own. And how is Charlie, as a matter of interest? Is he making progress?"

Jack frowned. "Doing as well as can be expected, apparently."

"I heard that he had deteriorated and was still unable to speak," said Bill. "In the circumstances, don't you think you should replace him?"

"Oh, I don't think we've got to that stage yet." Jack's expression brooked no opposition but Bill persisted.

"I think you're in denial. You need to appoint someone else."

"There's nobody else of Charlie's calibre, or with his medical experience," Jack responded tersely.

"Nick, let's continue. When do you think the Ultimate Care for Cancer Patients initiative will be implemented?"

"Well, I understand that it's already been implemented in patients over 75. For younger people, Charlie was trying to get agreement about what constitutes 'no hope of recovery with or without treatment,' and how on earth doctors can predict whether a terminal patient has six months or less to live. They just don't know."

76

"Well, we have to work out some new protocols, then. Such as, if two doctors agree that the likelihood of a patient surviving less than six months is more than, say 80%, they can go ahead."

"Yes, but," Nick said, colouring slightly, "I don't think you realize just how much objection we're getting from the relatives. They are beginning to make legal claims against the decision. There have been too many instances in the past of patients surviving much longer than their prognoses."

"Without legal aid there won't be too many of them," said Jack. "And if the rich want to prolong their relatives' lives, they can pay and go private. Nobody's stopping them doing that."

"I've heard of families selling their houses and bankrupting themselves to do just that," said Nick. "And of moving their elderly relatives quietly and quickly to other locations, to avoid the final stage of Ultimate Care. Of course, sooner or later they need a doctor and the minute checks are made on the website the game's up. I think they're really just trying to make their point."

"How is the new website functioning?" asked Alice trying to change tack before Jack totally devoured Nick. "What's it called again?"

Nick gave an embarrassed cough.

"lullaby.nhs.gov.uk"

There were a few stifled titters around the table.

"I don't think that's at all funny," said Jane.

"It's not meant to be," said Nick, "but we had to think up a name quickly."

Jack banged his fist on the table. "We're getting off the point. How many patients with progressive neurological diseases are on Lullaby?"

Nick rifled amongst his papers and pulled one out.

"Three hundred and twenty-nine."

"THREE HUNDRED AND TWENTY-NINE?" Jack's face was thunderous. "Is that all?"

"The medical assessments are taking a long time - we don't have enough doctors assessing. And so many people are

77

appealing. You can't lump them all in the same category –
some, with say Parkinson's, are in the early stages and not
ready for a way out. Others are practically terminal. The courts
are clogged with appeal cases."

Jack looked pensive. He hadn't reckoned on quite so many
appeals.

"Recruit more doctors for assessments."

Nick looked at Jack with a combination of contempt and
impatience.

"I'm sure it won't have escaped your notice, sir, that we are
already chronically short of doctors and despite increasing
training places at medical schools, the drop-out rate is so big
that we're not even replacing those who leave. Many died
during the Covid-19 pandemic. The situation gets worse by the
week."

"Can't we recruit more from abroad? I'm sure there are
doctors from many other countries who would love to work
here, wouldn't have major scruples about Ultimate Care."

They could hardly believe their ears. Bill cleared his throat.

'Perhaps you've forgotten the immigration curbs imposed
after Brexit? It was what the people voted for, after all. Limited
immigration?"

"Well, it should never have included essential jobs like
medicine and other health care workers.

Ridiculous." Jack glared at them all.

The incredulity persisted.

"But we passed that bill ourselves, with great opposition if I
remember. We only just got it through. You thought it was a
good idea at the time." Bill leaned back in his chair and looked
straight at Jack. "You were told at the time that despite more
training places we were losing doctors overall, and you chose
to ignore it. It was a fact that we largely managed to keep from
the electorate, too. People want home-grown doctors, sure, but
with the Health Service in such crisis, especially since 2020,
who'd want to work in it?"

For once Jack was short of words. He began to bluster but
his phone flashed and vibrated with an incoming private call

and he sighed with relief at the opportunity to deflect the conversation.

"Need to take this, it's from Charlie's wife. Hello, Debbie, how's it going?"

The Cabinet quietly talked amongst themselves while they waited. They despaired of Jack's short-sightedness. He finished the call and turned back to them.

"Not bad news, I hope?" asked Bill.

"Afraid so. The stroke rehabilitation unit say that he's not responding at all to the various therapies they're trying, he's in and out of consciousness and that he needs long term care in a nursing home."

Jane said "And who will pay for it?"

Jack looked as sick as a dog. "His wife will have to. Otherwise….well, I'm sure I don't have to spell it out to you."

Chapter 15

Kasia got up even earlier than usual to fit in her visit to Doris, who was not in the area Kasia normally covered. The Agency had persuaded her into taking on Doris because they just didn't have any local cover for her, and as Eric was again in hospital Kasia had a gap in her rota.

"It's only temporary," said Annie, the agency manager. "I've had local carers going in the last few days, but they're all on holiday or off sick at the moment."

"But it's a twenty-minute bus ride away from my other clients," said Kasia. That means forty minutes extra travelling time every day, even if the buses are on time."

Annie sighed. 'I'm sorry, but we have to try and cover so many more patients these days."

"It's not my problem," said Kasia. "I can only do so much in a day."

"We'll pay your extra travelling time," Annie's tone was wheedling.

"No." Kasia felt she had given more than her fair share of goodwill to the agency.

"We'll pay double travelling time? And 25% more for her visits?"

Kasia ground her teeth. This was hard to refuse. The agency must be really stuck.

"Fifty per cent?" she haggled.

The sigh at the other end of the line was audible. "Well.....OK."

"But you have to find someone else soon. For *me*, this is only temporary."

"Yes. Thanks, Kasia."

As she thumped the alarm button to turn it off, Kasia groaned. It only seemed like an hour or two since she'd gone to bed. She dragged herself into the shower and threw on her clothes, and decided that for once she'd have something to eat. She had just made coffee and put some bread in the toaster when a sleepy Stefan appeared. Kasia brightened up. She had forgotten how early Stefan got up. She wished she wasn't looking so scruffy, and smoothed her damp hair self-consciously.

"Hi," said Kasia.

"Hi." Stefan banged about, making himself a bacon sandwich. When he had assembled the ingredients and put the bacon on to fry had turned back to Kasia.

"Sorry, not really awake yet. How are you?"

"I'm fine, just tired as usual. Too busy."

Stefan nodded, deftly flipping his bacon over.

"Has that client of yours got anywhere with the lawyers I told you about?"

"No - I tried hard to persuade her but - well, she said it will take time, and she doesn't have much left. Also, her children are paying for her to see a consultant privately and perhaps for an operation. She's doesn't want them to, but her daughter came to take her to the hospital for tests when I was there a couple of days ago."

Stefan slapped his sandwich together, smothered it with tomato ketchup and sat down, munching hard.

"But I suppose you can't save them all."

Kasia said: "You don't see them as people, like I do. I see them every day, I am 'in their lives', you know what I mean?"

"You care too much," said Stefan. "You're a very caring person, but that doesn't get rewards in this life. Anyway, why are you up so early today?"

"The agency have given me a client out of my area, twenty minutes by bus each way, so I have to start earlier to fit her in."

"You see what I mean?" Stefan gesticulated with what was left of his sandwich. "You're - how do they say it here - a 'soft touch'? You should find a job where people don't take advantage of you so much."

Kasia, who was prolonging the conversation by slowly rinsing her mug and plate at the sink, turned and smiled at him.

"That's just where you're wrong! I refused, and they offered me double travelling time, and time and a half for her visit."

"Wow." Stefan regarded her with new respect. "That's a result. Maybe you can take me out for a drink some time, then."

Kasia's heart jumped. It was the first glimmering of a sign that Stefan liked her.

"OK, when I get paid. I'm off now, see you later."

Kasia could feel Stefan's gaze following her out of the door. She smiled to herself. She was beginning to think that it was time she had a bit of fun.

On the bus, she pondered Stefan's remarks and started to think about what other jobs she could do. It was really her clients who kept her going, and despite always being so rushed she couldn't really see herself waiting at table or working as a barista.

~

Kasia rang Doris' doorbell and waited. She could just make out a slow, shuffling noise on the other side of the door and eventually a peaky looking Doris on a walking frame opened the door to her. She was wearing fluffy pink slippers and a grubby-looking pink candlewick dressing gown and which contrasted starkly with her grey face.

"'ello .....oh it's you!" She smiled in recognition. "You were here the night I came home, you made me lovely scrambled eggs!"

"Yes, that's right. How are you doing?"

"Slow, dear, very slow. Having surgery as you get older is no picnic. I feel real fuzzy today, you know, a bit 'eadachey. And the number of people that agency 'ave sent me - almost a different one every time! They seem to be short of staff."

"Yes, they are, and they are taking on more and more clients. But one of my regular clients has gone into hospital so I have a gap; I'll be coming to help you first thing every day until they find someone regular locally again."

"That's good. Now, I know you only 'ave twenty minutes but I'd really love a bath, the other girls 'ave said there's not time, and I 'aven't had a good wash since I got out of 'ospital."

Kasia tutted. "They should not tell you that. It's important that you have a regular wash. I don't think a bath would be good with your bad hip, though? A shower is easier."

She helped her undress .

"Oh, you've still got the plaster on," said Kasia. 'When are you having the stitches out?"

"In a couple of days, I think. Doesn't look very good does it?"

Kasia prodded it tentatively. 'Looks like some pus is under this plaster, it's almost coming off." There was a nasty smell coming from it too.

"Do you have the number of your doctor's surgery, Doris? I should call them and ask the District Nurse to come urgently to look at this, I think it's infected. That could be why you're not feeling too well. You might need antibiotics."

"You could be right, dear. I'm really not feeling myself."

Showering Doris was not easy. She had a shower attachment over her bath, which dribbled pathetically and the hose leaked, and it was awkward for Kasia to get her in and out, but as she was a tiny, bird-like lady and not too heavy to lift She ignored the health and safety requirements.

"That feels so much better," said Doris afterwards. "Now, if you just 'elp me dress, I can rustle up a bit of breakfast myself. I took your advice, and got my daughter to order a grocery delivery from her computer. Marvellous, what you can do on computers nowadays, isn't it."

She sat down hard at the kitchen table, and winced with pain. She seemed exhausted by her shower.

Kasia laughed. "Yes, my generation wouldn't exist without the internet."

While they were talking, Kasia tidied up the kitchen without even realizing she was doing it, and noticed a pile of clothes on the floor by the washing machine.

"Would you like me to put on a wash before I go? I think your dressing gown could do with a wash too. I expect it's difficult for you to bend down isn't it?"

"Yes, thank you, dear, that's a great help. My daughter's meant to be coming over later so she can hang them up for me."

"Right, I'll be off now," said Kasia. I'll see you tomorrow morning."

It was pouring with rain and she waited ages for a bus, getting wetter by the minute despite her umbrella. She knew that there was another demonstration planned that day and prayed the bus wouldn't be delayed by it. In the centre of town, groups of people were assembling with banners and there was a lot of shouting through megaphones but the march hadn't quite got going and the bus was not held up. By the time it reached Mary's road the rain was easing off.

Mary looked more ill day by day.

"How are you today, Mary? You look tired."

"So do you!" said Mary, patting her on the arm. "We got the result of the MRI last night."

"Do you want to tell me?" Kasia busied herself making tea and toast for Mary. She couldn't bear to look her in the face when she knew the news might be very bad.

"Well, good news and bad. The tumour in my bowel is quite large but as far as they can tell it hasn't spread locally, or anywhere else. So my children want to pay for an operation."

"And will you let them?"

Mary sighed. "I just don't know what to do. It will cost around £10,000. None of my children earns a big salary and it means they won't get a holiday this year. And I'm eighty- four, I've got several health problems and there's no guarantee that an operation at my age will give me a longer life, or a better quality of life. Then there's the anaesthetic risk.....but I came through my hip replacement all right, didn't I? I just don't know."

"And if the NHS were going to pay for the operation? You'd go ahead with it?"

"I suppose so, although when I think of younger people that need things done it feels a bit selfish.

When I first heard the government's plans on rationing health care it seemed a sensible idea, but it's not so good when it affects you directly, is it?"

"If you were my mother, I'd persuade you to have the operation if it were free. I couldn't pay for it to

be done privately, but I would if I could."

She busied herself doling out Mary's numerous medications - blood pressure, heartbeat regulators,

diabetic pills, the egg cup was almost full. Mary had begun to sort out her own pills, but Kasia wasn't too happy leaving her to do it herself now she was so unwell, all her drugs were important.

Finally, she got Mary dressed and prepared to leave.

"How's Eric?" Mary asked.

Kasia sighed. "I don't really know, I haven't heard since he went into hospital. He was very poorly, and, um.....I'm not sure he's going to get any more treatment ..... well, you know what I'm trying to say."

"What are they calling it now? Ultimate Care?"

"Yes...." Kasia wasn't totally listening, she had caught a snippet of news from Mary's radio, which was always on in the background.

85

"Ridiculous name! It's more like….."

Kasia held her finger to her lips and nodded towards the radio. Mary stopped in mid-flow and they both listened. The demonstration which was taking place had got out of control very quickly and the police had moved in with tasers. Several people had been tasered and one of them had died. Ultimate Care had claimed its first victim.

Chapter 16

There was an expectant hum of conversation in the Cabinet Room. Jack was going to announce the name of the new Health Secretary and bets had been placed. Charlie Warwick was now installed in a nursing home and still couldn't speak. One or two glanced at their watches - Jack was late, which was very unusual. At last he burst into the room, his mobile clamped to his ear.

"Yes, yes, of course, but can you confirm you'll take it?"

All eyes turned to Jack, ears flapping. A big grin spread over Jack's face and he wound up the call with a "Great, great, see you later."

He sat down and beamed around the table. "That was a bit of a close thing, but I'm glad to tell you we've now got a new Health Secretary. He's getting here as fast as he can, so I think we'll leave the health business until he gets here."

"And?" Bill stared expectantly.

"Alan Holmes."

"*ALAN HOLMES?*"

He hadn't been anywhere on the betting list. He was a backbencher in a marginal seat.

"Where on earth did you drag him up from?" said Jane in her most caustic tone. "He's barely hanging on to his seat."

"Well, he trained as a doctor although he never practiced, which will be useful. Of course, he doesn't know nearly as many people as old Charlie did, but I think while we're implementing all these health reforms we need to have somebody with a bit of medical know-how."

"I should think Nick's got more know-how than Alan," muttered Alice. "He's been a dealing with it for long enough."

Jack looked withering.

"You know as well as I do that I can't make him Health Secretary."

All eyes turned to Nick, who was looking extremely relieved. His days in the hot seat were almost over.

"I can certainly give him the benefit of my time with Charlie and get him up to speed," he said. "And we really do need someone to take over soon at this critical stage of UC."

"Well, let's get down to business," said Jack, glancing down at his papers. "First up this morning, is...."

"Before you start," interrupted Bill, "I think you ought to know that a group of religious Members - Catholic, Muslim, Jewish, etc - are forming a Parliamentary Pro-Life organization. "They're talking about taking the matter of Ultimate Care to the High Court."

Jack looked unruffled. "Oh, I don't think we need worry too much about that. I've made great pals with the senior judges. They've assured me that all these appeals against UC will be turned down. Why do you think I gave them such a great new remuneration package last year?"

"As I think I've said before," began Alistair, "I've yet to be convinced that we are saving a substantial amount of money on Elderly Care when we're spending so much on all this other stuff...."

Jack cut him off.

"We need to get down to business. Alistair: Demonstrations, please."

He began wearily. "As you all know, a demonstrator died after a taser was used on him. I've just got the post-mortem report, which will be made public after this meeting. It shows that as the victim, who was 68, suffered from quite severe heart problems it cannot be proved whether he died as a result of the taser, or whether he just happened to have a cardiac arrest. Obviously, this is good news for us, although I take no pleasure from it. I'm not really happy about the use of tasers, for just this reason. There are going to be plenty more like this."

"The whole point" said Jack, "is to deter demonstrations. People are beginning to get the message now they know that they are likely to encounter water cannons, CS gas and tasers. We can't afford to be wimpish over this. The police are already stretched to the limits. Anything else?"

"Nothing urgent." Alistair shuffled his papers together.

"Mortuaries and crematoria?" someone shot out.

"Under control. Freezer facilities are now adequate and the average waiting time for cremation has reduced from six weeks to five."

"I had a constituent in my surgery the other day who'd had to wait eight weeks, and she had no idea where the body of her relative was," said Alice. "She was incandescent."

"Hmm, well, she was unusual; the waiting time really has come down a lot in most places. And nobody knows where the bodies go - we don't want them knowing they're in industrial freezer units."

"Can they be sure they're getting the right one back?" someone muttered.

"Can we get on?" said Jack. "We need to discuss Thursday's by-election. It's a marginal seat and we can't afford to lose it. We're losing popularity because of Ultimate Care. I just don't understand it; all the pressure to sort out elderly care, so we come up with a solution which means people with no quality of life can die with dignity, and massive amounts of care home fees saved, and then the public decide they don't like it!"

"I sometimes think you forget you're playing God with people," said Jane very quietly. "Of course it's a practical solution, but emotions can't help but enter into it. I often wonder if you have any."

There was a hush around the table; they were all so fearful for their jobs that nobody had dared to put this into words before.

"Well, of course, you're a woman," said Jack, giving Jane a benevolent smile.

"I'll pretend I didn't hear that."

"We're getting off the point. Regarding the forthcoming by-election, I think you're going up to Great Creeping later today to speak, and rally support for the party, Alice?"

"Correct."

"And although I'm so busy, I've decided to go up myself, the day before the vote."

This was a surprise. Jack must be really worried. He hated meeting the public, especially at the moment, for obvious reasons.

"Great!" said Alice. "Always good to see how the other half live, north of Watford."

There was a knock on the door. Jack himself got up to open it and ushered Alan Holmes into the room.

"Welcome, Alan, come and sit down."

There were no vacant chairs so one was moved from a corner of the room and a great deal of shuffling around took place so that he could sit next to Nick.

"OK, just a couple of other things to get out of the way before we move on." He turned to the Media Secretary, Peter.

"I do hope you're going to be able to tell me that you've found a film company prepared to take on the making of the information films."

Peter looked agitated.

"Propaganda, more like," said Jane.

Jack thumped his fist on the table.

"That's not helpful, Jane. Well?"

His pale blue, slightly bulging eyes fixed on Peter.

"Erm….well….I've got one interested. But he wants a huge bung to go ahead with it."

"Exactly how huge?"

"Ten million." He shuffled uncomfortably in his chair. "You did say, give them enough money and someone will do it."

"I had a few thousand in mind, not millions. Maybe another kind of incentive? A gong, perhaps? You could intimate one's in the offing, for services to film making, or some such."

"I'll try." Peter looked sick. He had as good as agreed ten million. Jack had told him to throw money at it.

"Right, now we'll move on to Health, as is usual for a Tuesday. We were just waiting for you to get here, Alan, but you haven't missed anything vital. Now then…" he produced a paper from his pile "Before Charlie's demise, he and I discussed another area where we think we can make considerable savings in health care."

"Which is?" asked Jane.

"Care of very premature babies."

Alan's jaw dropped slightly.

"Pardon?"

"Very premature babies," enunciated Jack very carefully. "Their care costs an enormous amount, and most of them have life-long health problems, so they keep on costing the health service money all their lives."

"And?" said Alan carefully.

"We need to raise the number of weeks gestation back to where it was before the doctors got so good at saving babies who weren't previously viable. We also need to be braver at telling the parents of babies born with severe problems that the kindest thing for them would be not to treat them."

Nobody quite knew where to look. Certainly, some adjustments could be made to save money in this area but Jack sounded like a modern-day King Herod.

"It used to be twenty-eight weeks," said Alice. "You surely can't mean to revert to that? Sure, babies of twenty-one or two weeks need months of intensive care and are often handicapped in some way, but there needs to be a compromise. I think they can safely save babies down to twenty-four weeks now."

91

"And just for your information," Jane was bristling with fury, "my daughter was born at twenty-three weeks and survived to live to a healthy adulthood. You just can't generalise."

There were murmurs of assent around the table.

"And I have five-year old twins who were very prem," said Alan. "Sure, they have a problem or two, but nothing that will impact their life too much."

Jane looked vindicated.

Jack said "Well, we'll have to sound out the medical profession, obviously; that's your job, Alan. We may be able to compromise a bit. And Nick will give you the benefit of his experience with Charlie as to how best to go about it."

Bill passed Alistair a note. He looked at it and nodded. On it was a crudely drawn skull and crossbones with a J below it.

Alan stood up suddenly, scraping his chair with a noise that put their teeth on edge.

"I'm sorry, Jack but I just can't do this. I can't take this job. I was tremendously flattered that you asked me, but I just don't have the courage of your convictions."

He made for the door. For once, Jack was speechless.

Chapter 17

Kasia was getting used to her early starts and the bus ride across town to Doris but she hoped the agency would find a replacement for her soon. She was so tired all the time. She arrived at Doris's house to find the curtains drawn, which was unusual as Doris normally woke early and managed to totter to the window to draw them herself. Her daughter hadn't got around to getting a key safe yet but left the key under a flowerpot. Kasia opened the door and gagged at the stale smell in the flat.

"Doris? Are you all right?"

She went into Doris's bedroom and pulled the curtains back. Doris was in bed, her tiny frame huddled under the duvet and her teeth chattering.

"Doris?" She shook her arm. Doris didn't respond. She finally opened her eyes and mumbled "I feel really 'orrible…….."

"Have you been taking your antibiotics?"

"No……. can't get out of bed…….made me feel worse."

Kasia wasn't sure what to do. She knew the GP wouldn't come out quickly so there was nothing for it but to call 999.

"I think we need to get you to hospital, Doris. You don't look at all well."

She dialled the number and sat on the edge of Doris's bed and held her hand while they waited for the ambulance. It was about twenty minutes before it arrived and Doris had stopped talking and seemed semi-conscious.

"What's the problem here, then?" asked the paramedic.

"She's been out of hospital about a week. She's had a hip replacement after breaking her femur. She was doing OK but the wound is infected. She's on antibiotics but she says she feels worse on them. She spoke to me when I arrived but now....."

The paramedic made a face as he pulled back the covers and looked at the operation site.

"Raging infection, by the look of it. She's probably not on the right antibiotics. And look at this here - she's got a rash almost everywhere. Could be an allergic reaction to them, or even septicaemia. We better get her to hospital. Have you checked the Lullaby website, Bob?"

The other paramedic was checking it on his tablet.

"All fine, she's not on the list; we can take her to A&E." They bundled her into the ambulance and Kasia tidied up a bit and gave the flat a good blast of fresh air spray. She tried to call the agency to tell them what had happened but the line was engaged. Then she made her way to Mary.

Kasia was struggling to open Mary's front door when her phone rang. It was Annie from the agency asking her if she could work the coming Saturday.

"No, I'm sorry," she said. "I have made plans for this weekend."

"We're so short of carers at the moment....." began Annie.

Kasia cut her off before she'd had time to pitch a sob story.

"You're always short of staff, Annie, but it's not my fault if the agency doesn't have enough people to cover the clients. I'm already doing Doris, and she's out of my area. It was only meant to be temporary, when will I be replaced? I'm really tired, you know."

"I'm working on it," said Annie. "I'll pay you double time for Saturday?"

"No, I can't." Kasia was firm.

"OK, I'll try someone else." She cut the call abruptly.

Kasia was going out with Stefan at the weekend, and even if she hadn't been she was too exhausted to think about working even part of another weekend.

Kasia turned off her phone and threw it into her bag as she entered Mary's bedroom. She was trembling with indignation.

Mary, who couldn't help hearing part of the conversation, raised her eyebrows.

"Good morning, dear. Trouble with the agency?"

Kasia took a deep breath.

"I've worked the last two weekends to cover someone who's ill, and they want me to do this Saturday. I haven't had a day off for nearly three weeks. She forgets we are human."

"And is it true that you have plans for the weekend?"

Kasia smiled for the first time that day.

"Yes! You remember Stefan, who got me the names of those lawyers for you? I thought it was a joke when he said I could take him out for a drink when I was paid, but he remembered."

"In my day," said Mary, "the man always paid on dates. You don't want to start that kind of thing."

Kasia sensed her disapproval. "Don't worry," she laughed, "He earns more than me and I'm sure he'll pay his share. Now, what's happening with you? When I came yesterday you said you had to make a decision about your operation."

"Seems like it's been made for me, dear. My children won't hear of me choosing the alternative, even though surgery will be so expensive. I'm going into a private hospital next Monday. Look at this!"

She produced a glossy brochure from her bedside table.

"Looks ever so posh, doesn't it? Look, you get your own room and bathroom, and they all look over the gardens. Bit different from an NHS hospital, isn't it?"

Kasia took the brochure from her and flicked through it.

"It looks great. I'm glad you're having the surgery Mary, I know you're worried about the cost but your children only want to do what they think is best. Right, let's get you out of bed."

She helped Mary to the bathroom, and was concerned that she seemed so weak and wobbly. She hoped the operation hadn't come too late.

"How long will you be in there?"

"Should only be four or five days, I think. I might get used to being waited on hand and foot and not want to come home! Oh sorry, dear, I didn't mean anything, you look after me very well."

"You'll be needing more visits than you have now," said Kasia. "The agency are so busy, I don't know how they'll manage. I asked Annie why they keep taking on more and she said that they have a contract with the local council, and they can't say no."

"They need to get this social care sorted once and for all," said Mary. "Every government has tinkered with it but haven't solved the problem. Until now, I suppose - if enough people are assessed for this awful Ultimate Care thing the numbers of old people will drop."

"Yes, it's too horrible to think about, said Kasia. "And it's not the way that *I* would deal with it." She patiently went through Mary's morning routine and left her drinking a cup of tea.

"See you tomorrow, Mary. Take care."

Kasia was just closing Mary's front door when someone from across the road waved at her and called "Kasia, Kasia.....

She crossed the road.

"Hi, it's David, Eric's son, do you remember?"

"Yes, of course, how is your dad doing?"

"There's been a terrible to-do because he was taken to A & E when he had his second stroke and he should have been taken to a terminal care home until his Ultimate Care papers were finalized." David was talking very quickly and was clearly upset.

Kasia went pink. She knew why that had happened. Perhaps it hadn't been such a good idea to try to give Eric more time.

"Anyway," continued David, "it's all done now. He....." He sniffed hard and wiped his eyes, embarrassed.

"Sorry. I'm finding it all really hard to deal with. It's....its happening tomorrow. You know what I mean.....we can't put it off any longer. I know it's probably the best thing for him, but that doesn't make it any less upsetting."

Kasia put her hand on his arm. "I'm so sorry. It must be very difficult for you."

"Not just me - what do I tell my kids? They're only six and eight. It's one thing to tell them that their grandpa's died, but quite another to try and explain how we know which day, and what time, he'll have his life terminated."

"Well, I'm sorry I won't be seeing him again," said Kasia. "I remember him before his dementia got so bad and he was a lovely man."

"Thank you," said David. "And thank you for your care. I know he wasn't always easy towards the end."

"Is he having a funeral? If I can, I would like to go but of course it depends on my rota. Perhaps you could text me the details? I must go now, as usual, I'm in a hurry." She gave him her mobile number.

"Of course, thanks Kasia. Goodbye."

David shook her hand and went into his Dad's house. Kasia tried to imagine how she'd feel if it was her own father. As a Catholic, she couldn't contemplate euthanasia - the church was very clear on matters of life and death. She couldn't imagine such a thing happening in Poland. But in England there wasn't going to be a choice for some people.

She checked her patient list. Another new patient, officially one to replace Eric, but the agency seemed to forget that meant Doris was meant to be his replacement, even if it was temporary.

The agency hadn't given her any notes about Peter, her new client, and she was annoyed. She liked to know something

97

about them before she saw them. She got out her mobile and phoned the agency, praying that Annie wouldn't answer. She was in luck, someone else did, and tutted when Kasia told her she knew nothing about the man she was about to visit.

"You really should have been given this information. I'm afraid he's been profoundly deaf since birth and his speech had never really developed properly. Do you lip-read or know sign language?"

"No, I don't."

"Pity. He has a pad and pencil to write things down, though. He also has Parkinson's disease and is struggling to manage now his wife is in a nursing home with dementia. I don't think it will be long before he has to go into one too, although I'm not sure he has enough money for both him *and* his wife. She needs 24/7 care so you know what that means if he can't continue to pay for her."

Kasia's heart sank.

"He needs regular 3-hourly medication. If he doesn't get it he literally freezes and can't move himself. He'll have had a shower and breakfast already from his first carer so this is really just a medication visit. OK?"

"What is the code for his key safe?"

"Oh, sorry, it's 1068."

Kasia thanked her and went on her way.

She let herself into Pete's house. There was no point in calling to him. He was sitting in the living room, holding a newspaper in his trembling hands. She tried to catch his eye to avoid giving him a shock but he was too engrossed to notice and she lightly touched his shoulder.

He looked up, startled.

"Hello, I'm Kasia, from the agency?" She hoped he could lip-read a bit. He grunted a greeting and Kasia looked him in the eye to say hello. it was going to be difficult to communicate with Pete. He said something unintelligible to Kasia and she shrugged. He could only speak in a whisper, and the words were difficult to make out. She handed him a pad of paper and a pen, and he wrote in wobbly capitals 'need toilet quick.' Kasia helped him up and steered him unsteadily to the bathroom. She could foresee big problems with his care when he was no longer able to write - how would they communicate? She'd heard that the next group of illnesses on the Ultimate Care programme was progressive neurological conditions, and she guessed that when Pete needed twenty-four hour care he would meet the protocols.

She helped him back to his chair, got him settled with his paper and finally gave him his coffee and medication.

"Are you OK now?" Kasia asked him.

He raised his eyebrows. It was frustrating. Kasia took his pen and paper and wrote the words down. He nodded, and patted her hand, waving goodbye tremblingly with the other.

She let herself out feeling very depressed. How on earth did anyone cope with Pete's problems? Then her phone rang and her heart missed a beat when she saw it was Stefan.

"Just reminding you about Saturday - you haven't forgotten you promised to buy me a drink?"

"Of course not......"

"I thought we could maybe go to the cinema and then for a pizza?"

"Yeess...." Kasia sounded a bit doubtful.

"Don't worry, I'll pay," he said laughing. "It was just a joke about you paying for me.

Kasia breathed a sigh of relief - quietly enough for him not to hear, she hoped.

"That would be great. What time?"

"Leave around 6.30? I'll bang on your door."

"Great. See you then,"

She smiled to herself and suddenly Eric and Pete seemed easier to deal with.

Chapter 18

Jack cornered Alistair in a basement bar in the House of Commons. One of the reasons Alistair had gone there was because he didn't think it was one of Jack's haunts.

"Hi, Al, just the man I want to see."

"Why?" Alistair asked bluntly, his tone defensive.

Jack put his hand on Alistair's shoulder and entered his personal space. Alistair tried to edge away, but he had his back to the bar counter. Jack lowered his voice.

"Al, you know I'm in a right fix trying to appoint a new Health Secretary."

"Well, it's not exactly the number one favourite job, is it?" Alistair picked up his pint.

"Apparently not, although I've never had trouble appointing people before; everyone wants the glory of a key government post. Anyway, I've come to the conclusion that I'm going to have to appoint within the Cabinet, and do a bit of a shuffle. And the man I'd like for the job is you."

Alistair choked on his drink. "Me? But I've no medical experience whatsoever, and to be honest, I'm not sure I fully agree with the Ultimate Care protocols. I really couldn't progress them. You'll have to ask someone else."

Jack's eyes narrowed. "I get to choose who does what, Al - you know that. I want you because I trust you. You've been a key member of the team. I need someone I can rely on."

"I don't think you can rely on me for this. Sorry. It's about time you knew that there is a lot of dissidence about UC. Not everyone shares your conviction that it's the only way to deal with the increasing elderly population."

"Are you telling me you're not committed to my reforms?"

Alistair shifted uncomfortably from foot to foot.

"I....well, I can understand the disquiet of the Church - churches - and the Muslims, the Jews and so on. It doesn't fit with their beliefs."

"And what is the alternative? I don't see anyone else coming up with a solution."

Alistair sighed. "Half the population is up in arms about it, you know that. And you've bludgeoned these protocols through without a proper parliamentary bill. You're treading on eggshells, Jack."

Their attention was diverted by 'Breaking News' on a TV screen. A massive demonstration taking place in Birmingham had got out of hand and police in riot gear were charging at the crowd. Clouds of smoke announced the use of tear gas. Two men fell down, seemingly as a result of being tasered. Jack tutted. Alistair looked sick.

"Is this the sort of thing you really want, Jack?" Alistair inclined his head towards the screen. "Civil disobedience is getting out of control - this is the third big demo this week."

Jack passed his hand over his face and for the first time in months looked genuinely concerned. Normally, he slid over unpleasantness with an oily smile. Alistair turned from the screen and back to look at Jack.

"Look, I've got an idea. I'm really not the right man for the job, and clearly Alan Holmes couldn't hack it either, but there is an ambitious backbencher I know who would jump at the chance. You probably don't know him that well, he was only elected at the last election, but I know for a fact that he's one hundred per cent behind U.C and he would be your man to

101

progress the protocols. Plus he has some experience in hospital management although he's not medically qualified."

"Who, then?"

"Robert Michel. Represents one of the Northern constituencies."

Jack looked thoughtful.

"I'm trying to picture him.....tall with red hair?"

"Tall and slim with auburn hair, yes."

"Hmm, well, his physique suits the post better than poor old Charlie, he really wasn't a good advert for

healthy living. Upset me hugely, him being taken ill like that."

Alistair looked doubtful. In his experience, Jack was rarely discomfited by anything, and Charlie's unfortunate stroke was more of a major inconvenience to his plan than anything else.

"Do you think we should run this past the rest of the cabinet before I ask him? We can't afford another embarrassment."

Alastair looked surprised. It wasn't like Jack to seek anyone's opinion about anything, but maybe he was learning.

"Yup, I think that would be wise. There will be others who know him who can back me up in my opinion that he'd be suitable - or not, of course, as the case may be."

"Good, good. I think maybe I'll have a drink now."

They sipped in silence. Alistair wished he could leave; being alone with Jack had become somewhat dangerous of late, you never knew what was coming next. The bonhomie they had shared whilst their party was in opposition had faded when they won power and Jack became more and more like a dictator.

~

The next Cabinet meeting was unruly, to say the least. As Alistair had expected, there was a noisy reaction when Jack proposed Robert Michel as the new Health Secretary. Alistair backed him up, citing his youth and enthusiasm for UC.

"But he's only been here five minutes," grumbled Bill.

102

"I've never even heard of him," said Alice.

"You need to be sure he won't accept and then withdraw, like Alan Holmes," said Steven. "You must emphasise just what the job entails at the moment. Not everyone can stomach it."

"Well, I know him quite well," said Peter. "And I know that he would be committed to the implementation of the new protocols regarding neurological conditions and so on. He's very pro - UC."

"Good, that's decided then. I'll speak to him as soon as I can."

Jack shuffled his papers.

"So, Nick, can you bring us up to date with the latest discussions with neurologists regarding the protocols around Motor Neurone Disease and Parkinson's?

Alistair noticed Nick flush. He seemed perpetually uncomfortable in Jack's presence. "I'm afraid that the working committee hasn't come to a unanimous decision as to what the protocols should be. Neurological conditions are notoriously capricious and a prognosis is always difficult. Just look at Stephen Hawking."

"Hmm, well, he's an exception." Jack wasn't about to make concessions. "What exactly have they agreed so far?"

"They're beginning to come to an agreement regarding at what stage of these illnesses patients can be processed for UC. It hasn't been easy. And of course, many of them have already opted for assisted suicide, which means that many of those who remain with zero quality of life are anti-UC. But we're slowly getting there."

"OK." Jack shuffled his papers again. "Well, when the new Health Secretary starts he must make this a priority and push for an early agreement. What about the premature baby protocols?"

"*That*," said Nick 'is a whole different ballgame. It's a very emotive subject and both doctors and midwives are in total disagreement about it."

"*I*, for one, as I've said before, am dead against it," interrupted Jane. Every case is different and you can't have a one-size fits all protocol."

"Can we let Nick continue?" Jack shot a malevolent look at Jane and nodded to Nick to continue. Jack was a misogynist and Alistair had had to work hard on him to appoint a couple of women in the Cabinet.

"Whilst many of them agree that the technology to keep extremely premature babies alive has made great strides in past years, several are concerned that these invasive procedures cause pain and distress and that the majority of babies have life-long problems. And others think that the gestation stage should be kept as it is."

"That's a generalization," Jane shot at him. "I think I've mentioned my own experience of having a premature baby before......"

"Not now, Jane," snapped Jack. He turned to Nick.

"Thank you, Nick for trying to hold the fort. But hopefully we'll have the new Health Secretary in place soon who will impress on those concerned with neonatal care that there must be reforms."

Alistair winced at the put-down. He thought Nick had done pretty well in extremely difficult circumstances. Jack smiled around the room. He seemed to think this was somehow a unifying gesture. Alistair nudged Bill, and made an 'I'm gagging' face. There was something about Jack smiling that was almost psychopathic; it induced nausea in him.

"OK," said Jack, 'Next on the agenda is civil disobedience, Alistair."

"I expect you all saw the demo yesterday, when people were tasered. Of course it's not the first time, but it's making the government more and more unpopular. The red-tops are saying that we're turning into a police state, and I can't blame them. The Police can barely cope; they're putting a lot of crimes on the back burner because they're so stretched. Unless more money is allocated, I don't see how we can keep on top of this." He looked pointedly at Jack.

"Well, I need to know how much the bean counters think we've saved on UC. We could plough that into policing, temporarily."

"I doubt it'll be anywhere near enough," said Bill. "At the last count, UC was costing more to implement than keeping people alive."

Jack shook his head impatiently.

"Yes, yes, I know all that, all new initiatives cost money, but there will come a break-even point soon, believe me." He rubbed his hands together. "Anything else that's urgent? I've got an early lunch with a very important person - you all know who!"

'Yes - you get along, Jack," said Alistair. "And try not to say anything he can tweet to the rest of the world." He smiled, to indicate it was a joke but Jack glared at him as he left the room, full of his own self-importance.

"Good luck with that," Alistair said under his breath.

The others laughed as they filed out. Alistair tapped a few of them on the shoulder as they passed and muttered "Could you stay a minute?"

When there were just six of them left he leaned against the closed door and said "I'd like to have a word with you all."

They sat back down.

"Now, then, I know you all pretty well, and I think all six of us feel the same about Jack. I think an awful lot of the Cabinet do, to be honest, but most of them are afraid for their jobs. Bill and I think we need to have a talk about how Jack's become totally out of order on everything. We think it's time to get enough members together to stage a vote of no-confidence. Time for someone else to take the lead."

There was dead silence for a few seconds. Then someone spoke:

"Yes, but we can't.....I mean he's so vindictive, heads WILL roll if he gets wind of any dissention."

"He can't sack the whole Cabinet," said Steven.

"But...." began Peter.

Alistair interrupted. "So, you're willing to put up with a leader who's effectively become a dictator? Who connives with doctors and judges to push through his monstrous ambitions? Ultimate Care is not democratic, and we all know it. Assisted suicide is one thing, but this?"

Alistair paused for breath, and looked around the room. "It won't be easy, but Bill and I have discussed possible courses of action. Jack has to make a monumental cock-up of something, to create a huge scandal. Something so serious that we can get him out. Even if we have to invent something - although with a bit of digging around I don't think we'll actually have to invent anything. Some of us have friends in the media."

"How can we be sure he hasn't got the Press in his pay? He seems to have fixed almost everyone else." Peter sounded bitter.

"He may have," said Alistair grimly. "But I don't think we can let that stop us. Finding a few sexual peccadillos for instance. But I think there needs to be something else as well, shady dealings, investment in dodgy companies, that sort of thing. We need to discredit his integrity."

"What integrity?" asked Bill. They all laughed.

"I should have said 'perceived integrity'."

"I have an old friend who works at the Post," said Steven. "He's written some stinging articles against Ultimate Care and other contentious issues. He loathes Jack's guts. He's good at investigative stuff. That's really what journalists are about, isn't it?"

Alistair looked around. "So?"

One by one they said "I'm in."

Alistair smiled. "Great. Let's go and drink to that."

106

Chapter 19

Saturday finally arrived. Kasia was exhausted and slept late into the morning. She got up, still feeling a bit tired, showered and washed her hair. Then she went out, bought a Polish newspaper and then went to a coffee shop and treated herself to a large cappuccino and a chocolate muffin - she intended to fully enjoy her weekend. She idly scanned the jobs column of the paper, wondering if she could find another job that was less exhausting. They were nearly all for domestic help, baristas and care workers.

"Hello, Kasia!" Kasia looked up to see one of the girls from the flat downstairs coming up to her table."

"Oh, Natasha, hi. I haven't seen you for ages. How are you?" She liked Natasha, who never seemed to have a care in the world.

"Oh, I'm good, thanks. But how about you? You always seem to be working."

"Yes, but not this weekend. And I have a sort of date tonight."

"Anyone I know?"

Kasia went pink. She wasn't really sure if she wanted to say.

"You're blushing....! Come on, tell me."

"You know Stefan? Who shares my flat with Anna and me?"

"Not the dishy Stefan - you lucky thing."

"Yes, it's very odd, we have lived there as friends, the three of us, for two years but just recently things seem to be changing. I was quite surprised he asked me out, he must have lots of girlfriends."

"Sure, but you're very attractive, Kasia. Don't put yourself down. Although, if you don't mind me saying so, you look a bit tired. Maybe some make-up tonight? And what are you going to wear?"

This had been worrying Kasia; she so rarely went out socially and she knew her wardrobe was very utilitarian.

"Perhaps I'll go shopping - I haven't bought anything new for months."

"Yes, go on, treat yourself. Well, good to see you, enjoy your date."

"I will." Kasia got out her mobile and tapped into her banking app to see how much money she had. She found that her balance looked quite healthy as overtime and lack of opportunity meant she hadn't spent much recently. She finished her coffee and headed for the nearby shopping centre, which was very busy. She went into a chain store she liked and wandered around. The music was deafening and after ten minutes her head was beginning to pound along with the loud music so she made an instant decision and paid. She was just leaving when she bumped into Natasha again.

"You again!" said Natasha. "Ooh, you've bought something - let's see."

Kasia fished out the skirt and top she'd bought from her bag. Natasha nodded approvingly.

"And I tell you what, Kasia, I've just been in the department store and they're promoting a new makeup line, and doing free makeovers. Why don't you go and see?"

"Oh. I *must* look tired."

Natasha pulled a face. "Sorry - I didn't mean that. Maybe you'd be better off having an afternoon nap and doing your own make up."

"I sure need to catch up on my sleep," Kasia agreed. "I start so early every day, and the agency keep giving me more clients. I'd love to find another job. I miss teaching, but I can't afford to take the Post Grad Certificate of Education course."

"I'm so sorry, I didn't realize how tough it was. I didn't realise you were a teacher - what a pity you're stuck working as a carer."

"I like it, in many ways. I have some really nice clients, but it's all rush, rush, rush and just when I think I've finished for the day the agency call and ask me to see an emergency client - like, you know, when someone has just been sent home from hospital."

"What age group did you teach?"

"The younger children - what they call Primary School here. Seems odd that now I take care of the elderly."

"I've just had an idea," said Natasha. "I have a friend who's starting up a nursery school. Maybe you could get a job there - I don't think you need post-grad qualifications for that."

"Really?" Kasia cheered up. "That's a fantastic idea. I hadn't really thought of nursery work. Small kids can be tiring too, but at least the hours are more regular and every weekend would be free. Can you find out more, and give me her details?"

"Yes, of course, I'll talk to her, and let you know." She looked at her watch. "Oh! I must rush, I'm meeting someone."

"Bye," said Kasia, "and don't forget to talk to your friend."

Kasia walked home feeling excited that at last there was a spark of hope about a new job. She now had a proper headache she took a couple of painkillers and went back to bed.

~

She awoke four hours later to find Stefan knocking on her door.

109

"Are you there, Kasia? We need to get going in around half an hour."

"Oh, sorry, I fell asleep. I'll get up now. See you in a bit."

She dragged herself out of bed, put on her new clothes and applied some make-up. She'd been rather alarmed that Natasha had commented on how tired she looked. She decided to leave her long hair loose and stepped back from the mirror.

"Not too bad," she said to herself as she grabbed her bag and went to find Stefan.

"Wow - you look great," he said. "Let's go. The film starts in fifteen minutes."

The film was a rom-com, and very funny. Kasia found herself crying with mirth and wiping her tears away with the back of her hand. Stefan silently produced a handkerchief and handed it to her. She glanced at him and he grinned, his eyes wet too.

"I really enjoyed that," she said as they left the cinema. "I can't remember the last time I saw a movie. It was so good to have a laugh."

"It was a real girls' film," Stefan teased her. She nudged him playfully with her elbow.

"Oh yes? I saw you too....... And you must be the only man in the world who still uses cotton hankies."

He laughed and took her hand. "I like proper hankies. I also have a Polish mother, remember?"

Kasia laughed. "Yes, things are a bit different here, aren't they? I think our parents would be a bit shocked if they saw how some people behave here."

"Probably, but I enjoy life here a lot more. More free and easy. Right, I'm starving. Is pizza OK?"

"That's fine by me. I haven't had a meal out for ages," she said. "Although this morning I had a huge chocolate muffin with my coffee."

Stefan glanced at her approvingly. "Well, you could do it more often, you don't have a weight problem, do you."

"No – it's just that there is never any time."

They settled into a corner table in the restaurant, and ordered.

"Wine?" asked Stefan.

"Well, I…..yes, why not."

"So, your job…." said Stefan. "You sound fed up with it. And what about all this euthanasia stuff? That must be affecting you."

"Yes, it's awful. And we're not supposed to call it euthanasia."

"So they think up this stupid name, Ultimate Care, which fools nobody. How about your own patients?"

"Clients," Kasia automatically corrected him. "We have to call them clients. I have one who is being 'processed.' I saw his son the other day and he was so upset. And another client, a lovely lady, has had cancer surgery paid for by her children because of the rules, she has other health problems and she's eighty-four. They told her that she would be left to get sicker, and that when she needed 24/7 care she'd be processed. So her children stepped in. I don't really want to have to deal with this stuff any more."

"You should look for something else. You have a degree don't you?"

"Yes, but I can't teach in the UK without a PGCE. But today I bumped into Natasha - you know, she lives in the basement flat. She has a friend who is starting up a nursery school and looking for staff. I think I could do that without the certificate. The kids would be younger, I taught seven to eight-year olds, but I don't mind that. She's going to talk to her friend about me."

"That's great - you must follow that up. You never seem to have any fun. You should be enjoying life more, like my friend Karl, and me."

Kasia laughed. "Yes, you and Karl always seem to be out. But you earn good money. Care work is not well paid."

"That's true, and that's why you should look hard for something else. Yes, in the building trade wages are good, but don't forget we both send money home to our families."

111

Kasia frowned. "Don't make me feel guilty. I'd love to send something home for my parents but it's impossible on my pay. Still, at least I'm not a burden on them."

"I'll drink to that." Stefan took a large swig of wine and topped up Kasia's glass.

"Hey, not so much! I will have a hangover. I already have a bit of a headache."

"Oh?" Stefan was concerned. "You didn't mention it?"

Kasia shrugged it off. "I've had it most of the day but I took some paracetamol before we came out so it's not so bad. I think I am just worn out. I spent half the day asleep."

"Well, Sunday tomorrow, so you can catch up on your beauty sleep again," Stefan teased her. "Oh, I didn't mean that....you're very attractive, Kasia." He took her hand across the table.

"No, I'm not that attractive," Kasia murmured, blushing.

"Let's do this again, I've really enjoyed spending some time with you instead of just nodding across the kitchen in the mornings when we're half asleep."

Stefan held her hand as they walked home, but said good night to her outside her room with a chaste kiss on the cheek. Earlier, Kasia had been hoping for a bit more, but now she was quite grateful as her headache was back in force, and she was beginning to feel rather unwell.

"Good night, Stefan, thank you so much. And for paying all the restaurant bill, you didn't need to." She gave him a hug.

"You're welcome. Sleep well."

~

When Kasia woke on Sunday morning she felt really ill. Her head was hammering, her throat was sore, she felt feverish and her limbs ached. She stumbled to the bathroom, collected a glass of water from the kitchen on her way back to her room and took two paracetamol. Then she fell back into an exhausted sleep, waking only to drink some water and take more. She had finished the packet and was wondering how she would get through the night when there was a knock on the door, and Stefan's voice said "Kasia? Kasia? Are you OK?"

"Not really," she croaked. "I think I have the flu. I hope you don't get it."

"Well, so do I….. but can I get you anything?"

"Do you have any paracetamol? I've finished all mine."

"No, but I can easily go down to the corner shop and get you some. I'll go now."

"Thanks." Kasia tossed and turned restlessly, every bit of her seemed to ache and she felt very hot.

Stefan was soon back, knocking on her door.

"Can I come in? I've brought you a mug of tea too."

"Yes, of course. Sorry, I must look such a mess," she said as he set down the tea beside her bed and extracted two paracetamol from the packet for her.

"Never mind about that, you look really ill. Here, take these. I'll leave the packet there."

She took the tablets with a swig of tea. "I really do feel awful. I don't know how I'm going to get to work tomorrow."

"You mustn't worry about that - you can't work if you're ill. I bet you never take time off, do you?"

"No, I've never had a day off. But I only get paid for the hours I do. I can't afford to take time off, the rent's due next week. I had a bit in hand but I bought some stuff yesterday. I didn't think then that I was going to be ill, I just thought I was tired."

"Look, if you're short of money, I can lend you some. Try not to worry, it won't help you get better."

She managed a smile.

"Thanks. Now go, before you catch this bug!"

"I think by spending yesterday evening with you I may already had caught it," he said. "Anyway, I hope you sleep OK. You need to drink lots of water."

"Yes, I know. But when I get up I feel all wobbly."

"I'll get you some more water." He disappeared and returned a couple of minutes later with a large jug of water. "There, that should keep you going for the night."

Kasia laughed. "It's a vase!" she said. "But never mind, it will do the job. I hope you rinsed it out first."

"Of course," said Stefan indignantly. She knew he was lying.

"Thanks very much."

"Good night, I hope you sleep OK."

"Thanks. Good night."

Kasia tucked down under her duvet and closed her eyes. She thought about Stefan and how helpful he'd been. She hoped it was because he was as keen on her as she was beginning to be on him. Then she thought about work, and how a few days off would put her in a tight spot with her money. She was a good at budgeting, she had to be, but there wasn't much wriggle room.

~

She had a restless night with some strange dreams in which a telephone kept ringing insistently. She finally woke up to find that it was her own mobile. As she picked it up, she noticed the time - 9.15 am. Of course, the agency.

"Kasia, Kasia, It's Annie, where are you? Did you oversleep? Your clients are waiting for you."

"I can't work today, Annie," she croaked. "I'm ill, I think I've got flu."

"But you've just had a weekend off - you should be full of beans."

"I can hardly get out of bed. I'm sorry, I have to take a sick day."

"One always feels worse first thing in the morning," said Annie. "I expect once you're up you'll feel better. Could you start at lunch time?"

Kasia couldn't believe her ears. "You don't understand - I have a fever, sore throat, I ache all over and I can hardly get to the bathroom, I feel awful. There's no chance I can work today, or tomorrow probably."

"I don't think you've ever taken a day off sick before, have you? You know if you don't work, you'll get no pay?"

Kasia sank back against the pillows and felt tears pricking her eyes.

"Yes, of course I know," she said through clenched teeth. "I am ill, I'm not doing this because I want a day off."

She cut the call without saying goodbye and tears streamed down her face. She thought of all the days when she'd felt a bit unwell, or just very tired, but still gone to work because she hated letting her clients down. The agency was impossible; she just had to find another job.

Chapter 20

Steven was having trouble getting hold of his friend Mike North at The Daily Post. He was beginning to wonder whether he had the wrong mobile number for him when, on his umpteenth attempt, the call was answered.

"North," barked a voice.

Steven was taken aback. This wasn't the Mike he knew and liked. He tentatively replied "Oh, hi, Mike, it's Steven." He didn't need to elaborate, they'd been friends since school although since Steven had been an MP they had got together rather less.

"Oh, hi, Steven, sorry to be so brusque. I've got an important deadline coming up, could I call you back this evening?"

"Sure. Speak later."

He was in a Regent Street bar when the call came. He didn't want to be having this conversation anywhere near other MPs.

"Great to speak to you," he said. "Sorry it's been so long, but parliamentary business never seems to end. Can we meet for a drink, or lunch perhaps? There's something I want to talk over with you. We need to be very discreet."

Mike laughed. "I get the message. Better be somewhere well away from Parliament Square then. Are you doing anything this evening? I'm trying to avoid getting home in time to go to a Parents' Evening."

"I said I'd be home for dinner, for once, but I can easily make an excuse. The sooner the better, as far as we're concerned."

"What do you mean, we?"

"Oh, don't worry, you're only meeting me, but I'm acting on behalf of several others. Listen, I'm in the West End, in a bar near Piccadilly Circus. We can't meet here, too noisy to have a proper conversation, but there's a great steak restaurant almost next door called Chez Vache - do you know it?"

"Yes, I do, I'll see you there in about twenty minutes."

Steven finished his drink, strolled along to the restaurant, and chose a table in a corner away from interested ears. He ordered a bottle of claret, leaned back in his chair and stretched his long legs. When Mike arrived they toasted their meeting and ordered. Over the starter they caught up with each other's news.

"So, how's life in the Cabinet, then?" asked Mike. "I imagine it's pretty gruelling."

"I'm enjoying it but it means long and unpredictable hours. It's making things a bit tricky at home, Pat's always moaning I'm never around. And look at me, my waistline's increasing by the week."

Mike grinned. You're still a good-looking bastard though, your height hides your weight."

Steven was, indeed, the handsome smoothie of the Cabinet. "Always rushing around, no time for proper meals, just grabbing sandwiches. And I see you've chopped minutes off your morning schedule by growing a beard."

Mike stroked his chin. "I grew it for charity but decided to keep it. The old scalp hair's thinning a bit so I thought I'd major on my face. And as for you, you should take a leaf out of Jack's book - he's always being papped enjoying his leisure somewhere."

"He lives a charmed life. It's us mere lackeys who do all the work. Still, I've got where I wanted to be so I can't complain.

How about you? A journalist's life is pretty erratic too, I'd imagine."

"Yeah, if I'm working on a big story to a deadline, like I was today, I can be up most of the night. And have you ever known a journo who didn't smoke and drink? But thank God for modern technology, it must have been far worse before the advent of computers. It means you can file copy from almost anywhere."

"And the kids? Jean was expecting another last time we met."

Mike pulled a face. "Yes, the 'afterthought' baby turned out to be twins. Born last November. We're finally getting a bit of sleep, but God, they're hard work. I've put my foot down about any more."

Steven laughed. "We stopped at two - Pat's not very good at pregnancy, lots of medical interventions, so she's happy to settle for what we've got."

The waiter brought the main course and when he'd gone Mike asked "So - to what do I owe this very pleasant meal?"

Steven leant conspiratorially across the table. "You must have guessed that it's about Jack and UC. Some of us had a very serious talk about him yesterday, and how we can get him out of office. This is all very hush-hush, the only other people who know we're meeting are certain members of the Cabinet."

He glanced around. "I don't think we're in danger of anyone overhearing but we need to keep our voices down."

Mike raised his eyebrows. "So?"

Steven gave him a pitying look. "Can't you guess the problem? Ultimate Care is splitting the country and the Cabinet. Jack's becoming more and more autocratic, virtually running the country without the consent of Parliament or the Party. You realise, don't you, that he and Charlie Warwick...."

"Yes, what exactly happened to him? Had a stroke, didn't he?"

"A bad one - poor chap is in a terrible way, half paralysed and can hardly speak. Needs 24/7 care. He'll never return to work. And if his wife can't afford to keep him in a nursing home he'll become a victim of his own policies. Ironic, huh?"

"Yes." Mike looked pensive. "Pity; a good chap gone to the bad. I always liked him."

"Yes, he was an affable guy, but too concerned with staying in favour. Jack used him mercilessly because of his background in the Health Service, and his contacts. That's how he managed to implement the UC protocols."

"He must be getting on a bit, though?"

"Yes, he's in his early seventies and I don't think he was planning to stand at the next General Election anyway. Parliamentary life is exhausting enough for someone of my age. Anyway, Charlie and Jack between them issued the protocols to the NHS and that was that."

Mike said "Didn't they have a problem getting doctors to implement UC? You know what people are calling it, don't you?"

"There are various names, and they all have ghastly connotations. But there *are* actually enough doctors around who are willing to carry it out. Those who aren't, aren't obliged to although Jack initially said they'd have their contracts terminated. There are various interpretations of the Hippocratic Oath."

'So what exactly are you planning with Jack?"

"Well, a lot of us at Westminster aren't at all happy about the whole UC business. It's not so much that we all *totally* disagree with him about not striving to keep certain categories of patients alive, but that it was not properly discussed and no bill was ever passed. If he can do this with the NHS, we're all very worried about what he might turn his attention to next. We just can't allow this lack of democracy to continue." Steven shook his head. "It's terrible."

"And so?"

"We feel sure that with a little digging around into his private life we can dredge up enough muck to get him out of power. No British politician has ever had a major scandal without having to resign. Ideally, we'd like some personal peccadillos as well as, perhaps, financial indiscretions to surface? I feel sure you could keep your antennae up and find something."

"Well, funny you should bring this up right now, because we already have someone following up a lead at the moment. Apparently, a friend of Laura, Jack's wife, let it out that they've had a major row. She thinks it's to do with infidelity, although Laura was being very cagey, as she would, I guess. You can't trust anyone nowadays, what with social media posts going viral so quickly."

Steven nodded. "Yes, I'm terrified to even email my own wife, these days, let alone post on Twitter."

"The financial thing, though, I'll to do some sniffing around. It's rumoured that he puts his earnings from speeches and so on into an off-shore trust, and that he invested in some extremely dodgy enterprises before he became PM. We need to prove that the investments were unethical, or that he avoided paying tax."

"Look," said Steven, "We're not too concerned with how much truth there is - just a whiff of scandal will bring people out of the woodwork and do the rest for us. Jack thinks he's invincible, he's got so much hubris he thinks he's as infallible as the bloody Pope. We need to knock him off his pinnacle."

"And who would take over?"

"Not me, obviously, too junior. Bill or Alistair, probably. But you never know with leadership elections."

"Too right. But what puzzles me is why nobody's publicised these dodgy financial dealings before. There've been rumours but they've not got into print."

Steven put down his knife and fork. "Well, there you have it. I think Jack's got some kind of hold over editors. He's sweet-talked the judges - nobody who's appealed the Ultimate Care decision has had it reversed - and also the doctors, or rather, he got Charlie to do that for him. He seems to have everyone in his pocket, so editors would be chicken-feed to him. He's a like a corrupt African ruler - favours are done, and I'm pretty sure money changes hands. Someone needs to stick their head above the parapet and publish."

"Interesting. I'll have a little chat with The Beast and see what vibes I get, without mentioning anything too specific. He may be dead against it."

"You mean your editor? Is that what you call him?"

"Not to his face, obviously. He's one of the old school. Hasn't long until he retires, although they say we'll never get rid of him, he'll die on the job."

"And what about the snooping?"

"Well, yes…. " said Mike. "The trouble is, I'm a bit too well known. Asking these kinds of sensitive questions is a bit risky when people know who you are. But we have a great junior reporter who's been on the paper a couple of years now, and he's ace at sniffing out this kind of thing. Like a terrier with a bone, he is. He should have been a detective. I'll take him out for lunch and have a man-to-man chat with him although if Jack's got half the country under his thumb it might be quite a struggle to expose him. He is, as you well know, very clever."

Steven gestured to the waiter for the bill. "Yes, he is."

Mike said "But I'm going to enjoy this. I've always thought him an odious man."

Chapter 21

Kasia got up to go to the bathroom and then wobbled into the kitchen to make a cup of tea before sinking gratefully back into bed. She felt terrible, and hadn't the energy to even do some toast. She dozed all morning and was awoken by a banging on the door.

"Kasia, it's Stefan. Can I come in?"

"Of course…but Stefan, what are you doing here at lunch time? You should be at work."

"The building job I'm on at the moment isn't far away so I thought I'd pop in and see you."

Stefan brought in a tray with a bowl of hot soup and some toast.

"Here you are, lunch. I figured you wouldn't be well enough to get anything to eat, let alone go out to the shop. Hope you like carrot and coriander, there wasn't much choice."

Kasia was almost speechless. She had been very much alone since coming to the UK and was used to looking after herself. She could hardly believe that Stefan had come back specially to check on her and bring her some food.

"Thank you….I don't know what to say, it's really nice of you. No, I definitely wouldn't have felt well enough to go out to the shop - I've been asleep most of the time and when I get up I still feel wobbly."

"And you've told the agency? How were they with that?"

Kasia sniffed. 'You won't believe this, but Annie just didn't understand that I was really ill, she suggested I come in later! I told her I could hardly get out of bed. So then she reminded me that if I don't work, I don't get paid. As if I could forget."

Stefan frowned. "I don't think that is right. If you have worked there for a long time - which you have - I'm sure you have employment rights."

Kasia sighed. "I have asked before, but they say we are all on something called 'zero hours contract' and have no rights." She laughed. "Zero hours! I wish. I must do about seventy hours most weeks. I'm supposed to have alternate weekends free but I worked three in a row recently."

"No wonder you're ill," said Stefan. "You're probably just very run down. Well, I must get back to work but I'll look in on you again this evening. You have my mobile number, so call me if you need anything."

"Thanks, Stefan – you're a star."

Stefan grinned. "No problem."

He went out and shut the door. Kasia ate half the soup and one piece of toast but couldn't manage any more. She listened to her iPod for a while but couldn't concentrate. She couldn't remember the last time she felt so ill. Towards the end of the afternoon she felt a little better as the latest dose of paracetamol kicked in and dragged herself to the bathroom for a quick shower. She felt she had sweated buckets and knew she was none too fresh. She had just got back to bed when Stefan arrived back from work. He brought her some more soup and toast, and this time she managed to finish them. Just eating made her tired again and she thanked Stefan and snuggled down under her duvet again.

~

Kasia was off work for several days, much to Annie's displeasure. Her first day back coincided with Mary's discharge

123

from hospital   after her cancer surgery, and she found her looking paler and thinner than ever.

"How're you doing, Mary?"

"It's so nice to be back in my own home, dear. The clinic was very nice, and I had a lovely room, but major surgery at my age is no picnic. And the bad news is that the tumour had spread and they had to take out more than they planned. They say I really need radiotherapy now, to make sure it's all gone."

"And when will you start that? You don't look fit enough at the moment."

"You don't look too hot yourself, dear, if you don't mind me saying so."

"Oh, I had the flu while you were in hospital, I was off work for nearly a week. This is my first day back."

"I'm sorry to hear that. You all work so hard in that agency, it's not good for your health. You still look at bit pale."

"Yes, well I'm looking into changing jobs. This was - how do the English say it - the last straw? The agency don't pay us if we're sick. My friend Stefan thinks it's against the law, but I don't know what I can do. Anyway, there's a chance I may be able to switch jobs and work in a new nursery that's starting up."

Kasia helped Mary to the bathroom. She was puffing a bit, and very bent over, and her walking was unsteady.

"Is your wound hurting, Mary? You're struggling a bit, aren't you."

"It's still pretty painful, dear. And the stitches are pulling. They are due to come out in four days' time. But I don't know who will do it - my GP surgery are saying that because I had the operation privately, I have to pay for all the after care, too. I'm not getting any help with the agency fees for my carers any more. I have to pay a nurse to take out my stitches, and I don't think there's any hope of me having the radiotherapy because I, or my kids, would have to pay for that too, and none of us can afford it. I know they had to scrape around to find the money for the operation."

"That's *terrible,*" said Kasia. "You are entitled to NHS care surely?"

"Apparently not. We didn't realise that by choosing to have the operation privately the health service would wash their hands of me. They say I would have fallen into the six-month cancer category - that means that I wouldn't have lived more than six months whatever treatment I had. And you know what that means."

"How can they know that? After this operation everyone hopes you'll live another few years."

"I can't tell you how worried I am; I don't want my children to have to pay out any more. I've only got my state pension and a little saved, but it will go very quickly if I have to pay for everything myself."

"Well, try not to worry too much, it will slow down your recovery. When is your daughter coming back?"

"She'll try to get back tomorrow or the day after - she brought me home from hospital yesterday but she had to get home because one of her children is ill. She had planned to stay a few days, until I get my stitches out, but.....the best laid plans."

"Hmm, you should really have someone here with you," said Kasia as she helped Mary dress. "You are very wobbly. How many visits have you booked today?"

Mary looked uncomfortable. "Only two, dear, morning and evening. I can't afford to have any more."

"This is just terrible," said Kasia. "I've seen the demonstrations and wished I could join them - I never seem to have time."

It was true to say that she'd also seen on television that there was a small organization that supported Ultimate Care. Her religion didn't allow for either assisted suicide or euthanasia and she didn't understand how people could ever think it was right. Elderly care was certainly expensive but even so....

"I don't see why you were entitled to free care before your operation, but now you're not. You'd have needed care even if you hadn't had the surgery."

Mary gave her a defeated look. "I'd either have died, or I'd have been processed for Ultimate Care. Either way it would have been the end of me."

"Don't say that, Mary."

"Well, it's true, isn't it? Maybe it would be for the best. I've had a good life, up until the last five years. This cancer will carry me off if I don't have radiotherapy - even if I did, there's no guarantee, is there? In my heart, I know that we all have to die sometime."

Kasia got Mary's breakfast and set out her medication. "You seem to be on even more drugs, Mary. What's this for?"

Mary peered at the packet. "Oh, they're antibiotics. I've nearly finished the course. You wouldn't believe what they cost on a private prescription. I hope I don't need any more."

Kasia frowned. "You need to get someone to ask questions about this. I have heard people are writing to their MPs to complain. You should get your daughter to find out how to contact him and write or email him or her. I'd offer to help you but I just don't have the time. I have to work overtime to make up some of my lost hours. I just hope I get the new job."

"I'll keep my fingers crossed for you. I'd miss you, but you're too intelligent to be working as a carer."

"Well, I'll be off." Kasia slipped her coat on. "My next client has been totally deaf since birth. It is so sad, but it is really difficult to connect with him. Oh, and you heard about poor Eric, didn't you?"

"No dear, I've been out of the loop for a few days while I was in hospital. Had another heart attack, has he?"

Kasia wasn't sure whether to tell Mary the truth. She knew she'd be upset, she'd known Eric for years.

"He had another heart attack a couple of weeks ago, I think you knew that. They took him to A&E because I pretended I didn't know he'd been processed for U.C. I shouldn't have done. They found out of course, and sadly he was processed."

126

Mary went pale. "Oh. Oh dear." She wiped away a tear. "That's terrible. He's the first person I've known who's been done away with. Because that's what it is, isn't it? It's murder, really, murder."

Chapter 22

Steven reported back to Bill and Alistair. They were pleased to hear that rumours were already circulating about Jack but were despondent when Steven mentioned that nothing ever got into print and Mike suspected that Jack had all the newspaper editors in his pocket.

"It seems likely," said Bill. "He seems to have everyone else under his thumb."

"Anyway, Mike's going to get an ace young reporter onto the job - says he's a real sleuth. And there's already a rumour about a possible affair. What I don't understand is why there's been nothing on social media. This stuff's so hard to keep under wraps now."

It was a Friday and Alistair was eager to get back to his constituency for the weekend.

"An MP's work is never done," he grumbled. "We slave away all week here and then have to go and do a Constituency Surgery on Saturdays. No wonder half the House is having an affair - they never see their wives or partners."

"I think maybe 'half' is an exaggeration," said Steven. "I wish I had the time and the money."

"Well, I know of one or two," Bill conceded. "I'm off in a minute too, I've got a special meeting set up by my agent this evening with the daughter of a woman in my constituency who had cancer surgery privately and is now being told she has been written off by the NHS and has to pay for everything herself. I don't think rationing was ever meant to go this far."

"My dad's got Multiple Sclerosis" said Alistair, "and at the moment he's not too bad but he will undoubtedly get worse. It's different when these protocols are knocking at your own front door."

"Someone told me that Jack's mum's got Parkinson's," said Bill. "Maybe that's something we should look into - like what stage is she at and how much care she gets."

"Really? Yes, good idea. Need to cover every possible angle. Well, I'm off, see you Monday."

~

Bill arrived at his constituency office late for his appointment due to travel problems to find a grumpy-looking woman sitting in the waiting room tapping into her mobile phone. She looked up as Bill entered.

"Mrs McCauley? I'm so sorry I'm late, blame Southern Region. Again. Please come through."

"Well, I suppose I'm lucky you could see me at all outside surgery hours, but I did explain to your agent that I don't live locally and that it would be difficult for me to get here on a Saturday morning, I usually work Saturdays. And I combined this with visiting mum."

"So...." Bill rummaged around in his briefcase to find the emails his secretary had printed off . "Ah, right, got it. This is about your mother, Mrs Mary Morris?"

"Yes. She's eighty-four and has a few health problems - diabetes, heart problems, blood pressure, arthritis - the usual for old people. She was diagnosed with bowel cancer but was told because of her other health problems she couldn't be treated. We - that is, my brother and sister and I - were devastated that she seemed to be written off like that."

129

"Hmm, it does seem a bit harsh," Bill murmured. "But these chronic conditions do cost the NHS a lot of money, you know. Type two diabetes can be prevented."

Mrs McCauley had a face like thunder.

"Her diabetes is mild, and under control, and also her heart condition - who doesn't have a degree of heart impairment at eighty-four? So we clubbed together to pay for the operation privately. It went quite well, except the surgery was more extensive than planned, but when she came out of hospital we were told that her daily carers had been cancelled, and her local surgery wouldn't take out her stitches."

BIll frowned. "I find this hard to believe."

"Well it's true - *and* we had to pay for a private prescription for antibiotics. We still haven't sorted out who will take out the stitches."

Her voice rose with her temper.

"And it hasn't been made clear who will now pay for her diabetes and heart drugs. It's downright inhumane. Nobody warned us that if we used private treatment we would have to continue to pay for everything privately. She's entitled to NHS care, even at eighty-four, surely?"

"Does she have any savings? Bill asked. "And what about her pension?"

"She has hardly any savings, and she just gets her state pension and a small widow's pension my Dad left. She lives in a council flat. Plus, the consultant says she needs a course of radiotherapy and that's out of the question. We've all sacrificed our holidays to pay for this surgery and we can't afford to carry on paying for her care privately. If she hadn't had the surgery and just been left to fade away, the NHS would have paid for her medication until the end, as I understand it. Wouldn't they?"

She was now red in the face with fury. Bill wished he'd done a bit more research into the details of who paid for what in this sort of situation. He couldn't help feeling that there were no clear rules about it and that every health authority now thought that it had the power to make the sort of decisions they would never have been able to make before. It was, at the end of the day, about saving money.

"I'm sorry that I don't have any ready answers for you. It's all very complicated, as you can imagine, and every Health Trust is looking at cases differently. I need to do more research with her own GP, and the Health Trust in her area. But rest assured, I'll do my best to get this sorted out, and ensure there are clear guidelines in future."

Mrs McCauley glowered at him. She got up and walked over to his desk, leaning across and putting her face close up to his. He recoiled back in his chair.

"Nothing 'in future' is going to help my poor old Mum, though, is it? You people in government make these cold-hearted decisions about whether people live or die without the slightest concern for the people involved. How would you feel if it was your mother, being treated like a clapped-out car, and thrown into the breakers yard?"

Bill was about to press the button under his desk to summon John, his agent, who was in the room outside, when Mrs McCauley suddenly crumpled like a deflated balloon, and started to sob. Bill looked on, helpless and appalled.

After some moments Mrs McCauley regained her composure and stood up and turned on her heel.

"This won't be the last you'll hear about my mother," she flung over her shoulder. "I'm going to the press. It's just the sort of thing the tabloids would leap at. And the BBC, for good measure."

They all say that, Bill thought. She'll calm down.

~

Later, in the pub, as Bill took a gulp of his gin and tonic, John took a sip of beer and said "Phew, that was tricky. I could hear what was being said through the door. It's getting really serious, Bill, this UC thing. Unpopular hardly covers it. I can't believe you're right behind your glorious leader on it, are you?"

Bill contemplated his drink. "Fundamentally I am, but I think it may have gone too far. Lots of us in the Cabinet aren't very happy with things. Jack's autocratic, he's getting dangerous and thinks he's invincible. Watch this space."

"You mean......dissention in the ranks? A vote of no confidence?"

"I.... I can't say any more. All very hush-hush. Don't breathe a word."

He drained his drink and slipped on his jacket. "See you in the morning, John, surgery at the usual time, I imagine?"

"Yes, 9.30, Bill. Sleep well."

As it happened Bill did not sleep well. He had been quite taken aback at Mrs McCauley's vitriolic tirade and had a feeling it was going to be the first of many. He tossed and turned, and asked himself for the first time why he had gone into politics.

The Saturday morning surgery was busy. There were several more complaints about health care and UC. By lunch time Bill was exhausted. He was beginning to feel rather angry, not to mention frustrated, that the implications of UC, and care rationing in general, had not been considered in detail. It seemed that every health authority was playing fast and loose with the rules and regulations that had governed people's care for a long time. He looked down at the pile of notes in his desk, cases which he had promised he would follow up, and groaned.

~

Monday morning came far too fast - he spent so little time with his family that his wife complained she felt like a widow. She had been amorous, for once, but he knew he had not acquitted himself well and had spent another bad night wondering how long his marriage would survive the current schedule. He travelled back to his lonely bachelor pad in London and threw down his case, then plodded wearily over to the House. He had bought a 'Clarion', and for balance, a 'Post' to read on the train but had spent the journey catching up on his sleep. He was just entering his office when Alistair panted down the corridor after him.

"Bill, Bill, hang on a sec - have you seen today's Daily Post?"

Bill fished it out from under his arm.

"No - I've got it here but I couldn't keep awake on the train and I didn't even glance at either of my papers. What fake news is it broadcasting now?"

"Sadly, I don't think it's fake," said Bill. "There's a long article about certain elderly people being denied healthcare in various ways, and one of them is a constituent of yours. Apparently her daughter came to see you? She says you were no bloody use at all, and her attack on the government in general is poisonous. "

"Was her name Mrs McCauley?"

"Yep, think that's the one."

"Oh shit."

Chapter 23

Kasia had managed to arrange an evening meeting later in the week with the friend of Natasha who was opening the nursery school. She didn't want to take off any more time from work as she was working flat out to bridge the gap in her finances. She was finding it hard going, as since her bout of 'flu she had been much more tired than before but had put off making an appointment with her doctor - something which she could ill-afford now that most people had to pay for appointments. She had confessed to Stefan that she was dragging herself through each day and had no energy left for anything else, even another date.

"Next week," she said to him, more than once. "I'm sorry, but I'm so tired."

It was Stefan who persuaded her to finally make a doctor's appointment. She knew it was sensible and went the following day. Paying for appointments had certainly minimised the long waits to see a GP. She had a chat with the doctor about having 'flu, her job and her tiredness.

"You're doing a very tiring job," the GP said. "I know you carers work long hours - I have a couple of nursing homes on my list and visit them fairly regularly. You need to be fit to do your job. This tiredness may just be the after-effects of a bad bout of 'flu, but you could be anaemic."

He handed her a form for a blood test. "I'll test for that, and for Glandular Fever. Let's hope you haven't got ME, that's really difficult to sort out."

Kasia was alarmed. "I have heard of Glandular Fever, a friend of mine had it, but what is ME?"

"It's very difficult to diagnose - another name for it is Chronic Fatigue Syndrome - does that make it clearer? It means you're tired all the time, but no medical cause can be found for it."

"Chronic Fatigue Syndrome," said Kasia slowly. "I hope I don't have that. I don't have time to be ill."

The doctor smiled and handed her a slip of paper with the name of an over-the-counter elixir on it.

"Take this until you get the results, it has some iron and vitamins in it and may help to give you more energy. I'll let you know the blood test results in a few days. If you're just anaemic, I'll prescribe iron tablets which should take care of it."

Kasia thanked him and left, and hurried to her first client of the day, who was Peter. She let herself in. It was strangely quiet. She was used to going into a client's house and calling out "Good Morning" to them but Pete's deafness made this pointless. It was the first visit of the day, which meant she had to get him up. He had deteriorated since her first visit. His trembling had got worse and getting him into the shower and the toilet was a real challenge. She had asked the agency to re-assess his needs - he couldn't live alone much longer.

She set off up the stairs, wrinkling her nose at the 'old person' smell in his flat - heaven only knew when it had last been cleaned. She was hoping he would not be too 'frozen' today and that he wouldn't take too long as she was running a bit late due to her doctor's appointment. Halfway up the stairs she stopped stock still, her heart racing, as a prone, pyjama-clad shape came into view.

"Oh no," she murmured as she forced herself up the last few stairs.

Peter was lying on the floor on the landing, his head bleeding. A little table had been knocked over and lying beside

Peter was a framed photograph of a handsome young couple, the glass broken. Kasia had seen it on the table many times; it was Peter and his wife, taken at their wedding 60 years ago. They made a handsome couple and every time she saw it she felt emotional, knowing that Peter's wife now had dementia.

She knelt down beside him and shook his lifeless form; it was pointless talking to him. He didn't flinch. He felt chilly and appeared not to be breathing as she felt for the pulse in his wrist. Nothing. She sat back on her heels and fought back tears. She was pretty sure he was dead. Conflicting thoughts ran through her mind. What a lonely way to die - but on the other hand he had been saved from the disruption of going into care. Or, she thought grimly, of undergoing Ultimate Care. She made one last attempt to find a pulse, then dialled 999. While she waited for the paramedics she called the agency. Annie answered, brusque as usual.

"What? Oh dear. Well, he was eighty-five, you know. And that's one off the books. When the ambulance has taken him away I'll give you the details of a new client we've just taken on. I was wondering who on earth could visit him today, so this is a godsend."

Kasia could not speak. Annie's hard heart and business-like attitude when dealing with, literally, matters of life and death, left her speechless.

"Are you still there?" asked Annie, unnecessarily loudly. "Kasia?"

"Yes, I'm still here. But I really don't think I could cope with another new client today, not after this. It's very upsetting......"

"Well, there isn't really much choice. We can't afford to be sentimental in our line of work, can we? No time for compassionate leave! Carry on to see Mary and then Doris and I'll text you the details of the new client."

"OK," said Kasia weakly, clenching her teeth. "Goodbye." She was so angry she was shaking. She knew she didn't really have a choice but the callousness of it all really distressed her.

She went down to the kitchen and made herself a mug of cocoa, something strictly forbidden unless a client offered it.

Normally she would never have thought of helping herself to a cup of tea or coffee, but today she didn't really care, and anyway who would know. She felt sure Pete wouldn't have minded. She then did something she'd never done before at work either - she called Stefan.

"Hi Kasia - you OK? You're not ill again, are you?"

"No, no. The doctor was very nice. I'm having some blood tests. No, it's just....." Her throat went dry. She didn't want to appear needy but she had to talk to someone after her awful conversation with Annie.

"Kasia?"

"Sorry....." She sniffed audibly.

"Look, wait a second, I'm up a ladder fixing a roof. I'll come down, so I can talk to you."

Kasia waited, wiping her eyes.

"OK - now what is it? Tell me."

"Oh Stefan, I got to my first client, you know, the deaf man with Parkinson's I told you about, and I found him lying at the top of the stairs. Goodness knows how he got there, it's normally so difficult for him to move around. Maybe he was trying to get to the toilet, I don't know."

"And is he all right?"

"No, that's just it, he's....he's dead. I'm waiting for the paramedics to come. So I called Annie at the agency - and...oh, she's so heartless, Stefan, she seemed quite glad he'd died because she'd got a new client who she wants me to go to instead. I couldn't believe it. I'm sorry, I just wanted to hear a friendly voice, I'm here alone with this man...." She finally broke down into loud sobs.

"It's not your fault," said Stefan.

"No, of course not, but she has no compassion, either for Pete, or for me. She expects me to carry on as if nothing has happened. It's not like you find a dead body every day, is it?"

"No, it's tough. I'm sorry."

Kasia heard an ambulance approaching down the road. "I have to go, Stefan, the ambulance is arriving. But it was good to hear a friendly voice."

"The sooner you get out of that job, the better," said Stefan. "Look, Kasia, tonight I'm taking you out for a bite to eat, and we can talk properly. I won't keep you up late. OK?"

"Thanks, that would be great, Stefan. 'Bye."

Mary could tell the minute Kasia walked through the door that something was wrong.

"You look very peaky, dear, what's happened?"

"Oh Mary, when I got to my first client, I found him dead. It was terrible. The agency just don't care…. I don't know how to deal with it."

Mary gathered her up in an embrace which a few weeks previously would have meant pressing her to a capacious bosom, but she had grown thin and sallow-looking with her illness.

"There, there, dear, you need a good hug, don't you? You can tell me all about it, you need to talk to someone."

She shuffled across the kitchen and filled the kettle, something Kasia normally did for her. She was glad she was recovering a little. They sat down at the kitchen table with their mugs of tea and Mary produced some chocolate biscuits.

Kasia smiled wanly. "Naughty, naughty, Mary, you know you shouldn't."

"I don't eat many," said Mary. "We all need a treat now and then, don't we. Here, come on, take one, I bet you didn't have any breakfast, did you? Now, tell me what happened."

Kasia felt better after she'd recounted finding Pete, and her conversation with Annie. Mary was bristling with indignation.

"That agency, they are beyond the pale. Much as I'd hate to lose you as a carer, the sooner you find another job, the better. Maybe in the meantime you could find another agency to work for?"

"I don't think the others are much different. They all have too many clients, and not enough workers. They charge big fees but the carers are paid a low wage."

"You'd have thought they'd be nicer to their employees if they want to keep them," said Mary. "I really don't know what the answer is. Anyway, we'd better get started, dear, or you'll be running late all day."

Chapter 24

Steven had a meeting organized with Mike from the Post to see what progress he'd made. It was over a week since they'd discussed delving into Jack's affairs. He figured he'd better take Mike to lunch or dinner as he was doing Steven a favour, even if he had said he thought Jack was an odious man. He arranged a dinner date with Mike and booked a Michelin-starred restaurant in a large hotel where he knew the tables were set far apart and voices would be muffled by the sumptuous carpet. Mike, predictably, was late. Steven ordered a good bottle of claret and stared around him while he waited. Most of the clientele seemed to be foreign, which wasn't surprising, and he noted some interesting combinations of old men and trophy wives. Most of the women had sharp cheekbones and a great deal of bling. He couldn't hear what was being said, which was annoying but at the same time reassuring - he didn't want anyone overhearing what he and Mike were going to talk about.

"Sorry, sorry," Mike said as he slid into his place at the table. "You know what it's like trying to get a paper to bed."

"Well, I don't, actually, but I can imagine." He filled Mike's wineglass and put a menu in front of him. "Let's order, shall we, and then we can enjoy a glass of wine before we start."

"Yes." Mike perused the menu. He set it down on the table as if he'd made a decision, and looked around him.

"Good grief, look who's over there!" He pointed none to subtly to his right.

"You'll have to fill me in, I don't really do celebrities."

Mike leaned closer, conspiratorially. "None other than Laura Hawthorn with a man who's not her husband."

"Christ! It might be her lawyer, I suppose. Thank god they can't possibly hear what we're saying."

"I wouldn't bank on that, not with today's technology, but we'll look on the optimistic side. How about sending her over a cocktail? "

"God no, I don't want to draw attention!" Steven glanced covertly at her again. "She hasn't seen me, too deep in conversation. I took the precaution of booking with an alias. I once took my secretary out to lunch after a particularly gruelling week in the House and the receptionist assumed the worst and alerted some bloody hack. She's a very good secretary but I don't fancy her one little bit. And of course, I'm happily married, like you."

Mike smiled. "Yes…...Well, do you want to hear what this bloody hack has dredged up for you? Or rather, my young sleuth."

"Spill the beans, then." Steven took a swig of wine and leaned closer in to Mike. Despite his precautions, he was still worried about being overheard.

"Well, Olly followed Jack on several occasions. On Thursday evenings he officially goes to see a tall brunette woman called Davina Hunt. It seems that she's a counsellor, not a girlfriend."

"JACK? Having counselling? Iron man, actually admitting that he needs help?"

"Apparently. But she also doubles as an alibi. He doesn't always visit her." He leaned back and sipped his claret. "He often loses his personal protection officers, tells them to go and get a meal, and gives them money to do it."

"So when this happens, where does he go?"

"I hope you're prepared for a shock. He goes to see a young man, not a woman. He goes to great lengths to cover up his visits to this chap, although of course there's no law against him having a male lover."

"I think my wife would take a pretty dim view of it," said Steven.

"But it's not what we were expecting, is it?"

Steven leaned across the table. "Who is this chap? Anyone we know?"

"No, no. Olly only saw him once. He looks Middle-Eastern. Young. Doesn't speak good English but very pretty. Tall, slim, saturnine, megawatt smile. His name is Hassan. We don't know where Jack met him but he seems to have taken him under his wing and installed him in a serviced flat in Sloane Street, far enough from the House not to be easily spotted. The bills are paid by an alias. Of course, he might be an illegal, and if so he'd want to keep a low profile. He probably doesn't know who Jack is, he's sure to have given him another name."

Steven whistled through his teeth. "How did your chap find all this out?"

"He tailed Jack for a week. Mostly, he lost him, but he got lucky once, and once was enough. He asked the concierge which flat Jack had gone to, saying he was a taxi driver and that Jack had left something in his cab. He pretended to take it up to him and when he came back he chatted to the concierge and learned quite a lot. He's pretty bemused by the whole thing too."

"He's sailing pretty close to the wind, if that's the case. Crazy! Surely Hassan watches TV? Goes on the Internet? And the concierge, surely he'd recognise him?"

"Obviously neither recognizes Jack. Jack arrives in a cab with darkened windows. Whilst in the cab, he puts on a baseball cap and a false beard. Beards totally change your appearance." Mike patted his pockets for his cigarettes before remembering he couldn't light up indoors. "Damn, I really could do with a smoke."

"Better for you if you don't," said Steven. "So come on, what else?"

"He doesn't go out anywhere in public with Hassan, obviously. When he's there, they order in a takeaway, and they have wine delivered regularly."

"What I don't understand," said Steven, signalling for another bottle of wine from the waiter, "is firstly, how he finds the time, and secondly, how has he got away with keeping this quiet? How long has it been going on?"

"We don't know for sure. The lease on the serviced apartment is renewed every month and Olly couldn't find out exactly how long the arrangement has been running."

"Well, well. He clearly thinks he's invincible."

"And that's not the only thing," said Mike.

Steven frowned at him to stop talking as the waiter arrived with the wine and uncorked it.

"Would sir like to taste it again? It's the same vintage."

"No thanks, just pour please." He was impatient to continue the conversation and his heart was missing the odd beat after what he'd just heard. The waiter finally left them alone.

"So what's the other thing?"

"We've discovered some unethical investments. Not illegal, mind you, but stuff which would go down badly with the public. He has offshore accounts all over the place, Panama, Guernsey, Cayman Islands. We're still working on what's feeding these accounts - some were quite easy to trace as they're just about legal, but nobody whose dealings are all totally above board needs so many offshore accounts. He has properties all over the place, presumably he made a great deal of money before he went into politics. Again, not illegal. But he has far more properties than he's open about, all rented out."

"And what sort of shares does he have?"

Their food arrived and prompted another pause in the conversation. The waiter fussed around and Steven was itching to get rid of him. Eventually they could talk again. Mike attacked his food with gusto and talked through a mouthful.

"Sorry, starving, haven't really eaten all day. So, he has a lot of investments in a palm oil company. One that evicts peasant farmers off their land. That's not good. He also holds investments in an armaments company, one that supplies dodgy foreign regimes."

"And Jack purports to be anti-war! But what I don't understand is that there are always rumours, and it hasn't been that difficult for your guy to dig all this up, so why has it not reached the papers, or social media newsfeeds?"

"Almost certainly they're in his pay. And have been threatened with the heavies, I suspect. He's the most corrupt PM we've ever had. He's slippery as an eel. I put the question to one of the paper's legal chaps over a coffee in the canteen the other day, and he looked very shifty and said that publishing anything about Jack was as taboo as the Royal Family used to be, in the past. He just said 'Dare not,' and drew his finger across his throat."

Chapter 25

Kasia somehow dragged herself through the day. Her new client was Geoff, and thankfully he was a cheery eighty-one-year old man with rheumatoid arthritis who had all his wits about him. By the time she reached home that night she was both physically and emotionally exhausted. Stefan was in the hallway of the flat as she came through the front door. Without a word, he took her in his arms and gave her a hug.

"I'm guessing you needed that," he said.

"You have no idea. That's the hardest part of having your family in another country - you really miss their support."

"Well, *I'm* here - and I've booked a restaurant I think you'll like for tonight."

"Tell me, where?"

"It's a surprise, but I'll be amazed if you don't approve!"

"OK – I just need to have a quick shower."

"You look fine."

"Stefan, if you'd been bathing and toileting old people all day, you'd want a shower."

"All right – you've got twenty minutes or so."

"That will be plenty. You just wait there."

Kasia reappeared a quarter of an hour later, wearing clean jeans and her newest top. She had taken her hair out of its pony tail and it bounced on her shoulders.

"Right, I'm ready to go. I'm wondering where we're going, though."

"It's a ten-minute walk. I expect you've guessed now, haven't you?"

"Stefan, there are about six restaurants within a ten-minute walk of here."

"Think pierogi.......and plaki....."

"Oh great, we're going to Polski Mama!"

"I thought you'd want something authentically Polish to cheer you up."

"You thought right – I love that place".

The proprietor greeted them in Polish and gave them both a hug. The restaurant hadn't changed much since it opened in the 1980s – you could have been in Warsaw or Krakow.

"It's almost as good as being at home!" said Kasia as Stefan poured the wine. "What a day. I hope I don't have too many more of those. That Annie at the agency is a complete cow. She....she was so *cruel* ....like these poor old people are just numbers on her computer. I told her I didn't feel I could cope with a new client after what happened to Peter but she told me I must be unsentimental and that in our job there is no place for compassion."

She took a swig of her wine and looked up at Stefan, a tear sliding down her nose.

"Now, Kasia, I'm going to get tough with you." Stefan reached for her hand across the table. "I know we've had this conversation before, but I am really going to nag you to find another job. If the Nursery School thing doesn't happen, promise me you'll look for something else. Because this job is killing you."

"Yes.....I know you're right. But I'll miss some of my clients, like Mary, for instance."

"From what you've told me, Mary may not live that much longer. I'm afraid, like Annie says, you can't afford to be too sentimental in your job, you shouldn't get so involved."

"I know, but it's difficult. Anyway I've got an interview fixed with Natasha's friend. The nursery isn't open yet but I'm keeping my fingers crossed for the job, whenever it starts."

They returned home, full to bursting with Polish dumplings and stew.

"Thanks, Stefan, that's really cheered me up."

She was reluctant to say good night. As she turned the handle of her door Stefan put out his hand to stop her. Suddenly she was in his arms, hugging closely. He drew away just far enough for his mouth to find hers. When he kissed her Kasia closed her eyes and melted into him. All the stress of the day drained away. This was something she had wanted him to do for quite a while, although she hadn't realized just how much until it happened. They stood locked together, Kasia hardly daring to breathe, until Stefan finally drew away.

"I should let you get some sleep."

"Yes, I should, but....." She didn't know what to say. Everything seemed rosier and she let go of her worries. "But I should like to do it again," she said.

He kissed her again, and then, detaching himself said firmly "we will do it again. But for now, goodnight. You need sleep. And don't have nightmares about Annie!"

After that, I'm far more likely to dream about you, thought Kasia. She felt a bit dizzy and her heart was thumping, but she felt much brighter and she hummed as she undressed. She had been wondering for a while whether Stefan would ever go beyond being a friend. Things were looking up.

The next day flew past, and the day after that Kasia was seeing Natasha's friend, Julie, for her interview. They had arranged to meet in a wine bar and despite Kasia trying to hurry through her last two clients she was still a few minutes late. She fought her way through the crowd, searching for a woman on her own. She realized she had no idea what Julie looked like. A young woman stood at the counter and she caught Kasia's eye.

"Kasia?"

"Yes, you must be Julie? I'm so sorry I'm late, I never quite know in my job when I'll be finished."

"Well, here you are now, don't worry."

"Which is why I'd like to find something else. I've almost reached the end of my patience with the agency."

"What would you like to drink?"

"A white wine please." They finally got served and moved to a corner table.

"Now, where were we? Oh yes, your work" said Julie. "Working with children would be rather different. You'd be going from one end of the age spectrum to the other."

Kasia smiled. "Yes, it would be a big change. So can you tell me more about the new nursery?"

"Sure. I've worked as a nursery nurse for some years. One of my aunts died and left me some money recently, and I thought to myself, this is an opportunity to do something a bit different. So I decided to open my own nursery - there's a huge demand for nursery places, as I expect you know."

"I'd like to get back to doing something with children."

"OK. So, I have some nursery nurses lined up but with such emphasis being put on early years learning these days I also need someone with teaching experience. Which is where you would come in. Natasha tells me that you are qualified in Poland but that you've not been able to get a teaching job in the UK?"

"Yes, that's right. The real problem is that I need to get the Post-Grad Certificate, and I just can't afford to take the year's course. I can barely make ends meet as it is."

"Well, you wouldn't need it for this job. From what I've heard so far, your English is very good. And you taught primary school children in Poland, didn't you?"

"Yes, I'm qualified to teach both nursery - I think you call it Early Years here – and primary classes in Poland. So how long do you think it will be before you can open the nursery?"

"I'm hoping in around six weeks' time, but the building is being adapted and knowing what builders are like it's more likely to be eight."

148

"And what would be my hours?"

"The nursery will be open from 7 in the morning until 7 in the evening, Monday to Friday; there will be a rota for the early starts and late finishes."

"I'm used to long hours and early starts. And" - here she hesitated a bit - "can I ask you about pay?"

"Of course." She named a figure and Kasia had to stop herself gasping.

"That would be marvellous - I am so tired of scrimping and saving."

"I've heard quite a lot about you from Natasha and you seem to have the right experience, but I'll need a couple of references. One could be the agency, and maybe you could get a reference from your last job in Poland? Preferably in English! And you may also need a criminal check - something which used to be a CRB but it's now called a DBS."

Kasia looked worried. "OK. But I'm not sure about asking the agency," she said. "They will be so annoyed that I'm leaving, I don't think I really want to ask them. I look after a lady called Mary, who is quite sound in her mind, and she seems to think well of me. Could she do it?"

"Well, I expect that would be OK. And how much notice would you have to give the agency?"

"I'm not sure – I'm on a zero hours contract, so I don't think there are any rules about it. I suppose it would be polite to give them a week. Oh, that's something I wanted to ask you - I would be a proper employee, wouldn't I, with paid holidays and sick pay?"

"Oh yes, you'd have a proper contract. No more zero-hours stuff. OK, then." Julie stood up and shook hands with Kasia. "I'll be in touch again soon. Now I have a couple of nursery nurses to interview – here comes one now."

"Thank you so much," said Kasia as she gathered her jacket and bag. "You can't imagine how excited I am."

She went home on cloud nine and found Stefan to tell him about the interview.

"Wow, that's marvellous, I felt sure you would impress her. I hope they'll pay you a bit more?"

"Yes, a lot more. The only problem is that she wants references. She wants me to get one from Poland. And the agency, but I really don't want to ask them. She said I could ask Mary."

"Oh Kasia, you must have more confidence in yourself. You can easily get a reference from Poland, and I'm sure someone there can translate it into English if necessary. And you should ask the agency – I don't see how they can refuse when you've worked so hard for them. You can explain exactly why you want to change jobs while you're at it. Maybe they will be more considerate to their staff."

"You're right. Although……"

Stefan silenced her with a kiss. Then he said:

"Hang on a minute," and went into the kitchen, returning with a bottle of Prosecco and two glasses.

"I just knew the interview would be successful." Then he took her hand and led her to his room.

Chapter 26

Steven couldn't wait to tell Alistair and Bill about his meeting with Mike but knew it would be safer to wait and meet them face to face. He texted them both to say "Meeting with Mike interesting. Tell you tomorrow. My office at 9.30?"

Two texts pinged into his phone almost simultaneously. Bill's said "Interesting or damning?" Alistair's said "Spill the beans."

He replied "Safer to wait, but you can let your imaginations run riot."

He had a restless night. He wasn't sure quite what they were going to do with the information now that they had it. It seemed unlikely that Mike's editor would run a story after what Mike had told them regarding the supposition that press was somehow in Jack's pay. Perhaps he'd even taken out injunctions.

He arrived at the House to find yet another demonstration about UC blocking the road outside. The police were trying, unsuccessfully, to disperse the crowd and many of the signs that were being held up bore the photos and names of the elderly who'd died. There were chants of 'Murder, murder.'

He found Bill and Alistair already waiting outside his office when he had finally got into the building.

"You're keen," he laughed. "Let me just unlock the door and get some coffee on the brew. My researcher won't be in 'til later, she has a dental appointment, luckily."

It was a very cramped office. It was dark and gloomy with a small, grimy window and heavy, old-fashioned furniture. Steven found it rather depressing and although he'd tried to cheer it up with plants and new curtains it was still rather like a Victorian accountant's den. There was barely room for three people and Bill perched on the researcher's desk, his short plump, legs dangling. He was the complete opposite to Alistair, who was tall and gangly, and folded himself into a hard chair.

Finally, when they were all seated with a coffee, Bill thumped the desk and said "Well, come on, spit it out."

Steven relished the moment of keen anticipation as he calmly took a sip of his coffee and put his mug back down.

"So......do you want the personal dirt first, or the shady dealings?"

"Shady dealings," said Bill.

"Personal dirt," said Alistair.

Steve outlined the investments to them.

"Palm oil producers are real shits," said Bill. "They've had such bad press lately - that documentary about displaced farmers starving in the cities left a bad taste in everyone's mouth. As for investing in companies that deal arms to dodgy regimes....he's just damn stupid."

"So what about the personal stuff? What we need is a mistress in the closet....."

"Oh, I can do much better than that," smirked Steve. "How about a pretty boy for a lover?"

Bill choked on his coffee. When Alistair had finished thumping him on the back and he'd regained his breath, Bill said "Are you serious? It goes against everything we've ever thought about Jack - he makes such a virtue of being macho. I've even heard him poke fun at gays. I find it awfully difficult to believe."

"Smoke screen." Steven took another slug of his coffee. "It would certainly explain why there are rumours about marriage problems, wouldn't it? By the way, she was in the same restaurant last night, with a man, and she got a bundle of papers out of a briefcase to give him. Maybe her lawyer. I was trying to keep a low profile, so I couldn't keep looking at them. Mike had a clearer view. Anyway, you haven't heard the half of it yet."

He proceeded to tell them about the young man in the serviced Sloane Street flat. Their mouths fell open.

"You got anything stronger than coffee in here, Steve? I feel in need of a medicinal slug of something. I know it's early, but....." Bill mopped his brow and fanned himself with a file he had been holding.

Steven crossed the room, took a key out of his pocket and opened the filing cabinet. He withdrew a bottle of whisky from the bottom drawer, and produced three glasses.

"Not for me, thanks," said Alistair. "I may be in shock, but it's really too early."

Steve poured two fingers into each glass and handed one to Bill. "Water?"

"No thanks." He took a large gulp.

"The thing is," said Alistair "I can't understand why rumours about Jack haven't been circulating if all this can be discovered by a junior hack."

"Oh, apparently there are plenty of rumours amongst journalists but they never get into print or onto social media. They think he's backhanding the editors. Not to mention the judges who are ruling against all the UC appeals, and god knows who else. He's just thoroughly degenerate."

"Where does he get the money to do that?" asked Alistair. "Is he drawing on Treasury funds?"

"We don't know for sure." said Steven. "He's got a lot of investment properties - they must bring in a fair amount. The question is, if we can't get this stuff out there to the public what on earth are we going to do with this information?"

"Can't we set up a fake Twitter account or something. Get rumours circulating, get people talking. Then we can grill him before a Parliamentary committee and hopefully bring him down." Bill was relishing the thought.

"I don't think it'll be that easy. From what my friend Mike said, there is some big cover-up machinery in place. I mean, we've known for a while that he's turned into a complete autocrat since he became PM but I'm not sure any of us had guessed just how powerful he's become. I think we have to go for the jugular, but in private.

"Mmm…." said Bill thoughtfully, "Maybe a little blackmail would be more effective, for openers? What I really want to see is him losing his cockiness. I want to see him sweat, I want him to suffer real stress."

"Well, the stuff about his dodgy investments is fact, isn't it? He can't dispute it. He might prevaricate about his male lover, he may think we have no evidence of that – and given that he uses a disguise when he visits this chap he might argue 'til he's blue in the face that it wasn't him. We really need to get some good photographic or video evidence."

"I'll ask Mike to send out young Olly again, this time with a zoom lens camera at the ready. You can often tell who someone is just from their rear view, or by their walk. And if we got a full facial I'm sure experts could run it through a facial recognition programme and confirm it's him."

Alastair drained the last of his whisky and finished his coffee. "We need to formulate a plan. And we need to talk to the other dissenters in the Cabinet and put them in the picture."

"I think we should be careful how many people we tell," said Bill. "We don't want the wrong people getting wind of this at the moment."

"I think we should keep it between ourselves, if you want my honest opinion," said Steven. "The fewer people who know about this, the better. So, how and when are we going to confront Jack?"

"I agree with Bill that a little blackmail is in order to begin with," said Alastair. "There is going to be serious civil unrest about Ultimate Care soon if we don't put a stop to it. We'll tell him that we have some damaging information about him which we'll make public, one way or another, if he doesn't ditch or fundamentally amend the UC protocols. He may prefer to resign than do that, it would damage his ego too much. I don't know about you, but my weekly constituency surgeries now comprise a huge number of UC complaints. I can't think how it ever got to this stage."

"I can," said Steve. "We were all too afraid for our jobs to materially oppose it. Our chickens have come home to roost and we simply must get Jack out of the top job."

"I agree," said Alistair. "We're definitely on track to lose the next election if we don't get a new, more moderate leader in place before then."

Steven's phone rang.

"It's Mike – I better take it. Hi Mike. Mm hm. Yes.....WHAT? Are you sure? Which companies? Yes, I....OK, right. Send through the details, will you? Speak later. 'Bye."

He turned to the others, a big grin on his face.

"Well, what do you know! This is the jackpot. Our dear leader has...."

He stopped in his tracks when the door opened and Steven's researcher came in. She looked from one to the other with a slight frown on her face, as if she guessed what they were up to. Steve hoped she hadn't been listening at the door.

"Hi Fiona. Hope you're in one piece after the dentist?"

She mumbled a reply through her anaesthetized mouth.

"I'll take that as a no, then. These guys were just leaving. Weren't you?" he said pointedly.

"Yes, I've got a meeting now," said Alistair. "See you soon." He shot Steven and Bill a meaningful look and tapped his watch, raising his eyebrows in an unspoken question. Bill nodded.

"Five pm, in Moncrieff's?" They nodded and left.

Fiona tutted as she cleared the coffee cups and glasses. "Whisky, at this time of day?" she muttered. "I suppose that's because you've seen the news flash."

"What news flash? I haven't heard or seen the news since I left home this morning."

Fiona fired up her computer and clicked onto a 24-hour news site.

"The Prime Minister has declined to comment", the interviewer was saying. "Now back to the studio."

A shot of the front door of 10 Downing Street faded from the screen and the newsreader moved on to another topic.

"So what was all that about? What has he denied?"

"Well, an American news channel has put out a story about him and his wife separating - his wife's filed for divorce. Sorry, it's really difficult to speak with my mouth frozen up like this."

Steve waited for her to start talking again.

"They say that she's cited infidelity, amongst other things. He's denying everything and saying it's fake news."

Steven whistled softly between his teeth. Maybe this wasn't going to be as difficult as they had thought.

Chapter 27

Kasia had a free Saturday and was sitting at the kitchen table with her laptop, composing an email to the school where she had last worked in Poland. Stefan was standing behind her as she sat at her laptop in the kitchen and reading what she had written.

"What do you think?" she asked Stefan.

"I think that it's a bit humble. Remember, they are obliged to give you one, and I don't think you need to sound apologetic. I'm sure you were a very good teacher, so there's nothing to worry about. Have you asked the agency yet?"

"No.....I just can't, I don't want to tell them I'll probably be leaving. It may be a few weeks yet, and I'm worried it will create bad feeling between us."

"I think you worry too much. They are so short of staff they are not very likely to make things any worse."

"Oh yes, they can. They could give me all the most difficult clients to visit. I saw it happen with another girl who told them she was leaving. Annie also said that one of my clients had made a complaint against me."

"I can't believe that....."

"I stood up for myself for once. I said that he had dementia, he didn't know what he was doing or saying, and I told her that he'd tried to hit me twice, and that I hadn't bothered to complain about *him*."

"Good for you. So are you going to ask Mary for a reference instead?"

"Yes, I've asked her - she said she'd be happy to do it and I'm I hoping she's done it by now. She's getting weaker every day, you know. Her family haven't been able to raise the money for her to have radiotherapy privately, and the NHS has abandoned her. I can't believe what's happening."

"I think that the NHS just has too many demands on it."

"Yes, you're right. Anyway, that's this email finished." She pressed SEND.

"So, what would you like to do today? How about the cinema this afternoon?"

"That would be lovely. Let's look and see what's on."

They scrolled through the films showing at their local cinema.

"I'd like to see this one." Kasia pointed.

Stefan laughed. "It's another rom-com."

Kasia's face coloured. "It's meant to be very good. Do you have a problem with it?"

Stefan squeezed her shoulder. "Of course not, I was just teasing. Yes, we'll aim for that one – we could go to the 5.30 and then have something to eat."

Kasia looked doubtful. She was still having to economise to make up the money she'd lost when she was ill. Stefan noticed her face and squeezed her shoulder again.

"It's my treat, silly. But I'll let you buy your own cinema ticket if it makes you feel better."

"Yes, that will be OK. Now, I need to go to the supermarket and buy a few things. Do you need anything?"

"Yes," said Stefan, "I'll come with you, I need to stock up on breakfast foods. I'm addicted to the English breakfast."

"Yes, the smell of your bacon cooking drives me mad in the morning. You know it's not very good for you, all that fat?"

"What?"

"My turn to tease you. OK, let's go. I'll just get my bag."

Her phone was ringing as she picked up her bag but she didn't manage to answer it before it stopped. She noticed that the caller was her mother and made a mental note to call her back. They were in the
supermarket when it rang again.

"Sorry, it's my mother, she called earlier. I'd better speak to her, I won't be long."

"If it's your mother, you'll be chatting until lunch-time." Stefan turned to scan the shelves but couldn't help overhearing the conversation in rapid Polish.

"That's marvellous!" he heard her say. "Yes, of course, you must arrange to come when I have a weekend off so I can show you around."

She finished the call and turned to Stefan, a big smile on her face.

"I expect you got most of that, didn't you?"

"Your parents are coming to London to visit?"

"Yes – my brother won some money on the lottery two or three months ago and is paying for my parents to come on a trip to London for their 30th Wedding anniversary. They've never been out of Poland, so you can imagine how excited they are."

"That's great – when did you last see them?"

"Around eighteen months ago. I went home for two days for my dad's 60th birthday. Since then I just don't seem to have been able to save up enough money to go, so it will be really great to see them in London."

"And is your brother coming too?"

"I don't think so, he and his wife have recently had another baby."

" I can see that makes travelling a bit of a hassle."

"Yes, my sister-in-law is a bit neurotic, I can't see her travelling with three small children. Right, what else do we need?"

Stefan's basket was full of eggs, bacon, sausages and croissants. Kasia's had all things healthy.

"You need more than that," he laughed, "You do a physical job like mine, you need more carbs." He grabbed a big bag of popcorn and a bar of chocolate. "We can eat these in the cinema. I'm going to fatten you up a bit."

Kasia wasn't sure how to respond. Stefan stopped to face her and touched her hand.

"Perhaps you haven't noticed, but to me it looks like you've lost some weight since you had 'flu. Seriously, you need to eat enough to do your job. I've been a bit worried about you."

Kasia stood on tiptoes and kissed Stefan lightly on the cheek.

"It's nice to have someone worrying about me. Thank you."

Later, at the cinema, Kasia ate half the bar of chocolate and some of the popcorn. They laughed their way through the film and as they were leaving Stefan put his arm around her and said "There, you're looking better already."

"Probably put on a kilo," grumbled Kasia.

"You can afford to. And now I'm going to make you eat a good dinner."

Her euphoria was short-lived and on Monday morning the agency called Kasia just as she was leaving to go to her first client.

"Kasia, this is Annie."

Kasia's first thought was that somehow the agency had got wind of her looking for another job. Her heart jumped.

"Yes?" she said cautiously.

"We'd like you to come into the office this morning at 11 o'clock – it' about the complaint."

"I thought we'd sorted that out. And what about my clients?"

"For once, we have a full complement of carers on duty and I've arranged for someone to cover two of your clients."

"Can't we discuss it over the phone?" she asked.

"No, we need you to sign incident forms and so on. See you later."

"But......" She sighed and put away her phone. She really didn't think it would be taken any further.

Mary could see that she was preoccupied during her visit.

"Something wrong, dear? I thought you told me you were getting on ever so well with that young man of yours."

"Oh, it's nothing like that, Mary. The agency has had a complaint about me and I have to go in later to see them."

"A complaint? I can't believe it."

"A patient with dementia pushed me hard. Now he's saying that I pushed him. I said to Stefan, I'm tired of being treated like dirt, I'm standing up for myself on this one."

"That's right, dear, you tell them. By the way, I've done the reference for that Julie, you know, the nursery woman. Here it is."

"Thank you so much, Mary, I'm - how do you say it, 'keeping my fingers crossed?'"

Mary patted her on the back. "You'll be just fine, dear, but I will miss you."

~

"And so," said Kasia, "he pushed me against the wall. I hit my elbow. Look. " She pulled up her sleeve to show Annie the bruise.

"Well, he says you pushed him first. He told his daughter about it."

"So it's his word against mine? And you're believing someone with dementia who doesn't know what day of the week it is?"

Annie sighed. "We have to investigate things like this. I'm not saying I disbelieve you but we have to fill in and sign an incident form. OK, so here it is on the computer – you dictate what happened to me, I'll type it

and then I'll print it off and you can sign it."

Kasia could barely contain her anger as she detailed what happened. She hoped with all her heart that she would get the job in the nursery.

161

"You know, I have had plenty of patients with dementia push me, or try to hit me, but I don't bother to report it. I think to myself, they are not right in the head, they don't really know what they're doing."

"Well, you should really report things like that," said Annie.

"It takes too long – it means I have to come into the office to do it, I don't have the time."

"I'm sorry, I know it's a pain. You work hard, Kasia, and you do a good job."

Kasia was so taken aback that she was speechless. She left the office, feeling a little guilty about changing jobs. But she knew she had to do it to save her sanity.

Chapter 28

Steven raced down the corridor to Bill's office. He burst in without knocking, out of breath.

"What on earth is it?" asked Bill.

"Fiona told me that a US news website has run the story of Jack's infidelity and divorce. It's all over the internet, which is great for us."

He pulled out his phone and logged on to the main news sites. Frustratingly, they gave few details.

"I'll try the US sites, It seems that his gagging injunctions are still in place in the UK."

Bill sat at his PC and searched in vain. "Can't see anything." He scrolled up and down. "Ah, yes, here it is. I guess a British PM's infidelities are not top of the US agenda."

'UK PRIME MINISTER'S WIFE SUES FOR DIVORCE.' It continued: "Jack Hawthorn, the UK Prime Minister, is being sued for divorce by his wife of sixteen years, Laura. Infidelity has been cited, although at this stage no names have been mentioned. The couple have two children, Harry 15, who attends the exclusive private school, Eton, and Cressida, 13. When not in London the couple have houses in…."

"That's enough," said Bill. "We know all the details of his family." He shut the page.

"So the chap she was talking to in the restaurant, he might have been her lawyer, who knows. Things are moving fast. What's our next move?"

"I've just had a text from Mike at The Post saying he has more information. I didn't want to tell you in front of Fiona. I think we've well and truly got him now. Mike says he's been taking bribes from construction companies to give them government contracts. We were damn lucky, somebody in one of those companies found out and blew the whistle, just at the right moment for us."

"Have you got specific details?" asked Alistair.

"He's just sent them through." He passed his phone over for him to see.

Bill whistled. "These are big companies. Fantastic. The Post is also looking into the Sloane Street flat business further. Trying to pump the concierge about Jack's movements, and his lover's."

"OK, so who's going to confront Jack? And when?"

"No time like the present. Let's catch him unawares."

Steven was more cautious. "I think we need to prepare ourselves a bit more. And Alistair's not free at the moment."

"But I'll ring his secretary right now and ask her when would be a good time?"

"Will all three of us go? We want him to feel outnumbered. Although I wonder if it wouldn't be better to do it at a Cabinet meeting?"

"I don't think so," said Bill. "If two or three of us confront him and can show him we've got something on him, he'll start to feel pretty insecure. Coming on top of the trauma of his divorce he'll really be under pressure."

"I don't see how he can talk himself out of this one."

"Absolutely. I'll ring his office now." Bill picked up the phone. Trying to get past Jack's various watchdogs was not easy, especially when he was asked what he wanted to discuss.

"No, I can't tell you, it's personal."

"I'm sorry, I have to be able to tell him the nature of your meeting. You can imagine things have gone a little crazy here after this morning's news. You don't want to talk about that, do you, because if you do, I can't….."

Bill cut her short. "No, it's nothing to do with that, but it's urgent and important, and I'm not at liberty to discuss it with you." He used his most authoritarian voice.

Steven smiled as he listened to the exchange. The secretary said something he couldn't hear.

"Can't it be later today? I don't think it can really wait until tomorrow. What do you mean, he's not in the House today? Where the hell is he, he doesn't have any outside engagements today?"

Bill raised his eyebrows at Steven as he listened to the answer. "All right, tomorrow at 10."

"Where the hell is he, today of all days?" asked Steven. "He can't run from the press, they'll be relentless. But who knows, by tomorrow we may have something else to pin on him."

"You're right." Bill gathered up his files. "Anyway, I can't spend any more time on this just now, but we're meeting at five, aren't we?

"Yes. See you later."

The bar was heaving and Bill had trouble locating Alistair, who was waving at him through a sea of people. The news about Jack's divorce was a hot topic and it seemed as if the whole House had flocked to one bar or another to chew the cud. He was glad that Alistair had got a bottle of wine and the glasses at his elbow as the queue for the bar was pretty long.

They settled in a corner. There seemed to be little risk of being overheard as the buzz of conversation was deafening. "By the way, Steven can't make it, something came up. But he forwarded me the texts about the business with the construction contracts." He showed Alistair, who raised his eyebrows. "This is just what we need."

"Absolutely. But before we get onto anything else, did your wife manage to contact Laura?" asked Bill.

"Yes. She was, understandably, in a pretty emotional state. Jenny didn't get much out of her, she just played it like a sympathetic political wife who understood the problems of marriage to an MP. But from what she *did* glean, Laura thinks it's another woman. Kept saying what she'd like to do to 'her.'"

"Right. So, we need to jot down a running order for our key points. First, the boyfriend, and what we know about that. We can play up the fact that Laura thinks it's a woman, and what a shock for her and everyone else when they discover that it's a man. Not that there's any law against it, of course, but......it's not the image Jack wants to project."

"Exactly. Second, whose money he's using when he bribes his minders to get lost for the odd evening? Is it from his own pockets? Third, the status of this chap. He seems to keep an extremely low profile, which suggests he may have something to hide. I think your suggestion that he might be an illegal immigrant may be worth mentioning, even if it turns out we're barking up the wrong tree. Or, even better, perhaps he's under age?"

"Long shot, but that would really stuff him."

"Right. Four, there's the dodgy investments. Especially the palm oil and the arms sales."

"Five, the newspaper gagging injunctions, and the probable bribes to the judiciary to turn down appeals against Ultimate Care."

"And last, the contract backhanders. Now we have specific names he can't bluff his way out of that one so easily."

"No. I'm just wondering, though," said Alistair "if he'll just flatly deny everything. We need concrete proof. Is the guy at The Post working on getting some photos? Maybe he'll have something more for us by tomorrow."

"Yes, he's on the case. For all we know, Jack may have been having wild parties in that Sloane Street flat. We need to get more on that aspect. It wouldn't be the first time that men high up in Government have procured prostitutes for sex, would it?"

"No. Could be as big as the Profumo scandal, if you remember that. Rocked the nation at the time."

"I'll drink to that." They finished off the bottle in companionable silence and made to leave.

"See you at 10 tomorrow then," said Alistair, a wicked smile on his face.

Chapter 29

It was a week before Annie got back to Kasia about the complaint. "I'm pleased to tell you that the family, having read your statement and had a chat with me, have withdrawn their complaint. I explained to them that people with dementia can act out of character, that they often get more violent, but don't fully realise what they're doing. They were shocked to think their father was capable of violence, but they accepted that personalities can change with dementia."

Kasia didn't realize she'd been holding her breath until she exhaled. She had been so worried that it would go against her DBS check and the last thing she needed was a blot on her character just now.

"But next time a client shows any violence to you, you really need to report it to us, so that if there are complaints we can immediately give our side of the story. Do you understand?"

"Yes. OK."

Hopefully, I won't have to worry about this sort of thing for much longer, she thought. Then it occurred to her that dealing with young children in this litigious age could also be hazardous. She hadn't heard anything more about her job at the nursery and she wondered whether she should give Julie a call, but decided not to. It may have taken a bit of time for the reference from Poland to come.

She told Stefan that evening that the complaint had been dropped.

"Great. Now you can concentrate on planning what to do when your parents come."

"Yes - I'm so looking forward to seeing them."

She pulled out her phone and showed Stefan a list of possible things that she'd noted down.

"And, of course I'll cook a meal for them here one evening, and I'd like you to eat with us."

"Are you sure? You know what parents are like with their daughters, they are always keen to get them matched up with a 'nice' boy."

Kasia looked a bit worried. "If you'd rather not meet them, I'll understand, but I've told them what a good friend you are and I know they'll want to meet you."

"I think we're a bit more than friends now, aren't we?" He gave her a big hug.

"Yes, but I don't want to give them the impression that things are *too* serious, you know what I mean?"

"Don't worry, I'll make sure they don't think they're about to hear wedding bells."

"So, what do you think from that list are the most important things to see? We can't do everything in two days."

"Why don't you ask them? They probably have a few ideas. Why not take them on one of those bus tours, on the top deck? Then they'd see a lot of places, from the outside at least, in a short space of time."

"Good idea, I hadn't thought of that. When you live here, you get so used to seeing the landmarks you don't really notice them."

"But I think definitely St Paul's or Westminster Abbey, don't you?"

"Are you sure? Maybe Westminster Cathedral."

Kasia said. "Perhaps, but It's quite modern. I think they'll want to see more historic buildings."

"I was joking," said Stefan.

"But your idea of the bus tour is really good, "said Kasia, "I wasn't looking forward to going on the underground with them, my mum's a bit claustrophobic."

The time seemed to go quickly by. Mary was getting worse, every day she seemed to have shrunk a bit more. It was hard to remember what a plump woman she'd been only a few weeks earlier.

"I'm so tired all the time," she said to Kasia one morning. "I know it will just get worse, until…until…." She sniffed, and wiped away a tear. "I didn't think I'd mind, I've had a good life, but now I know it won't be too much longer. When I need full-time care, I'll be processed, won't I?"

Kasia held her hand, noticing how frail and bony it had become. "Yes. I…I don't know what to say, Mary. I think it's so wrong, but I suppose one good thing is that you won't spend weeks in a lot of pain."

"That's what I tell myself, dear, it's the only way I can get my head around it. I'm already taking a lot more painkillers, and pain itself is so tiring. Anyway, what about you and that job in the nursery?"

"I haven't heard anything yet. I expect they're waiting for my reference from Poland, and I have to have a DBS check."

"DBS? What's that, then?"

"You have to prove that you haven't committed any crimes if you want to work with people like children and the elderly. I had to have one before I started work for the agency, but they've changed the rules a bit and I need another check before I can work with young children. Oh, and by the way, that complaint against me has been dropped - I'm so relieved."

"I should think so too," said Mary. "I was cross when you told me about that."

"Well, he does have dementia. It was him who pushed me against the wall, not the other way about. Right, let's get you dressed, and I'll get your medication."

She felt sad when she left Mary and wondered how much longer she'd got. Still, she didn't dwell on it for long because her parents were arriving the next day and she needed to get herself organized. She'd worked overtime the previous weekend so that she could have Friday afternoon off to meet them at the airport. They didn't speak any English and had never flown before so she was anxious to travel into London with them. Later, when she was home, she busied herself preparing dinner for the following night, and realized how long it had been since she'd cooked a proper meal. She usually had a supermarket 'ready meal.' Stefan appeared in the kitchen, sniffing appreciatively.

"That smells great, I can't wait to try it."

"Well, it's your recipe and it was great when you cooked it for me. Must be all that garlic! I haven't cooked anything like this for a long time, I'm out of practice. I've made enough for us to have some tonight."

"Great." Stefan put his arms around her from behind as she stood at the stove.

"Careful....."

"I think we should make the most of tonight, don't you, you're going to be busy with your parents for the next couple of days."

Kasia turned around and kissed him, then pushed him away.

"Yes – but later, I need to finish this."

She set off the next morning feeling more cheerful than she'd felt for a long time. She felt she had finally got over the bout of 'flu, and the iron tablets her GP had prescribed for her seemed to give her more energy. She was humming as she let herself into Mary's flat. It was eerily quiet.

"Mary? Mary? Are you all right?"

She sensed that something was wrong; usually Mary was waiting for her and called out 'Hello' when she heard her arrive.

"Mary?" her heart was banging against her chest.

She checked the bathroom, living room and kitchen before and heading for the bedroom where she found Mary lying down flat in bed, looking very pale. Sweat beaded her brow, and she was softly groaning.

"Thank goodness you're here, dear, I feel so weak today. I tried to get out of bed but my legs were too wobbly. And the pain – the pain's so bad today. I forgot to put my painkillers by the bed last night, could you get them for me – they're in the kitchen."

Kasia hurried to the kitchen to find them and came back with a glass of water and the pills.

"These are the ones, aren't they? The red and yellow capsules?"

"Yes, dear, thank you, give me two, would you?"

She swallowed them down and sank back down on the bed. "I won't be able to get up until they've started to take effect, dear. The pain is so much worse than usual."

Kasia wondered what to do; she couldn't wait around or she'd never be finished by lunchtime.

"In that case, Mary, I think I'll quickly make you some tea and toast, and come back in an hour or so to help you get up and dressed. Is that OK? I'd like to stay with you but I must get on, I'm finishing at lunch-time today so I can meet my parents at the airport."

"I'm so sorry, I'd forgotten they were arriving today. Yes, you go off and come back when you can, if you could just give me a cuppa and my diabetes medication. Except, I really do need a wee – I think I'll have to use that dreadful commode that arrived the other day."

"No problem." Kasia put the kettle on and some toast to brown, returning with the commode.

"You really need more help than us carers can give you nowadays, don't you? You're getting so weak. When's your daughter coming again?"

"At the weekend - tomorrow I hope. I just don't know what I'm going to do."

Kasia left Mary feeling dreadful. She phoned the agency.

"So?" said an irritated Annie. "What do you expect me to do? She's paying for her own care now, as you know, and if she needs more hours she'll have to pay for them. It's not our call."

Kasia grimly held on to her temper.

"I'm just informing you about how much worse she is. I don't want to be blamed for anything else. Her daughter's coming over this weekend, maybe it would be a good idea if you spoke to her."

"Yes, OK, I'll call her daughter. Go back later when her painkillers have kicked in and get her up."

"That is what I'm planning to do," said Kasia through gritted teeth as she cut the call.

She finished her other clients and headed back to Mary. She checked the time - she should just be finished in time to get to the airport. She let herself in and was relieved to see Mary looking better. She helped her through the morning routine, which took longer than usual, and finally left. She was still worried about Mary, but there was nothing more she could do.

Chapter 30

The next morning, Alistair vacillated between feeling buoyant and feeling apprehensive. He had waited a long time for something to stick on Jack, who had only just pipped him to the post in the last leadership election. Alistair had a good idea what Jack would be like before he became leader – they'd been at public school together, Jack a couple of years ahead of Alistair. But even Alistair could barely believe the single-minded brutality with which Jack pushed through selective euthanasia by conniving with Charlie Warwick.

Unfortunately, no photos had come through from Mike at The Post, but they had the ones of Jack arriving and departing the Sloane Street flat.

Bill knocked on Alistair's office door at 09.45. Jack could be quite volatile and they were both a little nervous. They quickly went over their notes together and then went along to Jack's office. They sat and waited; Jack was late, as usual. Minutes went by.

"Has Jack got someone in his office?" Bill asked Jack's secretary.

She looked embarrassed. "No, I'm afraid he hasn't actually arrived yet."

Finally, Jack appeared, sashaying into the room in an unhurried way.

"Oh hello, you two. I'm sorry, I'd forgotten I'd got an appointment with you this morning. Well, come in."

They entered his inner sanctum and he waved them into chairs.

"So?" he said.

Alistair couldn't believe that Jack could be so bright when his marriage was collapsing around him, and so publicly.

Jack was, as usual, impatient. "I suppose you want chapter and verse on my split with Laura?"

"Well," replied Alistair, "Of course, what happens in your marriage is really your affair, and I'd like to say that we're all really sorry about it. But that's not all – we're rather concerned about these accusations of infidelity on Laura's part."

Jack produced his most dazzling smile and gazed across the table. It was not returned. After a few seconds without any reaction it became more of a grimace.

"People in glasshouses, etc," he finally said. "How many MPs can put their hands on their hearts and say they have been totally faithful to their spouses? This House is notorious for it!"

"Accepted," said Alistair smoothly, "but we've been doing a little fishing of our own and have turned up some pretty interesting stuff."

Jack looked a little uncomfortable, but bluffed "you can't have the slightest idea who it is. What does it matter, anyway? Look at the presidents of the US – most of them involved with other women. Dirty linen washed in public…. nobody cares these days."

"Oh, so it IS a woman, then? We'd had information that you've actually been having some sort of relationship with….with a man."

Jack looked shell-shocked.

Alistair's mouth was getting dry, but he battled on. He had been a barrister but had never been so nervous in any court room as he was now.

"We've had you followed so we know what's been going on, and with whom. We're rather concerned about his immigration status, his age, and one or two other things."

This of course, were shots in the dark but Alistair was pleased to note that now Jack was looking really worried.

There was a split second's pause before he said "I haven't a clue what you're talking about. You can't prove a thing."

"No, but we can go public with all sorts of rumours which you'll have to defend. Our tail followed you to Sloane Street and chatted to the concierge at the flats. He found out quite a few facts about your friend. Seems he rarely goes out, and always looks nervous, as if he's half expecting someone to challenge him. He speaks poor English. Looks as if he's a kept man – he doesn't work, does he?"

Jack's bravado vanished. He sat silently for some seconds before running his fingers through his carefully barbered hair. Then he said, "so, I've discovered I prefer men to women. It's not a crime. But obviously I don't want this sort of stuff being aired in public, it's private and personal. And then there's Laura….."

Bill took over. "Yes, bad enough for her to find that you've been unfaithful, but when she hears it's with a man….." He let this hang in the air for a few seconds.

"How do you know she doesn't already know?" Jack bluffed. "I might have told her everything."

"Well, have you?"

"I might have."

He became defiant again. "This is ridiculous – where's your proof?"

"We have photographs," said Bill. "The beard was a nice touch, makes you look totally different. And the 'street cred' clothes."

He pulled out his phone, and began searching for the photos. He scrolled through them under Jack's increasingly agitated eye. His ebullience had quickly faded again.

Bill showed him.

"That's not me, doesn't look anything like me. It's rubbish."

Alistair pressed on, feeling more confident. "And we've also been doing some digging about your investments. I'm not sure how close an eye you keep on them, I imagine someone manages them for you, but you do seem to be investing in some morally abhorrent ventures. Like palm oil, for instance."

"No, you're right, I don't know exactly where my stockbroker invests my funds."

"Well, we think you should take more interest," said Bill. "Very careless. Especially since you also invest in companies that sell arms to the Saudis. Tut tut. You wouldn't really want that to go public, would you?"

Jack was frowning.

"Oh, there's worse." Bill was starting to enjoy himself. "We also suspect that you have High Court judges in your remit, and that they are paid to reject the appeals against Ultimate Care. If that isn't reprehensible, I don't know what is. And we are told that you have accepted bribes to award major construction contracts. Not what one expects of the Prime Minister."

"So, what are you going to do? This is little more than conjecture. Where's your real proof? I'm not sure where all this is going,"

"We think you should resign, Jack," said Alistair. "We will keep what we know to ourselves if you do so. You seem to be burying your head in the sand about how unpopular the party now is, and you in particular, mainly because of you and Charlie bulldozing through UC. If the details of all these matters become public you would have to resign anyway. This way you preserve your privacy, and the party keeps what's left of its reputation."

"That's blackmail. "

"Yes." Bill glanced at Alistair, the ghost of a smile on his face.

"I need time to consider things. God knows, I've got enough problems with Laura and the divorce without having to fight my corner in the Party as well. I can see you're just itching to step into my shoes."

177

"Well," Alistair smiled, "Of course I'd hope to be nominated in the next leadership election. Unlike you, I don't have any dirty secrets. I suggest you fill Laura in on the details before it becomes public knowledge."

"That's where you're so wrong, smartarse. The British press and news websites can't publish a word of it because they've all got gagging injunctions."

Bill said "Yes, that's something else we've discovered. But the Americans don't have any scruples. The public can log on to Fox News and read all about your seamy life. Those gagging orders will be totally ineffective soon when the details are all over the internet."

"So," pointed out Jack, "if, as you say, all these details are going to soon be public knowledge, what have I to gain from resigning? Blackmail just doesn't work."

"We're giving you a chance to go with some dignity, Jack," said Alistair. "Far better to do it now. Do you really want to exit the Prime Ministership with everyone baying for your blood? Whilst you're right about your sex life being your own affair, questions will be asked about this chap, whoever he is, how you met him, are you 'keeping him' like a mistress? What's his immigration status? How old is he? Does he even know who you really are? How much public money has been spent?"

"We're interested in the payments you make to your minders to lose themselves when you visit your friend," said Bill.

"I use my own money, of course."

Too late he realised that this was an admission of guilt.

"What about the newspapers? We've been led to believe that backhanders have been paid to editors to keep gossip out off the front pages. That the injunctions were also an opaque process."

Jack looked as if he was about to implode.

"I've had enough of this." And he got up and flung open the door.

"GO, the pair of you! I'll not listen to this drivel any longer."

They both rose slowly, savouring the moment.

"But I feel sure you'll think about our proposal, won't you, Jack? Just don't take too long." Alistair smiled sweetly as they left.

Chapter 31

Finally, Kasia finished for the morning and ran to the bus stop but she just missed a bus. When she got to the tube station there was a delay to the next train due to signalling problems and by the time she had changed onto the Piccadilly Line she was over half an hour later than she had planned. She sat on the train taking deep breaths and forcing herself to calm down. Her phone bleeped – great, she thought, Dad's picked up my message. But it was Stefan, asking her whether she got away on time.

She texted back – "Big delay, transport problems. Now on tube, around 10 minutes from Heathrow. Texted my Dad but no reply."

"Keep calm," Stefan texted back. "I'm sure they'll wait. xx"

She finally arrived at Terminal 2, thankful that she'd already checked which terminal. The flight her parents had taken had landed, but she saw that it had been late and she hurried to the arrivals area hoping her parents hadn't waited long. She was just in time to see them come through, pulling their case and looking anxiously around them.

Thank goodness, Kasia muttered under her breath and waved frantically.

"Hello! *Nad tutaj*!" They turned and saw her. Her mother had tears running down her cheeks.

"*To jest fantastywidziec was!*" her father said.

"It's fantastic to see you too," she laughed as she hugged them both. She felt guilty that she hadn't been home more often. They were both getting on, and they'd had a hard life. Her father looked older than his sixty-one years.

"I'm exhausted!" he said. "The excitement of flying was almost too much for your mother, she was so looking forward to it, but when they called us to board she had a panic attack. You know how she gets claustrophobic. I had to drag her on. But she was OK once we'd taken off."

"It was lovely," she told Kasia. 'Like sitting in an armchair in the sky. Just a bit smaller. And they came around with a trolley with free drinks and snacks."

"You were lucky," laughed Kasia. 'On most flights nowadays you get nothing, or you have to pay for it."

She took the case from her father and led them to the exit. She hoped her mother wouldn't have another panic attack on the tube. They were bemused by the ticketing system and how easy it was so easy to swipe your credit card in and out. Her mother forgot her claustrophobia until they were on the train.

"How deep are we?" she asked nervously. "What if there's an accident?"

Kasia thought of the bomb attacks of a few years back that she'd read about, but said "It's perfectly safe, millions of people travel on it every day. Just relax. At least we've got a seat. In the rush hour it's like a sardine can. Can you show me the hotel confirmation? All I know is that it's around South Kensington."

Her dad handed her the booking. It was one of a group of very cheap hotels. She tutted. Surely her brother could have booked something a bit better for a major wedding anniversary?

"Something wrong?" asked her Dad.

"No, no, it's fine, I know where it is." *Actually, they'll probably love it,* she thought. She couldn't think when they had last stayed in any kind of hotel. Her mother was easy to impress.

The tube train rumbled its way towards South Kensington with her mother getting more and more agitated. She got out her rosary beads.

"Nearly there," said Kasia. "After this we'll try and go everywhere by bus, but the buses are very slow."

The hotel room was much smaller than she'd imagined and even her mother, Zofia, was taken aback.

"Oh." She looked dismayed. "So small. But nice and clean."

"It won't do," said Kasia.

"No." Kasia's father walked into the corridor and headed for the stairs. "I'm going to see if there's anything bigger. I can pay the extra."

"I'll come with you, Dad, they won't speak Polish here!"

After sorting out the room Kasia left them to settle in and have a bit of a rest, saying she'd come back to collect them at 6 o'clock. She didn't have time to go home and the room was too small for three to relax. A local restaurant had been booked for dinner, for which her brother was paying, and she spent the time in a nearby café, having a cup of tea and catching up on her emails.

When she returned, her mother was wearing the outfit she'd worn for the wedding of Kasia's brother, Piotr, and her father had on his best, and only, suit.

"Er.....you both look lovely," she stammered. "But you didn't need to dress up so much."

Zofia beamed. "Well, it *is* our wedding anniversary. You're not going like that, are you?" she tutted.

Kasia thought she looked very respectable in black trousers and a crisp white shirt.

"For me, this is quite smart, I usually wear jeans and trainers. It can be a dirty job. Right, so let's go."

"Hmm, still not sure why you're working as a carer,' sniffed Zofia. "All that training to be a teacher."

"So you'll be pleased to know that I've applied for a teaching job in a nursery. I should hear soon if I've definitely got it. I've explained to you before, it's been hard for me to get a teaching job here because you need an extra qualification and I can't afford to do the course. Nursery schools are different."

Her father patted her on the shoulder.

"Don't take any notice of her, Mothers always worry."

You don't have to tell me, thought Kasia. That's something I haven't missed.

It was just a short walk to the restaurant but Jozéf seemed to be lagging behind.

"You OK, Dad?" she asked him. "You look a bit pale."

"I do have a headache. I expect it's the stress of flying with your mother," he joked.

"I have some paracetamol in my bag, I'll give you a couple when we get there."

The restaurant looked very smart and Kasia was relieved that her brother hadn't stinted on the venue, but Zofia was taken aback.

"Oh, Kasia, so smart! I am glad we put on our best clothes." She gave Kasia another disapproving look as they were escorted to the table. "Never mind, when you're sitting down nobody will know you're wearing trousers." For Zofia, trousers on women were a no-no for going out.

As instructed by her brother, Kasia asked for the wine list and chose a bottle of champagne. Zofia was overwhelmed – she'd only had champagne a couple of times before.

Jozéf was looking even paler and beads of perspiration were running down his forehead. He nudged Kasia. "The paracetamol?" he whispered. He didn't want to alarm Zofia, who always worried about everything.

"Sorry Dad, here you are. Don't use the champagne to wash them down…." She passed him the water. He popped the tablets and took a big gulp of water. He put down the glass and put his head in his hands, elbows on the table.

"You OK, Dad? Is it just a headache? You look really rough."

With much effort, he raised his head and took a deep breath. He forced a smile.

"Yes, I just have a headache, but it has got worse. I'll be OK, don't worry." His speech sounded a bit slurred, as if he'd had a drink too many. The waiter appeared and after a lot of translation by Kasia, and much discussion, they finally ordered. Jozéf said he wasn't very hungry but Zofia brushed aside his protests and ordered him a huge meal. Kasia was thankful they were eating in the flat the following night, she was finding it quite stressful. She realised how much she had got used to English food and customs in the time she'd been in the London.

"Tomorrow I've prepared something for us to eat at my flat," she said. "I expect you want to see where I live?"

"Of course," said Zofia. "We do, don't we Jozéf?"

He seemed to snap back from another planet. "Yes, of course. You said it was quite small, didn't you?"

"There are three bedrooms, a kitchen and bathroom."

"Tsk, tsk," said Zofia. "No living room?"

"No Mum, we use the living room as a bedroom. That way three people can live there and it makes the rent per person much cheaper. You have no idea how expensive renting is in London. The rooms are all pretty small, too. That's why I couldn't put you up there. Anyway, Piotr thought it would be great for you to stay in a hotel."

"Well I'm not complaining," said Zofia, "it was so kind of him to arrange this for us, but the first room we had was just too small."

Kasia was only half listening. She was racking her brains as to how she could tell them about Stefan without them getting too excited. "There will be my flat-mate, Stefan too. You remember I told you about him? We don't see Anna much, the other girl, she's a nurse, and on night duty at the moment."

Zofia frowned and Jozéf. sighed. He knew what was coming.

"You are sharing your flat with a boy? I did not know this."

"Yes, Mum, you did, I told you after I moved in. At first it was just Anna and I, but to reduce the rent we advertised for a third person. He's very nice, and easy to get on with."

Zofia sniffed.

184

"And what does he do, this Stefan?"

"He's in the building trade. He can turn his hand to anything. It's very well paid in England, they are short of skilled people like him."

Kasia was getting irritated. She started to ask her father how he was feeling but her mother interrupted.

"Not a professional, then, like you?"

"At the moment, Mum," said Kasia, mustering as much patience as she could, "I'm not using my training. Being a care assistant here is a minimum wage job. I have to do a lot of overtime to earn enough. But I hope that's about to change with the new job. I....."

She was cut short by Jozéf suddenly slumping in his chair, and slowly sliding under the table. Zofia screamed.

Chapter 32

After their meeting with Jack, Bill and Alistair drafted a memo to email to the rest of the Cabinet from Bill's account, outlining what had been said. Most of them were shocked to hear that the extent of Jack's misdemeanours didn't begin and end with adultery-induced divorce. Phones started ringing almost immediately, as well as emails pinging into Bill's inbox. They nearly all expressed disbelief about Jack's lover being male; it was something nobody could imagine.

"I'll forward these to your email, Ali. We've really opened a can of worms here. Most people put Jack down as a ladies' man. What a great smoke-screen that was."

Alistair quickly scrolled through them.

"Isn't it interesting how many of them have been secretly squirming silently over the Health reforms, all too terrified for their jobs to disagree . Now, after all these revelations, they're howling for his blood!"

Bill's phone rang again. It was Steven, whose friend Mike at The Post had set all this in motion.

"Just got your email, guys, a good job done. And I think we're beginning to get the proof you need to convince him that you're not dancing in the dark. You know how yesterday Jack just wasn't around at all in the House? Guess where he was?"

"Sloane Street?"

"Yup, all afternoon and evening. It was something that had obviously been arranged in advance, because it wasn't just him and Hassan. Three middle-aged men about Jack's age came - our spy couldn't recognise any of them. Then a minivan with around half a dozen youths turned up, some of them looked still wet behind the ears."

"What? Are you trying to tell me they were under age?"

"Sure looked like it."

"But how will we get proof?"

"The reporter, Olly, had great presence of mind. He waylaid the last youth as he was going into the building and asked him if he was going to Hassan's flat. When he said yes, he offered him money to take clandestine photos of the goings-on. He said he'd pay him as much again if he'd email him the pictures, and gave him his contact details."

"And?" Bill could barely contain his excitement.

"They've just arrived. Most are quite blurry, as you'd expect, and of course after a while someone noticed him snapping away and told him to delete them. He did, but he was pretty savvy and had already emailed most of them to his own account."

"Do the youths look under age?"

"Some of them do. Olly asked Darren – the boy who took the pics - how old they were. He said he thought between 14 and 17. Darren's 17, nearly 18."

"Wow, this is mind-blowing, Steve. Can you pop into my office now, Alistair's here too. I can't wait to see them."

"OK, give me ten."

When Steven arrived they loaded the photos to Bill's personal laptop so they could get a better look. Some of the photos were reasonably clear, others too fuzzy to see much.

"Either of you any good at enhancing photos?" asked Alistair. "These two look as though they've got Jack in them, but it's hard to be sure."

Steven leaned forward and took the mouse. "I can edit these a bit - can I just…."

"Sure." Bill moved off his chair to let Steven sit down. He expertly loaded the photos and whizzed round the app to enhance the exposure and colour saturation, and then sharpened them up. They all peered at the screen and viewed them one by one.

"Stop there." Bill pointed to a face with his pencil. "This is surely Jack? The light's not great but it's definitely him. And – OMG, just look at this."

Lowering their eyes they saw that Jack was being pleasured by two young men who were on their knees. One looked like the resident boyfriend and the other was very white, very pretty and very young. Jack's eyes were closed in ecstasy. They clicked onto the others and found two other photos with recognisable images of Jack. Behind him, in the murk of the darkened room, a tangle of bodies writhed on a sofa. In another shot, there were no people but a fairly clear image of injectable drug paraphernalia.

Steven sat back in his chair and they all exhaled the breath they'd been holding.

"Got him," said Alastair softly.

"Yes; and some of those lads must be under sixteen," said Bill."

"So, how do we proceed from here?"

"We need to contact the lad who took these photos. Do you think he'd be a witness? And does he know the other guys who went? How were they found? And how old they are?"

"Mike or I need to contact him to find out all that," said Steven "and set up a meeting with him. He'll be anxious to get the second tranche of his money so I don't see too much of a problem."

"And hats off to Olly. I guess the Post will get the scoop? After all, in a matter of such public interest it's hard to see how gagging injunctions can be enforced," said Bill.

"Yes," said Steven, "I'll contact this chap, I've got his email."

"And if he's reluctant to be a witness?" Alistair was doubtful.

"I expect a financial incentive will work," said Bill. "I wonder if he had any idea who Jack is?"

"Almost certainly not, he'd have given a false name. When you meet a public figure out of context like that you don't often recognise them. I don't suppose he's much interested in politics."

"Plan of action, then?" Steven was looking at his watch. "Sorry, but I need to be at a meeting in five minutes. Mike will have to be in on this, it's his scoop."

"OK," said Bill. "First contact Darren. Try and set up a meeting – you and Mike - and get details of how he and the other guys were recruited and get more details of their ages. If they're under age, we've got Jack in the bag. They'll be public uproar – we'll have a vote of no-confidence and he'll have to resign."

"And the police will have to get involved, he's broken the law," said Alistair.

~

Steven and Mike approached a run-down corner café in a Bermondsey back street that had seen better days. Part of the window was boarded up, graffiti adorned the side wall and a faded, tacky sign proclaimed that an all-day breakfast could be had for £4.99.

"Oh god," muttered Steven under his breath. "Looks like it's run by the local equivalent of the Mafia. Are you sure this is the right place?"

"Pretty sure." Mike consulted his phone. "Yep, Desmond's Dairy." He snorted. "Never have I seen anywhere that looked less like a flipping dairy. Well, let's brave it, then. I hope he's bloody here."

They entered reluctantly, knowing how out-of-place they both looked. A single client, an old man, sat in the corner. A very attractive black girl lounged behind the counter, inspecting her nails.

Steven assumed a confident air, strode over, and ordered a large Americano. "What about you, Mike?"

"I've never craved a gin and tonic more in my life," muttered Mike "but I'll make do with a double expresso."

The girl gyrated back and forth along the counter, slowly assembling the order.

"Will dat be to drink in, or out?"

"Drink in, thanks."

"Oooh. Kaaaay. Dat be five pounds thirty."

"Surely not….." began Mike. Steven nudged him in the ribs and produced a ten-pound note from a pocket with lightning speed.

"Thanks, here you are."

He deposited a large tip in the chipped cup provided for the purpose and they retreated as far away from the counter as possible.

"Could have had breakfast for that,' Mike grumbled. "Looks disgusting, too."

"Quit moaning, will you, it's a means to an end. Now, about Darren - did your spy…"

"Olly," Mike reminded him.

"Olly - did he think to tell you what colour Darren is? It would be nice to know who we're looking out for."

"He's white. About five foot ten, slim with blonde spiky hair. Multiple piercings. Tattoos. Shouldn't be too hard to identify. I just hope he turns up."

They sipped their coffee silently. The door opened and their eyes shot over to it. Another stunning girl came in, embraced the barista and commenced to relate some drama or other with much gesticulation. So fascinated were they that they almost missed Darren entering. He was dressed in a sleeveless, studded leather vest and matching trousers, and boots with steel toe-caps. He was holding a sturdy, black dog lead. At the end of the lead was a menacing, pit-bull type dog, snarling angrily.

Chapter 33

Kasia stopped mid-conversation and saw Jozéf disappear under the table with a mixture of horror and disbelief. He only had a headache…..Zofia's screams brought waiters running as Kasia got down on the floor with Jozéf. She tried to keep them away. "He needs air. Please, just let me deal with him."

"Dad, Dad – can you hear me?"

He didn't reply. His eyes were closed and his breathing was stertorous. His face looked rather droopy on one side. Kasia knew enough to recognise the signs. Zofia was hysterical and a waiter tried to calm her down, giving her water to drink. She knocked it out of his hand and babbled in Polish, getting so worked up she had a panic attack. He bent down to speak to Kasia.

"Your mother's hysterical, she's panicking…."

"I know, I can hear." Her mother was never much help in this kind of situation.

"Please call an ambulance for my dad, I think he may have had a stroke."

She put Jozéf in the recovery position and emerged from under the table to deal with Zofia.

"Calm down, mum – he's had a funny turn and I've asked them to call an ambulance."

Zofia was struggling to breathe and Kasia wondered if the ambulance would be taking both of them to A&E.

"Deep breaths, mum. Do you have your paper bag?"

She nodded, between gasps, waving towards her handbag. Kasia rummaged around and pulled out a well-used brown paper bag, her remedy for panic attacks. She held it over her mother's nose and instructed her to breathe. She alternated her attention between her mother and her father. Her heart was beating fit to burst and she wiped perspiration away from her forehead.

"Breathe slowly and deeply, Mum. Come on, one, two, three in, one, two, three out. Yes, like that, keep going, I need to look at Dad."

A worried-looking grey-haired man approached Kasia.

"Excuse me," he said, "I'm a doctor, can I help?"

"I think my dad may have had a stroke."

They both sank to their knees to look at Józéf.

"Yes, I think you are probably right."

He looked concerned.

"He needs to get to a stroke centre as soon as possible – if it's a clot causing it, and he can be given a clot-busting drug within four hours, he stands a good chance of recovery."

"Kasia…." Zofia took her head out of the paper bag long enough to wail "What is happening?"

Kasia stood up a little too quickly, banging her head on the table. She took a deep breath and explained to Zofia in rapid Polish about the urgency but, far from being reassured, Zofia launched into another episode of hysteria, and Kasia had to go through the paper bag routine with her again. She felt pulled in all directions and was getting impatient.

"Where is the ambulance?" she said to the doctor. "Why is it taking so long?"

He shrugged. "Funding cuts. Not enough staff. And too many calls for minor ailments."

Kasia took a sip of water and tried to get her thoughts in order. What a disastrous start to the weekend.

192

A couple of minutes later the paramedics appeared and the whole restaurant seemed to be staring at them, some of them muttering under their breath. Kasia stared back, as if daring them to speak. Embarrassed, one by one they turned back to their meals and conversation started to hum again.

The paramedics briefly examined Jozéf and then lost no time in loading him into the ambulance. Kasia bundled in her hysterical mother after him.

"We can't really take you both," said one paramedic. "There isn't the space."

"Please....look, you can see what a state my mother is in. She doesn't speak any English, they've just arrived from Poland this afternoon. I can't leave her here."

Zofia clung to Kasia like a limpet, crying. "What's he saying?"

Kasia translated, Zofia looked horrified and the paramedic relented. He could see she would hold things up if he didn't.

"OK, love, I can see you've got a big problem there, we'll squeeze her in."

Kasia nodded a thank you. "Which hospital are you taking him to?"

"The nearest with a specialist stroke centre is the London Metropolitan. Won't take us long."

They set off, the siren deafening them with its wail. The Friday night traffic was unbelievably bad and Kasia kept looking at her watch, frustrated.

"We're going so slowly. This traffic........"

"We should be fine unless there's serious gridlock somewhere. People are surprisingly good at getting out of the way when they hear the siren. Look, we're speeding up now we've got through that big junction."

Zofia moaned softly, stroking Jozéf's arm. She muttered something unintelligible in Polish.

"What did you say?"

There followed a frantic tirade in Polish during which Zofia's hysteria began to rise once more. Kasia clamped the paper bag

193

over Zofia's nose again, feeling she might need it herself if her mother didn't calm down.

They finally came to a halt outside A&E and Jozéf was briskly wheeled into Resus and several staff immediately clustered around him and went into an assessment regime as coordinated as a ballet. Blood was taken and sent off for analysis and a cannula inserted in his arm ready for a drip. He was connected to various monitors.

"OK," said the consultant, "Now we need to quickly get him into the CT scanner to assess exactly what's happened."

The trolley disappeared and Kasia and Zofia were left in the waiting area.

"What about all that food we ordered?' Zofia anxiously asked Kasia. "We didn't pay for it!"

"Don't worry Mum, they probably hadn't processed the orders, and in any case, no restaurant would be so grasping as to charge in these circumstances."

"And of course, they don't know where we live, so they can't send us the bill, can they!" said Zofia triumphantly.

"Of course," agreed Kasia, although she knew that her brother had provided his credit card number when he booked. It was unimportant now.

The wait seemed endless. Eventually the trolley reappeared and the consultant came over to talk to them.

"I'm afraid it's definitely a stroke. But it's a bleed into the brain rather than a clot. So although he got here very promptly we have to look at treating him for a haemorrhage rather than give him a clot-busting drug."

Kasia translated quickly to a distressed Zofia. Kasia patted her hand, and turned back to the doctor.

"I'm sorry, she doesn't speak any English. They've just arrived for a visit, it's their wedding anniversary and she's devastated."

"I'm so sorry. Could I speak to you alone and explain what happens next. Then you can translate for your mother."

"Stay here, Mum, I won't be long, I need to talk to the doctor."

"I'm afraid it's not looking too good," he said. "It's a significant bleed and has affected a fairly large part of his brain. We may have to operate to drain the blood and relieve the pressure but the normal procedure is to observe him closely for a while before we decide. Do you know if he's on any medication?"

"Yes, for his blood pressure, and something to regulate his heart beat, I think."

"Yes, his blood pressure is quite high. If it hasn't been controlled as well as it should have been, it may have contributed to the stroke. So, if you can follow me, we'll put him in an observation cubicle and see how he goes for the next hour or so."

They collected Zofia on the way. Kasia put her arm round her and tried to comfort her. She explained in Polish what the doctor had said, and they saw Józéf installed in a cubicle where a nurse came to monitor him. He had still not regained consciousness, which Kasia found worrying, but she said nothing to her mother, who had got out her rosary beads and was fervently praying.

"Would you like me to see if I can find us something to eat, Mum? I'm really hungry because I didn't get any lunch."

"I can't eat at a time like this! Perhaps a cup of coffee, though."

Kasia set off on what turned out to be quite a long walk to find the coffee bar. Her mind was buzzing. How was she going to cope with her hysterical mother while her father was at death's door? And what on earth would she do if he actually died? If only Piotr were here. She chewed at her nails, frowning as she pondered what to do. There was only one thing for it - Piotr would have to come over and share the load. The barista was about to pack up for the night but she managed to persuade him to make two last cups of coffee and she picked up two packets of sandwiches.

Having said she could not eat anything, Zofia suddenly decided she was hungry when she saw the sandwiches and started to eat one, complaining all the while how terrible it was compared to Polish sandwiches. The nurse popped in and out, checking the observation readings. A heart monitor beeped relentlessly and annoyingly. Every now and then it would screech and a nurse would hurry to check what the problem was.

"The doctor says you told him you thought that your father was on something to regulate his heart beat. It certainly seems a bit erratic - do you know if he's had his medication today?"

Kasia asked Zofia, who shrugged. "Do you even know the name of it?" Kasia asked her.

"No, I don't understand all this medical stuff," Zofia said. "But I know he takes all his pills twice a day, morning and evening."

Kasia turned back to the nurse. "They flew over from Poland today. He most likely had his morning dose before he left, but we were out to dinner when all this happened so I'd be pretty sure he won't have had the second dose."

"OK, that's helpful," she said. I'll ask the doctor to write him up for something. We've already given him something to lower his blood pressure because it was pretty high."

"What will happen if he doesn't regain consciousness?" Kasia asked.

"We may have to operate to ease the pressure. Time will tell."

Zofia stopped eating to ask Kasia "What's she saying?"

Kasia wearily explained and started nibbling nervously at her sandwiches and coffee. The task of constantly having to translate everything, combined with the stress she was under, was exhausting. The food slowly helped her feel a bit better.

"Have you phoned Piotr?," asked Zofia suddenly. "He must know. He must come."

"It's the next thing on my list, Mum. I've hardly had a chance yet. I'll try now, before they go to bed."

"Oh, I don't think you should phone him just before bed. He might not sleep."

Kasia closed her eyes and counted to five. She fished out her phone and dialled the number.

Chapter 34

"Darren?" asked Mike.

"Yeah. You Olly's friend? How do. DOWN, Poppet, DOWN! SIT!" he bellowed.

The dog continued snarling but sat. Darren poked it with his toe and it stopped snarling and panted wheezily. It strained menacingly at the leash. "You don't wanna mind Poppet, she's still a puppy really. Wouldn't hurt a fly."

He held out his hand to Mike, who could barely bring himself to shake it, so solidly was it covered with tattoos.

"Hi, I'm Mike, a colleague of Olly's."

"Yeah, the one who's been snooping around our little club? What's his game then?"

"We're just trying to amass evidence against someone in your.....um, *Club*. "

"And who's this?" He indicated Steven.

"He's a friend."

"Yeah, well, first things first", said Darren. "I need the second instalment of the dosh for those pics. I'm not 'ere to answer questions. You're not the f-ing police, are you?"

"No…." Mike stalled.

He handed over an envelope, which Darren opened. He proceeded to count out the money, very slowly, then pocketed it and handed back the envelope.

"The thing is," began Mike, and stalled. The presence of the boy and the dog was very disconcerting.

Steven picked up the thread. "There may be more where that came from, if you *were* interested in answering a few questions. And yet more if your answers were useful to us and were prepared to give a statement."

Darren frowned.

"What kind of statement?" he asked suspiciously.

"Something which will confirm things about who was there, whether crimes may have been committed. That sort of thing."

"I'll 'ave a large latte and a chocolate muffin, love," he called across to the barista.

"I'll get that," said Mike quickly putting money on the counter. Shall we all sit down?"

"If ya like." He lowered his lanky frame into a chair, his leather clothes creaking as he moved. The dog sniffed at Steven's feet, then relaxed and continued wheezing.

"I dunno" said Darren. "Don't want to be involved with anyfing dodgy. 'Oo are *you*, anyway?" he asked Steven.

"Oh, I'm.....well, I'm not the police. I'm.....actually a Member of Parliament. We'd just like to establish the identity of one of the men at your 'Club'. And we're interested in the age of the youths you were with, and how you all came to belong to this 'club'. You understand that if any of them were under 16, an offence will have been committed?"

"Christ, nobody bothers about that sort of fing any more," Darren replied. "So, how much if I give you the answers you want?"

Steven and Mike glanced at each other. They'd talked about this earlier but couldn't fix on a sum. Olly had given Darren a hundred and fifty before the photos, and they'd just given him the same again as promised, but having met him, Steven felt that a bigger incentive might be in order.

"Three hundred now, and another three if you sign a statement?"

Darren sipped his latte and pretended to consider.

"Yeah, suppose so. Don't want to 'ave to give a statement really, though."

"How old are you?" asked Mike. He already knew, but wanted it from the horse's mouth.

"Seventeen."

"Can you prove it?"

"Yeah...." He rifled through his pockets and came up with a provisional driving licence.

"This do?"

They both peered. "OK, Thanks," said Mike. "Now then, if you're seventeen, you've nothing to fear. It's only under-age boys we're concerned with."

"Are you *sure* you're not the pigs?"

"No, as I said, I'm a journalist," said Mike. "Now, I'd like you to look at these pictures - I've had the ones you sent printed and enlarged – and tell us if you recognise this man."

Mike showed him the photo with the clearest image of Jack on it. He'd taken off the false beard for the party.

Darren looked long and hard.

"I seen him in that flat before, mind, but I've no idea who he is. Seems to have pots of money, anyway."

"What's his name?"

"Calls 'isself Sam."

"Right. And this man here - the one with the dark complexion - do you know anything about him?"

"Well, it's his flat, innit. Hassan. He lives there. Seems very friendly with Sam."

"Do you know how old he is?"

Darren shrugged. "Dunno. But he looks well over sixteen in real life, more like twenty, I'd say."

"Right. Thanks. Now." He went back to the picture of Jack.

"These two boys who are – um – with Jack, what do you know about them?"

"Well, that one's called Jayden, and that one's Farrell. They're both in care, and I'm pretty sure Jayden's fifteen and Farrell" here he indicated the very young, pretty youth who barely had any pubic hair "is fourteen, cos he said something about his fifteenth birthday coming up soon. Ere, show us those other pics, there's another lad who's only fourteen, Wesley, 'is twin. He's with the same foster parents."

Mike handed him the photos and Darren thumbed through them until he stopped at one and indicated another adolescent.

"Do you know where they live?"

"Nah, anyway they keep moving you around when you're in care. They can't wait to live on their own. But I know which school, it's the same one I was at."

"Can you tell us which one?" asked Mike.

"Well, I *can*, but they're 'ardly ever there. It's Manchester Road Comp. So....you think anyone's going to bovver about them under age boys, do you? Kids in care are targeted all the time, girls *and* boys. But I'm sure you know all that, if you're a *journalist*." This was delivered in sarcastic tones.

"OK," hurried on Mike, you've really been a great help. "I'd just like to ask about the drugs."

"Nuffin' to do wiv me," Darren said quickly. "Although that's the way to make your fortune. Me, I don't touch 'em, my dad died of an overdose. It would kill my mum if I took 'em too. Let alone dealt 'em."

"So who supplies them?"

"The guy who's flat it is, I s'pose. There's always all sorts of stuff there to inject or swallow, or snort."

"So when you say 'always', do you mean these evenings happen often?"

"I've been to two or three."

"And how did you get to know about them?"

"Friend of a friend," said Darren vaguely. "These fings are kept pretty quiet."

"And what about the boys in care? Have they been groomed?"

The lad shrugged. "Dunno about that, but they used to be in a proper kid's 'ome and everyone knows that's where you get kids for this sort of stuff. Offer 'em money, or a new phone, say it's easy work. When they get there, if they don't wanna do it they give 'em drugs to loosen them up."

Steven and Mike exchanged glances.

Darren caught the exchange.

"I don't need no drugs. I feel like an old'un compared with these wet-behind-the-ears babies."

"Seventeen isn't very old…." began Mike.

"I'm eighteen in two months. I got a disabled mother, a young brother and sister, no father, no qualifications. I 'ave to make money where and when I can. Nobody can bring up three kids on disabled benefits. I just switch off my mind when I'm with these perverted old gits."

Mike smiled. "I admire you for wanting to look after your family. It must be really difficult." He fished in his pockets, glad he'd gone to an ATM before the meeting. He fervently prayed that the editor would reimburse him.

"Right, so here's three hundred. If you give us a signed statement - which we really need - there's another three hundred."

Darren's face clouded over. Finally he said: "Well….OK."

They exchanged glances.

"Wanna do it now, do you?"

"No, we can't do it here, we need to get it typed up. Somewhere more private."

Reluctant as they were to let the boy out of their sight until they had something in writing, they agreed they couldn't do it there; Darren would have to come into the Post's offices.

"Can you come into the Daily Post offices and do it now?"

"Nah, I got to do a courier job for someone in 'arf an hour. Gimme the address and I'll get there later."

Mike handed him a card. "This is the address. You will come, won't you?"

"Yeah, but don't forget the money, will ya."

"What time can you make it? And can we have your mobile number? We've only got an email address for you."

"Yeah, OK."

Darren glanced at the time on his phone.

" 'Bout two o'clock?"

"Yes, should be OK."

"How do I find you?"

"Ask for Mike North at the reception desk and I'll come down and get you."

He glanced at Poppet.

"And maybe leave the dog at home?"

Darren shook his head. "Can't do that."

"Can I ask why?"

"She goes everywhere with me. She cries if I leave her at 'ome and it drives my mum mad."

"What about when you go to these parties? You don't take her there."

"I got a mate who 'as 'er those nights. Can't ask him today, he's got to see his Probation Officer."

Mike sighed. "Well, OK, but would it be too much to ask you to muzzle her? I can't help thinking she's a breed that ought to be muzzled in public."

"She 'ates it," he said, as if that were the end of the matter. "But don't worry, she'll be good as gold." He picked up his motor cycle helmet and left the café. Steven turned to Mike.

"I'm not enjoying this one bit. Do you think he'll turn up?"

Steven shrugged. "He's our only hope."

Chapter 35

Kasia had great trouble getting hold of Piotr, her brother. She dialled several times and the call went straight to voicemail. She felt desperate to share the awful news with someone and dialled again and willed her brother to answer. Her mother got hysterical on occasions like this and Kasia felt like she was the adult, and her mother the child. The language problem didn't help. When Piotr finally answered, he was in bed, and very tetchy.

"Where have you been?" demanded Kasia. "I've been trying to get hold of you for ages."

"Oh, one of the kids hid my phone down the sofa. When I finally found it, the battery was flat, it's just re-charging. So, are they having a good time? Was the restaurant I booked good?"

"Never mind all that, there are much bigger problems."

"Oh, don't tell me, Mum had a panic attack on the Underground?"

"No…yes she did…but…look, that's not why I'm phoning. I've got *really* bad news. In the restaurant, Dad collapsed."

"What?"

"Dad, he collapsed before we'd had the meal. He's had a stroke. He's in the hospital, in the emergency department."

There was a long pause at the other end of the line.

"A stroke? Seriously? How bad?"

"Pretty bad. A bleed, rather than a clot, which means it can't be treated with medication. They're observing him to see how he goes, but if he gets worse he may have to have surgery. Although that wouldn't guarantee that he'll get better."

"Can he speak?" asked Piotr.

"No, he's unconscious, his face is twisted and they think he's paralysed down one side. He hasn't said a word. It started with a headache and I gave him some paracetamol, and we ordered the meal. He got paler and paler and then suddenly collapsed so we called an ambulance. One of the other diners was a doctor and he helped me. Mum caused uproar by having a panic attack in the restaurant. It was ghastly, Piotr, I'm exhausted, trying to deal with both Dad, and her."

"It would be difficult for me to take time off work just now," he said guardedly.

"Well, me too," said Kasia. "I negotiated this weekend off but on Monday I need to work again. I don't know what to do. I can't leave Mum alone in that hotel either, I'll have to sleep there with her tonight, if we ever get away from here. After the weekend, I don't know where she'll sleep. You *have* to come."

"Can't she sleep in your flat?"

"Piotr, you've never seen my flat, but it's too small for an anxious, hyperventilating woman like Mum. You simply *have* to take some time off. I really need you to come and help me sort things out, I can't deal with this on my own. Dad might die, or be in hospital for quite a while. You did take out travel insurance for them, didn't you?"

Piotr was silent for a moment.

"No…" he said slowly, "I didn't. I figured we still have reciprocal health arrangements with the UK, and we didn't need it. After all, it was only a weekend, and they were both fine when they left. I couldn't have anticipated that Dad would have a stroke, could I?"

Kasia sighed wearily.

"That's exactly why you need to take out insurance, stupid. To cover unexpected things. Well, he's fine in an NHS hospital at the moment and getting good care. But you know they have this thing here, Ultimate Care? People who need 24/7 care are given a terminal injection if they fit certain criteria. In that case, we'd have to get him home, fast."

"What do you think he chances of him recovering are?"

"It's hard to say at the moment. They're going to do another scan in the morning to check on the bleeding in his head. If it's no worse, they probably won't operate. Please come over tomorrow - apart from anything else, he may die and you wouldn't have had a chance to say goodbye. I think the stroke is a bad one, but it's hard to get the staff to tell you very much. They always seem to be optimistic."

"Well….OK, I'll see about getting a flight."

"Right, I must go, Mum's waving to me. Call me when you've booked a flight."

"OK. Bye. Love to Mum. And Dad, of course."

Kasia walked down the corridor towards her mother, who was waving frantically at her from outside Jozéf's room.

"Quick, Kasia, come, he woke up!"

She hurried to his bedside and held his good hand. The other was curled inwards in an unnatural position. His eyes were open but he looked very frightened. He was trying to speak but just couldn't get the words out.

"Don't try to speak, Dad." He gave up and just raised his eyebrows.

"You've had a stroke. You're in the hospital in London. It's affected your speech and one side of your body. Can you understand what I'm saying?"

There was the merest movement of his head. Zofia clasped his other hand, tears running down her face.

"Oh my darling Jozéf, what are we going to do? We were going to have such a lovely weekend. Try to move this arm…."

"Mum, don't ask him to do that. He probably can't and you'll distress him if you carry on like that."

The nurse appeared. "He's woken up?"

"He's opened his eyes. He can't speak but he seems to understand what we're saying."

"Do you have any pain?" asked the nurse.

"He doesn't speak English," said Kasia, and translated the question. Again, the merest shake of the head.

Zofia addressed him, letting out a torrent of Polish. Jozéf's eyes showed panic.

"Please Mum, don't - he can't answer except for yes and no. How do you think *he* feels? He knows he's ruined the weekend but it's not his fault, is it?"

There were more tears and the nurse tactfully shepherded them outside, saying she needed to attend to him.

Kasia blinked away her own tears. She felt the burden of responsibility crushing her and wondered what on earth was going to happen. The nurse came out of the cubicle and nodded to them, indicating that they could go in again. They sat, one on each side of the bed, holding his hands.

"Yes, and what is this I've heard about killing off old people here?" said Zofia. "There was a programme about it on TV recently. They are killing people suffering with dementia and some other conditions, I think?"

Kasia thought of Eric and Mary. "Yes," she said quietly. " Some of my own clients have died because of this policy. I do not agree with it."

Zofia sniffed. "Terrible, just terrible. Thank goodness in our country it will never happen. The Church would never allow it. This seems to be a godless country, no?"

"Compared to Poland, yes. Mum, I finally spoke to Piotr. He's going to try and get over here as soon as he can."

"How will he afford it?" lamented Zofia.

"Mum, he won the Lottery! He has money."

Jozéf was trying to speak again. Kasia patted his hand and said: "Don't try to speak.

Are you uncomfortable?"

He shook his head slightly. His eyes pleaded with her but she couldn't understand what he wanted to say.

"Just try to relax, Dad."

A drunk was shouting down the corridor and Kasia put her head round the door to see what was going on. Two policemen were trying to restrain him. She almost missed her phone ringing with all the racket. It was Piotr.

"OK, so I've booked a flight leaving at 7am tomorrow. It's landing some place called Luton. Do you know it?"

"Yes, it's an airport out of London, sort of north west. You'll need to get a train into London but there will be plenty of them. Come straight to the hospital, it's called The Metropolitan. You can google it."

"How will I find you all?"

"I don't know where he'll be tomorrow but I'll text you and let you know. Bye."

Suddenly, Jozéf's whole body twitched and gave a shudder, and groaned. His eyes closed and his breathing changed.

"What has happened now?" screamed Zofia. "Get the nurse!"

Kasia rang the bell. Nobody came. She went out into the corridor. It was Friday night, and chaotic. Staff scurried about, patients lay on trollies in the corridor, groaning, machines bleeped, buzzers went off and constant announcements were coming over a loudspeaker. She looked around for the nurse who had just left them but couldn't see her anywhere. Zofia joined her and tutted impatiently.

"It's like a zoo here, Kasia. Why does nobody come?"

"The Health Service is overworked and underfunded, Mum. But I agree that it's awful."

She caught sight of Jozéf's nurse and waved to her.

"You need to come, he seems to be unconscious again, and his breathing is very odd."

The nurse went in to examine him and then scurried off again. "I'll be back, I think we need to scan him again."

Suddenly it was all action. Jozéf. was wheeled away to the CT scanner with Kasia and Zofia trailing behind.

"We think he's had another bleed," the nurse told them over her shoulder. 'If so, I think they will take him straight to the operating theatre."

Kasia translated. Zofia shook her head and looked defeated. She just had time to pat his hand before Jozéf disappeared through some double doors.

"Let's wait here," said Kasia, indicating a couple of chairs in the corridor. "Then we can corner someone as soon as they've done the scan."

Finally Jozéf was wheeled out of the Imaging Department and a doctor came to speak to them.

"He's definitely had another bleed into his brain and we're going to take him straight to theatre to release the pressure."

"What are his chances?" Kasia whispered.

"I'm afraid I just don't know."

Chapter 36

Steven was in Mike's office at the Post, pacing up and down and glancing frequently at the clock. Two o'clock came and went.

"I don't reckon he's coming, do you? I can't stay here all day, there's a vote in The House later this afternoon."

"I'll text him," said Mike. "Assuming he gave us the right number, of course."

They waited. The phone buzzed. Steven grabbed it.

"Phew. He says he's on his way, stuck in traffic. Be about another ten minutes."

Finally, Reception buzzed up to say there was a youth to see Mike.

"He's a bit rough looking," she whispered. "And he's got a horrible looking dog with him."

"Yes, I know all about the dog. I'll be right down."

He walked into a fierce altercation in the reception area; a security guard was shouting at Darren that he couldn't bring the dog into the building.

"Do you have a muzzle for this dog? Because it needs to be muzzled in public."

Darren sighed. "She's a Staffie, not a pitbull." He picked up Poppet and kissed the end of her nose.

"You see? And she's just a puppy, wouldn't harm anyone."

"No dogs allowed in here unless muzzled. It's the rule," said the security guard.

Mike had a feeling this rule had just been made up but he said "It's OK, I'll handle this." He turned to Darren. "I *warned* you didn't I? Do you actually *have* a muzzle?"

"Yeah. It's on the bike. I'll get it."

He picked up the dog and departed sullenly. Mike prayed that that he would come back.

He sidled back in, the dog muzzled. He looked nervous.

"So….watcha want me ter do?"

"If you could come upstairs, Steven's up there too."

He led Darren to an interview room where Steven was waiting and motioned him to sit down. He opened his laptop.

"OK. All we'd like you to do is to say again what you told us this morning – where the party took place and who was there that you know the names of. And their ages. Also about drugs being freely available. And what you know about the man called Sam. I'm going to type it as you speak." Steven was going to covertly record it on his phone, too.

It was a tedious process, teasing out the relevant information and getting it down in a grammatical form. The clock ticked on, and Steven looked anxiously at the time.

"There!" Mike saved the document. "Now I'm going to insert the photos, and then go next door where there's a printer. Then I'll come back and get you to sign it."

Darren looked relieved. "O…K….And the money?"

"I've got it here - I'll hand it over as soon as you've signed."

He went away and took two copies, one for him and one for Steven.

"Here," he said, re-entering the interview room. "Read it through, and then sign it, if you would."

"You said it would be anonymous," pointed out Darren. "If it's got my name on it, it's not, innit?"

"I thought we explained that we need a signature to prove that a real person, who was actually there, who made the statement. But we promise that when and if the story gets into the paper, the source will be given as anonymous. Most of all, we need it for private reasons, to trip up an important person who shouldn't be doing this. Do you understand?"

"Well.....'spose so. But I'm, like, thinking, six 'undred ain't much if this is so important to you." He sat back in his chair, resting one foot on the opposite knee. His fingers drummed the table. "Make it a grand, and I'm all yours."

Mike and Steven exchanged glances. They hadn't bargained on Darren wanting more. "Excuse us a moment," said Mike and steered Steven outside the office.

"Christ, what are we going to do? I don't think I'm going to get any more money out of the Post."

"Yes," said Steven, "but we're so near....Look, I'm prepared to cough up the extra money myself. This is too important to let it slip through our fingers."

"Beyond the call of duty, if you ask me, but OK, if you're sure. Can you nip out now? You'll have to go to a bank, you won't be able to get that amount out of a cash machine."

"Not sure the bank will give me that much, either."

Mike fished out his own cash card and wrote the PIN on a Post-it. "Get as much as you can on mine too."

Steven left and Mike went back to Darren. "We've agreed you can have a grand. But that's definitely our last offer."

A slow smile spread across Darren's face.

"Right."

"So, just read it and check you're happy with the facts as I've set them down, then sign it. Mike will be back with the rest of the money in a minute."

Darren skimmed through the document at great speed. Mike wondered if Darren could actually read to any useful standard.

"Seems OK," he said. Where do I sign?"

"Just here, under where your name is typed. Have I spelled your surname right?"

"Yeah." He laboriously scrawled his name in wobbly lower-case print on both copies and handed them back.

"There. So just hand over the dosh, and I'll be off."

He shifted nervously from foot to foot, anxious to be away. Mike willed Steven to come back quickly, he wanted Darren to be gone as much as Darren did.

Steven came in, out of breath and put the cash down on the table. Mike produced a bulging envelope containing the rest of the money. This time, Darren did not bother to count it, but stuffed everything in his pocket, scooped up the dog, and left, throwing a "Bye" over his shoulder as he went.

Steven sighed a huge sigh of relief.

"Wow! There were times when I thought we weren't going to manage that."

He picked up his copy. "Needs to be kept under lock and key."

"Yep," said Mike. "I've deleted it from my laptop and got it on a memory stick, which will remain on my person for the time being. I've got the audio version on my phone. Now I have to discuss with The Beast when we can run this. Not until after you've confronted Jack privately, though. Keep me posted."

~

Steven burst in to Bill's office, waving a folder.

"We got it!" he exclaimed triumphantly. Bill's secretary jumped, then muttered something about it being polite to knock.

"Sorry. Bit excited."

They closeted themselves in Bill's inner office and Steven took the document out of the folder with a flourish and laid it on Bill's desk.

"One signed statement," he said. Bill whistled.

"I'm impressed. I really did wonder whether he'd turn up, and if he did, whether he'd go through with it. Let's have a look."

He flipped through the pages. "He sounds quite articulate?"

Steven snorted. "Er, no, it was like getting blood out of a stone. We tidied up the grammar a bit, otherwise it would have been tricky to read. We're not too sure how literate he is - he skimmed through it at great speed and just look at the signature!"

"See what you mean. Anyway, now what? How are we going to do this? We need to get the Cabinet together and drop the bombshell. It won't be that easy, at least half of them are loyal to Jack."

"I really don't see," said Steven, "that faced with the photos, how he'll have a leg to stand on. There's nothing wrong with him having a gay boyfriend in but the underage sex can't be overlooked. Or the drugs."

"I think we should talk to Jack first, Alistair and I," said Bill.

"What about me?"

"Not sure if I know what you mean, old boy."

"Don't take that patronising tone with me. I *met* Darren, Mike is *my* contact at The Post and it was Mike and *me* who did all the legwork."

He knew he sounded belligerent. But he had been looking forward to confronting Jack and he was eager to see the look on his face when he saw the photos. He wanted to wipe off his smug smile and see him sweat.

"I'll talk to Alistair," said Bill, "and let you know." He picked up the folder.

"No you don't....." Steven swiped it out of his hands and made for the door. "If you want another copy you'll have to ask Mike. Or be more inclusive. I know you and Alistair are vying to be PM and Chancellor but you're not there yet, and you can't treat those of us beavering away to help get rid of Jack as lackies."

He stomped out. Like some others in the Cabinet, he wasn't sure if Bill and Alistair were altruistic in their aim to remove Jack, or whether they were more interested in boosting their own careers.

When he got back to his office, he rang Mike.

"I'm not happy with the way Bill's going about this business - I feel I've - well, *we've* – been used. I've refused to hand over the statement and told him he'll have to get his own copy out of you."

213

"And what do you want me to do?"

"That's entirely up to you," said Steven. You need to make it clear that it's the property of The Post, because I'm going to keep my copy under lock and key. It was your guy, Olly, who followed him, your editor who made some of the money available to pay Darren, and your office who typed up the statement. And it's you who's going to write the exposé. But it's me who facilitated it, and I want to be there when Bill and Alistair confront Jack. So I'm going to make life difficult for them."

"OK, I'll deflect him for the time being. Keep me posted. Sorry, gotta go, deadline approaching."

"Sure, but we must meet for lunch or dinner soon, I definitely owe you one. 'Bye."

Bill called Mike at the Post and got his voicemail. He left a message. He tried again, and got voicemail again. The third time, Mike picked up. "Yep? Mike North here."

"Ah, Mike! It's Bill Travers. We've never met, but of course I know all about you and your colleague's excellent detective work regarding Jack Hawthorn's activities, and I'm really grateful. As you can imagine, we want to confront Jack as soon as possible about this – not least because the under-age sex is an offence. Then it will be a police matter. Now then, Steven's shown me the statement but he's being very difficult about handing it over. I don't think you can publish anything until we've confronted Jack privately and the police have been informed, so I'd be really grateful if you could see your way to giving me a copy."

"Sorry Bill, I'm on a deadline here, I can't discuss this at the moment. I'll get back to you ASAP." He cut the call.

Bill banged down the phone in frustration. He knew he'd just have to be patient, or persuade Steven to hand over his copy of the statement. He sought out Alistair in the bar later and told him what had happened. Alistair was fuming.

"Who does he think he is? And why won't Mike North give you a copy?"

214

"Well, he might, he just said he was on a deadline and couldn't do anything at the moment. I'm worried the Post will break the story before we've confronted Jack and he's resigned."

"But I thought Jack had the Press in his pocket, and they couldn't do anything unless they got the injunction removed? But does that really matter? I don't see how they can enforce the injunction if Jack is shown to be breaking the law."

Bill took a long swig of his beer. His face was stormy.

"I feel like it's all slipping out of our control, Ali. I'm not at all happy."

~

While Bill and Alistair were plotting in the bar, Mike finished the article he was writing and sent it to the sub-editor. Then he called down to the Big Chief and asked his secretary if he was available.

"Will be, in about five minutes. Do you want to come and wait?"

"Be right down."

He picked up his copy of Darren's statement and walked the three flights to the office of the Editor-in-Chief, Gideon Faraday. He had an explosive temper and generally Mike steered clear of him. But today, he couldn't wait to reveal his scoop, and was optimistic that Gideon would run it, injunction or no injunction - it was definitely in the public interest.

Contrary to the laws about smoking in the workplace, Gideon was drawing on a noxious French cigarette and had a half-full tumbler of scotch at his elbow. He was the archetypal editor – florid complexion, overweight, and a glass of whisky always at hand. He put out the cigarette, waved the smoke out of the open window, and sat down again.

'Hi there, Mike, long time no see.",

"Hi, Gideon, er....no, we haven't spoken for a while."

Mike placed the folder on the table.

"My protégé Olly Banks, and I, have been doing a bit of snooping around Jack Hawthorn. The paper has actually partly bankrolled it, I'm not sure how aware you are of that but I'm sure you'll think it was worth it. I'm not going to say that it was my idea - I've a friend in the government and he thought that there was more going on than meets the eye over Jack's divorce. He and his colleagues are anxious to get some dirt to stick on Jack. He's getting so autocratic that he's virtually become a dictator, and they're desperate to get him out. Anyway, just read this."

He slid the statement across the desk and watched Gideon's face as he first flicked through the pages, then went back and read them more carefully. Finally, he looked up, smiled and took a large gulp of whisky before setting down the glass with exaggerated precision.

"This, Mike, is pure dynamite."

Chapter 37

It was a very long night. Józéf was in the operating theatre for three hours but Kasia and Zofia wanted to stay until he was safely back on a ward. Kasia had just about persuaded her mother that they really should go and get some sleep when a doctor put his head around the door of the Visitors' Room.

"Oh, you *are* still here. I thought maybe you'd gone home."

Kasia glanced at the clock on the wall, which displayed 2.30 am. "We were just about to, now I'm glad we stayed. How is he?"

"We drained some blood to release the pressure and he's stable but unconscious, I'm afraid...." He stopped as Zofia clutched onto Kasia's arm and began wiping her eyes with what was left of a tissue. Kasia quickly translated, then turned back to the doctor, who was searching the room for a box of tissues. He spotted one under the table and handed it to Zofia.

"So what are his chances, do you think?"

"It's always difficult to know in cases like this, it's really too early to say."

Kasia nodded. "What about us getting him home to Poland? My parents are just here for the weekend, they're due back home on Monday. I've lived and worked here for about two years and my brother's coming over tomorrow for a couple of days, but I have to work. My mother can't speak English, and after the weekend she has nowhere to stay. And…and….she has no money for hotels….."

She tailed off, a wave of hopelessness washing over her. Her mother demanded in rapid Polish what was being said. Kasia tried to explain.

"Sounds like you've got your hands full," the doctor said. "But I'm afraid there's not really any more to be done tonight. If I were you I'd go home and get a little sleep."

"But - " Kasia put her hand on his arm as he made for the door, "Do you think we'll be able to take Dad home?"

"Well, he's definitely too ill to move at present, you'd need an air ambulance; maybe you could later on, when he improves." He did not say 'if' although the possibility that Jozéf. might not recover hung between them.

"I expect the charge nurse will know more about this than I do, I'll get her to come and speak to you."

A few minutes later, a nurse arrived with three cups of coffee and motioned them to sit down.

"Hello, my name's Sylvia. I'm in charge of the department tonight. I understand that you'd like to take your father home to Poland?"

"Well, yes…..We're afraid that if he stays here and needs long-term care, he'll be processed for..for…." She couldn't bring herself to utter the awful words.

"Yes, well that is, of course, a possibility. How much do you know about this?"

"Too much," said Kasia. "I'm a care worker, some of my clients have been processed." She looked at the floor, remembering Eric, and felt sick at the thought of Mary's likely demise.

"Oh dear. I'm sorry. Do your parents have travel insurance?"

"No. My brother forgot to buy some." Kasia felt anger rising in her. She was too ashamed to admit that Piotr had not bothered. She had first-hand experience of how suddenly life-changing events can happen and had told him to make sure he got insurance.

218

Sylvia sighed. "I'm really sorry to tell you that although we have reciprocal health care arrangements with Poland, it's really for the treatment of acute conditions, and doesn't extend to repatriation. I'm afraid you'd have to bear the cost yourselves, and it can run to thousands of pounds if you need private air transport."

Kasia felt too distressed to translate for Zofia. She crumpled a tissue in her hand. She was feeling tired and wobbly and wished her mother were better at coping with this kind of thing.

"I'm sorry, I just don't know what to do."

"Do you have any other family?" Sylvia asked.

"Yes, my brother, he's arriving in the morning, but he won't be able to stay more than a couple of days."

"Well, I should wait until he comes, and then talk it over with him. But it sounds like you may not have a choice, your father will be looked after here, on the NHS, for the time being. Then you may have to make decisions."

"Thank you. I'll tell my mother."

She explained to Zofia, carefully editing what she said so as not to distress her mother too much. But there was no getting away from telling her that repatriation costs would not be borne by the UK.

"Can we see my dad before we go home?" she asked Sylvia.

"Yes, of course, but I should warn you he's hooked up to lots of drips, tubes and drains." She inclined her head towards Zofia. "Do you think your mother would cope?"

"I don't think she'll go until she's seen that he's still alive. I'll try to keep her calm."

Sylvia led the way down an endless corridor. She asked them to wait while she had a word with his nurse and then beckoned them into the room. Józéf. was barely visible under the machinery attached to him. He was deathly pale. His chest rose and fell almost imperceptibly and the monitor on the wall showing his heart tracing was erratic. An alarm went off.

219

"Don't worry about that," said his nurse, "It's very sensitive, and overall his heart rate and his blood pressure are OK."

They stood in tearful silence, each holding one of his hands. The ventilator huffed and puffed, the monitors hummed and the intravenous drip infused with agonisingly slow drops. He looked grey and old and Kasia couldn't help remembering what a lively man and playful father he had been just a few years back, when she and Piotr were young. She sighed and massaged her eyes, and said "Say goodnight, Mum, we need to get some sleep. They'll call us if there's any change."

Kasia was already awake when her mobile shrilled. The current dilemma played itself like a repeating video across her brain. She opened her eyes to the unfamiliar hotel room. She took in the orange walls, and the daylight slicing through the inadequate window blinds. She fumbled with the phone, noticing that there were a couple of messages. Then it rang.

It was Piotr. "Hello…..Where are you?"

"I'm on the train coming into London. You said you'd text me to tell me which ward to go to when I get to the hospital."

"I'm sorry – we had such a late night and you woke me up. I'm at the hotel with Mum."

"How was Dad when you left him?"

"Just out of surgery – unconscious but stable. The staff said they'd call if there was any change" – she quickly glanced at her messages – "but they haven't. He's on Intensive Care Unit 2, it's on the 11th floor."

"OK. And when will you get there?"

"As soon as I can although Mum hasn't really woken up yet, she put in ear plugs and slept through the phone ringing. We'll grab a coffee and a croissant and then come over."

"Right. I'll see you later."

She glanced at her phone again. One of the texts was from Stefan, who'd been pretty worried when she didn't return to the flat. In her panic, she had completely forgotten to tell him what was happening. She felt terrible, and quickly replied, briefly explaining the drama of the previous night.

Then she gently touched her mother's arm. "Mum, time to get up. Piotr's here, he's on his way to the hospital."

Zofia was groggy and disorientated. "What? What are you telling me?" She struggled to get the ear plugs out.

"It's time to wake up. I'll put the kettle on, a cup of coffee will wake you up."

Zofia looked at her watch and tutted.

"It's only half past seven, I don't feel as if I've had any sleep at all. But we must get there to meet Piotr. Did he have a good flight?"

"I don't know, I didn't ask. It was on time, anyhow, he's already on the train from Luton."

"Did you tell him where Dad is?" Zofia asked anxiously. "Does he know he's on the Intensive Care ward?"

"Yes, of course, I told him; no need to worry. I said we'd have a shower and something to eat and go over to the hospital."

She managed to get Zofia to the hospital without her having another panic attack, even though the tube was crowded. Standing at the end of the carriage where the window in the intercommunicating door was open, her mother clutched her rosary beads with one hand, her lips moving silently, whilst she hung on for dear life with the other.

They finally got to the ICU and Piotr was there, waiting outside. Zofia hurried up to him and gave him a big hug. Kasia found herself feeling irritated – Piotr was her mother's favourite, even though he rarely did anything to merit this.

"Hey! How're you doing?" he greeted Kasia.

"Stressed. Thank God you're here. Have you been in to see Dad?"

"Yes, I was with him for half an hour, then the nurse asked me to wait outside. He's still unconscious and they're worried about his blood pressure, it's too high even though he's on medication."

Zofia tutted. "What do they know? His blood pressure's been up for years. It's no problem."

"Mum, it probably contributed to his stroke. Smoking doesn't help either, especially that awful strong brand that he likes. But there's nothing to be done now. Let's go in."

Józéf looked much as he had the previous evening.

"How long will it be before he regains consciousness?" asked Piotr.

"He may not. They just don't know. We have to make plans. I suggest we go down to the café in a few minutes and talk this through. He might be like this for a while."

They settled down at a corner table.

"Now then, what are we going to do?" Kasia asked her brother.

"I think we should get him home," said Piotr. "We've got reciprocal health care with the UK so it shouldn't be a problem."

"Actually, it's a BIG problem." Kasia stirred her coffee slowly and deliberately and tried to keep a lid on her anger. "The arrangements we have don't extend to getting sick people home. Because you didn't take out travel insurance, *we* would have to pay, it would be thousands of pounds."

"He might not make it, then we won't have to make that decision, will we?"

Kasia shook her head in disbelief. "I can't believe you said that. We're working on the presumption that he will recover enough to go home."

Zofia dabbed at her eyes. "Yes, really Piotr, how can you even think that. And anyway, you have the lottery win. You'd spend some of that for your dad to get home, wouldn't you?"

Piotr said quickly "I don't think I've got enough left for that, Kasia says it would cost thousands."

"Surely you have most of it left?"

Piotr said nothing and shook his head. "Well, if you can't do that, I'll need to stay here for a while. Kasia says I can't stay in her flat, it's too small, so I'll have to stay in that hotel for longer. You can help me out with that, surely?"

Piotr shuffled uncomfortably in his chair.

"Well, the thing is….."

"Yes?" said Kasia and Zofia in unison. "You won 250,000 Euros didn't you?"

"Um... well.... We bought a few things for the house, and for the kids....and had a nice holiday....and then there was your weekend away.....and my air fare to London."

"And?" Kasia's tone was icy.

"There isn't really any left."

Chapter 38

"Can we run it?" Mike asked as his editor picked up the statement and flicked through the pages. "We're all convinced Jack's got an injunction against the Press – are we right?"

Gideon sighed. "Yes, and I've abided by it - there were both financial advantages *and* penalties involved so I've *had* to. And I've kept it quiet - but since news of Jack's adultery and divorce was made public on foreign news sites, I reckon it's open season. There's no doubt that the man in those photos is Jack. He's breaking the law and apart from anything else the whole business is repugnant; he's the bloody PM, for God's sake. We can't have someone with such bad judgement running the country. I'm going to speak to our legal advisers and see what they say."

"Right. Now then, I've got the Chancellor, Bill Travers, repeatedly calling me for a copy of this – he and the Home Sec, Alistair Radley, want to confront Jack personally but I've kept him off my back so far. The MP Steven Woolwich is my contact in the House – we're old mates, go back years. It was with him I got this statement from the youth. He has a copy of it too and although Bill and Alistair have seen it, I gather from him that he's keeping hold of it as he wants to be there when they confront Jack; he's pretty pissed off with them, says they want all the glory themselves."

"So that's the plan, is it? To confront Jack and get him to resign?"

"Originally, it was, yes - but that was before we gathered this latest info. Previous to that, they just thought he had a boyfriend, which is not illegal. And also some dodgy investments. They've already confronted him about that, and he laughed in their faces and told them to bring him some proof. But should we take it to the police?"

Gideon considered. "No. I want to break this scoop in the paper. It can't go in tomorrow's edition because I'll have to get the legal guys to OK it, but we'll get it in the day after tomorrow. I'll talk to them, while you write the article. Then let the police investigate, and do their worst. Bugger Bill and Alistair. They'll get their moment of glory when Jack's deposed - one or other of them will end up as PM."

"Just one thing, though. Steven and I promised Darren, the lad, that his name would be kept out of it, and I'd like to attribute the statement it to an anonymous source. He comes from the kind of background where you don't want to be seen associating with the law."

"That's fine, although of course these things have a habit of coming out eventually."

He had a sudden thought. "But can we trust this Darren chap? What's to stop him telling his story to other papers, or putting it on the internet?" He reached for his Scotch.

'Don't worry," said Mike, "he doesn't know that it's Jack Hawthorn we're after. He knows him as Sam, and he clearly didn't recognise him as PM from those photos. But I doubt politics is Darren's first concern, he probably doesn't even know who the PM *is.*"

Gideon pushed the file across the desk to Mike.

"OK, have it finished by lunchtime tomorrow. And thanks, Mike, great work!"

He stood up and leaned across the desk and shook Mike's hand, who left the Chief's office with a warm glow. This kind of thing didn't happen very often. He decided to get up early and write the article in the morning when he was fresh. He tried to call Steven to arrange to meet him for a drink - or maybe dinner, Steven certainly owed him one. He had no intention of being at his desk and available to answer the phone in case Bill called again. Let him sweat. The call went to voicemail and he left a message and went to the nearest pub and ordered a drink. He could overhear someone protesting loudly about Ultimate Care, apparently his father had just been told he fitted the protocols and the guy was clearly incensed. That was something that Jack's government had introduced, thought Mike grimly, without any concern for folks' sensitivities.

He had just taken a sip of his second drink when Steven rang.

"A good day's work, Mike, but I'm exhausted. Where are you drinking? Yep, I can meet you there in about twenty minutes. I'd love to stand you dinner, but I'm absolutely whacked, and if I don't get home at a reasonable time tonight I may have a divorce on my hands. We'll do it another night, yeah?"

"Yes, fine, but I'd like a quick drink to tell you what the Big Chief said when I showed him the statement."

"OK, see you soon."

Both nursing pints, they retreated to a corner of the bar and looked around to make sure nobody was watching them, or could easily overhear them.

"The Ed wants to run the story the day after tomorrow. He has to run it past the legal guys."

"I was wondering about the injunctions. Do you think he'll be able to go ahead?"

Mike laughed. "You should have seen him, like a foxhound scenting the prey. He's absolutely dying to unleash this onto the country and he couldn't care less whether you lot in the House confront Jack first or not. I've had Bill bending my ear all day, wanting a copy, but I've put him off so far and told him I'm too busy to deal with it. As for the legal issues, the Ed's take on it is that if Jack's marriage demise is all over the internet it's open season. Nothing could be higher on the 'in the public interest' index.'"

Steven's lip curled. "Good. I've no intention of letting them get hold of *my* copy either. I suddenly felt I'd just been their lackey in all this, their attitude made me sick. Maybe it *would* be better if all hell just breaks loose, Jack will have to resign anyway. He'll probably be charged and released on bail, which is a shame. There's nothing I'd like more than to see him banged up right away. Second only to, maybe, seeing his face when confronted with our evidence."

"Me too," agreed Mike. "Although from what you say, it doesn't sound like you're Bill and Alistair's best fan either."

"No, well, as much as we all want to get rid of Jack, the Bill/Alistair Dream Team has its own problems.," said Steven. "They'll be canvassing under the 'Abolish Ultimate Care' banner. But between you and me, I'm not convinced they'll bin it. Alistair is quite anti, but I think Bill's right behind it, whatever he says."

He gazed into his pint thoughtfully.

"I hate it too," said Mike, "but my dad's in a nursing home and the fees are killing me and my brother."

"The problem is," said Steven, "the country's on its knees, and this policy, odious though it is, is beginning to show big savings on elderly care, now that the teething troubles have been ironed out. But of course it's a huge moral dilemma for many."

"And how do you feel personally about it, Mike?"

"I'm in two minds. We don't let animals suffer, do we? I'd hate to be burden on my family, or on society, if it were me. I know I moaned about my dad's care home fees, but I sometimes look at the shell of the man who used to be my dad, and I'm not sure if it wouldn't be kinder to help him slip away."

"Well, as I said, it's a big dilemma" said Steven. He put down his glass. Well, that's me done. I'd better get home before I'm toast."

~

Bill and Alistair were staying late at the House and were conferring in Bill's office.

"That fucking Mike chap!" said Bill. "He hasn't got back to me, and last time I called they said he'd gone home. He's screening calls on his mobile, naturally."

"What about Steven?"

"He's not in the house, or answering his phone. Blasted chap." Bill was furious.

"You can't blame him for wanting a piece of the action, I suppose, but to snatch the file away like that and storm out - he's behaving like a toddler."

"But what are we going to do? said Bill. "Can we confront Jack without the statement in our hands?"

"We could" said Alistair thoughtfully, "but he'd probably say exactly what he said last time - bring me some proof."

"The thing is," said Bill, "will the Post run the story before we've had a chance to confront Jack? At this rate, it might. I think we should track down Jack and tell him what we know now. When he realises that it's going to be a police matter, he'll surely resign?"

"I just don't know." Alistair sounded pretty frustrated. "We've got so near, and yet we're still so far......Do you know, I think maybe we'll do nothing for the time being. If it's in the news tomorrow or the next day we won't have to do anything. Jack will resign and we can put our plans into action. Why should we warn him? We've tried once and he's demonstrated just what a conceited arsehole he is. He thinks he's so clever, and that nothing can touch him."

"OK." Bill slapped Alistair on the back. "Let's sleep on it, shall we?"

~

Mike set his alarm for six o'clock the next morning, much to his wife's disgust. "What the hell.....? You never surface until 9."

228

"Got a very big story to write. Needs to be in by lunchtime. It's a scoop but I can't tell you the details. There'll be big ructions tomorrow."

"Sounds interesting." She yawned. "See you later." She snuggled down and for a moment Mike was tempted to have another hour in bed. But he was excited about the story and wanted to leave plenty of time to get it right. He made a cup of tea and settled down with his laptop at the kitchen counter.

Two hours later he'd got the first draft. He reworked it, slashing whole paragraphs and amending sentences. By ten o'clock he felt he'd cracked it. He pressed 'SAVE' and went upstairs to shave and dress. Then he sat on the Tube hugging his laptop bag, thinking that if the passengers knew what a newsworthy bomb he was holding, their bored expressions would soon change.

Gideon was on the phone when he entered his office. It was a heated conversation and he was puce in the face, although whether from the conversation or the half-empty bottle of whisky on his desk Mike could only guess. He eventually slammed down the phone and sighed.

"That was number one legal eagle. He's not happy about things but I've stressed how important this scoop is, and they're going to consult some more before making a decision."

"What about the fact that Jack's private life is all over the internet already?"

"It gives *some* precedent but they're still worried. I've not shown them the statement but of course I had to tell them the nux of the matter."

"Right. Well, I've got the piece here – he tapped his laptop – do you want to read it on my laptop or shall I email it to you? I suppose I could print it out, but....secrecy is all, just now."

"Do you know how to send it encrypted?"

"Not a clue. I seem to remember we had a memo from the IT department a few months ago about encrypting, but I haven't used it yet."

"Me neither," said Gideon, but......MANDY!" he shouted. His secretary appeared looking harassed, wearing a 'what now' expression.

"You got that bumph about encrypting copy? We need it now."

"Um, yes, I'll have a look, I printed it out. I think I know where it is."

"You'd better," muttered Gideon, taking a gulp of Scotch.

Mike watched him covertly. It was barely half past eleven, a bit early for the hard stuff. He looked flushed. He wondered how any secretary could work with Gideon, day in, day out. He was a nightmare, but a damn good editor.

Mandy reappeared holding a file. 'Here it is. Do you need some help?"

Gideon gave her a withering look. "No thanks, I'll be fine. I *can* read."

He handed it to Mike. After Mandy had left he said "Whilst I can read, you're younger than me, and forced to be more tech-savvy. Have a go at encrypting it and then email it to me."

"Um, yes....I think I'll do it in my own office, if that's ok?" He knew he wouldn't be able to concentrate with Gideon scrutinising his every move. He moved towards the door.

"Shouldn't be too long," Mike said with more certainty than he felt.

In the event, it proved fairly simple and he saved the document with multiple passwords. He emailed it to Gideon and felt a sense of anti-climax: he was impatient, unable to settle to anything else. They were at the mercy of the legal team now.

Chapter 39

Kasia and Zofia stared at Piotr in disbelief.

"What do you mean, there's none left?" Kasia glared at him. "I expected you to spend some of it on stuff for the family, but 250,000 Euros? How can you have got through that much?"

Piotr shrugged. "It's not difficult, once you start replacing tacky furniture and buying clothes, and toys for the kids; having a nice holiday; it soon goes. We did put quite a lot into a into a pension fund but I can't get at that."

"Are you telling me," shrieked Zofia, "that you haven't put anything aside in the bank for a rainy day? NO? You are a stupid boy. First, you scrimp on our trip by not getting travel insurance, and now you're telling me you've spent 250,000 Euros in a few months?"

Piotr looked at his feet .

"Teresa made me put some into a pension fund but I can't get at it. I do have a little in the bank but it won't go far here. I wasn't to know Dad would have a stroke in London, was I? It was meant to be a lovely treat for you….."

"Not such a lovely hotel," Zofia cut in. 'Now I understand why. Pah!"

She sat down heavily and tutted. Kasia turned to Piotr.

"Come outside with me. We need to talk." They left Zofia breathing deeply.

Kasia said "I just don't believe this. You don't have any liquid cash?"

Piotr nodded miserably. "What I have won't go far in London. A cheap hotel is a couple of hundred pounds a night. She'll have to stay with you, you'll just have to squeeze her in."

"So, she can share Stefan's double bed, can she? I only have a single."

"Why don't you ask Stefan if you can swap beds, just for the time being?"

"Piotr, if I put a double bed in my room there will be no space at all. Bad enough sharing with Mama, but to squeeze into my little room? You wait 'til you see it."

"Maybe you can swap to Stefan's room for a while, share his bed with Mama?"

"I don't think he'd be happy about that, he pays more rent than me because it's a bigger room. But I'll call him and see what he says. I don't see any other way around it. Can you get a refund on the return air ticket?"

"No, I booked a basic flight, not a flexi. So I'll have to fork out for another, *when* she - or they - go home. And about this Stefan – how friendly are you with him?"

Kasia narrowed her eyes. "He's my boyfriend. I told you that."

"Yes, but how serious is it? I was thinking maybe you could share his double bed and Mama could have yours."

"*What?* Mama would have a heart attack."

"Just because she was born in the dark ages," moaned Piotr. "Things have changed. And I'm assuming….."

"Yes?" Kasia wasn't going to make it easy for him.

"I…er….imagine you're sleeping together?"

Kasia reddened. "None of your business, but yes. Although we're trying to keep things low-key."

"Seems like a good solution to me."

"No, Piotr, the best solution would have been taking out travel insurance, and keeping some of your win aside for emergencies, which is what this is."

"Why can't we just take Dad home? He'd be well looked after there."

Kasia raised her eyes to heaven. "We've been through all this. He'd need an air ambulance, not a seat on a commercial flight."

"But what about this awful euthanasia thing they have here? If we don't get him home, he might meet their rules. We can't let that happen.'

"I agree," said Kasia, "and don't mention Ultimate Care in front of Mama, she'll have another panic attack and I really can't cope with any more. What am I going to do with her?"

"Well, you call Stefan and I'll go back to be with Mama. One step at a time. Once Mama has somewhere to stay for the time being, you can go back to work. We don't know how long Dad will be here, do we."

Stefan picked up immediately he saw Kasia's number on the screen.

"Kasia! How's it going?"

"Terrible. My brother arrived this morning, but he's useless."

"Oh. But how's your dad?"

"In a coma. No change there. It's accommodation, Stefan, that's my biggest problem at the moment. My mum will have to come and stay in the flat, there's nowhere else. I wanted to talk to you about sleeping arrangements. I was wondering....."

"Why don't you share my room, and your mother can have yours?"

"Yeah, that's just what Piotr suggested, but she'll freak out if we do that. I don't have to tell you how our mothers are about that sort of thing. I was wondering...." She swallowed hard, it was a big ask. "I wondered if we could possibly swap rooms for a bit, so that I could share the double bed with her? We can't move it into my room, there isn't space."

"Of course we can. I'll swap over our stuff today, no problem."

"Oh, Stefan, thank you so much. You're a star."

"I wish I could do more to help. Would you like me to come over to the hospital?"

"That's really sweet of you, but it would be much better if you could sort out supper for the five of us tonight, we'll be bringing Piotr back for a meal but he'll stay in the hotel. We can have that casserole I made. And maybe do some rice and green beans to go with it? Then I won't have to think about food."

"OK, no problem."

He thought he could hear her crying.

"Kasia? Kasia.....I love, you, Kas. I'm blowing you a kiss down the phone. Try to stay positive, you're doing just great."

"Oh Stefan.....'Bye."

She went back into the café to tell them what they'd arranged. Zofia noticed her red eyes and looked at her suspiciously.

"He must be a good friend, to do this for you."

"I told you Mama, he's very kind and helpful. Please can you just be grateful we've sorted something out, and stop criticising."

Zofia went very red in the face, opened her mouth and then thought better of it. Piotr looked more cheerful. *It's all right for him, thought Kasia, he'll go back to Poland on Monday and leave me to sort out this mess.*

They sat silently at Jozéf's bedside and waited for something to happen. Piotr started to get restless.

"Do we *all* need to sit here?" he said. "Why don't we take it in turns. Maybe I could see something of London?"

"OK," said Kasia, "but take Mama with you, she should see something while she's here as well. I'll stay here and we could meet up at lunchtime?"

"Yes, OK, great. Come on, Mama."

"Oh I don't know," Zofia blustered. "What if he wakes up?"

"He'll either stay asleep until we get back, or he won't," said Piotr. "You probably won't miss much. They say he's stable, he's not going to die in the space of two hours."

234

Kasia was torn between chiding Piotr for his lack of feeling and being relieved that she might get a couple of hours of peace and quiet.

"Yes, go and see something. Why don't you go to Buckingham Palace, you might be in time to see the changing of the guard."

"That's a good idea. Right. Off we go, Mama."

He put his hand under Zofia's elbow and helped her up, and steered her towards the door.

"There's a fantastic Austrian patisserie near the Palace, Piotr, take Mama there, she'll love it. It's called".....she thought for a minute "Helga's, I think."

"OK, I'll try and remember that. 'Bye."

The door closed and Kasia breathed a sigh of relief. She rang Stefan again, hoping for a longer chat but he didn't answer. She wandered around, straightening things, putting things in the bin, willing her dad to wake up, but he slumbered on. His nurse took some observations and smiled at Kasia.

"Do you think he'll ever wake up?" Kasia asked.

"Impossible to say, I'm afraid. But I'm afraid you have to prepare yourself for him perhaps never regaining consciousness."

"And if he doesn't....if he needed 24/7 care....he'd be processed for Ultimate Care?"

"I suppose it's possible. I don't know what rules apply to foreign nationals, it's a bit of a grey area. You'd do better to take him back to Poland."

Kasia sighed, not wanting to go into it all again. "Yes, I know."

She went to get a drink from a machine in the corridor and returned to her dad's room. She felt so helpless, sitting there watching him. His breathing seemed to have changed and she bent over him anxiously, stroking his hand while the clock ticked away the minutes. Then she called Stefan again.

"Hi, Kasia, did you call before? I was in the middle of swapping over our stuff and I couldn't get to the phone."

"Sorry to interrupt you, I'm really grateful for what you're doing. But I need to talk to you without the others hearing."

There was a thump while Stefan obviously put down something heavy.

"OK, I'm all yours."

"I'm just so worried about what's going to happen to Dad. They say he could be like this for a long time. The thing is, Stefan, if he stays like this they will want to move him to a nursing home after a month, which we can't do because the family don't have the money."

"What about Piotr's Lottery money? Couldn't he help?"

"He's spent it all. No, don't ask.......I'm so worried about what will happen to Dad. Nobody seems to know what rules apply to foreign nationals."

"Right." Stefan was thinking. "Look, when I've finished swapping over our stuff and made up the beds....."

"You don't need to do that, I'll do it when I get back."

"You won't feel like it by the time you get back. No, what I was going to say was, I'll do some research on the internet and see what I can find out. I don't really see how your dad can be subject to the same rules as citizens of the UK. And we could try the Polish Embassy."

"Thanks Stefan, that would be great. Of course, he may not survive....but it would be good to have the information."

"Right. I'll speak to you later. Kisses."

The nurse returned to do Józef's observations.

"His breathing seems to have changed," said Kasia.

"Yes, and his oxygen saturation levels have fallen. His pulse has slowed, too."

She shone a torch into his eyes to check whether his pupils were retracting, and sighed.

"His level of unconsciousness seems to be deeper," she said. "I'm so sorry."

She sat and stared at Józef; the thought of him dying so comparatively young was unbearable. She put her head in her hands and wept.

Chapter 40

The afternoon dragged on. Steven called Mike's mobile to see what was happening and on hearing the disconsolate tone in Mike's voice, knew immediately that he had no good news.

"No decision from the legal eagles, then?"

"Not yet. It's very frustrating."

Then his landline started ringing and he grabbed the receiver saying "Hang on, Steven, this may be The Beast."

Steven overheard Mike's side of the conversation with Gideon.

"Yep....yes, right.....oh. So what's the form?"

There was a long dialogue during which he could hear Mike say 'yes' and 'no' several times until "OK, that's fantastic. I'll get onto it." Mike cut the call to the editor and went back to Steven.

"It's all systems go," he told hm. "The legal department isn't *entirely* happy and I've got to change a couple of things in the copy, but basically they're planning on running it in tomorrow's edition."

There was a whoop down the phone from Steven. "We've done it! Do you know, I saw Jack in passing this morning and I looked at the self-satisfied expression on his face and thought, you just wait, you haven't a clue what's coming!"

"So what are you going to do about Bill and Alistair? Are you going to give them the statement?"

"I'll offer, but unless they let me go with them when they confront Jack I'm not letting it out of my sight."

He said goodbye to Mike and called Bill. "What's your plan re. Jack?" he asked. "I can tell you that the story's going to run in tomorrow's Post, written up by my friend Mike. Are going to confront Jack first?"

"No, actually we've decided not to. After all, if the story comes out in the media tomorrow we won't need to do anything, will we? He'll be interviewed by the police and he won't have any option but to resign."

Steven felt deflated. Even if it happened as Bill predicted, he would have liked to have been there when they flourished the statement and photos under his nose.

"Oh. I thought you were looking forward to seeing him crumple."

"We were, but there is a certain satisfaction in the 'We warned you' scenario too. He was so bloody dismissive and cocky that we had no real proof, it'll hit him like a sledgehammer tomorrow when he wakes up to all hell breaking loose."

"O...K..." said Steve slowly. "If that's the way you want to play it. 'Bye for now."

Bill hung up and hurried along to Alistair's office and barged in.

"Start the leadership campaign right now! The Post's publishing the story in tomorrow's edition, which means it'll be online later tonight when it's gone to press. We've done it, Ali, we've done it!"

~

Mike stayed up until he could access the web edition of the paper. He read his article, annoyed to find that the legal bods had edited one or two more things out, but by and large he was pleased with it. He went to bed, knowing that the morning would bring a shitstorm. He woke early and sure enough, his phone was full of texts and emails, which he flicked through, clicking only on a couple as he wanted to get onto the internet. His wife was in the kitchen, glued to her laptop.

"When you said it was a big scoop, I had no idea it would be anything like this! It's unbelievable. How on earth did you get the facts? You been to one of these parties yourself?"

"No, of course not, I sent one of the junior reporters to snoop on Jack and he managed to get one of the boys going into the flat to take photos and send them to him. But what I want to know is what's happening to Jack?"

He searched the news channels but there was nothing. Mike was baffled - he had imagined more action from the police, although it was still early, he supposed.

He didn't have to wait long before Gideon called. "Didn't you get my text? The police want to interview you."

"ME?"

'Yes, apparently they're not satisfied that this is genuine. They were calling me at home at the crack of dawn. They want to see Darren's statement...."

"You asked them to keep his name out of it, didn't you?" interrupted Mike.

"Yes, I did, although I'm pretty sure they'll want to see him too. I don't see how we can keep him out of it, no matter what you told him They want to see both you and Olly to verify everything. Until they do, they're not confronting Jack."

"Oh really!" Mike was exasperated. "If he wasn't the PM they'd have been battering down his door long ago."

"So you need to be at The Post's offices at nine."

"What about the flat in Sloane Street? Surely they'll suss that out."

"Well yes, but you can bet your bottom dollar Jack will have warned his friend. By the time they get there he may be gone, and any evidence with him. They'll still have the Concierge to question, of course. He can confirm certain things. Anyway, those photos are proof enough."

"All right, I'll be there. I must say, I thought things would move a bit faster. Bye."

"I expect you got the gist of that," Mike said to his wife. "I'd better get a move on."

His mobile immediately rang again. Predictably, it was Steven.

"Read your article, Mike, great stuff. What's happening?"

"I've got to be interviewed by the police before they'll go to Jack. And I'm not sure we can keep Darren out of this, either. They will want to verify it all with him, although I'll do my best to keep his actual name out of the papers."

"Let's hope he doesn't run scared."

"Agreed. Keep me posted."

~

At Number 10, Jack stumbled into the bathroom, bladder bursting, head banging. He really shouldn't have done the coke last night, but now he and Laura were living apart he could take it whenever he wanted, and he found it hard to resist. He lurched back into his bedroom and seeing that it was still early, sank back into bed. Immediately, there was an insistent banging on the door. Bill had found the intercommunicating door between numbers 10 and 11 open, and had decided to surprise Jack. The door was usually kept locked on Jack's side but it gave Bill a chance to slip in without getting past the security guys.

"What're you doing here?" growled Jack as he staggered back to bed.

Bill flourished a copy of the Post under his nose.

"What rubbish are they dishing up today?"

Bill pointed to a front-page article. "It's about you. It's pretty damning."

"Give me my glasses," growled Jack. "Can't see a thing."

Bill didn't know that Jack wore glasses, he'd never seen him with them. Presumably he normally wore contact lenses. He could tell from the fug in the room that Jack hadn't had a mug of cocoa and an early night. He left the paper on the duvet, handed Jack his glasses, and took a step back.

240

Jack tried to focus on the article and took some time over it. He looked a wreck. His face turned even paler as he read. Then he snatched off his glasses, threw the paper down the bed, and shouted "It's rubbish, all of it. I'll sue."

"You need to think carefully about that, Jack. Since Alistair and I confronted you, we've gathered more proof, including photos of you in a very compromising position."

Bill paused. He was enjoying this immensely. "At least they didn't print those. And we have a statement from a young man who was at one or more of your little parties in Sloane Street."

"It's all rubbish, all a fabrication. They can't publish stuff like this about me, there are injunctions. That's why I'm going to sue."

"I understand that this was all run past the Post's legal department, and in view of the fact that the internet is already rife with accusations and rumours which originated in the US, they felt they were not really breaking fresh news."

"But accusing me of...of....fucking boys....I haven't seen that anywhere on the internet."

"Well, that's as may be, but if I were you, Jack, I'd consider your situation. It can't be long before the police interview you. After that, you'd have to resign."

"Hey, not so fast!" Jack frowned. "Why should I resign - they need to prove these allegations."

"I think you'll find they'll be tested in court, Jack. Come on, admit it, this is curtains for you. I told you, we have proof in the form of a signed statement and photographs. You're not going to be able to wriggle out of this one. How can you keep denying it?"

"I wish Laura was here, she'd help me sort this out."

"*LAURA?* Don't you think she'll be shocked to her bones when she finds out you actually prefer men? Or boys, perhaps I should say."

"*GET OUT!*" screamed Jack. "You evil, plotting piece of shit! You just want to be PM, don't you? *GET OUT!*"

Bill went. He trod softly down the stairs, whistling softly as he went, and called Alistair.

241

"I've popped in to see Jack,' he said. "I found the intercommunicating door open and couldn't resist it. He's in a right state. Still trying to deny everything. Absolutely ridiculous. I need to call Steven, to find out if he's spoken to Mike North yet this morning. It was a great article, wasn't it?"

"Yes," said Alistair. But I just don't understand why the police are being so slow."

"I'll call Mike," said Bill.

Mike was just arriving at The Post's offices when his mobile rang and Bill's name popped up on the screen. The last person he wanted to hear from, but he answered.

"Mike? It's Bill here – congratulations on the article. But we don't understand why the police haven't moved in on Jack yet – at least, there's nothing on the web."

"That'll be because they want to interview me, and Olly, who did the scouting. And see the signed statement the boy gave us. Seems they can't quite believe that someone in Jack's position would do such a thing."

"It doesn't totally surprise me" said Bill. "He, Alistair and I were at school together, you know."

The implications of boarding at a public school hung in the air.

"Well, it's a waiting game at the moment, I'm afraid," said Mike. "We're due to see the police at nine. Once they've seen the photos I don't think they'll have any choice but to arrest him. Pity they couldn't have put the photos in the article! He'd do himself a favour if he'd resign right now."

"I'm sure you're right, but I've already seen him this morning and suggested that. I got nothing but abuse."

"Right. Well, must go, Bill. Goodbye."

The Metropolitan Police had sent two of their most senior detectives to talk to Mike and Olly. They listened gravely as they set out exactly what had happened, and when they saw Darren's statement and the photos they were convinced.

"Right," said one, "I don't think we have any choice but to bring the Prime Minister in for questioning."

"This is one of the best days of my life," the other muttered sotto voce to his colleague.

Mike heard it and smiled.

Chapter 41

Jozéf's condition didn't change during the rest of the day. They all went back to the flat for supper and Kasia introduced her mother and Piotr to Stefan, who had smartened himself up for the meeting. Kasia was grateful, and Zofia looked him up and down as Kasia had known she would.

"I'll put on the kettle and make some tea, or coffee if you prefer? And I have a chocolate cake here. It's from a supermarket, but it looks good."

"I'd prefer coffee," said Zofia, relieved that she could speak to Stefan in her native tongue.

"And I guess you'll have tea?"

Kasia nodded. She had picked up some English ways in her two years in England.

"Come with me, Mama, this is where we'll be sleeping. Stefan has changed our things around and put clean sheets on the bed."

Zofia stared around the room. "Stefan did all this?"

"Of course," laughed Kasia. "Young men are quite domesticated nowadays. He's a good cook too."

Zofia sniffed. "Woman's work, really," was her only comment.

Kasia sighed. "Well, I'm very glad we haven't got to do all the rearranging. I don't know about you, but I'm tired."

Zofia's mind had moved on. "But all my things are at the hotel!" she suddenly said. "I have nothing here."

"Piotr will bring them to the hospital in the morning, won't you? I can lend you a nightdress and a toothbrush for tonight. Come on, let's have that tea."

Stefan had excelled himself by finding matching mugs and plates for the cake.

"Mm, not bad," said Zofia as she tried the cake. "But not as nice as the strudel I had in that coffee house this morning."

Stefan just smiled. "Did Piotr take her to Helga's?"

Kasia nodded.

"Yes, it's a wonderful place."

Kasia had been putting off the moment when she would ask Stefan if he'd managed to find out anything about the Ultimate Care protocols for non-British nationals. She raised her eyebrows at him and whispered "Any luck with your search?"

He nodded.

She turned to Zofia.

"Mama, we need to talk about what happens to Dad. Stefan's been trying to find out about the rules. You know that if Dad needs care 24/7 we'll have to pay for it in a nursing home. Or we take him home – but we don't have the money for either."

Zofia tutted. "Well, I don't really understand all this. It's barbaric. So what did you find out?" she asked Stefan.

He produced a sheet of paper which he had printed off the internet.

"I'm sorry, it's in English, but I'll translate."

"It's quite ambiguous. It says that the UC protocols apply *only to citizens of England,* which I found actually meant that Wales and Scotland have their own rules. Later it says that foreign nationals living in England without settled status, and visitors, can be subject to the same rules as the English. There is maximum of one month when the NHS will provide care to citizens of those countries with whom they have a reciprocal health agreement. After that, if they are not repatriated, It seems that they are subject to the same rules as the English.

It strongly urges that all visitors have repatriation included in their health insurance."

He turned to Piotr. "I understand that you didn't take out any travel insurance."

"No, stupid boy! He tried to save money," said Zofia. "So, we have a month. What can we do?"

"Well, all attempts to appeal UC decisions in the High Court have so far failed. And that's just citizens of England – no foreigners have tried. There's a lot of stuff on the internet questioning if judges are being bribed by the government to fail all appeals. But to get back to repatriation, some people have had it paid for by their governments if they don't have insurance, or can't afford it. I'll have to check this out with the Polish Embassy."

"What about lobbying the local MP? Someone at the hospital suggested that to me," said Kasia.

"Hard to see how that could help when appeals all seem to fail, but let's see who ours is, I've no idea," said Stefan.

He searched the internet for a couple of minutes, then sat back in his chair and whistled softly.

"Well, guess what, it's Jack Hawthorn."

Zofia looked blank. Kasia said:

"*WHAT*, the Prime Minister?"

"Yes, apparently this is his constituency. It says he has a local 'surgery' on the first Saturday morning of the month. But I wonder if it's worth seeing him. I think he's the one who introduced Ultimate Care."

"I think we have to try. Dad is an unusual case."

Zofia looked distraught. Kasia put her arm around her and said "Don't worry, Mum, we'll sort it all out," although hopelessness sat in the pit of her stomach. Stefan shot her a look and shook his head slightly. It seemed unlikely.

Zofia slumped in her chair and dabbed her eyes. "Oh dear, it's so awful."

Stefan got up and produced a bottle of wine from the fridge. "I've got something here that will cheer us all up. And Kasia made a casserole, so I'll heat that up and do a few vegetables."

Zofia whispered, "Nice boy, Kasia, and so useful."

Kasia smiled to herself. She had been sure Stefan would win her mother round. Stefan poured the wine and they chinked their glasses and drank to Józéf.

"What do you think of the casserole?" Kasia asked Zofia when Stefan had served up the meal.

She looked thoughtful. "Not bad," she eventually said. "Really quite good, darling."

"I cooked it, but it's Stefan's recipe," said Kasia.

"Oh, it's very good, Stefan. Who taught you to cook?"

"I taught myself. I just bought a cookery book. My mother always said that if you can read, you can cook."

"Well, sometimes there's a little more to it than that," said Zofia.

Not totally won over then, thought Kasia. She rummaged around the freezer and found some ice cream for dessert.

"And before you ask, no, I didn't make it."

"Well, even I don't make ice cream," said Zofia.

After doing the washing up they all decided to have an early night. Kasia didn't sleep very well even though she'd phoned the hospital at 10 pm to ask how Józéf was, and was told there was no change.

In the morning Zofia insisted on going to Mass and it was lucky that they knew where the church was, as they never went. Kasia always relished a lie-in if she had a Sunday off.

"Can you ask the priest to say some special prayers for Józéf?" Zofia asked Kasia. "What's his name? Do you know him well?"

Kasia and Stefan exchanged glances. "No, he's quite new, we don't know him," lied Stefan quickly. "It's not like home, people are more distant here."

He quickly checked his phone to find the times of Sunday Mass. "We'd better get going, there's a Mass at 10.30."

After Mass, Zofia insisted on talking to the priest and asking him to pray for Józéf's recovery. Kasia translated, shifting uncomfortably from foot to foot, embarrassed that her mother assumed she was a regular at the church. The priest made no comment about never having seen Kasia before and promised to remember Jozéf in his prayers.

Arriving at the hospital they found the intensive care unit in some chaos.

"We're moving your Dad to a high-dependency unit as he's stable and they need the bed for a more serious case.," said the Sister. "They've taken him off the ventilator, which is good news."

They followed the procession of Jozéf's bed, porters and nurses holding drips and other pieces of equipment, and took the lift to the floor above, which seemed equally busy. Jozéf was settled in a corner and different nurses busied themselves checking him over. Finally, Kasia, Zofia and Piotr sat down beside the bed. He looked very peaceful and was still in a coma. Piotr was restless as usual, and Kasia suggested to him that they go down to the café to discus their options.

"This is going to be a real problem, is it?" said Kasia, as she sipped her tea.

"Seems like our best option is to put pressure on our own government to get him home," said Piotr.

"Yes, it seems the most likely solution. If that fails, we'll try and see our MP at his next surgery in a couple of weeks' time. The problem is, Piotr, our MP's the Prime Minister, which we'd forgotten, and he's the one who introduced the Ultimate Care thing."

"Yes, I can see that might be a big problem. By the way, Mama thinks Stefan is wonderful!" said Piotr.

Kasia laughed. "Oh, I think he's a hit. She couldn't get over him being so domesticated."

"Even *I* have to help at home now that Teresa has gone back to work after maternity leave." said Piotr.

"Well, that's only fair. Our parents are a different generation, things have moved on. So, better get back upstairs I suppose. Maybe we can persuade Mama to come out for a little while. We could take her on the London Eye, we have two tickets already and we could buy another. Then we could have lunch on the South Bank."

"Agreed. She enjoyed seeing the Palace yesterday, once I'd dragged her there."

But Zofia was not be budged. "No, I must stay. What if he wakes up?"

Kasia sat down and took her hand. "Mama, it's not very likely. And we may as well use the tickets on the London Eye, they're expensive. We're booked for 2 pm. It takes about half an hour, then we can have lunch and come back here later in the afternoon."

"No, I'm staying here. You go off with your brother, you haven't seen him for ages."

Then Kasia's phone rang. She didn't recognise the number and frowned as she pressed answer.

"Yes?" she said tentatively.

"Oh, Kasia, hello, it's Julie - the nursery job you applied for? I hope you got my email."

"No, I don't think I did," said Kasia. 'I've been a bit busy, my father is ill. When did you send it?"

"A couple of days ago. You say your father's not well?"

"Yes, he's in hospital at the moment, here in London. "

"Oh dear, that's a worry for you. But I'm pleased to tell you that your references were very good and I'm offering you the job. I'm sorry, it's been quite a while since we met, hasn't it?"

"Yes," agreed Kasia, thinking what a lot had been going on since then.

"So," continued Julie, "I've managed to get the alterations to the building done in record time and we're opening on Monday 24th. Will you be able to start then?"

"Yes….yes I hope so, but things are a bit unpredictable at the moment. Can I call you back tomorrow?"

Julie sounded put out. "I really need a firm yes at this stage, Kasia. You seemed so keen to get the job."

Kasia's heart sank. "Yes, I really am, it's just…..I have a lot to cope with at the moment. Please can I call you back tomorrow when I've sorted my head out? I promise I'll call you first thing."

She said goodbye and briefly closed her eyes and tried to sort out her conflicting emotions. The last thing she needed at present was getting to grips with a new job.

Chapter 42

Bill called his secretary and told her he'd be into the House a bit late. He hung about by his front window and waited - he wanted to see the police arrive and arrest Jack. He planned to go next door and give the impression that he was trying to help Jack, but really he just wanted to watch the circus. Time dragged on, and he dashed into the kitchen to make a coffee. His wife, Tessa, was sitting at the counter top and took a sip of tea as she pulled the Post towards her, scanning the front page.

"What the hell……" She looked up at Bill from the paper with wide eyes. "Is this true? Did you know about it?"

Bill looked like the cat who'd got the cream.

"Yes, of course, but for obvious reasons I couldn't tell you. Looks like we might be moving next door."

"Not if Alistair has anything to do with it," replied Tessa, "I can see the mother and father of all competitions between you two."

Tessa paused her reading to take another sip of tea. "Well, Jack *is* a bit of an autocrat," she said, "but this? I'm almost speechless. The last time I saw Laura, she was a bit tipsy and she told me 'in confidence' that she suspected Jack had a mistress. She intimated that their sex life was pretty crap, but you'd think she might have had an inkling that he preferred boys!"

"He's certainly a dark horse. I must say, I'd never have suspected."

"It says here that there are photos to back up these accusations. Have you seen them?"

"Unfortunately, no. Thereby hangs a tale. Steven Woolwich…"

"What, the Communities Sec?"

"Yes – he has a friend at the Post, Mike North, who sent one of his news-hungry junior reporters to tail Jack. An insider at a gay party was paid to take some photos, and later he gave them a signed statement, with the photos. But I haven't actually seen it, although God knows, I've tried hard enough."

"Wow," said Tessa. "This is a big day. Shouldn't you be in The House?"

"Yeah, but I'm waiting here until the police turn up. They can't be much longer."

As he spoke the wail of police sirens rose to a crescendo, screeching to a halt outside. Bill smiled. "I'm going to enjoy this."

He slid through the communicating door again and searched for Jack, finding him in the living room, and was relieved to see that he had dressed, although he still looked very rough. He was nursing another large mug of coffee.

"Can I be of any help?" he asked in oily tones. "The police have arrived. Looks like you might need a friend."

Jack began to spout a stream of invective at Bill but before he'd got very far the door burst open and suddenly the room was full of both uniformed and non-uniformed officers.

Jack almost dropped his coffee mug.

"Are you John Edward Hawthorn?" asked one of the detectives.

"You *know* that I am," said Jack.

"Right, sir, I'm arresting you on suspicion of having sex with minors, that is, persons under 16, on 10th March, and other occasions."

He went on to formally arrest Jack and to give him the statutory arrest warnings while Jack collapsed into the nearest chair, shaking his head.

"Is all this really necessary?" he muttered. "After all, I *am* the Prime Minister."

His astounding hubris was evident, even at this late stage.

"Probably not for much longer," said the detective. "Please accompany us to the police station where we'll need to question you."

The entourage traipsed down the stairs.

"Would you like me to come with you?" called Bill after him, hoping he would not.

"No thanks," snapped Jack. "You turncoat."

Bill slipped back next door where Tessa was waiting to find out what was happening.

"They've gone off to the police station," he said. "I'd better get to The House, I suppose. It will be chaos."

Tessa brushed his cheek with a kiss and he grabbed his briefcase and headed off, texting Alistair as he went. Alistair was waiting for him in his office when he arrived and they sat down together in front of Sky News. There were some jerky frames of Jack getting into the car outside number 10, obviously amateurly shot with a phone camera. A police statement had been released about his arrest, but nothing else.

"I expect they'll charge him later, but let him go on bail," said Bill. "He'll have to resign at some point today."

"Did he say anything to you?" asked Alistair.

"He was pretty unpleasant to me."

But he was smiling as he said "I offered to go with him to the police station, but he declined, and called me a turncoat. And I am; we both are, but nothing has given me greater pleasure than seeing his initial disbelief, and then amazement as they led him away."

Alistair could barely contain his excitement. "Well, bring on the leadership contest," he said.

Bill suddenly realised that Alistair, who'd been his accomplice all these weeks, was now his enemy. Only one of them could be PM.

"Whoa there, one thing at a time. Need to talk to the Speaker first, I think."

The corridors were buzzing. As Bill had anticipated, chaos reigned but there was a tangible air of expectation. They finally tracked down the Speaker, Angela Debden, who was being besieged. She beckoned Bill into her office and firmly shut the door against the braying crowd. Alistair slipped in behind him.

"You," she indicated Bill, "are Secretary of State, and officially Deputy PM. We need to draw up a plan of action. If you agree, the day's Order is to be scrapped and there will be an emergency debate about Jack, and whether he should resign."

"Surely that's a foregone conclusion?" said Alistair. "He can't stay in power after this. We've gone to great lengths to make this happen, he HAS to resign."

"Nevertheless, a debate will take place, and a vote. At 2pm. I agree, I can't see many dissenters. You two are perceived as his most loyal supporters, so if you want him out, I'm sure everyone else will too. But we have to follow protocol. If he resigns, there will be no need for a Vote of No Confidence. So, excuse me, I've a lot to do before two o'clock."

"OK. Let's get to work." Bill turned on his heel and headed back to his own office, whistling as he went.

~

At noon Jack was slumped in his cell, his head still hammering. He'd managed to get a cup of tea and a stale sandwich out of his custody officers but so far they hadn't come up with any Paracetamol, despite his frequent requests. He was still incredulous that the Post had managed to get hold of the story and he couldn't imagine how; he'd been so careful with the disguise, the blacked-out car windows and shaking off his minders. He wondered if the minders had trailed him without him knowing. He thought they rather liked the nod, nod, wink, wink way he implied that he wanted some time alone with his lover. They had no reason to suspect he preferred men, he'd even said 'her' and 'she' several times on purpose. He began counting the tiles along the wall, anything to take his mind off this unexpected turn of events. Where was his bloody solicitor? You'd have thought that the PM being taken into custody would take priority over everything else. He didn't believe they could prove anything, there would need to be witnesses, photos to back up statements, and heaven knows what. He felt confident he could tell them it was a pack of lies. He didn't believe there were any photos.

The door to the cell finally opened and his solicitor, Harry Fraser, came in.

Jack jumped up with an energy he didn't feel.

"Thank God you're here, you've taken your time. Now get me out of this hole as fast as you can."

"And good afternoon to you too, Jack."

He sat down and got out a legal notepad.

"I thought I'd better read the Post's article carefully and make some notes before I pitched up here. Seems like a bit of a mess."

"You surely don't believe any of it, do you?" Jack blustered.

Harry didn't answer directly.

"My job is to represent you, not decide if it's true or not. So, you deny the whole thing, do you?"

"Of course," spluttered Jack. "What do you think!"

"I think there's no smoke without fire. So, first things first, you are saying you've never visited this flat in Sloane Street?"

"Never."

"Your lover doesn't live there?"

"My security detail will tell you that she lives in Fulham. They know I visit once a week."

"I've heard that you visit a psychotherapist there once a week, not a mistress?"

"Of course, stupid, it's a decoy."

255

Harry sighed. He wished, not for the first time, that he wasn't Jack's lawyer. The trouble with politicians was that they couldn't tell the difference between lies and the truth. It was no wonder so many political marriages broke down – trust was in short supply.

"It's all getting a bit complicated. Explain. Truthfully, if you can manage it."

"I say I'm going to see this shrink lady but it's a front for visiting my girlfriend."

"It's a bit of a stretch from that to drug-fuelled orgies with underage boys, Jack. They say there are photos, and that you've been identified from them."

"You can edit photos to look like anyone. They could put my head on another body and say it's me. Surely you know that?"

"Yes, I suppose so. Technology moves so fast. It's making the collection of evidence easier in many instances, and harder in others."

"Hmm, yes, I guess. But that's only one part of the evidence. OK, let's move on. Now then, you've had gagging injunctions in place on all newspapers for a while, haven't you?"

"Yes, and the first thing we're going to do when I get out of here is sue the blighters."

"But bearing in mind these injunctions, don't you think The Post would have to be absolutely certain that they were publishing a true story, and that it would have been passed by their legal department? They wouldn't want to risk an expensive court case, would they?"

"They're still breaking the injunction."

"Yes, but a lot of facts about your private life have already been published on the Internet, and of course something like this is in the public interest."

"How's that , then?" said Jack, sulkily. "This is my private life."

The door opened and a detective came in.

"Hello. I'm Detective Inspector Towers. We're taking you up to an interview room now, Mr Hawthorn, so you can give a

256

statement and answer some questions. Good, I see your solicitor has arrived."

"Yes, and we've hardly had a chance to say hello," bluffed Jack. Can't you delay it for half an hour?"

The detective gave him a scathing look.

"I'm afraid *we* set the agenda here, *sir*. Follow me."

"So I take it you're going to plead not guilty?" hissed Harry in his ear as they were led out.

Jack raised his eyes heavenwards. "Of course."

Chapter 43

"Who was that?" asked Piotr.

"I applied for a new job, teaching in a nursery school. They had to get references, and a crime check. It's taken a few weeks and I'd almost forgotten about it, especially with Dad being ill. The nursery is new and it opens on Monday 24th. Julie, who runs it, wants to know if I am accepting the job and if I can start then."

"So what's the problem? How much notice do you have to give the agency?"

"Oh, that's fine, I don't have a contract, although it would be polite to give them a bit of notice. But with all this going on I'm really not sure I can cope with a new job as well. And I've waited so long to get out of the care agency."

"I'm surprised, I thought you liked the work."

"I've tried to make the best of it and do a good job but it's so sad, Piotr. All these old people who can't cope on their own, with families either not interested or living a long way away. They don't get nearly enough help, sometimes we only get fifteen minutes with them. It's very, very tiring, the pay is awful, and now some of my clients are having to go through the protocols for Ultimate Care. I just had to get out."

"You need to take this job, if working as a carer is getting you down so much. You only have one life."

"I know, I'm not going to turn it down, but I just wish that I didn't have to start quite so soon."

"Well, let's go and do the London Eye, and try to forget everything else for a couple of hours."

Kasia had been in London for two years but had never been on The London Eye - there always seemed something more important to spend her money on. It was a clear day and they had an excellent view. Kasia pointed out some of the landmarks she recognised. The half-hour went too quickly and suddenly they were being told to get off.

"That was wonderful. I feel much more clear-headed."

"So, let's go and get a bit of lunch. There are lots of restaurants around here, what do you fancy?"

"I'll go anywhere as long as you're paying. You said that you do have a bit of money? I can't believe you've got through almost 250,000 Euros."

"I told you, I invested some of it, Teresa made me, but I can't liquidise the money for years, it's in a pension fund. It was just too much of a temptation to buy things we have never been able to afford. And the holiday, of course."

Kasia sniffed with disapproval. "You didn't confess that one to Mum or me, did you?"

"I....I didn't want to, I felt a bit guilty because I knew you haven't been able to get home for a long time. Anyway, I paid for this weekend for Mum and Dad, didn't I?"

"I suppose you never thought to offer to pay for a break for me too?"

He looked sheepish. "No....I'm sorry....I wasn't sure if the reason you hadn't been home was that you couldn't afford it, or whether you had made your life here and didn't want to come back. I envy you being away from Mum, with her criticism and disapproval. Teresa is really fed up with her interfering with the way we bring up the children, not to mention her dramas and panic attacks, and then there's her slavish following of the Church."

Kasia smiled. 'No, I admit I haven't missed that. But she asks in every phone call if I've met a 'nice man' and when I'm going to give her some grandchildren. She can't imagine another way of life for a woman."

"Perhaps you'll get together with Stefan and do her a favour, eh?"

"Perhaps. I don't feel ready for all that yet. I'm not even thirty."

"No, well I wouldn't have married so young if Teresa hadn't got pregnant."

"No, it wasn't your finest moment, but I think Mama's got over it. Giving her two grandchildren has redeemed you."

After lunch they made their way back to the hospital where Zofia was in a high state of excitement.

"He opened his eyes! He tried to say something, but I couldn't understand him."

"And now? He looks just the same."

"It was just for a few seconds."

Kasia went to speak to his nurse. "Does this mean things are more hopeful?"

"I didn't actually see it myself; your mother insisted he had a brief moment of consciousness, but"

Kasia understood from her tone that it may have been her mother's wishful thinking.

"I know, she does dramatize everything. Don't worry, I'll try not to get her hopes up too much."

She went back into the room. Zofia had her back to her so she shook her head at Piotr.

"What are you doing about getting home?" Kasia asked her brother. "Did you book a flight yet?"

"No, I thought I'd stay another day and if there's no change I'll go home on Tuesday. I really don't want to take any more time off work, we're really busy at present and I can't afford to lose my job."

No, you certainly can't, thought Kasia.

"I'll have to call the agency this evening and tell them that I can't work tomorrow, and that I'll be leaving for another job They won't like that it at all."

'Well, you'd better call the nursery school woman and accept the job before you tell the agency," said Piotr. "Perhaps you could take all this week off, you know, compassionate leave or whatever it's called."

"I can't do that. If I don't work, I don't get paid. And it would be unfair to the others. They'll have to re-do all the rotas and try to find a replacement, although I wish them luck with that. We're already understaffed."

"But it's not *your* problem, is it. You are too kind-hearted for your own good sometimes."

Zofia, who had appeared not to be listening, suddenly said "You've got a new job, Kasia?"

"I thought I'd mentioned that I'd applied for one. I heard this morning that I've got it, and that I'm to start on Monday 24th."

"But you can't! You have to take time off work while your father is ill."

Kasia sighed. "I can't afford not to work, Mum, I have hardly any savings and I have to pay the rent and my share of the bills. And eat of course." She knew eating was high on Zofia's list of priorities. She looked at her father.

"He seems to have fewer drips and tubes," she said.

"Yes, the nurse took out some this morning," said Zofia. "But he still has to have the fluid drip and that...that...thing." She waved vaguely to the catheter bag hanging from the bed frame. "They will take out the stitches in a few days."

Yes, thought Kasia, *and then what*. She slipped out of the door to find Jozéf's nurse, Linda.

"I see you've removed some of his tubes and things," she said. "Will he stay here until the stitches come out of his head?"

"I imagine so, but it's not really up to me. There's a huge demand for high dependency beds, as you can imagine, and as soon as he requires less care he'll be transferred to a normal ward."

"Do you mean...." Kasia trailed off and started again. "Do you mean a geriatric ward?"

Linda smiled. "We call them 'Care for the Elderly' wards now, but yes. And of course, now that we have a faster flow of

261

patients through these wards, there will almost certainly be a bed soon."

"Do you mean that because of Ultimate Care, nobody stays long on them?"

Linda looked uncomfortable.

"Well, yes…..yes, that's the situation. Don't think for a minute that I agree with it, I came into nursing to care for the sick, but it's not like we have a choice. There are strict protocols and the doctors have to implement them."

"It's just that we're not certain whether they will apply to my father. After all, he's not a UK citizen. But on the other hand, we don't have the money to either bring him home, or to pay for a private care home here. We seem to be in Limbo."

"I'd say you need to do some serious research on this," said the nurse. "Yours is not a typical case. You could appeal to the courts?"

Kasia laughed a cynical laugh. "Oh yes, my boyfriend has been doing some research. It seems that not one single appeal case that's been heard has been allowed. There are rumours that the judges have been told not to allow any. We thought we'd lobby our MP, and see what he can do. He must be able to do *something*, surely?"

"Good idea. Is he any good?"

"I've no idea, my boyfriend says he's the Prime Minister, so I can't think he'll have a lot of time, but we're going to try to talk to him at his next surgery."

"You mean it's Jack Hawthorn?"

"Yes. Why? I've not really taken much interest in UK politics so I was surprised we had the Prime Minister as our Member of Parliament."

Linda laughed. "Haven't you heard the news? It's been all over the papers and the internet. Seems like he's been playing around, and not with another woman."

"What do you mean?"

"The Post broke a story on Friday about him going to gay orgies and having sex with underage boys and taking drugs.

He was arrested and questioned by the police. They've let him out on bail."

Kasia didn't know what bail was, but she said nothing.

"I can't believe you haven't heard anything. He's resigned as Prime Minister, but he's still an MP. And did you know that he was the prime advocate of Ultimate Care? Him and the ex-Health Secretary."

Kasia felt quite shocked. "I've been so involved with my parents coming over and then my dad collapsing that I've been too busy to look at the news. I can't believe that any Prime Minister would be so stupid."

"Nor me. Anyway, it can't do any harm for you to speak to him. It will be ages before the trial and he hasn't been thrown out of his seat - yet. But of course, he probably will be, and it may be a while before someone else is elected in his place."

"I see," said Kasia slowly, feeling her heart sink. Thanks."

She went back into the room and told Piotr. He knew nothing about the UK political system and wasn't really interested, until Kasia explained that if Jack Hawthorn had to stand down as an MP, as well as Prime Minister, they wouldn't be able to get to talk to him about Jozéf..

"Well, really," said Piotr, "these British politicians. *Gay orgies?* Unbelievable."

"I must call Stefan and talk to him about it," said Kasia.

She went outside and called Stefan. He took ages to answer and when he did there was a lot of background noise. She thought she could hear female voices.

"Where are you?" she asked.

"Oh, just in the pub around the corner having a beer with a couple of people."

"What people?"

"Polish friends – two of the guys from work and some others."

Kasia heard a female laugh. "Sounds like an interesting group," she said, not wanting to sound jealous, but feeling a twinge just the same. "Anyway, I was wondering if you'd heard the news about the Prime Minister? It could affect us."

"Yes, I only just heard this morning, you know I don't bother with the news, and I've been busy."

This made Kasia feel guilty.

"Yes, yes of course. But you do see that we might have a problem, don't you? If he has to resign as an MP there won't be anyone for us to talk to until a new one is elected. By then it will be too late."

"Oh, you mean we won't be able to speak to him at his surgery?"

"Exactly. Oh Stefan, it really is all too much."

She heard him excuse himself from the group and go somewhere quieter.

"I know it's a setback, Kasia, but don't despair. Don't forget I'm going to call the Polish Embassy tomorrow, to ask about repatriation. In the meantime, try to stop worrying."

"OK. And not too many beers, eh? Give my love to anyone there who I know." She told herself that it was nothing to worry about, the female voices were probably just friends of his work-mates.

Chapter 44

Jack, Harry and Chief Inspector Towers tramped up a dank staircase to the interview room and were joined by a second detective. The two of them faced Jack across the table and Harry sat to one side, notepad in hand. DI Towers started by turning on the tape and stating who was present. Harry nudged Jack and hissed into his ear "Just answer 'no comment' to everything, understand?"

Jack affected not to hear.

"John Hawthorn, you have been arrested on suspicion of having underage sex and taking illegal Class A drugs on Thursday March 10, at 45 Elton Court, Sloane Street and on other occasions, dates not known. Perhaps you can tell us what you were doing on the evening of this year? That's last Thursday."

"I.....I went to visit a lady called Devina Huntley."

"And I understand that this lady is a psychotherapist whom you visit on a regular basis?"

Jack hesitated. "Not exactly. Well, she *is* a psychotherapist.....but she's a front.....she's actually my girlfriend. She's an alibi."

"And where does this lady live?"

"South Kensington."

"Not Sloane Street?"

"No."

"So perhaps you can explain how you were seen outside Elton Court, which is a block of serviced apartments on Sloane Street, on the evening of 10 March at around 7pm?"

"That's impossible." Jack snapped his mouth shut. Harry glared at him.

Towers sighed. "If I told you I had a written statement to the effect that you were seen to draw up outside this building in an MPV and enter the building, what would you say?"

"But….." Jack checked himself. He really didn't believe that with his disguise he would have been recognised. He began to sweat.

"Who gave that statement?"

Harry was sending him frantic signals, but Jack was ignoring them.

"A junior reporter from The Daily Post who had been tailing you for a while. He saw through your disguise. Furthermore, he states that you were alone in the aforesaid vehicle, i.e. nobody from your security detail accompanied you."

"On Thursday evenings they knew I went to see Devina and we agreed I would give them the slip. A man has to have some privacy, for God's sake."

"Having spoken to your diary secretary, I gather that Thursday evenings were blocked out on a regular basis and that you did actually see Ms Huntley as a psychotherapist on some of them – but that on others, you went nobody knows where. We've been led to believe that you regularly gave your security team some cash and asked them to 'get quietly lost' on certain Thursday evenings. Do you deny this?"

"No." For once Jack was stumped for further comment. His head was spinning. He felt sick. It was clear that someone was on to him, the cast-iron alibi he thought he had invented was looking a bit flimsy. How had he not noticed the tail? And a junior Post reporter to boot, what a humiliation. He contemplated his fingernails.

"Did you not, on some Thursdays, proceed to Sloane Street instead of consulting Ms Huntley and took part in" – here he cleared his throat – "sexual encounters with men, some of whom were under the age of consent?"

"Definitely not."

There was an audible sigh from Harry, who had to watch his client implicating himself further and further.

"And if I told you…." here Towers pulled towards him a folder which had been lying on the table "that we have a signed statement here, complete with photographs, of yourself engaging in homosexual acts with young boys?"

"I'd say you were completely barmy."

"Please may I have a word with my client?" asked Harry. 'Could you turn off the tape for a moment?"

Towers did as he was asked.

Harry leaned towards Jack and whispered urgently in his ear: "For God's sake, Jack, you're digging yourself an enormous grave here. Just answer 'no comment' to any further questions before you implicate yourself to a degree from which there's no return."

"But…" started Jack defiantly.

"NO COMMENT," repeated Harry and made a 'button your lip' sign.

"I object to this line of questioning and my client will be answering 'No Comment' to all further questions. To interrogate the Prime Minister like a common criminal is preposterous."

"And why might that be?" asked Towers acidly. "We are all common before the law."

The questioning continued for some time but the detectives got nothing more out of Jack.

"I shall shortly terminate this interview," said Towers, "but before I do, I would just like you to take a look at these photographs." He opened the folder and put it in front of Jack.

"Are you the man, marked with a white arrow, in these photographs?"

Jack looked at them against his better judgement and could not believe what he saw. Turning a sickly shade of grey he quietly said "No comment."

Jack was taken to the Magistrate's Court where he was charged. He pleaded 'Not Guilty' and was released on bail. He and Harry fought through the crowd outside, got into the nearest taxi and headed back to number 10.

They sat in the kitchen nursing mugs of tea, Jack looking totally shattered. He was in shock and the first stirrings of fear had developed into a pain in his chest.

"What a fuck-up. I thought I'd been so careful."

"So you *are* guilty." Harry looked thoughtful. "I'm afraid it's the end for you Jack. You can't possibly withstand a scandal like this. It's no good protesting your innocence and waiting for the trial. The Brits only need a whiff of something like this to turn against someone in power, even someone who was once popular."

Such was Jack's hubris that he just looked belligerent. He took his phone, which had been silenced all morning, out of his pocket and glanced at the screen. There were dozens of messages, voicemails and emails. He threw the phone onto the table.

"I can't cope with all that at the moment. I need my secretary – can you get her for me?"

"Yes – but what are you going to do, draft your resignation speech?"

"I don't think it's come to that." Jack shook his head as if he couldn't believe he'd been the engineer of his own misfortune.

There was a knock on the door.

"Can you get it, Harry, I really don't want to see anyone just now."

Harry went to the door. Jack heard Laura's voice and put his head in his hands. She charged in past Harry and stood in front of Jack, incandescent with rage .

"Well? What have you got to say for yourself?"

"Nothing much," said Jack, in a nonchalant tone. "In case you haven't heard, I pleaded 'Not Guilty'."

"You bastard! Nobody could have been more surprised than me to find that you were into *boys*. And I'm your *wife*."

"It doesn't have to be one or the other," muttered Jack. "Lots of people are bi."

Laura chucked her bag on the floor with a thump and sat down at the kitchen counter. "Harry, could you get me a large G&T, and then leave us alone? Thanks."

He silently obliged and left the room.

Laura turned to Jack.

"You are a prize PRICK! How you could do all this stuff when you're the Prime Minister, you must have realised that it would catch up with you sooner or later? And as for the children...." Here she broke down and fished out a hankie, noisily blowing her nose. "They'll be mincemeat at school. How *could* you."

"Can I remind you that I pleaded 'not guilty'?"

"Oh, don't be ridiculous. We both know you've been unfaithful, you admitted it. You just kept the details to yourself. What's the point of pleading not guilty? I heard they've got proof." She took a large slug of her gin.

"I can't believe at this late stage you think you can wriggle out of this. As for me.....what am I supposed to do?"

She gulped down the rest of the gin and tonic in one go.

"My life's been wrecked - in the space of a few hours it's been made impossible. Journalists hounding me day and night. It was bad enough when we announced we were splitting up, but now..... Do you ever think of anyone but yourself?"

Jack felt too exhausted to summon up any words.

"Well, do you?" screamed Laura as she threw her glass at him.

~

Meanwhile, at the House, Bill and Alistair were in Bill's office glued to the BBC News website, waiting for updates. The latest news flash said that Jack had been taken to court to be charged. They both fully expected that before long they would hear whether he'd pleaded guilty or not, and whether he'd drafted his resignation. The rest of the House seemed in turmoil, MPs were barely able to believe what was happening and the bars and cafes were buzzing.

Finally, the BBC announced that Jack had been charged with having sex with underage boys, also using Class A drugs, and that he had pleaded not guilty and been released on bail. There was no mention of a resignation.

"He should be here," said Bill. "He needs to face the music. *Surely* he'll resign now. I'll try to call him."

The call to his mobile went straight to voicemail. He tried going through the official phone channels at number 10, only to be told that Jack wasn't taking calls at present.

"Well, tell him it's his Chancellor here, and on behalf of the rest of the House, I need to speak to him. NOW! Get him to call me back."

Bill looked out of his window. A crowd was already beginning to gather; a local Ultimate Care protest had morphed into a 'PM must resign' demonstration and someone had even managed to create a couple of banners in the short space of time since his court appearance had been made public. His phone rang. He saw it was Jack and took his time over answering.

"Jack! At last. Bit of a pickle, isn't it?"

There was an exasperated sound at the end of the line.

"Are you coming into the House today, Jack? When are you going to resign?"

"I don't see why I should resign before I've been tried by a judge and jury. I have to be *proved* guilty."

"I really don't think you have any choice."

"Oh, fuck off. Bastards, all of you."

Bill covered the mouth piece and muttered to Alistair "He's completely deluded – he thinks he can carry on until a court has found him guilty."

Alistair snorted. "Let me talk to him." He took the phone from Bill.

"Come on, Jack, the game's up, they're baying for your blood here. You really don't have an alternative. You're done for."

Jack cut the call. Alistair looked at Bill and shrugged. "I really do wonder if he's all right in the head, don't you?"

Chapter 45

Stefan finally managed to speak to someone at the Polish Embassy but he wasn't much help. Yes, they had helped one or two people in Jozéf's situation to get home, but all cases were judged on an individual basis.

"Citizens are warned to be sure to take out travel insurance, including repatriation costs, for just this sort of situation."

"Yes, I'm aware of that." Stefan gritted his teeth and silently cursed Piotr. He wondered how someone as sensible as Kasia could have such a hopeless brother. Not only was he irresponsible, but he didn't come across as having much feeling for his parents, either.

"So can you tell me what sort of circumstances the people who were repatriated were in?"

"Oh, generally victims of accidents who were recovering quite well and just needed extra seats on the plane. Severe strokes are a different matter, you'd need an Air Ambulance. I suggest you wait and see how your father gets on – is it your father? He may improve."

"My girlfriend's father, actually."

"Well, as I said, I'd wait and see."

"But he only has a month of free NHS care, and after that we're worried he might be subjected to the Ultimate Care rules, which is why we're anxious to get him home."

"In the event of him being processed, you would need to go to court with your case and plead for exemption on the grounds of non-citizenship. If they ruled that he was subject to UC like UK nationals, we would then look into helping you."

"And who would pay the lawyers?"

The official sighed. "You would, I'm afraid."

Stefan clenched his teeth in frustration. It just wouldn't be an option.

"OK, well thank you for the information. I know from research that nobody has yet won a case in the High Court. It looks like we're on our own with this. We're going to try and speak to my girlfriend's MP, that's the next step. I've been told that a couple of politicians have taken up cases like this."

"I wish you luck. Good bye."

~

Kasia had taken the day off to make sure Zofia knew how to get to the hospital and back on her own. They met up with Piotr in the ward, where he informed them that he was going home that afternoon.

"But you said you'd stay until Tuesday,!" Zofia could hardly believe it.

He looked shamefaced. "Of course, but I looked at the fares home – it's much more expensive buying a single fare, you know, and fares tomorrow seemed to be much more expensive than today."

Kasia opened her mouth and shut it again, and took a deep breath. She was almost beyond words, where her brother was concerned.

"OK, you bugger off home, and leave everything to me. I don't know why I thought you'd be any use here."

"You have Stefan," said Piotr, sounding defensive. "He'll help you."

"Just as well," snapped Kasia. "Right, you stay here with Mama, and I'm going outside to make a couple of phonc calls. I need to tell Julie at the Nursery that I'm taking the job, and

273

call Annie at the agency to give in my notice. All I got this morning was her voicemail when I called to tell her I couldn't work today."

She flounced out. Piotr tried not to meet Zofia's eyes. He waited for a torrent of abuse but she simply sighed and said "A man has to do what he has to do."

Piotr felt just a tiny twinge of guilt.

"Yes, but Kasia has to work too," he pointed out. "You will have to get yourself around London alone, and maybe help with the cooking and so on. She works long hours, and she can't do everything." Much as he felt that he should try and stick up for Kasia, he was itching to get away. Jozéf's death didn't look imminent and he felt he could do little good by staying – he hated hospitals.

Kasia reappeared looking a bit more cheerful.

"All sorted," she said. "Annie was furious, but when I told her what my new job was, and the salary, there wasn't much she could say. And I managed to have a word with Dad's nurse, she says his condition's just the same. The consultant does his round this morning, so if we hang about we should be able to have a word with him."

The consultant, when he arrived, appeared to Kasia to be rather distant, in a hurry and full of his own importance. He was accompanied by a cohort of medical students and only nodded vaguely in her direction before studying Jozéf's notes. He instructed one of the students to examine Jozéf and guess what the diagnosis was, and then carried on talking about Jozéf as though Kasia, Piotr and Zofia weren't there. When he turned to go, Kasia intercepted him and asked what he thought the outcome was likely to be.

"He's in a deep coma following a major stroke, which I'm afraid isn't a good sign after three days. You may have to prepare yourself for the possibility that he won't recover and will need long-term care. I understand he's here on a visit from Poland?"

"Yes, and we're worried what his situation is regarding long term care, as a foreigner, I mean. We understand he'll have at least four weeks of care here."

"Yes, I believe that's the case. Good morning." He swept past and onto the next patient.

"But…." Kasia started, but it was clear he wasn't prepared to give her any more of his time.

"What a rude man. What did he say?" demanded Zofia.

Kasia repeated his words. It was nothing they didn't know already. She tried to cheer up Zofia by reminding her that Stefan was going to try to get through to the Polish Embassy today, and that they'd arranged to speak during his lunch break.

I'm sure they'll help," said Kasia. "After all, that's what they're there for, isn't it?"

~

They settled into a routine, Kasia leaving early for work each morning, and Zofia getting herself across London and spending most of the day at the hospital. She complained incessantly, about the crowds on the Underground, the nurses at the hospital, Kasia's long hours. The language barrier didn't help but Kasia was surprised at how many English words she had quickly learned. Jozéf was no better, and no worse. It seemed that he could remain in a coma indefinitely.

The end of the second week finally arrived. Kasia was booked to work the weekend, her last two days with the agency, and really didn't want to but she needed the money. Also, it provided a bit of a respite from Zofia. By Sunday she was exhausted and dreading starting at the nursery on Monday, where she knew she would have to be on top form. She hadn't done any teaching for two years and was beginning to feel nervous. Stefan cooked them a chicken for Sunday dinner and tried to boost Kasia's confidence about the new job over the meal, but Zofia was no help.

"I don't know what you're worried about," she sniffed. "You taught for years in Poland, and these are very little children, yes?"

"Starting a new job is always stressful, Mama. And the nursery is new, it's actually opening tomorrow. I was supposed to have an induction day this week but I couldn't take the time off."

"Still, if everyone is new, it won't be so bad, will it?" said Stefan. "Nobody will have settled in. You'll be fine, and it's what you really want. Working for that agency has worn you out, you remember how ill you were with flu? Half of that was just exhaustion, I'm sure."

Kasia smiled weakly and held out her glass for more wine. Zofia tutted under her breath. "Maybe not such a good idea to drink too much wine, Kasia, if you want to be on top form tomorrow."

"It's relaxing me, and will help me sleep." Kasia was, for once, defiant. Living cheek by jowl with her mother was driving her mad. Stefan filled her glass and winked at her. He had been managing her mother very well, which had helped.

Kasia chinked her glass with Stefan and then her mother. "Here's to my new job!"

"When are you going to see your MP?" Zofia asked.

"We just hope we still *have* an MP," said Stefan. He tried to explain about Jack and why he'd had to resign, although he skimmed over the worst details of the sex parties. Zofia still didn't really understand.

"Anyway, we're going next Saturday morning, that's when he holds his 'surgeries.' Although as he introduced Ultimate Care I'm not sure how helpful he'll be."

"Maybe he'll take it up as a cause, to boost his popularity," joked Kasia. "He sure needs something to turn the tide of hate against him."

"England is a curious place," said Zofia. "This could never happen at home."

Stefan exchanged glances with Kasia, who raised her eyes to heaven.

"I think you'd be surprised, Mama," said Kasia. "These things happen everywhere but perhaps at home they wouldn't be made so public."

They had an early night and despite the wine Kasia didn't sleep well. Her mind would not stop going around in circles – she felt she was being pulled in so many different directions. The sleeping arrangements didn't help, as Zofia snored and was a restless sleeper. Kasia tried to get as far away from her mother as possible, clinging to the edge of the bed. She'd put in ear-plugs but they didn't totally shut out the noise. She missed the physical closeness with Stefan as for the last three weeks they hardly dared even exchange a kiss. Her mother always seemed to be hovering, there was nowhere to get away from her and the flat felt so claustrophobic.

Although she was still rather tired in the morning, Kasia was also excited, and the adrenaline gave her a buzz. She trawled through her wardrobe for something to wear; Julie had specified no jeans. Zofia pointed out that small children could mess up her clothes as easily as the old and infirm, and she stopped searching for something smart and grabbed a pair of cotton trousers and a shirt, both of which Zofia insisted on pressing. Kasia grabbed a piece of toast, blew a kiss to Zofia and Stefan, and hurried off.

"I hope she knows what she's doing," fretted Zofia to Stefan later as he too left for work. "She may find she doesn't like it, she used to teach older children, sevens and eights."

"Mm?" said Stefan, who had been wondering when he and Kasia would be able to have sex again. He wanted to help Kasia but he was beginning to wish he hadn't got so involved. It was taking up a lot of his time and he was beginning to get impatient to get on with their lives.

"Oh, yes," he finally said, "but the carer's job was beginning to depress her. And then there's Ultimate Care. Of course, she doesn't believe in it, and she saw some of her clients, who she'd got fond of, dying."

Zofia nodded. "Yes, it is a terrible thing. We have to make sure Jozéf gets better, or gets home."

Stefan remained silent. It was going to be a battle.

Chapter 46

The Commons chamber was crammed to bursting point, and buzzing with expectation. Bill was feeling elated; he was sure he would win the leadership bid. The debate started and it was a noisy and unruly affair. The House was dividing into pro and anti-Ultimate Care factions. The anti-brigade couldn't wait to get rid of Jack, and were delighted at the unexpected turn of events. Bill and Alistair were both purporting to support them. However, a few minutes into the debate a messenger came into the chamber and put a note in the Speaker's hand. She held up her arm for silence.

"Ladies and Gentlemen, I have some important news. A few minutes ago the Prime Minister read a short speech outside number 10, resigning as Prime Minister and leader of his party." There was uproar, and she held up her hand for silence, to no avail.

Online news feeds had broken the news simultaneously. Sky and BBC news had hastily dispatched film crews to broadcast Jack's announcement, from outside number 10. He looked exhausted, and dishevelled, despite some last-minute tidying up by Harry. He stood unsteadily at the lectern and read from a prepared text without making eye contact with the crowd.

"I regret to tell you that due to certain accusations about my private life I have been pressured into resigning from my position as leader of the Party, and Prime Minister of this country. Whilst I strenuously deny the charges, the scandal they have provoked would appear to be incompatible with my office. I anticipate that a senior member of my Cabinet will soon be elected in my place and prove to be a worthy successor."

There were shouts of "Who? Who gets your blessing, Jack? Who do you want to succeed you?" and "Are the accusations true?" but Jack ignored the questions; he felt unable to string any more words together. He turned and disappeared through the front door.

The MPS were all checking the announcement on their mobiles. The Speaker shouted for order.

"There is therefore little need to continue with this debate as the matter has been taken out of our hands. The Right Hon. Bill Travers, Chancellor of the Exchequer, First Secretary of State, will act as Prime Minister until such time as a new leader of the party has been elected."

Bill, looking smug, waved a hand vaguely round the chamber.

Jane Dawes, Secretary of State for Transport, stood up and waved her order paper.

"Perhaps we could use the time to discuss Ultimate Care? There was never a law democratically passed about it and at least half of MPs don't agree with it. My weekend surgeries are full of distraught constituents."

Alistair stood up. "If I'm elected the next Leader and PM, I'll review it."

"Order, ORDER!' bellowed the Speaker. "The House is adjourned."

They drifted out, most pleased to be finished with official business for the rest of the day, but although emotions had been running high there was now an atmosphere of anti-climax. Bill caught up with Alistair.

"What was that all about? You want to stop UC when it's beginning to really save money?"

"Well of course I do – I thought you did too?"

Bill shrugged. "I'm not 100% behind it but I think it's a juggernaut we can't stop – just look at the savings on elderly care we're making now. How do you intend to fund it if we stop UC? Sorry, but I think you're being naive. We've come too far down the road to reverse now."

Alistair was bewildered. "But I thought that we were singing from the same hymn-sheet here, Bill? It was one of the main reasons we were so determined to get rid of Jack, wasn't it?"

Bill's face seemed to close up. "Sorry, old chap, but it's dog eat dog in this business, as you know only too well. From now on we're enemies, I'm afraid, until the leadership election is over."

With that, Bill turned on his heel and strode away. He still believed that after the first couple of rounds of voting for a new leader, the race would be between him and Alistair - they were easily the two most popular members of the Cabinet. And Bill was quite prepared to stage an all-out war. A dirty one, if necessary.

Bill's phone rang the minute he reached his office. It was Steven.

"I've just had a call from my pal Mike at The Post. You'll never guess what."

"It seems to be that kind of day," mused Bill. "Surprises all round. Tell me."

"Our mole, Darren, the young guy who took the photos…."

"Yes, I do remember," Bill cut in, not without sarcasm.

"Well, now that Jack's resignation is all over the news, Darren has just connected 'Sam' to Jack."

"I suppose he wants more money, now that he realises how important those photos were?"

"Not quite. He says he's got some video footage of the party. Apparently the quality of the frames isn't very good because of the poor lighting but he reckons it's good enough to tell it's Jack. Jack reckoned that the police can't prove it's him because, as we know, it's possible to fiddle around with digital photos and put a head onto another body. But if they can identify him from a video they have the definitive proof they need."

"Wow," said Bill. "This is a development none of us anticipated. Very good news. We've definitely got him nailed now."

"The Editor's got Darren coming into The Post's offices later today to see for himself although he'll have to hand it over to the police, of course."

"But why didn't he offer the video before?" asked Bill. "Seems a bit odd."

"A good question," said Steven. "I think maybe we underestimated his IQ level. He obviously decided to keep something back in case it came in useful for extracting more money at a later date."

"Right. Still, the story in today's Post has done the trick and precipitated Jack's resignation already so from our point of view we've achieved what we set out to do."

Steven laughed. "Yeah, you're right there. So now we can look forward to you and Alistair battling it out in a leadership contest I guess?"

"I'm sure there'll be other contenders for the leadership," said Bill smoothly. "However, I'd be surprised if doesn't come down to just Al and I. I only just missed it last time."

"I should watch out, if I were you," was Steven's response. "A lot of people are saying that the next leader should be a woman. We haven't had one for a while, and the feminist lobby is quite powerful."

"Hmm, well, we'll see. Can you get your friend Mike to call me direct after the Editor's seen the video?"

"Why?" Steven was being difficult once again.

"Well, I'd just like his initial reaction to it. Of course, what I'd really like is to see it for myself."

"This video, at the moment, is for the Editor and then, of course, the police. I don't really see why you should be involved. You're not PM yet, you know."

Bill was silent for a moment while he digested what Steven had said. He didn't like being told what's what by someone he considered junior to him. He had thought that Steven could bring some influence to bear because of his friendship with Mike but he decided not to make an issue of it.

"OK, well can you let me know if there are any new developments?"

"Sure," said Steven. "Bye."

Bill decided not to tell Alistair just yet. He was going to have to put some distance between them while the leadership contest was going on. He sat in his office pondering how much support he had in the party and knew that Alistair was also pretty popular and it might be a close-run thing. He hadn't admitted to anyone just how much he wanted the top job – he figured it wasn't tactically sound to appear too ambitious but secretly he was desperate to be in charge.

Chapter 47

Kasia was enjoying her new job at the nursery and adjusting to looking after humans at the other end of the age scale. To begin with it was exhausting, as any new job is, but working with other adult colleagues was a tonic. So many of her old clients had suffered from some level of dementia that normal conversation had often been difficult. As tiring as small children can be, it was coping with her mother that caused her the most stress. Every evening Zofia prattled away at full speed, recounting every minute of her day and reporting the minutest signs of improvement in Jozéf. Zofia berated Kasia for not visiting her father every day, but she stood firm with her, saying that she was simply too tired to go every evening.

The Saturday of Jack Hawthorn's constituency surgery finally arrived.

"It would be much easier if just Stefan and I went, Mama," said Kasia. "You won't understand what's going on and it would be simpler if I didn't have to keep translating."

"No, no, I am *coming*," she insisted.

Stefan gently touched her arm. "Zofia," he said "You mustn't pin your hopes on this meeting. This is the man who introduced Ultimate Care - and I have discovered that he and the Health Secretary did it without a vote in Parliament. He's a ruthless man. But as our MP he is obliged to listen to our problem and see if he can help."

"Not just ruthless," sniffed Zofia with disdain, "But no morals, either. Really, I don't want to deal with this man but I am interested to meet him just the same."

They arrived and gave their names to Jack's agent. The waiting area was already crowded but they soon worked out that, like them, whole families had come together and they were fourth in the queue. Stefan went to a café down the road and came back with coffees and three large slices of cake. They hadn't had time for much breakfast and he thought it would keep Zofia sweet. He was getting adept and handling her so as to keep the peace between her and Kasia. Finally, a door opened and discharged a weeping couple. The agent called "Miss Jablonski, please."

"This is us," said Stefan, helping Zofia up, and they went in and sat down on three very hard chairs. Jack, they noted, was sitting in a comfortable padded swivel chair. He ignored them - he was reading something and tapping the end of his pen on the table, looking grey and haggard. Stefan was quite shocked at the change in his appearance from the suave man pictured on his website.

Jack finally looked up at them and said "So, how can I help you?" They were appalled that he didn't bother to stand up, let alone shake hands and Kasia took an instant dislike to him. She glanced at Stefan who indicated that she should start things off.

"My name is Kasia Jablonski. I am Polish and I've lived and worked here in London for two years. This is a friend, Stefan, who's been helping us with our problem, and my mother, Zofia. She and my father came to visit London about three weeks ago for a weekend and my father had a stroke and has been in hospital since. He is unconscious and the doctors think he may stay as he is for a long time. Poland still has a, how do you say it?......"

"Reciprocal," said Stefan.

"Yes, that's it, a reciprocal health arrangement with the UK but it doesn't include getting patients like my dad back home. Unfortunately, he doesn't have travel insurance. After a month he won't qualify for free care here and we can't afford either a care home, or an air ambulance to take him back to Poland."

"Oh dear," said Jack, "Not a good situation to be in." It was hard to tell whether he meant this as a statement of fact, or a criticism.

"Well, yes, it is."

"The point really is," cut in Stefan, "because he needs 24/7 care, if he stays here it seems that he might be processed for Ultimate Care."

At this point Zofia interrupted, demanding to know what was being said. Kasia took a deep breath to calm herself down. This was exactly what she had feared if Zofia came. She rapidly translated and asked her mother to keep quiet.

Kasia continued: "What we really need to get clear is whether a foreigner can be processed for Ultimate Care, because it is really a rule for English citizens. It seems so unfair."

Jack appeared to be doing some rapid thinking. He didn't really know much about the small print relating to UC, but he wasn't about to admit it.

"Yes, on the face of it, it does seem unfair."

On the face of it? thought Kasia. It was totally unfair, whichever way you look at it.

Jack had a thought and his face brightened up. "Of course, the answer is to speak to the Polish Embassy. They will arrange for him to be taken home. That's what they're here for, to help their citizens who have problems." He smiled with his mouth but not his eyes, as if the matter was closed.

"It's not as simple as that," said Stefan firmly. I've spoken to them, and they say that since the UK left the EU they have not had a case like this, but that they wouldn't pay for his transport home and that Kasia's parents should have taken out travel insurance for a situation like this. Kasia's brother booked the flights but didn't think insurance was needed."

286

Jack looked bored. "Well, I really don't see how I could help." He appeared to ponder the problem. "If he's selected for Ultimate Care you can appeal in the courts."

Stefan fought to control his rising anger. "I expect you know, sir, as well as I, even though I am just a Polish immigrant, that *nobody* has so far won an appeal about Ultimate Care. And" - here he leaned forward in his seat - as I've already said, this family have no money for legal affairs."

Jack sighed impatiently. "OK, leave this with me and I'll speak to the Health Secretary about your case and get him to clarify the position concerning foreigners. Give all your details to my agent and I'll be in touch."

"Thank you," said Kasia. "But it is quite urgent....my dad's had three weeks of his month of free care already."

"Well, I'll do my best."

They all got up. "Thank you," said Kasia and held out her hand. Jack ignored it. When he was sure they'd left, he went to find his agent.

"Is that it? I thought there was someone else waiting."

"They had to go. Family dramas. What do you think you can do to help the Polish family?"

"Bloody foreigners," said Jack. "I'll have to be seen to do something, but really, if he's processed, he's processed. They should have taken out insurance. They all think they're a special case, these people."

Kasia was blinking away tears as they walked back to the tube station.

"I can hardly believe how rude he was. You could tell that he couldn't care less about Dad. I felt like we were just being a nuisance to him."

"He did say he'd speak to the Health Secretary," said Stefan. "That must be a good thing?"

"We're no nearer getting him home, fretted Kasia. "In a week's time they could start processing him for UC. If he doesn't regain consciousness, that's what will happen.

"I think we should go to the Polish Embassy again," said Zofia. "I'll go too, and make a scene. You are very a nice boy, Stefan, but I can imagine you were very polite and did not make enough fuss. The Embassy is there to help Polish citizens who have a problem. We have a big problem. Surely they can't sit back and watch this happen ? It's not right at all."

"Yes," said Stefan, "but I've had another idea - I also think that we need to go public about this. We could go on social media; we could even try to get a newspaper involved. They love cases like this, where the ordinary man is up against the State. And the fact that our MP is Jack Hawthorn is another reason why they would be interested – he's in enough shit as it is."

"That's a very good idea," said Kasia. "But I do think we need to go back to the Embassy too, like Mama said. I will have to ask Julie if I can have some time off next week."

"Right. So we have a plan of action. First, we go back to the Embassy and put more pressure on them. Then we put out something on social media, and contact one or more of the papers. I've got a mate who really knows about how to work social media, and how to get noticed. I'll call him and get him involved – he owes me a favour, as it happens."

"Oh?" said Kasia, raising her eyebrows. "And what would that be?"

Stefan just laughed and said "Nothing to concern you!"

"And," said Kasia "I've thought of an angle we could use, along the lines of how so many Poles worked with the British in World War II – you know, is this how we repay our Polish friends, that sort of thing."

"That's brilliant, Kasia. We definitely have to be a lot more pro-active."

Zofia smiled for the first time in a while.

"I have to hand it to your generation; you really know your way around all this modern technology."

Chapter 48

The leadership contest was continuing apace. To Bill's surprise, seven contenders had announced their intention to stand, including three women. Jane Dawes, the Transport Secretary, was one, and she was fiercely opposed to UC. Bill was beginning to doubt his own confidence that it would be a shoe-in. The pro-female lobby was much stronger than he'd estimated, and Jack's misdeeds hadn't exactly strengthened the case for another male leader. Still, in the end it would come down to experience, he reckoned. Things had cooled somewhat between him and Alistair, for obvious reasons, but he hoped that shortly they'd be back working together as PM and Chancellor, privately hoping, of course, that it was he who'd be Prime Minister.

The fact that several of Jack's constituents had formed a group and made a public proposal for a Recall Ballot came as no surprise to Bill or anyone else. It was interesting, he thought, that there were such strong feelings about it – notwithstanding that Jack had broken the law concerning sex with minors, he wondered whether, if Jack had been involved in a heterosexual orgy, the public reaction would have been quite the same. He was still on bail and there was no date set for the trial. The police had triumphantly seized the video taken by Darren, but he had not reaped the rewards he'd hoped for. Aside from publishing a new, damning article mentioning the video The Post hadn't been able to capitalise on it very much - it wasn't the kind of thing you could put in the online edition and it was now the property of the police. Still, it just about wrapped up the Prosecution's case. Bill had no doubt that Jack was done for.

"Guess what's the latest with Jack," Bill said to Alistair during one of their now rare conversations in one of the Commons' cafes.

"I've already heard," said Alistair. "Memoirs, my foot! What's he ever done to crow about?"

"Maybe he'll treat us to a blow-by-suck account of his parties," said Bill drily.

"Hmm, more likely he'll try to make out he was the best PM of recent times. The conceit of the man is astounding. Still, it'll give him something to do when he's ousted from his seat."

"Do you think that's a certainty?"

Alistair laughed. "No doubt at all, I'd say. Any crime which a member of parliament is almost certain to be found guilty of is probably reason enough, but this? Now they've got video evidence he's a dead duck. But, much as I dislike him, I don't envy him going to prison. He'll be hounded morning, noon and night, and possibly physically attacked."

"Knowing Jack," said Alistair, "He'll smarm all over the prison officers and his life will be a bed of roses. I bet you, as the ex-PM, he'll get all sorts of privileges that ordinary prisoners don't get."

Bill shrugged. "I don't see why he should be treated as anyone special. Aren't we supposed to be all equal under the law?"

Alistair said "sure, but we both know what a charismatic person Jack can be when he wants to."

"Well, back to the fray," said Bill. "I must say, I'm pretty pissed off at the number of women who've thrown their hats into the ring. I thought Jane Dawes would be the only one."

"Sh, you don't want anyone overhearing you say that! Very un-PC. I certainly think Jane is too hot-headed to be leader, but the other two in the running are more measured. Well, I must go." He popped a final mouthful of ham sandwich into his mouth, drained his glass of beer and strode off.

~

Meanwhile, Jack was impatient to unload the problem of Józéf onto someone else. He didn't care at all what happened to Józéf and the Jablonski family but he went to see David Michel, the new Health Secretary, who was a great deal more efficient and pro-active than Charlie had ever been, but lacked his Irish charm. Jack missed Charlie. They'd worked together for several years and his relaxed personality had always been soothing. He was in a care home and Jack had heard rumours that due to Charlie's gambling habits there wasn't much money in the family. It was possible that Charlie might become a victim of his own protocols. Jack was nervously greeted by David when he appeared in his office.

"So, what can I do for you?" David asked, pushing an untidy pile of folders to the side of his desk.

"Oh, it's just a pesky problem to do with the father of one of my constituents." He described the family's dilemma. "I guess the crux of the matter is whether, as a foreigner, he can be subjected to the same rules and regulations for UC as Brits are, given that the family are poor as church mice and cannot afford to get him home, or pay for care."

David sat back in his chair. He had large, bushy eyebrows, which appeared to twitch uncontrollably when he was thinking hard.

"Hmm, tricky problem, and I'm not sure I know the answer. You and Charlie dreamed up this thing, I would've thought you'd dotted all the 'i's' and crossed all the 't's'."

"I never did concern myself much with the finer details. I think we all assumed that if a foreigner had been assessed for UC and was too ill to be transported home by the normal means, the insurer would foot the bill. Or their Embassy."

"So there isn't any travel insurance?" David was appalled. "How can people be so short-sighted."

"No, apparently not, and they have no money to go to Appeal, either.

David sighed. "Isn't the Polish Embassy willing to help?"

"Apparently not, although I don't think there's been a definite decision; just a lot of discouraging noises. The point is, David, can foreign nationals be subjected to the same rules and regulations as our own people? It's a technicality really, isn't it?"

"Yes, and one which should have been sorted out a long time ago. I can't believe this is the first case like this."

"It does seem unlikely. Perhaps you could check if there are any precedents?"

"Er, yes, I'll try." David had more than enough to do coping with a threatened nurses' strike.

"Great. I can pass this over to you and leave it in your capable hands then?"

He handed David a sheet of paper with the details.

"Oh." David sounded put out. "As I said, I'll see what I can find out, but….."

"Just one small snag," said Jack, turning on his heel and pausing. "He only has a week before his month of free care expires, so it's kind of urgent. But maybe he'll die before then."

David closed his eyes and took three deep breaths. Then he summoned his researcher.

"I've got a little job for you to do."

The researcher had a great deal of trouble turning up any useful information. She reported back to David that it appeared that foreigners were not treated any differently. Three foreign nationals had been in the same position as Jozéf and had been taken home by air ambulance. Either their insurers had paid, or their embassies. David called Jack to tell him.

"I think this family's best option is to harass the Polish Embassy. There don't seem to be any exceptions to the rule, which seems a bit harsh, if you ask me."

"Well, don't blame me," retorted Jack.

"So who should I blame?" asked David, his tone icy. "You dreamed up this scheme, you and Charlie Warwick. Seems you didn't really think it through."

"When you're PM," said Jack, "you don't concern yourself with the finer details, you create the big picture and let others sort out the trivia. To be frank, I find sorting out my constituents' little problems very tedious."

"Pity you became an MP then. Because what we're supposed to do is *represent the interests* of the constituents, not treat them like a nuisance."

A couple of weeks previously, David would not have dreamed of talking to Jack like this but he had been disgusted by his behaviour and knowing his days were numbered he really didn't care any longer.

"I'll bid you goodbye, then. Thanks for the info." Jack hung up. David wondered if he could intervene in this one case and instruct the hospital to keep Jozéf alive until they'd found a solution. At that moment, his researcher, Imogen, came into his office and said "Look at this, David." She passed over her phone, which was on the Sky News app page.

"Look, here - the family of the Polish man have gone public to The Post about their plight. And kicked up a storm on Twitter, a hell of a row is brewing up. It seems up until now, nobody realised that foreign visitors were also subject to UC if they couldn't get home."

"Yes, that sounds interesting. I've got to go down to my constituency for the night but I'll deal with it tomorrow."

Chapter 49

"Wow!" said Stefan that evening as they first clicked through Twitter and then checked comments on The Post's website. "I never thought we'd get this much interest."

Jozéf's plight had gone viral. Zofia frowned. "So what is happening? I don't understand what all this is." She waved a hand in the direction of the laptop.

Kasia tried to explain about social media.

"It's really good news, Mama. So many people agree with us, that the UC laws are wrong, and definitely shouldn't apply to foreigners. If lots of people make a big noise about it, the rules will have to be changed."

"But they won't change in time for Papa, will they. He only has a few days left."

"A lot of people are saying that the Polish Embassy should be shamed into paying to fly home people like Papa."

"That's great, but what if people are too ill to move?"

"We don't know yet, this has all taken off over the last day or two. One step at a time." said Stefan.

He produced a bottle of wine from the fridge. "I think we have something to celebrate! Things are really moving now. Only problem is, we don't have any supper to go with it."

"Yes, we do," said Zofia proudly. "I left the hospital early today and stopped to buy a few things. It was difficult, finding things in an English supermarket, but I found a lovely Polish assistant in there and she helped me. I've made a pie."

Kasia was surprised, not because her mother couldn't cook, but because it meant she'd been food shopping alone. She was beginning to realise that her mother had hidden depths. Zofia had already surprised her by getting to grips with travelling around London, and now she'd been food shopping. Of course, this could just mean that she didn't appreciate her and Stefan's culinary skills, but still. She wondered whether her father had overshadowed Zofia all their married life. She certainly seemed to be more independent since he'd been ill.

Stefan's phone rang. "Yes...yes...oh really? That's fantastic. OK, OK, yes, thanks."

"That was one of my work-mates, he's been fantastic about publicising Józef's situation. Looks like other newspapers are picking up the story, too. It's even overtaken Jack Hawthorn's downfall."

"That's marvellous. I feel we're getting somewhere at last. "But we still haven't heard anything from Jack Hawthorn's office."

"Yes...well, I wouldn't be surprised if we don't. He didn't seem as if he was going to bother about it, did he? He seemed a prize prick, if you ask me."

Kasia nudged him hard and indicated Zofia with an inclination of her head.

"Sorry," he muttered. Zofia affected not to notice, and she set the pie on the table and they sat down to eat. Kasia's phone rang and she frowned at the screen. "It's not someone on my contact list, I'll leave it." It went to voicemail, and when Kasia had finished eating she listened to it. Her face fell. "I'll put it on speaker so you can all hear," she said. They all listened and Zofia was impatient for a translation.

"It's...it's the Health Secretary's office. Apparently Jack Hawthorn asked Mr Michel to go through the small print to try and see exactly what the UC rules say about foreigners. That was his researcher - of course he delegated the research to her, and she says she can find nothing about exemption from the rules for people like Jozéf. She's liaised with the hospital authorities at the Metropolitan Hospital and they say he's had 23 of his 28 days free care and will be processed for UC in a few days' time unless we can take him back to Poland or put him in a care home."

Zofia put her hand over her mouth and let out a low moan.

"No….no, they can't, have they no mercy? It's not fair, it's just not fair…."

Kasia put her arm around her.

"Don't worry, Mama, we're getting such a lot of support now that it's gone public, a petition's been started. I don't see how such a public show of support can be ignored."

"Well, I hope you're right," sniffed Zofia. "Five days isn't long."

Stefan was busy updating his social media posts which prompted a flood of support. Suddenly he stopped short and gave a low whistle.

"Just look at this!"

He handed the phone to Kasia, who stared at the screen, unable to believe her eyes.

"I don't believe it, this is marvellous!"

"What, what?" Zofia impatiently grabbed Kasia's arm. "What's happened?"

"Someone's started a crowd-funding page with £1,000. A Pole, who's lived in the UK for years and has

a very successful business. He wants us to use the money to put Jozéf in a Care Home until we get enough to take him home, or, to take the case to the Appeal Court. Other people are adding to it, there's already nearly £3,000 in it. It's unbelievable - if we get enough we can just take him home!" He swept Kasia up into his arms and waltzed her round the kitchen. "At last, we're really getting somewhere!"

They all slept better than they had for days and in the morning the crowd-funding total was up to £7,000.

"It's just the breathing space we needed," said Stefan to Kasia as they bolted down some breakfast. "We can transfer him to a care home short-term while we arrange transport back to Warsaw and find a care home in Poland. Right, I must go. Keep in touch during the day, won't you?"

"Of course, if I get a minute between reading picture books and taking toddlers to the toilet. Sometimes I wonder if it's so different from working as a carer," she laughed.

"I guess the difference is that you can put a toddler on the naughty step," said Stefan.

"Bye, Zofia." Before he opened the front door he put his arms around Kasia and gave her a long, slow kiss.

Whenever Kasia got a chance she checked the crowd-funding page on her phone. It was still growing and she discovered that colleagues at the nursery had read about her father's plight and some had donated small amounts to the fund.

"But why didn't you tell us what was going on?" Julie demanded. "I had no idea until yesterday what a fix you were in."

Kasia blushed. "Well, I don't know you all very well yet, and it seemed to be my problem to sort out. Until the last couple of days when things went public we'd no idea that we'd get such support."

"I can't believe they're inflicting these rules on foreigners too," said Julie."

"They do emphasise to travellers that they should be sure to take out travel insurance, but my brother's such a cheapskate he didn't bother – he figured that not much could go wrong in a weekend." She shook her head.

"Look," said Julie, "This must all be so stressful for you, I think you should take a couple of days off, you must have a lot to sort out."

Kasia could hardly believe her ears.

"Oh Julie, that would be marvellous, but I've only just started here - I can't possibly take time off so soon." Even whilst saying it, she was thinking how fantastic it would be to have some time to research care homes for Jozéf while they decided what to do next.

Julie said "Well, we're very light on numbers at present as we've only just opened, and for the next few days we could manage without you, if it would help."

"It would be a huge help."

"Off you go, then," said Julie. "Keep us posted."

Kasia thanked Julie profusely. "I'll update you later today," She said over her shoulder as she let herself out.

She went straight to the hospital where Zofia was surprised to see her.

"What are you doing here? Have you taken time off work?"

"Not exactly - Julie, you know the lady who runs the nursery, asked me if I'd like some time off to get Papa sorted out. I couldn't believe it, but she almost insisted. The nursery isn't full at present so they can manage without me for a couple of days. What I'm going to do is find a care home where we can put Papa temporarily until we can get him home. The crowd-funding total is growing all the time and as soon as we have enough money for an air ambulance, we can get him back to Poland."

Zofia nodded. "I have to say, that I am being constantly surprised at how the kind the British people can be. I did not think they were like this."

Kasia smiled. "I have come across many who aren't, Mama, but when they take a cause to their hearts they can be incredibly generous. Now, I'm going to find someone to ask how I go about finding a home."

She was lucky to find the ICU manager at the nurses' station.

"Excuse me – I'm Jozéf Jablonski's daughter. I don't think I've seen you here before."

"No, I've just got back from leave. What can I do for you?"

"I don't know if you know this, but my father's situation has gone public on social media sites and in the papers, a crowd-funding page has been set up and already has a lot of money donated, because it doesn't look as if the UC rules are going to be relaxed in his case."

She stared at Kasia. "Good heavens, I didn't realise we had him here, on this ward. I've heard about him, of course."

"Well, the thing is, I need to find a care home for him, but I don't know where to start."

"Nor me, I'm afraid! But I'll phone down to the social workers office and get one of them to see you."

"It's getting quite urgent, can she see me this morning?"

"I'll call her right now. I'll ask her to come up to your dad's room, shall I?"

"I'd prefer to see her in her office," said Kasia. "My mother's with him, and she can get a bit hysterical."

Kasia waited as the call was made.

"You're in luck, she's just had an appointment cancelled. She could see you in twenty minutes. Her office is on the ground floor, in Block B, room 203."

Kasia thanked her and headed off through the maze of corridors. She finally found the right office and was greeted by a brisk, skeletally thin woman who looked like she was extremely stressed.

"Hello, I'm Cathy. And your name is?"

"I'm Kasia Jablonski. My father's name is Jozéf."

"So, I gather from the ITU Sister that you want to find a care home for your father?"

"Yes, although it will only be temporary. We're hoping to get him home to Poland soon."

"Is your father the man who's been in the papers, the one they want to process for UC?"

"That's right. We only have a few days of free care left but because the crowd-fund is growing all the time we hope it won't be long before we can afford an air ambulance to get him home."

"Whilst getting a placement in a home is easier than it used to be, vacancies in high dependency care homes can still be tricky to find," said Cathy.

Kasia was surprised. She'd imagined their only problem would be finding the money for care, not whether a home would accept Jozéf.

"How long will it take?"

"Well, I imagine you'd want to look at a couple of places before making a decision, even if it is only going to be short-term."

Together they filled in the form and Kasia signed it and gave Cathy her contact details. Cathy printed out a list and handed the paper to Kasia.

"Here's a list of homes which had a place when I enquired a few days ago. You could start with those, and I'll try and contact you later with a couple more. Would you be able to look around soon? Vacancies often don't stay free for long, even nowadays."

"Yes, I've been given a few days off work to try and get something sorted out. Thank you for your help."

"It's a pleasure. I can't emphasise enough the need to act quickly on this; the level of care your father requires is not available in many homes."

Kasia hurried back up to the ICU to tell Zofia the good news.

Chapter 50

By the time David got back from his constituency the next day, Józéf's plight had gone viral and the government was getting a great deal of bad press. Emotions were running high and suddenly it seemed that the nation's main preoccupation was with an unconscious 61-year old Polish man who was soon going to have no choice over his fate.

"Have you *seen* the papers this morning?" Imogen waved copies of four dailies at him and he glanced at their front pages.

"Why didn't you call me?" David demanded.

She raised her eyes to heaven. "Believe me, I tried. You had your mobile switched off. But I really don't see how you can have missed the news, it's everywhere."

David was silent for a minute. "It seems that I did. But I *have* been thinking about it. I was going to say that we should intervene at the eleventh hour to restore confidence in the government but, as the public are raising the means to get this chap home, we may as well save ourselves the trouble."

"It won't save your face, though, will it?" Imogen was incredulous. "Are you actually *serious*?"

"Look, this was pushed onto me by Jack, who couldn't be bothered. It was always unlikely someone like Jack would help in this sort of case; he pushed it onto *me*, saying that the Health Secretary should deal with it. Well, now I don't really need to, do I? Things weren't helped by the fact that there don't seem to be any hard and fast rules about it. I didn't have a clue what I was going to do, and now I don't need to do anything."

"Until the next case," murmured Imogen as she left.

David put a call through to Jack's office but was told he wasn't in the House so he put the matter out of his mind and turned his attention to other matters. Nurses had again voted for strike action. After the Covid-19 pandemic they'd become much more militant about pay and conditions and hundreds had resigned. They attributed the loss of so many medical personnel to the lack of adequate personal protection equipment, a recurring problem during the outbreak. He also had a problem with the BMA, who had a growing number of doctors refusing to carry out UC. Threatening them with dismissal wasn't an option as the country already had depleted numbers of doctors. There were, in fact, many doctors who were happy to end a life which they considered lacked any quality, but there were some vociferous exceptions. The Department of Health had made a big issue of re-interpreting the Hippocratic Oath: the motto 'Do no harm' was not contravened, it said, by ending the lives of people who complied with the protocols - in fact, it was doing them a kindness. Naturally, there were many who disagreed with this and David's next big task was to win them round. He was due to deliver a speech at the upcoming BMA conference and getting it right was consuming a great deal of his time. He was not running for Party Leader; he shuddered at the increased responsibility and time it would involve. After the Coronavirus pandemic the post of PM had become a poisoned chalice – that is until Jack came along, whose ambition outpaced any qualms he may have had. David's phone rang.

"Sorted out that Polish man, have you?" Jack asked.

David took a deep breath. "My researcher and I have looked long and hard at the protocols and regulations and can find absolutely nothing relating to foreign nationals. Seems that whoever drew up the small print overlooked that. However, since the media have pounced on it and run with it, to the extent that they've created a crowd-funding page to finance his transport home, I don't really think the government needs to do anything at all, do you?"

Jack grunted. "Well, I couldn't care less, old boy, but yes, I'd say we've been let off the hook here, don't you?"

David agreed. He couldn't wait for Jack to be Recalled and out of the House.

Chapter 51

Trying to find a care home for Jozéf was pushing Kasia's patience to the limits, not helped by Zofia's anxiety. Cathy had given her a list of homes which, in theory at least, took patients requiring the level of care which Jozéf needed. None of them had an immediate place. Kasia took to the internet to search for more and spent a frustrating afternoon checking another five homes to see if they had a place, and if they were equipped to provide the sort of care Jozéf needed. Two of them were full, one of them had an immediate place, and two others were expecting to shortly. Kasia surmised that this meant they had residents at death's door. She found this difficult to explain to Zofia without being graphic, and Zofia had a fit of hysterics, screaming:

"You mean, they wait for someone to die, then put a new person in the warm bed? Oh Kasia, this is terrible."

Kasia sighed. They had already looked at two of the homes, both of which Zofia had found lacking, and Kasia hadn't been fully satisfied with, either.

"It is just how things are, Mama. It is an awful thing to say, but before Ultimate Care, we might have waited weeks or months to find him a place. You have no idea."

"But why? They are so expensive, who can afford them?

"In the past patients who were paid for by their local authority were charged a smaller fee than those who were paying their own way. So, those self-pay patients were subsidising the publicly paid-for, which was very unfair. Now, because the number of people needing publicly funded 24-hour care is almost nil, they can charge the full price, which is good for all the homes still in business."

Zofia sniffed. "It all seems totally immoral to me."

"But we need to get a move on. This home is the most expensive but it has an immediate vacancy and it's on the edge of London - we can get there on the Tube."

This would be the third one they'd viewed, and she was desperate to make a decision.

"Oh, not a long Tube ride......" wailed Zofia.

Kasia felt drained by her mother's constant complaining.

"If you like, I'll go on my own," said Kasia, praying her mother would agree.

"I can't let you go on your own, and make a decision without me. What next!"

Next, thought Kasia as she silently fumed, will be a murder. Right here.

The home was called 'Bishop Gabriel's Lodge' and stood at the end of a tree-lined avenue, a good ten minutes' walk from the Underground. It was an imposing house which must once have made a splendid home for an affluent family, with a well-tended garden. They were ushered into a small sitting room off the hall. Zofia stopped and looked around, impressed. It was expensively furnished and a vase of fragrant roses stood on one of the immaculate glass table-tops.

"Well, I suppose it would do. It looks all right from here."

Kasia bit back what she wanted to say and merely said: "Mama, it's a palace compared to the tiny flat you live in at home. Papa is unconscious, he won't be able to appreciate where he is, will he? And the quality of the care is the most important thing, not the décor."

"I suppose so. And he wouldn't be here for long, would he?"

"Well, we hope not, but I don't know how long it will take to arrange his transport home." Something else I'll have to sort out, she thought, cursing Piotr for fleeing back to Poland. "The main thing now is to get him out of the hospital and into a home before his month of free care is up."

Zofia shrugged and sighed deeply and was about to speak again when the door opened and an attractive young woman entered the room. She had immaculately styled hair, and was wearing a sharp suit and vertiginous heels. She trailed an aura of Chanel No 5 and looked nothing like the matron of a care home.

"Good morning Mrs Jablonski, Miss Jablonski. I'm the manager." She extended a limp hand to Zofia, then Kasia.

"Hello, you're Miss Redhill who I spoke to on the phone?" asked Kasia.

"Indeed. Please call me Helen."

Kasia said "I should explain that my mother speaks very little English and I'll have to translate. She can be quite ...." She searched for the right word – "Quite emotional, I think is the word."

Helen's eyes met Kasia's and she moved her head slightly, acknowledging the problem.

'Please sit down. Would you like some coffee?"

Kasia was rather taken aback – the other two homes they'd looked at had been very brisk and business-like. There were no offers of refreshments.

"Thank you, that would be lovely."

Helen pressed a bell switch above the highly ornate fireplace and in due course a tray of coffee and biscuits arrived.

"Now, then...." She took some papers out of a folder. "I have the application forms you emailed me. Yours is a very unusual case. But of course, we've all read about it in the media."

"Yes, we've been so lucky with all these wonderful people sending money so we can get Papa out of hospital and then, we hope, home to Poland."

Helen gave her a piercing look.

306

"Yes. Still, I need to run through the financial side of things. There is a registration fee of five hundred pounds. Our basic weekly fee is two thousand pounds. For someone requiring your father's level of care, this will incur a five-hundred pound weekly supplement."

Kasia's head was spinning at these eye-watering sums. Helen continued "The minimum charge is one month's fees, which must be paid in advance, and there will be no refund if he stays a shorter time. I'm assuming that the monies accrued from the crowd funding could meet these costs?"

Zofia nudged Kasia. 'What's she saying?" she whispered in Polish.

Kasia shushed her. "I'll tell you in a minute, it's just about the fees."

"Can we afford it?" Zofia whispered back.

Kasia nodded, although it a was close call. When she researched the home on the internet, it only quoted the basic fees. However, she was betting on the crowd-fund continuing to grow. There wasn't enough money yet to pay for the air transfer.

"OK." Kasia took a deep breath, trying to get her head around it all. "Perhaps we could have a look around?"

"Of course." Helen set down her cup and stood up. Kasia swiftly finished her own coffee and said to Zofia "We're going to look around now, Mama." They followed Helen, who showed them the lounge, dining room and one of the bedrooms.

"Of course, your father won't be able to make use of the public rooms, but it gives you an idea of the standard of accommodation."

Kasia was speechless at the opulence, and Zofia was too amazed to comment. It was like a luxury hotel, with deep pile carpets, expensive and tasteful drapery and a hushed atmosphere. In the lounge, several expensively dressed and beautifully coiffed ladies were playing bridge and there was a drinks trolley in the dining room. The bedroom they were shown was spacious and nicely furnished, with views of the garden.

"Very nice, all very nice," murmured Zofia. "I think this is the one, Kasia."

But Kasia was not to be swayed by the décor and furnishings.

"So, would my father be in a room like the one you just showed us? It seemed more like a hotel room."

Helen looked a little uncomfortable.

"No, he'd be in the 'Care Plus' wing, as he'd require special equipment and so on."

"I think we need to take a look at that, too," said Kasia firmly. "I worked as a carer until recently, so I know what might be required for a patient like my father."

They were led down a long hallway and passed a door marked 'DEMENTIA UNIT.' Helen kept up an inconsequential chatter as they went. Finally they were ushered through a white door marked "CARE PLUS" Here the deep pile carpet was replaced by synthetic carpet tiles and there was a smell of rose-infused disinfectant in the air. Helen opened the door of room number 5.

"A nice, bright room, quite large, as you can see, so there is space for things like hoists. It has its own bathroom of course and most of the fittings of the rooms in the Luxe Wing. But obviously the carpeting is more suited to ill patients, spillages and so on. I'm sure you understand."

Kasia's eyes swept around the room. Certainly, it didn't have the luxury feel of the other room they'd been shown, but it was perfect for Joseph's needs. Zofia whispered something in Kasia's ear. Helen raised her eyebrows at Kasia, who translated. "I think my mother's very impressed, although of course it's the most expensive home we've looked at. And this is the room you're offering?"

"Yes, we actually have two rooms like this vacant at present."

At these prices I bet you do, thought Kasia..

"Excuse me, while I speak to my mother."

She said in rapid Polish: "It's definitely the nicest one we've seen, Mama, but so expensive!"

308

"But we have enough in the crowd-funding thing to pay for a week or two here, and the airlift home?"

"Not quite….I think we will pretty soon. I just feel they're charging too much. But we'd be happy for him to be looked after here, wouldn't we?"

Zofia nodded. "Yes. Yes, we definitely say yes, Kasia."

Kasia was still a bit torn. It was ideal, but she felt she was being taken for a ride with the charges, perhaps because they were foreigners. Still, what option did they have? She turned back to Helen.

"We're both very happy with things here, so can we make definite plans."

"Of course." Helen beamed. "Come into my office and we'll do the paperwork."

Her office was obviously almost paperless. A large glass-topped desk stood by the window with lovely views, and on it was an Apple desktop. There was nothing else. A plethora of potted plants sat on the window sill and a brocade sofa lined one wall. Kasia wondered if Helen used it for afternoon naps, she certainly didn't look like a manager who got her hands dirty.

From a hidden drawer under the desktop, Helen produced some forms for them to sign. "And of course, I shall be asking you for the deposit, to secure the place. The deposit, due now, is the registration fee and fifty per cent of the first month's fees. The balance to be paid before admission."

"I'm afraid," said Kasia, "The deposit is a bit of a problem. We have an accountant dealing with the fund for us, he's giving his services free, and I shall have to get him to transfer the money into the Home's account, if you can give me the details."

"We do have a credit card facility," said Helen, "We really need the deposit paid before things go any further."

Zofia was making faces, trying to attract Kasia's attention. Kasia shook her head at here, and said firmly to Helen: "I simply don't have a credit limit that's high enough to cover it, I'm afraid. As I told you, I was working as a care worker for an agency until a couple of weeks ago. I've just changed jobs and should be able to get a higher credit limit soon, but at the

309

moment.....I'll ask the fund administrator to transfer the deposit later today."

Helen visibly bristled. She obviously wasn't used to anyone challenging her.

"Very well then, but if it's not, you may lose the place."

She handed Kasia a piece of paper with the bank details. "And when can we expect your father to arrive?"

"By the weekend, when his free care runs out. Friday or Saturday. I understand that I have to arrange a private ambulance to bring him here. I can let you know the exact details when I've made the transfer arrangements."

"Perfect." Helen smiled with her mouth, but not with her eyes. "I'll see you out, then."

On the way back to the Tube, Kasia said to Zofia, "It's a really nice place, isn't it, Mama? But what did you think of Helen?."

"A hard-nosed lady. You handled her very well. She didn't look anything like a Care Home Manager, did she. Anyway, at last we've found somewhere we both like, even if it's very expensive. After all, it will only be for a week or so."

Yes, and we have to pay a registration fee AND the first month's fee, just for that short time, Kasia thought. She would take a bet that the care workers got paid the minimum wage. *Someone* was making a lot of money.

Chapter 52

Kasia recounted their visit to the home to Stefan over supper.

"Honestly, Stefan, if you could have seen her, this Helen woman. She looked like a fashion magazine editor going to watch a cat-walk show. She obviously isn't involved with the practical side of things at all."

"But the Home was very nice," chipped in Zofia. "*Very* nice, wasn't it Kasia?"

"Yes – and very expensive."

"Well, tell me," said Stefan. Kasia told him the figures. He put down his knife and fork and stared at her.

"You have to be joking! Do you think it's all a con, that she knows about the Crowd Funding and has made up these figures? It is normal to have a registration fee?"

Kasia shrugged. "I checked with Cathy, the social worker at the hospital, and she said they were entitled to request one, but that normally it would be a lower sum. And usually a deposit is paid to keep a place on the waiting list, if they don't have an immediate vacancy."

"And the surcharge because he needs a high level of care?"

"It seems they can do what they want. But I think it's very misleading to advertise the weekly fee on their website without mentioning that it's the basic amount, and that it could cost a lot more, depending the condition of the patient."

"Not to mention that she knows he won't be in there for long, so you get no rebate from the monthly fee if he's only there a few days. It's outrageous," said Stefan.

"Well, we don't have much choice. They have an immediate vacancy and we're in a hurry. He's moving there on Friday."

Stefan frowned. "That only gives you a day and a half to organize the money. Did you speak to - what's his name - Thomas Whitby, who's administering the fund?"

"Yes, he's doing a bank transfer to the home for the deposit. The rest will be transferred on Friday. The next thing I have to do is book a private ambulance to get him there. Then we need to get care organized back home before we book the Air Ambulance transfer - when we've got enough money in the fund."

"Please tell me you're not putting Piotr in charge of that?"

"I don't have a choice. It's really difficult to organize it from here, and someone needs to look around possible nursing homes. But don't worry, I've had a word with Teresa and she's agreed to go with him so we can get a woman's opinion."

She finished her meal, put down her cutlery and leaned on her elbows, putting her head in her hands and massaging her temples.

"What's the matter?" asked Zofia anxiously.

"Nothing, Mama, it's just that my head is spinning trying to sort all this out."

"Get off to bed then, don't worry about all this....." She waved a hand in the direction of the dirty dishes and pans. "Stefan and I will clear up. You'll feel better in the morning."

The first thing Kasia did the next day was to call the private ambulance company. It wasn't too surprising that they'd heard about Jozéf, and they seemed very keen to take the booking. So much so, she wondered if they were planning to arrange for the Press to take photos, as a publicity stunt for their company.

"OK, so we pick him at 11am from The London Metropolitan Hospital on Friday, he's in ward 23B, and we take him to Bishop Gabriel's Lodge in North London. Can I have a credit card number to confirm the booking, please?"

Kasia hesitated. She was frustrated at having to refer everyone to the accountant of the Fund.

"We won't take any money off the card right now, it's just a surety for us."

"All right, in that case I'll give you my personal credit card number. But I'll send you details of who will actually pay the bill."

She gave him the number.

"OK, all set, madam. Will we see you personally on Friday?"

"Oh yes, my mother and I will be going with him."

Kasia called Thomas Whitby, the fund administrator, who confirmed he'd wired the reservation fee to Helen at Bishop Gabriel's and he reassured her that there was enough money in the fund to cover the rest of the fees.

"Is the money still coming in?" asked Kasia anxiously. "We need a whole lot more to finance the Air Ambulance."

"Don't worry, it's building nicely. A few more days should do it."

"OK." She felt reassured. "One other thing.....the ambulance company that I've booked for tomorrow – they knew all about Dad, and seemed very keen to do the transfer. I wonder if they're going to use the opportunity for publicity."

"Nothing wrong with that," said Thomas. "It would be great if they had a camera crew outside the hospital when you left, that sort of publicity is priceless."

"O.K...." said Kasia slowly. "I was hoping they wouldn't, but as you say, there's nothing wrong with publicity, it might prompt more donations."

"Exactly! Would you like me to call them and check it out?"

"Yes, thank you, that would be good of you."

"So, good luck, I hope the transfer goes smoothly."

313

"I can't thank you enough, Thomas. Bye."

When Kasia and Zofia arrived at the hospital later that day they told the staff that they would be transferring Józéf at 11am on Friday morning. They sat and held Józéf's hand for a while but there was no reaction. Zofia sighed and stroked his forehead.

"I never thought it would come to this," she said. "He's only just retired. We were so looking forward to it. Life hasn't been easy, you know. You have an education, something we didn't have a chance for. Manual labourers get old before their time in Poland."

"Yes, I know Mama. It's awful for you. I saw it all the time as a carer. But he *may* recover. I know it doesn't seem very likely but we will just have to hope and pray. Now, I have to leave you to go downstairs and speak to Cathy, the social worker, to update her with everything."

Kasia related her encounter with Helen Redhill to Cathy, whose normally humourless face cracked into a smile. "Yes, I've met her. Quite something, isn't she! Made me feel I was in the wrong job. nursing homes must be a lucrative business if she can afford shoes like that."

"Anyway, I just thought I'd let you know, we're transferring him on Friday morning. I've booked the ambulance and the Fund Administrator is dealing with the finance. Thank you so much for your help."

"You're welcome. And all just in the nick of time; I checked, and his free care runs out the day after tomorrow."

"Yes, the Crowd Funding is like a miracle," said Kasia. I don't know what we'd be doing if that hadn't happened."

"I hate to say it, but I'm afraid you'd be dealing with the bureaucracy of UC."

"Yes. That's something we couldn't bear to think about."

The next morning it seemed as though half of London's paparazzi were camped outside The London Metropolitan.

"What's going on?" asked Zofia.

Kasia smiled. "You'll see." She deliberately hadn't told her mother about the possibility of publicity, to avoid the inevitable drama.

"The ambulance isn't here," fretted Zofia.

"Don't worry Mama, it's only quarter to eleven. They won't want to be hanging around too long because parking is difficult."

When they reached the ward, the staff had prepared Józéf for the journey and were almost ready to wheel him downstairs. Kasia was handed a plastic bag.

"What's this?" she asked.

"Oh, it's just the clothes he was wearing when he was admitted. He didn't seem to have anything else."

Kasia peeped into the bag and wished she hadn't. For a moment she pictured her father as he had been when they went to the restaurant on his first night in London - before he collapsed - looking smart and a bit uncomfortable in his only suit, which she hadn't seen him in since Piotr's wedding. She swallowed a sob and handed it to her mother.

"Can you take this, I just want to say thank you to the nurses. It's Papa's clothes."

Thanks having been given all round, Kasia and Zofia and Józéf headed for the lift accompanied by two nurses and a lot of resuscitation equipment. The lift made a frustratingly slow descent to the ground floor, where one of the nurses hurried outside to see if the ambulance had arrived. She waved to the paramedics, who opened the rear of the ambulance and wheeled out a trolley. Then, as Kasia and Zofia followed behind Józéf's bed as it was pushed out of the doors, they were met with a popping of flashlights and a small crowd of people holding 'STOP ULTIMATE CARE' placards. Someone called "Well done, you beat the system!" but there was also a group of noisy protesters holding a placard which read: "WHAT ABOUT THE BRITS, THEN?" and shouting "'Crowd fund UC victims!"

315

A reporter thrust a microphone under Kasia's nose and asked her how it felt to be able to get her father out of hospital and home soon to Poland. She shielded her eyes from the flashes and couldn't think what to say. Finally she took a deep breath and stuttered

"It's marvellous. We are very grateful that people have….um….supported us by spreading our story on social media…..and in the newspapers. It's….um…..been amazing. And of course all the fantastic people who have….um….been so generous giving money so we can, er…. get my father home. A big thank you!" The crowd cheered.

"And when will you get him home to Poland do you think?" asked another, thrusting his microphone at her.

She batted it away and said "I'm sorry, I can't say any more now. Excuse me."

She went to move towards the ambulance but Zofia turned back to the second reporter and spoke into the microphone in a rapid torrent of Polish. She smiled at the crowd and clapped. They cheered back. Kasia couldn't quite believe her ears.

"Mama," she said," trying to pull her away. Zofia ignored her and threw her arms up and said in English "Thank you all very much!"

Embarrassed, Kasia steered her mother towards the ambulance, where the paramedics were expertly transferring Jozéf inside. Kasia and Zofia followed them in.

"Turn around and wave, Kasia, wave," instructed Zofia. "Give them a nice picture."

Reluctantly, she joined her mother in enthusiastically waving as the doors closed on them.

"I saw BBC and ITV written on the cameras," said Zofia excitedly. She'd been watching a lot of TV soaps while she'd been in England. She didn't understand much but she could often get the drift of the story. "We're going to be on TV!"

~

When they climbed down from the ambulance outside Bishop Gabriel's Lodge Kasia breathed a sigh of relief, and said to Zofia "We're here at last."

"Excuse me...." Helen was hurrying towards them. "Just a moment...."

"Is there a problem?" asked Kasia. She didn't like the look on Helen's face.

"I'm afraid there is." She addressed the paramedics. "Hold on there, please don't bring out Mr Jablonski yet."

Kasia stood and stared at Helen, a wave of dislike washing over her.

"What is it?"

"We don't seem to have received the balance of the payment due. I'm afraid I can't let him in until we do."

"But....I don't understand. I only spoke to Thomas yesterday. He was all set to transfer the money."

"Well, whatever the reason, it hasn't reached our account. It's the strict policy of this group of Care Homes that no new client can be admitted before we have the money."

"But you can't leave him in the ambulance!" Kasia was aghast. "This is ridiculous. We'll get him inside and then sort it out."

Helen positioned herself at the back of the ambulance, blocking Józéf's exit. Zofia clutched at Kasia demanding to know what was going on. Her face contorted with fury, and she advanced on Helen, shouting at her in Polish. Helen, unable to take a step backwards because of the ambulance, held up her hand to fend her off.

"Please tell your mother to back off," she said coldly to Kasia. "and can you contact your Mr Whitby, please."

Kasia pulled out her phone and, with shaking hands, dialled Thomas' number. It went to voicemail. She took a deep breath.

"No answer. I'll try again." This time he picked up.

"What? That can't be right, I did the transfer last thing last night, on line. The website said it had been accepted and that it would be in the Home's account in two hours."

317

"Can you get hold of the bank and sort it out? The Care Home manager is forcing us to keep my father inside the ambulance until the money's here."

"I hope you're not serious?" Thomas couldn't believe his ears.

"Sadly, I am."

"Why don't you get this on video? It would be dynamite on social media. Meanwhile, I'll get on to the bank and find out what's gone wrong."

Kasia turned to tell Helen what Thomas had said and found her mother already filming Helen obstructing the ambulance. She had to smile, even in the stress of the situation. She didn't think her mother knew how to take videos on her phone. Helen was furious.

"Delete that this minute. How dare you!"

"How dare YOU?' retorted Kasia.

The standoff continued until Thomas called Kasia back and said he'd sorted it. The transfer had been queried because of its unusual circumstances.

"It's done," said Kasia to Helen. "We can bring him in now."

"Oh no you don't. You all stay here while I go inside and check the account on the computer."

"I think maybe we picked the wrong home after all," Kasia said to Zofia. "This woman is unbelievable."

Eventually, Joseph was wheeled inside and installed in his room. Helen appeared and hovered at the door, clearly regretting her earlier actions.

"He looks very peaceful," she said. "You can stay as long as you like with him. Would you like me to get someone to bring you tea or coffee?"

"Tea," said Kasia. She seldom drank alcohol, but at that moment would have given anything for something stronger. "Thank you."

"Oh, don't thank me, it all goes on the bill," Helen said as she withdrew noisily on her high heels.

Kasia ground her teeth and didn't bother to translate for Zofia.

Chapter 53

The fund had at last reached the amount needed to get Józéf home. Piotr had been looking around nursing homes in Warsaw and had found a home suitable for Józéf .

"Did you get the details of the nursing home I emailed you?" he asked Kasia.

"Yes, it looks nice - well, as nice as any state-run home can look. Not quite up to the standards of Bishop Gabriel's although I can't wait to get him out of that place. The care seems good but it's more like a five-star hotel with no ambience. So when can this place take him?"

"They have a place now. I think someone just died there. Do you want me to accept it so you can get on with transferring him home?"

"Yes....but could I speak to Teresa first. No offence, Piotr, but I'd like a woman's opinion on this place."

Piotr sighed. "All right - hold on." His wife came to the phone.

"I'd just like your opinion of this place, Teresa. Women look at these things differently."

"I thought it would do very well, Kasia. The Matron was very warm and pleasant and the staff we met seemed friendly and professional. The rooms are simple but adequate. I don't think we'll do any better. The patients looked happy enough, those who were in the public rooms."

"OK, thanks. Could you tell Piotr to confirm the place and that I'll go ahead booking the Air Ambulance. I'll let you know the date and time."

Kasia told her mother that they'd decided on a nursing home in Warsaw and that it had an immediate vacancy. She'd already shown her the details Piotr had emailed.

"I would have like to have seen it first," she fretted. I don't like it that you and Piotr decided."

"Mama, you know that it's impossible. We have to have a place ready to take him when we fly him home."

"He could go into a hospital for a few days, couldn't he?"

"It's a possibility, but don't you think he's had enough changes? Teresa has looked at it too, and she approves."

"Hmm, Teresa." Zofia sniffed. 'What does she know?"

"I'm sorry if you don't approve but it's all organized now. I just need to book the Air Ambulance."

"And we can go with him?" asked Zofia.

"Yes, of course, but I won't be coming, I need to get back to work."

Zofia looked like she might be on the verge of another panic attack. "I can't go alone!" she wailed.

"You can, you won't be alone, there will be a doctor and nurse on board. They will be with you and Papa right until you reach the nursing home, they'll be in the ambulance with you for the land transfer too. Anyway, Mama, I've noticed since you've been in England that you've been much more independent. It's been good for you in many ways to have to do things on your own. When you get home you won't have Papa to depend on. You'll need to be strong for him."

"Yes, I suppose so. I, too, am surprised that I managed to travel across London on my own, and to go shopping in an English supermarket. And talk to the TV newsmen! It looked good on TV, didn't it? But it will be so good to get home."

Kasia was busy with her laptop and set about getting quotes from various companies which arranged air ambulances.

"Look at these," she said to Stefan. "Who would have guessed that there were so many companies doing this? How in earth do I choose?"

"Look at the reviews, first. Don't necessarily choose the cheapest. See exactly what they all offer, and if it differs. What's the average cost?"

"Looks like around £10,000, which is what we were budgeting on. I need to check what extras there might be. If they're anything like the nursing home we might be looking at twice that."

"If I were you I'd call a couple and talk it through with them. You can often judge companies better if you have personal contact with them. Are you going with him?"

"No. I really have to get back to work. I've told Mama, she wasn't pleased, but it can't be helped. I pointed out to her that she'd have to be the strong one now, and I think she is probably more capable that she thought she was."

"Where is she now?"

"She popped out to the corner shop for some milk."

Stefan took Kasia in his arms, held her tight and had just begun a serious kissing session when the front door slammed, announcing Zofia's arrival.

Zofia sensed she'd interrupted something and disappeared into the bathroom with a disapproving sniff. Stefan gave her a final kiss and murmured "To be resumed. Not long now. It will be nice to get back to normal."

Kasia made some phone calls and eventually decided which company to use for the flight and booked it for two days' time. Then she called Helen at the Nursing Home to tell her the date and time of the flight.

"Oh. We're sorry to be losing him so soon, " she said.

I bet you aren't, thought Kasia, you'll be well in profit from this patient.

"And what time will he be picked up from here?"

Kasia realised that she'd been so focussed on booking the Air Ambulance that she'd forgotten to arrange a road ambulance for transfer to the airport. She wasn't going to admit it to Helen and said, "Oh, I haven't finalised it yet, I'll let you know."

She cut the call and took a deep breath. She had formed a deep dislike of Helen and couldn't wait until Jozéf left her care and was on the way home. She called the private ambulance company, who greeted her like an old friend.

"Hallo Kasia, another trip so soon?"

"Yes, the Fund has enough money now for us to get my father home. Partly due, I'm sure, to the publicity outside the hospital. I hope you got some good press, too?"

"Well, you know what they say, there's no such thing as bad publicity."

" Good. So, the transfer will be from the nursing home to Heathrow Airport. The flight's at 14.30 the day after tomorrow. What time do you think you need to pick him up from the Home?"

"Better make it 10.00 to allow for traffic, and getting him processed at the airport. There's a lot of red tape associated with these flights. Who's accompanying him?"

"Well, both my mother and I will go to the airport with him, and then my mother will go on the flight. I'm staying here, I need to get back to work."

"OK, that's booked in. Has his condition changed at all?"

"No, it's much the same. Thanks, Chris."

It was a Saturday and so Stefan was able to go with Kasia to the airport to say goodbye to Jozéf and Zofia. The ambulance took them to the Medical Centre and they had to say their goodbyes there, before Zofia and Jozéf went airside.

Kasia took her father's hand and held it for a long minute. Then she bent and kissed him. "Goodbye Papa. Please get better for us all, especially Mama."

She fished a tissue out of her bag and turned away, crying quietly. Then she put her arms around her mother, and hugged her tight. Zofia was also crying.

"Oh Kasia, I don't know what I'll do without you. I wish you were coming with me."

"I know, Mama, but you have medical people on the flight, and when you get Papa into the nursing home you can relax a bit. And Piotr will be there."

She wondered just how much help he'd be, but she felt she'd borne the brunt of the past few traumatic weeks and that it was definitely his turn. She knew that she now had to make her departure and not dither. Stefan kissed Zofia on both cheeks, Kasia gave her mother another hug and they left, hand in hand, blowing kisses as they went.

That evening they went to Polski Mama for a meal and Kasia relaxed for the first time in weeks.

"I can't tell you what a relief it is. But, you know, I think all this has done Mama good. She's beginning to learn she can't play the drama queen all the time and that she's got to get to grips with making decisions a lot more."

"Yes, but it's a good job she had you organizing everything. Have I got you back now? I feel that for the last few weeks you haven't quite been on the same planet as me."

"Yes, I'm sorry. I know I've been distracted. I couldn't have done it all without your support, though. You were marvellous with Mama."

When they got back to the flat, Stefan teased, "talking of decisions, which bedroom are you sleeping in tonight, then?"

"I think you know that, Stefan."

David was having a quiet coffee in his office, looking at some NHS spending projections. He felt a huge sense of relief that Alistair, who had fought the leadership election pledging to re-assess Ultimate Care, had narrowly won. With Alistair in charge, David hoped that his role as Health Secretary would become a little easier. Alistair had promised that UC would be suspended pro tem while the matter was properly debated and voted on in Parliament. The rules about foreigners would be clarified. Bill had said little about UC during the campaign but it was widely known that despite his reluctance to either endorse or approve it he had no intention of making any changes.

After a long spell in a nursing home, Charlie Warwick had suffered a second serious stroke and died, not a moment too soon as his widow was about to run out of funds for the care home fees. Charlie had apparently been a little too keen on betting on the horses. The irony of almost suffering the fate of his own UC protocols was not lost on the Cabinet. Despite their fondness for him, many of them had not been keen to attend the funeral as Jack had loudly voiced his intention to go. There was a general feeling that he was somehow tainted, and nobody wanted to be seen fraternising with him.

Jack had, as expected, had been Recalled and a by-election was to be held. His trial was being prepared, in which there was a huge amount of public interest. The evidence against him seemed overwhelming. David took another sip of his coffee and felt that finally all was coming right in his world. His reverie was interrupted by Imogen bursting in.

"Sorry to barge in, but you have to have a look at this."

She showed him her phone. He quickly took in the BBC News notification under the 'BREAKING NEWS' banner.

'IS COVID-19 MAKING A RETURN?' 9 suspicious deaths in London and Birmingham.'

David put his head in his hands. "Oh no. Please tell me this is fake news."

"I'm afraid it's verified. I called the Chief Execs at both the hospital trusts concerned. The symptoms are the same, and the disease seems just as deadly."

"But....but everyone is vaccinated now. We haven't had a case since we ended the vaccination programme. And why hasn't anyone called me direct about this? I'm the bloody Health Secretary."

"Believe me," said Imogen drily, "Your phone will be red hot any second."

She scrolled down the screen further and continued to read.

"Oh God.....Oh fuck.....you really don't want to see this."

His mobile and his landline began to ring simultaneously.

He ignored them and grabbed her mobile from her. What he read sent panic searing through him.

'At first evaluation, the virus seems to have mutated. Scientists are saying that the current vaccine will not protect against it.'

ACKNOWLEDGEMENTS

Many thanks go to the tutor and members of my writing workshop for their invaluable feedback and suggestions, and to family and friends for their encouragement.

ALL PROCEEDS FROM THIS BOOK WILL BE DONATED TO NHS CHARITIES

Printed in Great Britain
by Amazon